W9-CZS-150

	DATE DUE		

30408000002357

FIC
SHU

Shusterman, Neal.

The Shadow Club
rising

Woodland High School
Henry County Public Schools

THE SHADOW CLUB RISING

Woodland High School
800 N. Moseley Dr.
Stockbridge, GA 30281
770-389-2784

NEAL SHUSTERMAN

speak
An Imprint of Penguin Group (USA) Inc.

SPEAK
Published by Penguin Group
Penguin Group (USA) Inc.
345 Hudson Street, New York, New York 10014, U.S.A.
Penguin Books Ltd, 80 Strand, London WC2R ORL, England
Penguin Books Australia Ltd, 250 Camberwell Road,
Camberwell, Victoria 3124, Australia
Penguin Books Canada Ltd, 10 Alcorn Avenue, Toronto, Ontario, Canada
M4V 3B2
Penguin Books (N.Z.) Ltd, 182-190 Wairau Road, Auckland 10, New Zealand

First published in the United States of America by Dutton Children's Books,
a division of Penguin Putnam Books for Young Readers, 2002
Published by Speak Books, an imprint of Penguin Group (USA) Inc., 2003

10 9 8 7 6 5

Copyright © Neal Shusterman, 2002
All rights reserved

THE LIBRARY OF CONGRESS HAS CATALOGED THE DUTTON EDITION AS FOLLOWS:
Shusterman, Neal.
The Shadow Club rising / by Neal Shusterman.—1st ed.
p.   cm.
Sequel to: The Shadow Club
Summary: Even though he has disbanded his Shadow Club, formed to play
mean-spirited tricks on his enemies, fourteen-year-old Jared finds himself sus-
pected when a popular boy at school becomes the target of new pranks.
ISBN 0-525-46835-8
[1. Practical jokes—Fiction. 2. Clubs—Fiction. 3. Schools—Fiction.] I. Title.
PZ7.S55987 Sj 2002   [Fic]—dc21 2001045206

Speak ISBN 0-14-250089-5

Printed in the United States of America

Except in the United States of America, this book is sold subject to the
condition that it shall not, by way of trade or otherwise, be lent, re-sold,
hired out, or otherwise circulated without the publisher's prior consent in
any form of binding or cover other than that in which it is published and
without a similar condition including this condition being imposed on
the subsequent purchaser.

For Erin Dayne

ACKNOWLEDGMENTS

The Shadow Club would not have risen had it not been for the following intrepid individuals, whose support and encouragement paved the way for this book: Dr. Steve Layne, whose passion for *The Shadow Club* convinced me that it deserved a sequel; Stephanie Owens-Lurie, whose support and editorial wisdom has been a guiding light throughout my career; Kathleen Doherty, who first rescued the Shadow Club and saw the potential for a sequel; Frank Hodge, whose dedication to children's literature has touched thousands of hearts from coast to coast; Jeff Sampson, David Ruskey, Rachel Morgan-Wall, and all my other on-line fans, whose ideas and enthusiasm continue to inspire me :); and Dr. Donald Levy, for his friendship and expertise on allergic reactions. And my children, Brendan, Jarrod, Joelle, and Erin, who are a critical audience for all my first drafts and a constant source of joy and inspiration.

THE
SHADOW
CLUB
RISING

T HE SEA AND I have never been friends.

We're more like neighbors who nod politely in passing while keeping a respectful distance. There was a time when the sea and I battled. It was a night lit by the flames of a burning lighthouse, when the surf was charged with an offshore storm. It was the moment of my greatest triumph, and my deepest failure—triumph because I beat the sea, cheated death, and saved a kid's life; failure because I finally had to admit my guilt for every awful thing the Shadow Club had done. It wasn't just admitting it to others, I had to admit it to myself. If you know what happened—and you probably do, since it's no secret in this town—then you already have your own opinion of me. If you don't know about it, well, all the better, because maybe you won't judge me before you get to know me.

There are times now when I'm drawn to thoughts of what happened. When my mind is quiet, I start thinking about that day. I have this shiny seashell, about the size of my fist, that I found on the beach when I was little. Sometimes I'll lie on my bed and toss it up and down, fidgeting with it while I think about things I should probably try to forget. They say you can hear the ocean in the spirals of a seashell, and I used to believe it with all my heart. But now, of course, I know it's just echoes of the world around you, caught in the twisting spiral. Which maybe explains why I *do* hear the ocean when I put my ear to the seashell these days. Not just the ocean, but the roar of the flames from that burning lighthouse—two things still caught in the spiral, echoing round and round in my own world.

That's the way it was with the Shadow Club. We thought it was all over, but it had only just begun. The fires, the war against Tyson McGaw, all the dark and dastardly pranks—they were nothing compared to what happened next. In the end we had all confessed to the things we had done—we thought that by purging ourselves of the guilt, it would all just go away. Of course we knew we'd have to pay for the things we did, but even then there was relief in knowing that once we paid our debts to society, we could gather up our lives again and move beyond it. But anger and hatred and resentment—those feelings are as slippery as a greased pig: hard to handle, and even harder to catch when they get loose. Feelings like that don't die easily—they just move on to other people if they can't have their way with you.

Like I said, we'd thought it was over, until February, when everything crept up on us, slamming into us from behind like a traffic accident.

It started, like so many things in my life seemed to have started, with Austin Pace. But this time things were a whole lot different. . . .

The Iron Maiden

I HAVE A BIKE, but I don't ride it much. In our town there are too many hills, and the roads aren't paved as well as they should be. The shoulders are littered with rocks broken loose by the rains and the roots of tall pines. I've always relied on my feet to get me places. In the mornings I run to school, even in the winter, when my nose and ears grow so cold that they feel numb all through first period.

Now that I was officially off the track team, all that running I did to get from place to place meant a whole lot more to me. But on this particular day I didn't run, I walked, because I wasn't in a hurry to get to this destination.

It was the middle of January. Cold to me, but then nowhere near the deep freeze that other parts of the country got. While other places were getting blizzards, we'd just get rain, and when snow did fall it never lasted. The only white Christmas we ever see is from the fog that rolls in from the ocean.

It was getting dark as I walked along the winding, tree-lined road that led to the homes on the hill. My social studies teacher said that in Third World countries the higher up you are on the hill, the poorer you are, because it means that you don't have any water or electricity. But not so in the world I live in. The homes up the hill have pools and big yards and picture windows with million-dollar views. Austin Pace lived about two-thirds up. Not high enough to be in a mansion, but high enough to be able to look down his nose at two-thirds of the rest of us, which he had always done quite well.

Three months ago I had been indirectly responsible for breaking his ankle—and now I was going to his house for dinner. I had to admit I couldn't have come up with a worse punishment myself. I kept reminding myself that I wasn't *actually* the one who spread those sharp rocks on the field—rocks that cut up his bare feet and mangled his right ankle. *That* had been Cheryl Gannett—my life-long friend and now ex-girlfriend. She had done it for me without my knowledge or consent to get Austin back for all the nasty things he had done to me. She did it because I was the second-best runner—all the members of the Shadow Club were second best at something. I had to admit that none of the indignities he had made me suffer came close to the vicious games the Shadow Club had played. Austin had once apologized for treating me the way he had. That was in the nurse's office, after I carried him off the field. He reneged on his apology later, though, when he found out I was partially to blame for his injury. "Pain makes people delirious," he said, and claimed he hadn't meant a word of it.

So then why was I being invited to dinner? I asked myself. Had Austin finally accepted my apology? Or was it because my parents paid his uncovered medical expenses with the money they had set aside for buying me a car in a couple of years? Maybe he felt bad because I had resigned from the track team as part of my penance for the Shadow Club's deeds. Or maybe, I thought, he invited me over to dinner just to poison me.

And so I walked instead of ran.

"Oh, it's you," said Allison, Austin's younger sister, as she opened the door. She said it with such contempt, it was clear she had been practicing saying that for most of the day.

"Come in, Jared," said Mrs. Pace, with a smile that was way too inviting. Her husband sat in the background, reading in an armchair—but the moment I stepped over the threshold, he quickly folded his newspaper and went into the other room. Austin was nowhere to be seen.

"Please, make yourself at home," Mrs. Pace said. There was enough brightness in her voice to light up the Astrodome.

This is all too weird, I wanted to say. *Can I go now?* But instead I just said, "Sure." And I sat down, trying to look comfortable, even though I felt as if I were sitting on a bed of nails.

"We're having pot roast," Mrs. Pace said cheerfully. "You eat meat, don't you?"

"He probably eats it raw," said Allison.

Austin came downstairs, slowly hobbling. The truth was, he had been walking just fine for the past few weeks, but whenever he saw me, his limp mysteriously returned. That was okay. After what the Shadow Club had done to him, if he wanted to rub salt in my guilt, he had every right to do it, so I played along.

"Still hurts?" I asked.

"Only when I move."

I offered a slim smile, but I couldn't hide just how uneasy I was about this whole dinner. He seemed to take some comfort in my discomfort. I stood up, putting out my hand to shake, knowing that he wouldn't take it. Seeing me put down my hand unshaken seemed another moment of satisfaction for him.

"I want you to know," he said, "that this wasn't my idea. It was my mother's."

The dining table was set for five, but only four sat down when dinner was served. Mr. Pace did not join us—although I could hear newspaper pages turning in another room.

As Mrs. Pace brought out the serving dishes, I found myself grabbing the food far too quickly—not because I was hungry, but because I wanted to occupy my mouth with chewing, so I wouldn't be forced to talk. Austin seemed to have the same idea, but his sister had different plans.

"So," Allison asked, "what was it like being suspended?"

I looked down at my plate, wishing the meat was a little tougher so I could continue to chew for a few minutes without having to speak. "It gave me a lot of time to think," I answered.

"I thought you had to have a brain for that," Austin said.

"Now, Austin," his mother said, "Jared's our guest tonight."

"So you keep telling me."

The newspaper turned in the other room.

Finally I broke down and asked the question that had been plaguing me since I had received this invitation. "I hope you don't mind me asking, Mrs. Pace, but . . . why am I here?"

"For dinner, of course," she said.

It was Austin who explained. "The self-help book my mom's been reading says we have to make peace with all the people we hate."

"And," added Allison, "there's nobody we hate more than you."

"More string beans, Jared?" asked Mrs. Pace.

Back in seventh grade I did a report on medieval torture

techniques; people stretched on the rack, or made to stand in the dagger-lined shell of the Iron Maiden. I should have included "Dinner With the Paces" in my report.

I continued to stare into my food, moving my fork around and around until the potatoes became a brown sludge lagoon beside my island of meat.

"Listen," I said, unable to meet their eyes, "the Shadow Club was a mistake. What we did was wrong. And I'm sorry."

"You're sorry?" said a man's voice behind me. I turned around to see Mr. Pace standing at the threshold of the dining room. "You think that ruined ankle and the scars on Austin's feet will go away just because you say you're sorry?"

"No," I said, forcing myself to look him in the face, no matter how small it made me feel. "But I'm sorry anyway."

After he left the room I could still feel his eyes on me.

"I've lost my appetite," said Austin, dropping his fork on the plate with a clatter. Then he stormed away, remembering his limp halfway out of the room, leaving me to be killed by his mother's kindness.

I ate quickly, said a polite thank-you, and headed for the door—but even as I did, I knew that I couldn't leave like that. I knew I had to say something to Austin, though I didn't know what it would be. I found him in his garage, which had been converted into a game room, playing pool by himself.

"You're still here?" he said, shooting at the nine ball and missing completely. Either he wasn't very good, or my presence was throwing his game off. "What is it you want?"

I took a deep breath and spoke, not sure what I would say until the words came tripping out of my mouth. "I stepped down from the track team, I've apologized a thousand times, but it doesn't seem to make a difference. What is it going to take to even up the score between me and you? I want to know what I can do to make you happy, because whatever it is, I want to do it. I owe that to you."

Austin put his cue stick down. "You can't stand the fact that I hate your guts, can you?"

"I guess you have every reason to hate me," I admitted. "Me, Cheryl, Randall, and the others."

Then Austin took a step closer, and said, "Then let me hate you . . . because that's what makes me happy."

"How was dinner with the Paces?" my dad asked when I got home.

"Fine," I said. It was a one-word response that said nothing. Things were like that between me and my parents these days. Although I had always been able to talk to them before, ever since the disaster at the lighthouse, there was like this no-fly zone between us, and we really couldn't talk the way we used to. It was as if they didn't quite see me when they looked at me now. I don't know what they saw. It's very unsettling not to be able to see yourself reflected in your own parents' eyes, if you know what I mean.

"Just fine?" my dad said, pressing me for info.

"Yeah. Fine."

He opened the refrigerator like he wanted something to eat, but he was just pretending so that he didn't have to look at me. I knew that trick, because I often did it myself.

"Everything okay at school?"

"You mean aside from the casualties from the elephant stampede?"

Now he stared at me with one hand on the open refrigerator door.

"I'm kidding, Dad."

He shut the door. "You have your mother's sense of humor."

Funny, because Mom always accused me of having *his* sense of humor. Lately neither of them would take credit for me.

As I went to my room, I began to think about the ex-members of the Shadow Club. Cheryl, who had taken my offhand comment about forming a club for second-best kids and turned it into reality; her younger brother, Randall, who had always been hundredths of a second away from first place on every swim team he'd ever been on; Darren Collins, who never saw the glory he deserved in basketball; Jason Perez, whose dreams revolved around a trumpet solo he'd never been asked to perform; Karin "O. P." Han, who was always One Point away from having the highest grades in school. Abbie Singer, who was almost, but not quite, the most popular girl around. And then, of course, me—the king of the silver medal in the hundred-yard dash.

It all seemed so important just a few months ago, but when you terrorize your enemies the way we did, you lose your taste for blood—and although I still had the urge to be better at what I did, I no longer had the need to be better *than*.

It all came down to this: I could deal with myself now. I had come to terms with the things we had done . . . but that look of hatred on Austin's face—that was something I still couldn't deal with.

"Do you hate me, Tyson?" I asked from the threshold of his room that night. It used to be our guest room, but now Tyson was a permanent guest.

He didn't answer my question. Instead he held up the drawing he was working on. "How do you like this one?" he asked. It was an intricate pencil sketch of a city skyline.

"I like it," I said with a sly smile. "It's not on fire."

"Ha-ha," he said. I think I was the only person who could joke with him about that—perhaps because I had been there during the last blaze he had set, when he burned down his house and nearly took both of us with it. I don't take blame for everything in the world, but a good part of that was my fault, too, because I was really the one who had pushed Tyson to do it.

I took a look at the drawing. It was good—all his artwork was good—and, like I said, the fact that he didn't draw anything burning was a good sign. So many of his sketches and paintings had everything from airplanes to buildings to people being consumed by flames. His psychiatrist said it was good for him to air his demons through his artwork, but it still didn't make it any less creepy.

How Tyson ended up with my family is something I can take a little bit of pride in. After his lighthouse burned and I rescued him from drowning in the ocean, he had been taken away from his foster parents. They were the third ones he had lived with since his real parents died when he was just a little kid. With no one else willing to take him, he would have been stuck in Pleasant Haven Children's Home, which was neither pleasant nor much of a haven—it was just a last-stop orphanage with a deceptive name. I was the one who insisted that we take him in—that *we* become his new foster family. Although my parents were definitely not too keen on the idea of an angry pyromaniac kid in the house, they knew I owed him even more than I owed Austin. In spite of the history between Tyson and me, even Social Services agreed that placing him with us was better than sending him to Pleasant Haven. When I was younger I always kind of wanted a brother. Of course Tyson wasn't what I'd had in mind, but I sort of liked it.

Tyson turned a page in his sketch pad and started a new drawing, forgetting, or pretending to forget the question I had asked when I first stepped in.

"So, Tyson," I said once more, refusing to let him off the hook, "do you hate me?"

He shifted uncomfortably. "Yeah, sure," he said. "Maybe a little."

"Maybe a lot?" I pushed.

"I don't know," Tyson answered. "Somewhere between a little and a lot—but closer to a little—and anyway, I wouldn't have come to live here if I didn't like you more than I hated you."

I smiled. "You can't stand me when I drag you out of your room in the middle of the night." Tyson grunted like a bull. Part of my penance, as far as Tyson was concerned, was setting my alarm for 1:00 and 4:00 A.M., then hauling Tyson out of bed to take a leak, with the hope of breaking that nasty little bed-wetting habit of his, which I had so thoroughly announced to the entire school.

"How do you deal with it when people totally hate your guts?" I asked.

"Very badly," he answered, and I realized what a stupid question that was to ask him—a kid who always went ballistic at the drop of a hat. "Is this about Austin?" he asked, knowing where I had gone to dinner that night.

I nodded. "I thought he might give me time off for good behavior, you know?"

"More like life with no chance of parole?"

"No," I said, "more like death row."

And then Tyson said something that I'll never forget.

"Sometimes people see you the way they want to see you," he told me, "no matter how hard you try to change it. It's like they'd rather twist the whole world just so they can keep seeing you the same lousy way."

It wasn't long until I knew how true that really was.

Alec Smartz

THE LETHAL BREW that the Shadow Club had set to simmer would have boiled over eventually, no matter what anyone did—I'm convinced of that—but it was the arrival of a certain person in town that really turned up the heat.

When some kids move into a new neighborhood, they make no ripple at all. They just slip into the back of the classroom while no one's looking, or simply replace someone else who just moved away. Then there's the kid whose entrance is like a cannonball jump into a still pool. Alec Emery Smartz Jr. was that kid.

Alec was slim, good-looking, and entered school on the top level, socially, academically, and even athletically. Although he wasn't the tallest kid in school, something about him gave you the impression that he was. He rode into our school in a mythical kind of way and quickly became legend.

Now, just to be clear on this, I had no problems with

Alec. Well, maybe just a little one when it came to him and Cheryl—but I'll get to that.

I first saw him in the office while I was filling out a tardy slip, because, well, punctuality has never been my strongest point. Alec was having a conversation with Principal Diller like they were golf buddies or something. Principal Diller asked if there were any extracurricular activities he might be interested in, and Alec responded in an "aw shucks" kind of way, saying, "I don't know—there are lots of things I like to do."

"Well, I'm sure you'll make a lot of friends here," Principal Diller said. Then he caught a glimpse of me and made sure Alec walked in the other direction. I pretended like that didn't bother me.

From that first time I saw him, I sensed Alec would be the epicenter of seismic activity in our school. It was the way he held himself, and the way he looked at you. Like he already belonged, before even making an effort. And then there was the name—"Alec Smartz." It was one of those cruel parental jokes that would be an eternal mystery. But then on the other hand, it was so obvious that only a moron would try to take advantage of it. Whenever some kid tried to call him "Smart Alec," he would say in a total deadpan, "Gee, that's clever. Nobody ever thought of that before," making the moron feel even more stupid than he was before, if that was possible.

But I guess, in a way, Alec Smartz was condemned to be

what he was, the same way so many people became slaves to their name—like our music teacher, Mr. Musiker, and the guy who runs the fruit stand down on Pine Street, Mr. Groesser.

It was a few days after dinner at the Paces that I made a point of meeting Alec rather than just see him brush past, or hear people whisper about him. I wasn't quite sure what the whispers were about, but I was getting more and more curious.

It was one of those rare mornings when I was actually on time. He and Cheryl were locking up their bikes. Apparently Cheryl had forgotten her lock at home, so Alec was chaining both of theirs together. I'd be lying if I said it didn't make me a little bit uncomfortable. He and Cheryl had been spotted together on several occasions since his arrival in town.

"Hi, Cheryl," I said, which was pretty much the limit of our conversations these days. Cheryl and I had been best friends for most of our lives, and for a short time we were more than friends, but now, well, I didn't know what we were. Accomplices, maybe. Co-conspirators. I missed our friendship but had no clue how to get it back.

"Hi, Jared," she said in a strained sort of way. "Have you met Alec?"

He shook my hand. "Nice to meet you."

"Yeah."

He was much friendlier than I had imagined he would be, but I should have guessed that—after all, Cheryl would never hang out with a creep.

"I hear you're a runner," he said.

"Was."

"Still are," said Cheryl. "He's just not on the team this year, that's all."

I offered no further explanation.

"Maybe we could go jogging sometime," Alec suggested.

"Jared doesn't jog—he runs."

Alec glanced toward the school. "Listen, I gotta go—the soccer coach wants to talk to me before class. It was nice meeting you." And off he went with a confidence that divided the packs of kids in his way.

I turned to Cheryl, wearing a smug little grin.

"Don't look at me like that," she said.

"Like what?"

"Like you know something." Cheryl checked her kickstand. "And anyway, I can be friends with anyone I want."

I had to laugh. "I didn't say anything about you and Alec!"

"But you were thinking it."

"Then you need more practice at reading minds."

Cheryl blew into her hands to warm them, and now that I had caught my breath from the long run to school, I was beginning to feel cold myself.

"So what do you think of Alec?" she asked.

"I think he's OK."

"Everyone likes him."

"He seems like a likable guy."

The first bell rang, and Cheryl turned to hurry into school, having never been tardy in her whole life.

"Cheryl," I called to her before she got to the school steps. When she turned, I said, "I think you two look good together."

She gave me her famous prosecutor's gaze, ready to deny that they were "together" at all, but instead she just said, "Thanks," and went inside.

I had to admit I wasn't lying. I thought they really did make a nice couple—and it really ticked me off.

Our school's just a block away from Pine Street—which was unfortunately the only street in town where all the pine trees had been cut down and replaced by sycamores. The street was lined with shops and cafés that had died when the mall opened up a few miles away, and then were reborn when people decided malls were boring and quaint little street shops were cool.

Among the various cafés was Solerno's Pizzeria, a place run by an old grimace of man whose taste buds must have been removed, because his pizza had more salt than the ocean, and enough garlic to keep the town free of vampires. Still, when compared to the school cafeteria, Solerno's was a world-class restaurant, and so kids flocked there during lunch, hoping for a thick slice of god-awful pizza, and hoping to catch miserable old Solerno in a less awful mood than usual.

That same afternoon, I ran into Alec and Cheryl at Solerno's during lunch. Alec was actually talking to the old man, suggesting that he change his selection of spices. I have to tell you, I would have laid down and worshiped Alec myself if he got through to Solerno, but, true to form, the old man threatened to hit him with a broom.

Still curious as to what made Alec tick, I sat down with him and Cheryl, and we suffered through our pizza together.

The conversation didn't go much of anywhere, until Cheryl decided it was time to get cute.

"Did you know Jared has a hidden talent?" she told Alec. "He can drink soda through his nose."

"Oh, c'mon, Cheryl, I haven't done that since fifth grade."

I have to admit, it was something I was once rather proud of—and although it always gave me one heck of a brain-freeze, it was worth it to impress friends and disgust adults, back when I was ten.

"Now *that's* something I'd like to see," said Alec. "I'll bet you can't do it anymore."

I don't know what came over me then. I guess I'm still a sucker when it comes to being challenged. So I took a deep breath, shoved my straw up my left nostril, pinched the right one closed, and began to guzzle. Drinking soda through your nose is like riding a bicycle—it's a skill you never quite forget. I downed the entire cup in fifteen seconds flat.

Cheryl laughed and applauded, and I felt . . . well . . . stupid for having actually done it.

"Cool," said Alec.

And that's when I thought I saw something change in him. The grin on his face was the same, but something about him suddenly shifted, and grew colder. Or maybe it was just my brain-freeze.

"I can do that," Alec said.

Cheryl laughed. "I wouldn't advise it. You should leave it to the professionals."

"No, really," Alec said, and before any of us knew it, he shoved his own straw up his right nostril—making me realize how completely asinine I must have looked—and began to drain his Dr Pepper into his face.

"Alec . . ."

It was a second before he gagged, coughing a spray of fizzing soda all over us. Some girls at the next table got spritzed; a guy behind us stood, fully prepared to give him the Heimlich; and from behind the counter, Solerno said, "You puke uppa my pizza, you don't getta no more!"

Alec quickly regained his composure, if not his dignity.

"Don't worry about it," I told him. "It takes years of hard work to master."

But he said, with a harshness hidden deep within his smile, "Practice makes perfect."

I looked at Cheryl, who just shrugged as if it were nothing, but somehow I knew better.

———

It only took a few days more until I knew all I needed to know about Alec Smartz. The stories circulating around school painted a whole gallery of pictures.

Painting number one: **Still Life With Algebra.**

Mr. Kronisch, our math teacher, gave bears of exams that were the subject of many a nightmare. For this reason his midterms were called the Kronisch Inquisition. Alec, being new, isn't expected to take the test, but he does anyway. He aces it, throwing the curve so far into orbit that everyone else's score goes down half a grade.

Portrait number two: **Self-portrait With Saxophone.**

While still scouting out the school those first few weeks, he wanders into Mr. Musiker's room during a mostly pathetic band rehearsal (which is no great surprise, since our band's rehearsals are always mostly pathetic).

"Do you play an instrument, Alec?" Mr. Musiker asks.

"A few," he responds, then proceeds to borrow Chelsea Morris's alto sax and plays a number that could get him a recording deal with the jazz label of his choice. You can almost hear the blood draining from all the wanna-be band stars in the room.

Portrait number three: **Alec at the Bat.**

Alec wanders innocently onto the baseball field—but by now I've come to realize that Alec doesn't really "wander" anywhere. All his casual arrivals are as well calculated as his answers on the Kronisch Inquisition. Today the baseball team is getting ready for the upcoming season.

"You interested in going out for baseball?" the coach asks.

"Well, it's not my sport," says Alec, "but I'll give it a try." Long story short, now there's a new shortstop, and a grin on the coach's face that has never been seen in all his years of coaching our losing baseball team.

When asked how he got so good, Alec says, "Nowhere in particular. I'm just good in any sport that involves a ball." It's a statement that makes all the coaches drool, and all the jocks run for cover.

When someone enters a school with as much noise as Alec did, emotions are bound to run high—in both directions.

"I don't like him," I heard Drew Landers, the star swimmer, say, obviously anticipating the day Alec Smartz "wandered innocently" up to the pool.

"I don't trust him," Tyson said, and for once Tyson's paranoia was reflected by many others.

"I heard he was a genetically engineered cyborg," said Ralphy Sherman, who had never uttered a word of truth in his life. And what was scary was that some kids believed him.

I had my own theory, however. Simply put, Alec Smartz was just plain *good*. It was the kind of "good" that was not locked into a specific sport or subject. Alec was one of those rare individuals whose talent was like a suitcase he could carry through anyone's door, whether it was the door to the music room, the math room, the gym, or even the door to a pizza place, where he inhaled a can of Dr Pepper through his nose one week after seeing me do it, breaking my twelve-ounce record by four seconds.

Whether he worked hard to be so good I couldn't quite say, but that didn't matter because he made it look easy. In fact, he seemed to get his jollies by making everything look so easy that the rest of the world looked bad.

Thanks to him, the entire school now qualified for membership in the Shadow Club.

Freaks Like Me

NOBODY SEES THEMSELVES as "the bad guy." Even the nastiest, most evil people are heroes in their own minds. I thought I was still a pretty good guy. In the past, whenever I had screwed up, people never got too bent out of shape. "Your heart's in the right place," they would always say, and that's how I still felt about myself. Even when my brain took an extended vacation, I could be forgiven, because my heart was in the right place. Of course the Shadow Club's victims would never believe that, but I just assumed that everyone else who knew me would. Sometimes it takes a good left hook to open your eyes.

The fight started as Tyson's—not mine. Although it was now harder for kids to whip Tyson into that fighting frenzy he was so famous for, it wasn't impossible. Those same kids who had always tormented him now worked overtime to make him nuts. Like Tyson said, people see you the way they want to see you . . . and sometimes they manage to turn you into the very thing they want to see.

It was just before lunch, when everyone was most irritable, that our school's designated nuisance, Brett Whatley, heaped one too many rude remarks on Tyson's head. By the time I happened by, they were already into it, swinging full force, and bouncing back and forth across the hall in a locker-bashing brawl. I have to admit, I seriously considered just walking the other way, and letting the fight take care of itself . . . but like I said, my heart was in the right place. See, if Tyson won the fight, he'd probably be suspended, and if he lost the fight, he'd be drawing pictures of things burning again. I couldn't let either one happen, and since no teacher arrived to break it up, I took it upon myself. I pushed my way through the chain of spectators, squeezing myself into Brett and Tyson's airspace, and taking a nasty elbow to the ribs from Tyson before he realized it was me.

"Back off!" I yelled at Tyson, loud enough to break through his anger.

"But . . . but he called me a—"

I turned to Brett, before Tyson could finish. "You want to fight someone, Brett, why don't you start with me?"

And for an instant Brett Whatley looked scared. The kid was practically a head taller than me. But here he was, backing away from me.

It only lasted a second, though, until he remembered that he had an audience.

"Well, if it isn't Jared Mercer," he sneered. "I should have known I'd find you holding Tyson's leash."

He couldn't even come up with an original insult. He stole that one from *Star Wars*.

"Why don't you get a life and lose it," I told him.

"You and Tyson deserve each other—you're both a couple of losers."

Although I thought I was immune to Brett Whatley's brainless taunts, they were starting to get to me.

"Just leave us alone."

He crossed his arms, sensing he had the upper hand. "Why? What are you gonna do, Mercer, put a bomb in my locker? Or maybe just a razor blade in my sandwich."

Hearing him say that knocked the wind right out of me. Those comments came so far out of nowhere that I thought I had somehow missed part of the conversation. "What?"

Then a voice from the sidelines chimed in as well. "Maybe he'll just break your kneecaps in your sleep."

And someone else said, "Or maybe he'll just kill your dog."

I looked at the faces of the kids around me. I couldn't tell who had spoken—but by the look of distrust on their faces, it could have been any of them. Some of them even backed away, as if I might actually do those things to *them*. These were kids I knew, kids I had studied with, played with, and joked with for years. Now they were kids I suddenly didn't know, or at least they didn't know me. Did they really believe I was capable of such awful things because I had been in the Shadow Club?

Brett sneered at me, sensing the support all around him. "You know, there's a word for freaks like you," he said.

But whatever word he had in mind, no one was hearing it today, because I launched at him with both fists swinging. "I would never do those things!" I screamed as I fought him, making each word strike home with another wild punch. "I would never . . . never . . . never . . . never . . . never . . ." Finally Tyson pulled me away—*he* was the calm one trying to cool *me* down.

"Did you hear what he said?!" I screamed at Tyson. "Did you hear?!" I began to get furious at Tyson. How could he be so calm? And then someone else grabbed me, spinning me around. I was ready to fight with this new assailant as well . . . until I realized who it was. I was standing fist to face with our vice principal and guidance counselor—Mr. Greene.

Brett was sent to class.

Although *he* began the fight with Tyson—although everyone knew that Brett created every disaster he was involved in—he was let go, and I was brought in for disciplinary action. Me, alone.

The fury had left me by the time I landed in Mr. Greene's office. Now there was a knot in my gut that spread out through my whole body, as if my entire body was clenched like a fist.

"I can see you've made no effort to clean up your behavior," Mr. Greene said to me.

"So, I got into a fight—so?"

He said nothing.

"I mean, everyone fights once in a while," I added, "and I haven't done anything wrong for months!"

He swiveled calmly in his chair. "At least not that we know about."

"What's that supposed to mean?"

"It means that you played me for a fool once before, and I won't let it happen again."

It took a moment for me to process that.

"Kids like Brett Whatley are easy," he continued. "With Brett you always know exactly what you're getting. You know what fights he'll pick, what insults he'll throw. You know what he's going to do before he does it. He's predictable, and in my book that makes him pretty harmless."

I looked down at my shoes. "I don't think so."

"But you, Jared, you're not like that. When you pull something, you don't leave a trail behind you—there's no 'smoking gun.' You're quiet . . . and you're sneaky. In my book, that makes you dangerous."

It was all coming into focus now as he spoke: what he thought of me—how he saw me. The category he had me filed under. This wasn't about the fight, was it? The fight was just an excuse to bring me in—so he could read me this little riot act. It was as if these past three months had meant nothing. As if the only reason I hadn't been in trouble since then was that I simply hadn't been caught.

"Just because I'm quiet doesn't mean I'm sneaky."

"And just because you show remorse doesn't mean that you're really sorry for anything."

"I *am* sorry!"

"I wish I had a reason to believe that."

"You'll never have a reason!" I shouted at him. "Because you don't want to find one!"

He considered that and, for a moment, I could see him squirm a little. It was his job to peg kids, and he was good at what he did. So good that he would never accept being wrong. Whatever label he had chosen for me, he would fight to the death to make sure it stuck like a *kick me* sign tattooed to my butt.

"You don't know what's inside me," I said to him, feeling my eyes moisten, but I refused to be brought to tears.

"You're right, Jared, I don't," he said. "And that's what scares me."

Great Balls of Fur

IT TAKES EVERY ounce of your strength not to become what they make of you. Your spirit could implode under the pressure the way mine did that day with Brett . . . but in a way that opened my eyes, letting me see the trouble brewing around me—trouble that everyone else was blind to.

The Winter Carnival was a tradition in our town, started by a mayor too cheap to pay for a summer carnival. Since no one else wanted to throw a carnival in the dead of winter, we ended up with twice the rides at half the price for two whole weeks instead of just one. This year I got a weekend job at one of the carnival ticket booths to take my mind off things. You learn a lot working at a ticket booth. The conversations of people in line make you a local expert, because the ticket booth is a crossroads for all the town gossip. Who was getting married and who was likely to get divorced; who was cheating on his or her spouse and who was cheating the government. I learned so much about Alec Smartz that I could have written his biography. There were the kids who were impressed by him—younger kids mostly—seventh and eighth graders idolized him. There were the girls who vied for his attention and were endlessly irritated by the fact that Cheryl got most of it. And then there were the others. The ones who neither worshiped nor fawned. The ones who were not amused. *"The way he plays that saxophone you'd think he was born with it growing from his mouth,"* they would say, or *"What, does he have a homing beacon in his baseball mitt?"* It wasn't so much their words, but the way they said them—oozing with hatred. A girl whose name I didn't know talked to me as I sold her tickets, telling me how Alec became the overnight star of the chess team.

"He keeps stomping on you until you stop moving," she said. "He doesn't just beat you, he *squashes* you." And she was right. It was like anyone with any talent was a cockroach he had to crush. "Someone ought to do something about him," she said. "Someone ought to put him in his place."

Then she winked at me. "Of course, it would take more than one person to do it right," suggested the chess girl. "Make it so it would stick. It would take kids with *experience* in that sort of thing."

Now I realized why so many of the conversations about Alec were loudly spoken in my direction. *Someone ought to put him in his place.* More than one person had suggested that to me, and with it came the unspoken threat, *"If you don't, Jared, then we will."*

"Here are your tickets," I told her. "If you want more, go to the other booth across the park. Don't come back to me."

I saw Alec and Cheryl at the carnival that Sunday just before my shift ended. They had already been to the midway, because Alec was carrying around this huge blue giraffe he had won at one of the games. Although he could have left it somewhere, he made a point of lugging it around as he zig-zagged through the carnival, in case there was anyone left who hadn't seen that he had won it. I imagined him sitting in his garage for weeks on end hurling footballs at tires, or tossing coins at little glass plates, so when it finally came time for the real event, he would do it in just one shot, making it look like anyone should have been able to do it. I was the one who noticed all the looks he got—the wide-eyed looks from those in his fan club, and the narrow-eyed glares from those who resented him.

When my shift was over I wandered through the fair, trying to convince myself that I really wasn't looking for Alec and Cheryl. His big stuffed giraffe was sitting propped up against the rail of the bumper boats. The line had already emptied out onto the semicircular dock of the bumper-boat pool. I hopped the rail and handed a few ride tickets to the attendant. He pointed me to one of the last available boats that actually worked, then started my engine with a pull cord, like a lawn mower.

Bumper-boat racing is more or less an individual sport. One person per boat, and everyone out for themselves. Even when you try to do it in teams, it's never long before your own teammates turn on you without warning. The little inner-tube boats began to bounce around like angry atoms in a mad scientist's brew, with everyone trying to keep away from the ice-water fountain in the center of the tank. You'd think someone would realize that getting drenched in the middle of winter wasn't anyone's idea of a good time.

Alec and Cheryl were in different boats, spinning circles, and careening into everyone around them. They hadn't seen me yet. I worked my way toward them, giving full throttle to the gutless boat engine.

By the time I reached the far side of the pool, Cheryl had been carried off in a current of boats. I floored my accelerator and hit Alec from behind, sending him spinning around and bouncing off the side wall. It got his attention.

"Jared!" he said, calling out over the noise all around us. "I thought they had you locked up in the ticket booth."

"I escaped."

He bumped me, and before I knew it we were moving in a circle around the outer edge of the pool, bumping each other.

"So, how do you like our school?" I asked him.

"You came to the bumper boats to ask me about school?" he said, sideswiping me.

I came around, pinning him against the dock. "I came to tell you something you might be too busy to notice."

"I notice everything." He tried to squeeze his way past, but I stayed just in front of him, keeping him pushed up against the dock.

"You might not notice *this*."

"Come on, Jared," he said. "I paid good money for this ride—those were my last tickets."

"I'll give you new tickets," I said to him. "Just listen."

I leaned forward, getting as close to him as I could, and said as quietly as I could under the circumstances. "You need to watch yourself," I told him. "Because there are some people who aren't too happy with your success. I just felt I should warn you."

Then his face hardened as he looked at me. "Are you threatening me?"

But before I could answer I was hit so hard from behind that my boat spun circles, and my head was slow to catch up. It was Cheryl.

"You were a sitting duck," she said. "It was my moral obligation to nail you."

The ride attendant called the boats in, and the kids that resisted got pulled back to the dock with a long hook. Alec hopped out of his boat, but my knobby knees were stuck. He came up to me, leaned over me, and said, not too loud, but loud enough for Cheryl to hear, "Don't think I don't know about you and those awful things you made Cheryl do in the Shadow Club."

"What's this all about?" asked Cheryl, but before I could explain myself, Alec put his arm around her and led her away.

"He's just a little jealous, that's all," he said. "He'll get over it."

I didn't even try to stammer out any further explanation, because I knew that no matter what I said or denied, I would look as guilty as a corporate executive in a news interview. So I just sat there with my legs uncomfortably wedged into the tiny boat until the carny came to shoo me out.

It began less than half an hour later.

There were several versions of the story, but when you put them all together you come up with this: Alec and Cheryl were sitting in the heated dance canopy, eating hot dogs and listening to a bad country western band. There were other kids at the tables around them, and a few people on the dance floor. Everyone was having a good old country time, until Alec started taking a few sips from his Dr Pepper. He complained that it tasted funny and very innocently took off the plastic lid, to reveal that the Dr Pepper shared the cup with a hair ball the size of King Kong. In fact, if you believe the various accounts, the cup had more hair than soda. In a few seconds Alec's face went through every shade of the visible spectrum before he leaped up, accidentally dumping the table and the hairy Dr Pepper right into Cheryl's lap.

Some say he puked right then and there, while others say he puked all over the dance floor. Still others claim he puked all over the lead singer's shiny red boots, but wherever his cookies landed, the fact that he tossed them was not in dispute. The story spread so quickly that a sonic boom echoed through the phone lines, and by morning the Furry Pepper Incident, as it was now being called, was quickly becoming a town legend like the Shadow Club itself . . . and that had me more scared than I had been in months.

I know what it's like to be trapped in a burning building—to have the smoke blind you, and the air turn into a furnace as you struggle to open a door—everything so far out of control that you can't even control your own bladder. I also know power. I've watched my will run unchecked, wreaking havoc among friends and enemies alike. I know how good it feels to be in control, and to feel that control reach beyond the limits of yourself until you feel larger than life. I know helplessness and I know power—and if I had my way, I would never want to be in either of those places again, because while one might burn your body, the other burns your soul.

If anything good came from the Shadow Club's dark adventure, it was the knowledge that I was capable of incredible acts of bravery, as well as profound acts of malice. Knowing the bad stuff is there is a good thing, I think, because you can always see it coming. You can protect yourself. You can chase it away before it takes hold and does any damage. But you can't fight what you can't see—and far too many kids didn't see the Furry Pepper Incident for what it really was . . . who didn't know that even the Great Flood began with a single drop of rain.

"Did you do it?"

Cheryl accosted me in a dead-end hallway in the math department. We were both late for class, but then, what choice did we have? Neither of us were willing to talk about this during passing time, when ears with the sensitivity of Geiger counters were hyperextended to hear gossip.

"Do you *think* I did it?" I asked.

"Are you going to play games with me?"

I shifted my heavy math book to my other hand.

"I suppose if I pleaded 'the fifth' you'd take my silence as guilt, wouldn't you? Why are you even asking if I've already been tried and convicted?"

"Did you do it?" she demanded again.

I found myself getting more and more angry that she, of all people, thought I was still capable of that.

"If I had a new girlfriend," I asked her, "would you put a clump of Bigfoot in her Coke?"

"No," she said, grimacing at the thought. "Of course not."

"Then how could you think that I would?"

She stood silently for a moment. I could see her shoulders relax. "So you're saying that you didn't do it."

I held out my book. "Do you want me to swear on my math book?"

"No," she said. The second bell rang, announcing that we were officially late without an excuse. "Alec says you threatened him."

"I *warned* him that there were some kids who aren't too happy with him. He just assumed I meant me."

"Are you . . . jealous of him, because he's going out with me?"

I wish I could have flatly denied it. I mean, what kind of moron admits to his former girlfriend's face that he's jealous? I guess I was that moron.

"Yeah," I told her. "Yeah, I am, a little . . . but that's *not* what this is about."

And then, to my amazement, she said something that no one had said to me for a long time.

"I believe you."

I should have shut my mouth then—quit while I was ahead—but of course I didn't.

"Actually, I kinda like Alec," I said. "I mean, he's an okay guy, once you get past his perfection problem."

She looked at me sideways, and that one look told me I was done for.

"Just what do you mean by that?"

"Well, just . . . um . . . that he's weird about being good at everything."

"There is nothing wrong with aiming high."

"There is when you're hunting ducks with a bazooka." By now I was so far into it there was no sense pulling back. "I mean, overkill must be the guy's middle name. It's like he would die if someone else got to be the center of attention."

She crossed her arms in her prosecutor posture.

"If he's so totally into himself," she said, far too calmly, "then why is he helping *me* run for class president?"

I stumbled over my own thoughts for a moment, wondering when she had decided to run, and why I didn't know about it. There was a time when I would have been first to know.

"That's great," I said. "I'm glad he'll be helping your campaign." And then I added, "Prove me wrong about him— and I'll eat my shoe."

"You're on," she said, shaking my hand. "Only I get to pick which one—I want to make sure it's nice and grungy."

She turned and strode off to class, but I couldn't let her go—not yet, because there was something I had to tell her— something I had been thinking about since the moment I heard about the hair ball.

"I've been thinking of reconvening the Shadow Club."

My words stopped her dead in her tracks, but she didn't turn around. She just stood there for a few seconds, her back still turned.

"I thought maybe we could all get together and stop things from happening to Alec," I told her.

"You won't need to stop it, because nothing else will happen," she said, and continued on to class.

The administrators of our school district haven't quite come to grips with the twenty-first century, or even the twentieth, for that matter. Our desks are the same shellacked, pen-carved relics they used fifty years ago. There are still holes for inkwells in the corner. We're not required to wear uniforms, but every Friday we still have to dress up for assembly. We also have that rare animal called a "junior high school"—seventh, eighth, and ninth grades all together, leaving only three grades for our senior high school. If it were up to our district superintendent I'm sure we would all be in little red schoolhouses that dotted the coastline.

I really didn't mind the junior high school thing. I mean, sure, I wanted to be in high school, but there was something to be said about never having a freshman year. Our town has only one junior high and one senior high—massive buildings across town from each other—built in the days when schools were giant institutions like prisons, which meant that few things would change when I made the move from ninth grade to tenth grade, other than the length of my run every morning. Same basic kids, same basic attitudes—and what you sowed in kindergarten, you were still reaping in twelfth grade.

Since the senior high had only one feeding school, it had been decided some years ago that during the winter lull after Christmas vacation and before the standardized tests, elections would be held for next year's class president. Whoever won the honor in ninth grade would walk right into senior high, master of tenth grade.

Nominations came during the next Friday's assembly. The assembly featured a former state representative who was so old we were afraid he would expire before his parking meter outside. Following him were our official presidential nominations. It was common knowledge by now that Cheryl planned to run. She had weathered the storm of the Shadow Club far better than I had. Rather than earning her the label of "questionable kid," as it did for me, her involvement left an aura of awe around her. It was just the kind of quality that could get a person elected, and she knew it. Of course you couldn't nominate yourself, and so when the call came for nominations I quickly raised my hand to nominate her. Turns out I didn't need to. Alec held his hand high right next to her. He drew the principal's attention as he always drew everyone's attention. He was called on first.

"I nominate Cheryl Gannett," he said.

"I second that," shouted someone else.

"I accept," said Cheryl as if there would be any doubt.

I observed as the nominations went around the auditorium. In all there were about a dozen, but when push came to shove, few of them were seconded, and so those kids names never made the list. In the end it was Cheryl, Tommy Nickols, who was expected to be the school's valedictorian, and Katrina Mendelson, who had been trying to get elected since fourth grade. As the principal called for final nominations, one more hand went up. The hand belonged to Calvin Horner—a snively kid with a bit of a speech impediment and teeth almost as yellow as his hair. I wondered what on earth would possess him to stand up and speak in front of a crowd when it was always such a chore for him to answer a simple question in class.

"I would like to nominate Alec Smartz for class president," Calvin said.

There were more seconds than I could count, followed by a low afterburn of grumbles from those who were not pleased. I turned to see Alec shrug innocently at a gaping Cheryl as he said loudly, "I guess I accept."

That's when I saw Calvin Horner give a little nod to Alec, making it very clear that this was not a spontaneous act.

On Monday I came to school with a shoe box under my arm and approached Cheryl at her locker. Holding it like a waiter with a tray, I pulled off the lid.

"Canvas or leather," I said. "Your choice."

Inside, of course, were one of my dress shoes and a sneaker so grungy it could be considered hazardous waste.

"Oh, shut up."

I had to admit I felt bad for her, and guilty for having rubbed her nose in it. I shoved the shoe box under my arm.

"Sorry," I said. "I mean . . . I'm sorry Alec wasn't really behind you. It would have been great if you could have worked together."

"Actually," said Cheryl, "things will still work out. Chances are that one of us will win, and the other will take second place, which means we'd be each other's vice president."

"I don't think so," I said. "Two possibilities—assuming Katrina or Tommy don't pull it out—either (A) he'll win and you'll be his vice president; or (B) you'll win, and he will melt like the Wicked Witch of the West."

"Well, now you're just being nasty."

"No, I'm serious. Alec is not a vice presidential kind of guy. He might say so now, but that's just because he doesn't believe it will ever happen."

She slammed her locker, incredibly angry about how sure I was, and maybe a bit bothered by the knowledge that I was right. "That's your opinion," she said, "and if I didn't want your vote, I would tell you exactly where you could put that opinion."

There was a commotion farther down the hall. I didn't take much note of it until we both heard the name Alec

Smartz mumbled more than once. We went over to find out what was going on.

"Did you hear what happened to Alec?" said a kid who was anxious to tell anyone who would listen.

"What?" asked Cheryl apprehensively.

"He got skunked," the kid said. "Him and his whole family."

Cheryl's first reaction was relief that it hadn't been anything really bad, but that relief was quickly overshadowed by suspicion. "Wait a second . . . skunks aren't out this time of year—"

"Maybe he went poking in a hole where it was hibernating, or something," I suggested.

"Nope," said the kid, "it happened in their van. They got in it this morning, the skunk popped out from under a seat, and the rest is history."

Suddenly I got that same sense of looming doom I felt when I first heard about the hair ball in his soda. Unless skunks had acquired the ability to teleport, it was clear that it had been intentionally slipped into the Smartzes' family van.

Alec didn't show up for school that day, but he was there the next day. Although he tried to act as if nothing was wrong, that burned-rubbery smell of skunk surrounded him like killer BO, no matter how many demusking baths he took. And as for that minivan, it couldn't have been more totaled if it had fallen off a cliff.

Although Alec didn't accuse me to my face, the accusation was there all the same. It was in the way he looked at me—or refused to look at me. The second day after the skunking he came up to me as we were leaving English class, one of the few classes we had together. He didn't just bump into me—he made a point of coming up to me, and, although he hadn't said a word to me in two days, he looked at me, grinning in a way that I couldn't quite read, and said, "Nice shirt."

I figured he was just trying to bother me, you know, the way you say "nice socks" to someone whose socks are perfectly fine, making him wonder for the rest of the day what the heck is wrong with his socks. I just stored it away in my brain.

The weird thing Alec said wasn't the only thing bothering me. In fact, he didn't bother me as much as the looks I got from other kids—suspicious glances that were more obvious than ever before.

As I pulled books from my locker the next day, someone behind me said, "Good one, Jared!"

I spun on my heel, but when I looked at the kids around me, I couldn't tell who it had been. It could have been any of them. All of them. A hallway full of faces convinced that the Shadow Club and I had been responsible for the skunk as well as the hair ball.

That afternoon I slipped messages into six different lockers—messages that called the Shadow Club back from the dead.

The Ghosties

SOME PLACES, LIKE some people, age well, and others don't. They fall into disrepair and disrespect. That's how it was with the old marina. The old marina was on the north end of town, about a mile past the lighthouse ruin. The place wasn't exactly a picture postcard. The water was slick with a perpetual oily scum, and speckled with bits of trash. The wooden piles that held up the fishing pier had been eaten away, making the pier a use-at-your-own-risk kind of place. Of course, there were still die-hard fishermen—old-timers mostly—who set out from the marina every morning before dawn, but otherwise the place was a desolate relic of another time.

At the far bank of the inlet sat the half-submerged skeleton of a ferry that had been washed up during a storm, ten years back. On the south side of the inlet was a seawall made of eroding concrete, dripping rust from the reinforcing iron bars that now lay exposed to the sea. Just above that seawall, overlooking the marina, was the Ghosties.

The Ghosties was a graveyard of sorts—a boatyard of the

damned. Fishing boats, sailboats, cabin cruisers, you name it, they eventually found their way up to the Ghosties. Of course, few people would admit that when they towed their boat there, they were bringing their vessel to its eternal rest. The boats were brought here for repairs, or for storage. They sat in rusted trailers with flat tires, or cradled in scaffolding, waiting for their owners to return. But those owners would die of old age, or move on to other hobbies, leaving the forlorn boats to haunt the Ghosties, tortured by a beautiful view of the ocean that they would never set keel in again.

The sight of the old boats had always impressed me. They looked so much larger on dry land than in the sea— vessels that seemed so natural when bobbing with the tide, and so awkward and alien when dragged up on dry land.

The Ghosties had always been a great place for hide-and-seek when I was younger. Kids used to play it all the time here, until some kid fell off the seawall and drowned. After that the Ghosties had been fenced off . . . but when you live near the ocean, it doesn't take long for the salt air to rust through a chain-link fence.

"So what do you think?" Tyson asked as we meandered through the maze of abandoned boats.

"It'll do," I told him.

It had been his idea to meet here rather than at the Shadow Club's old meeting place—that old foundation in the woods we had called "Stonehenge." Too many bad memories there—and besides, if people were starting to suspect us, that would be the first place they'd look. This secret meeting required a new secret place.

"This way," said Tyson, leading me between the peeling hulls, until we came to the remains of a tugboat left to rot within a steel cradle barely large enough to hold it. It was clearly the largest boat in the Ghosties, and it sat there like a monument, just by the edge of the seawall, overlooking the ocean.

A swell smashed against the seawall some ten feet below, sending salt spray across the old boat's hull. "Someone bought it for salvage, I think," Tyson said. "They gutted it and left its shell up here."

On its lower hull was a hole about two feet wide. No doubt this tug had an interesting story to tell, but I suspected it never would.

"I used to come here when things got real bad," Tyson said, poking his head up through the hole in the hull. "Great place to go when you don't want to be found. Have a look."

I leaned into the hole in the hull. The space smelled of mildew and diesel fuel, but I couldn't see a thing.

Then I heard the far-off rattle of the rusty fence, which meant either our meeting was about to begin, or we were being chased away. I hurried off toward the sound, but found myself lost in the maze of boats. It was Jason Perez who found me, rather than the other way around.

"Hey," he said. I turned around to see him keeping his distance. "So, like, where are the others?"

"You're the first."

"Oh." He didn't seem to like the idea of being first. "I hope you know, I ditched band practice for this." He took a few steps closer, and so did I, hoping the discomfort between us would fade with each step. It didn't. "Are you sure the others are coming?"

"No."

"Well, if they don't show," he said, "I'm bailing. I don't even know why I came in the first place."

"I'm glad you did." I reached out my hand to him, and he looked at it for a long moment. Finally he accepted it, shaking halfheartedly, but then he tensed as he saw someone over my shoulder. I turned to see Tyson coming up behind us.

"It's okay," I told Jason. "I invited him."

"Oh . . . uh . . . nice to see you, Tyson."

"Yeah, yeah." said Tyson. I guess you couldn't expect any more from the two of them. I mean, the last time they were this close to each other, Jason and the others were trying to drown him with their bare hands.

"So . . . like, you're a member of the club now, Tyson?" Jason asked.

"No . . . I'm kind of an independent observer."

"There is no club!" said a voice behind us. We turned to see Darren Collins coming out from behind a broken catamaran. "The Shadow Club doesn't exist, and I'm guessing we're here to make sure of it."

"You guessed right," I told him. I have to admit I was surprised he had come at all. Of all the members of the club, he was the one who had pulled the farthest away from the rest of us. He wouldn't talk to us, wouldn't acknowledge us in class. It wasn't so much a cold shoulder, as a "no shoulder." It was as if the only way he could get past it was simply to cut the Shadow Club out of his life. He played basketball the same way—blocking out everything but his teammates, the ball, and the basket. That's what made him so good.

Abbie showed up next, looking as beautiful as ever, dressed one week ahead of the fashions. "OK," she said, "I'm dying to find out what possible reason you have for getting us all together."

Karin "O. P." Han showed up with Randall. She didn't say much, but as with the others, her eyes darted to Tyson, and looked away, ashamed.

"My sister chickened out," Randall said. "Cheryl's not coming."

"Big surprise," said Darren.

"Too bad," I said, trying to hide how disappointed I really felt. "But we can do this without her."

"Do what?" asked Abbie.

"Duh," said Randall, his same old obnoxious self, "figure out which one of us is pranking on Alec Smartz."

Everyone glanced at one another with the same suspicion that the other kids in school heaped on us.

"What makes you so sure it was one of us?" I asked him.

He looked at the others, one by one, and then his thoughts seemed to turn in on himself. "I don't know," he said. "I just figured . . ."

And that was half the problem right there. If even the members of the Shadow Club believed it was one of our own, how would we ever gain one another's trust again?

Tyson and I led them up to the old tugboat and through the hole in the hull. When our eyes had adjusted to the light spilling in from the hole below, and the dozens of little separations in the old boat's wooden planks, we found ourselves in a strange and very private world. The empty shell of the tugboat's keel was like an upside-down attic. Although the space was about thirty feet long, and seven feet high, it still felt claustrophobic. I didn't like it. Rats hide in forgotten places like this, I thought. And I'm not a rat. The fact that we had to hide at all made me regret having even called them together. I mean, was Alec Smartz really worth all this trouble? And if my heart really *was* in the right place, then why was my spirit confined to the moldering shell of an abandoned boat?

"We didn't do anything to Alec Smartz," I said, once everyone was up inside our new meeting place. I didn't ask them, I told them. If there was one thing in this world that

I knew, it was that all of us—even Randall—had come through the ordeal better than when we started. None of us would pull that sort of mean-spirited prank on anyone ever again. Although it was dim in the shell of the old boat, I could see enough of their faces to know I was right.

"So, like, we're supposed to prove our innocence before the whole world blames us, right?" said Jason.

"It's not about proving our innocence," I told him. "It's about stopping the pranks."

"How are we supposed to stop the pranks if we don't know who's pulling them?" asked Darren.

"We do some detective work," I said. "We find out."

"Why should we care a rat's butt about Alec Smartz, anyway?" asked Randall.

"Because we started it. None of this would be happening if we didn't start the pranks last fall."

"Statistics show," said O. P., "that the most notorious of criminals often have copycats—and sometimes those copycats are worse than the ones they're copying."

"Oh, come on," said Abbie, tossing back her hair, "we're not exactly serial killers."

"No," said Tyson, "but you came pretty close to killing me."

Tyson had been so quiet, sitting all the way up toward the bow, that we had almost forgotten he was there. It sobered us up a little bit.

"We set the pattern," I told them. "We were the ones who put the idea in people's heads, and now they're picking up where we left off. I don't know who it is, but I do know that the pranks are going to get worse and worse, just like they did the first time. When we formed the Shadow Club, it's like we let something loose in this town that didn't die when we burned the charter."

"You mean like a demon or something?" asked Randall.

"Now you're getting me all spooked," said Jason with a nervous chuckle.

"Call it what you want," I told them. "A demon—or just a bad idea—but either way it's not going away until we find a way to shoot it with a silver bullet."

"I thought that was for a werewolf," said Jason.

"Get a clue," said Abbie.

I let the thought sit with them for a few long moments. The wind blew across the hole in the hull, like someone breathing across the mouth of a bottle, and the whole tugboat began to resonate with a faint deep moan.

That's when Darren said, "I'm outta here." He stood up, balancing himself on the slanted floor beneath him. "I've got better things to do than start dreaming up problems that don't exist."

I was too stunned to say a thing.

Abbie stood up next. "I mean, really, Jared, you've got yourself all worked up into a panic for no reason."

"What a waste of an afternoon," said Randall.

"Wait a second," I said, just beginning to see how totally I had misread them. "Don't you care at all about what's happening?"

Jason shrugged. "People were pulling pranks long before the Shadow Club existed," he said. "Just because they're doing it now doesn't mean we, like, *inspired* them or something. It probably has nothing to do with us."

"Yeah," agreed Abbie. "Alec Smartz has made as many enemies as he has made friends."

I looked to O. P., who had seemed to be more on my side than any of the others, but now she looked away. "I think maybe you're being too paranoid, Jared."

I stood there watching them leave, not sure what to say that could convince them they were wrong. That, yeah, maybe I was paranoid, but sometimes that cleared your vision more than it clouded it.

"The Shadow Club's dead," said Darren. "Let it stay that way." Then he slipped out through the hull, leaving Tyson and me alone. Tyson didn't move from his little perch way up at the bow. He must have sat in that spot when he used to come here by himself.

"That went well," he said.

"Oh, shut up."

I thought the meeting was over, but when Tyson and I slipped out through the hole, we were met by an unexpected guest.

"I could have told you they wouldn't go for it," said

Cheryl. I turned to see her standing just a few yards away. I wondered whether she had been there all along, listening, or if she had just arrived in time to see everyone else desert.

"Easy for you to say, now that they've all gone." I was a bit angry that she hadn't done anything to help, but also grateful that she decided to come after all.

"They've got nothing to gain by helping you find the new prankster. The further away from it they stay, the better for them."

"That's what they think, but they're wrong. It's going to come back in their faces, the way it's come back in mine."

A wave broke on the seawall below us and sent up a burst of foam that soaked Tyson.

"Oh, man . . ." Tyson used it as an excuse to leave, but I knew he felt uncomfortable being there—a kind of third wheel between Cheryl and me. When Tyson was gone, she took a step closer.

"Alec thinks there ought to be a new club—one that will cancel out the Shadow Club."

"One that *he's* in charge of?"

"It could be a good thing. All right, I'll admit he's a little bit conceited, but his heart's in the right place."

Hearing that made me suddenly feel the chill of the ocean breeze.

"Does he know how much you stand up for him?"

"No," answered Cheryl, "but he knows how much I stand up for *you.*"

That shut me up real quick. On the one hand it felt good to know that she would still stick up for me. On the other hand, Cheryl always knew the exact words to say to win a conversation with me. Lately reading her had been like looking into a one-way mirror. I could only tell what was behind her words in a certain rare light, which wasn't shining today.

I couldn't look her in the eye, so I turned and stepped over to the ledge, where the seawall rose from below and met the flat mesa of the Ghosties. It was an unguarded precipice, and I marveled at how stupid we all were to play here when we were little. I longed for that kind of stupidity again, when I didn't know enough to see danger around me. Far off I heard the fence rattle as Tyson made his way out of the Ghosties. The sound brought me back to the here and now.

"Maybe we'd better go," I told Cheryl.

Another wave sprayed up over the ledge, dousing us, as if the sea itself was trying to chase us away. I heard the fence rattle again, and figured it must have just been the wind. We turned away from the tugboat, and left together, but it was painfully obvious to both of us that we were very much apart.

The next afternoon, I went with Tyson down to the community pool. One of my many New Year's resolutions had been to teach Tyson to swim. I figured it was one small way to try and make up for the part I played in almost drowning him last fall.

At first I took him to the pool several times a week, but, like all New Year's resolutions, my resolve faded pretty quickly. I hadn't given him a lesson for more than three weeks. But now, with so many things squirming around in my brain, I welcomed the chance to focus my thoughts on something else. I dragged Tyson down to the pool, with him resisting all the way.

"It's cold." "I'm tired." "I got too much homework." "I think I got an earache."

Tyson was never an eager learner when it came to anything, but today I wasn't taking no for an answer.

Our local pool had a personality all its own. First of all it wasn't even called a pool, it was called a "natatorium," which I guess was a gymnasium for swimming. With a fancy name like that, they could charge two bucks to get in. The natatorium had an Olympic-sized pool, and huge windows that were always so fogged it defeated the purpose of having windows in the first place. As for the pool itself, well, it was about as clouded as the windows. I used to wear goggles when I swam, but stopped because I got tired of looking at all those unidentifiable bits of floating organic matter. There are just some things I'd rather not know about.

Tyson had managed to master the dog paddle pretty early on in our lessons, and now he proudly huffed and puffed his way through six laps like a Labrador, while I swam a fairly lame, but effective crawl.

"Listen, do you want to learn to swim or not?" I snapped as he tried to climb out of the pool.

"What do you call what I just did? That was six laps!"

I pulled him back into the water. "Six dog laps," I corrected. "That's not even one human lap, Fido."

In the lane beside us, which was reserved for the more serious swimmers, someone did a quick flip turn and splashed super-chlorinated water up my nose.

"Ughh!" I sneezed and tried to clear my burning sinuses.

"Serves you right," Tyson said.

When I looked up to see who had splashed me, I caught sight of Drew Landers, our school's number one swimmer, peering out at me from beneath his armpit for an instant, as he stroked forward, toward the deep end of the pool.

"He did that on purpose!" I said.

"What, is like everyone out to get you now?" Tyson said. "You're starting to sound like me. That's scary."

"Tell me about it."

Drew Landers, however, did have a reason to hold a grudge against me—after all, the Shadow Club had pranked him exceptionally well during that first round of pranks, when it all still felt like fun, before it started getting dangerous. We had paid Drew a midnight visit, and peeled back the grungy socks from his feet as he slept. Then we painted his toenails red and put the socks back on. He didn't take them off again until swim practice the next day, and, let me tell you, it made quite an impression on the swim team—not to mention the coach, who scheduled him an immediate visit to Mr. Greene for tender guidance. I had to admit, though, Drew did manage to turn the whole situation around. Rather than clean off his toes, he painted every other toenail white, so his feet proudly displayed our school colors of red and white. He said it was a sign of school spirit. Since he was the team captain, and one of the cool-defining personalities of our school, the entire swim team followed his lead and went the rest of the season with red-and-white-painted toenails. I think this is how really stupid traditions are born.

"C'mon," I told Tyson, trying to forget about Drew. "I'll teach you the crawl."

"Tyson McGaw never crawls."

"Then Tyson McGaw drowns."

"Have you ever known a dog that drowned?"

He had a point, but he wasn't getting out of it so fast. "Would you like it better if I called it 'freestyle'?"

"Yeah. I could get into freestyle."

I tried to work with him on the rhythm of his breathing, but then took another blast of water in the face. It gagged me, and I coughed up like half a lung. When my eyes cleared, I saw Drew Landers standing in the pool beside us, doing some sort of swimmer's stretch with his arm behind his head like a contortionist.

"Your stroke bites the biscuit," Drew told me. "If Tyson wants swimming lessons, he should have asked me."

"Yeah, right," said Tyson. "Like you'd care."

Drew only shrugged. "It's a community service," he said. "Community service always looks good on your permanent record."

"Thanks, but we're doing fine by ourselves," I told him, and tried to get back to the lesson. I hoped Drew would just push off and continue his laps, but he didn't.

"I hear you've been pranking on Alec Smartz."

I took a deep, slow breath, and tried not to let anger seep into my voice. "You heard wrong."

"That skunk was rank and righteous!" Drew said. "Was that the first time you ever skunked someone?"

"No!" I insisted. "I mean yes! I mean neither! I didn't do it!"

"Hey, you know what they say: *He who denied it, supplied it.*"

"No," said Tyson, "that's for farts."

Drew shrugged. "Skunks, farts, not much of a difference, is there?" Drew reached up and did his contortionist stretch again. "Can't say Alec didn't deserve it, though—the way he's been strutting around like he's God's gift to whatever."

"If you hate him so much," I said, "then how do we know that *you* didn't do it?"

Drew slipped his goggles back on. "Because I lack the psycho-factor—but not you. In fact, put the two of you together and there's enough psycho to make national head-lines."

I was going to say something back—something truly wise and profound, or at least just flip him off, but before I could, he slipped back under the water and pushed off, swimming away as silently as a shark.

"That really ticks me off," I grumbled.

Tyson nodded. "Wanna go on a rampage?"

I shivered, feeling cold with half of my body out of the water. "That's not even funny."

The Microscope
and the
Magnifying Glass

I HAD TO accept that, in the real world, there was no such thing as being innocent until proven guilty. Everyone was happy to assume I was guilty, and I was the only one who could prove my innocence. That would take some serious investigation.

I'm not much of a detective. I used to read all those three-minute mystery books, but I never had the patience to figure them out, so I'd just turn to the back to find the answer. I always seemed to miss the details that were most important. While Tyson wasn't stupid, he was no great brain either, and so together the two of us felt less like Holmes and Watson, and more like Beavis and Butthead.

The hair ball trail was cold. There was no sense even trying to solve that one. So Tyson and I spent the next afternoon on a skunk-out. Cheryl had been right when she said that skunks weren't out this time of year, and even if they were, it would have taken quite a lot of effort to catch one. Seemed to me that the skunk had to come from the Nature

Center. It was a small building down a dirt road, famous for grammar school field trips, and an adopt-a-snake program that hadn't gone over very well. Tyson and I saw what we expected when we went in: metal cages filled with everything from guinea pigs to porcupines, and glass aquariums that housed iguanas and many an unadopted python. The ranger, or whoever it was who ran the place, wasn't there, but we did find one of our classmates, Jodi Lattimer, cleaning out a rabbit cage.

The half grin on Tyson's face as we approached testified to the crush he had on Jodi. She was one of those down-to-earth girls who never seemed to have a problem with being elbow deep in compost. She was pretty but found a variety of ways to hide it. Today it was a denim baseball cap turned backward to cover her long blond hair. She was the kind of girl I might have had a crush on if I hadn't known Tyson was already there.

"Hi, guys. What's up?" she said. I stepped forward, trying to figure the best way to say this without sounding too terribly stupid. "We were wondering if you, by any chance, had misplaced a skunk."

She grinned, knowing exactly why we were asking, and Tyson grinned back, probably thinking her smile was for him. "You mean had a skunk been *stolen*, don't you?" she said.

"Naah," said Tyson. "Can't steal a wild animal, they belong to everyone." I rolled my eyes.

"Well," said Jodi, "apparently somebody thought this

skunk belonged to them." She went on to tell us that some-body had pried open a back window and had run off with it a few nights ago. "God knows how they got it out of here without it spraying all over them—unless, of course, they drugged it."

We went around the side of the building to the window that had been pried open, searching for footprints or some-thing, but the ground was hard, dry, and covered with dense pine needles. Nothing to give away who it might have been.

"We don't have much to go on," commented Tyson.

Jodi crossed her arms and smirked, "Come on, you guys, the way you're talking you'd think you were investigating a murder."

"Maybe we are," I said. "After all, the skunk hasn't been seen since it escaped from Alec's van."

She laughed at that, and then I noticed Tyson starting to get all fidgety, annoyed that I had made her laugh instead of him.

"If you want to do a real investigation, you ought to talk to my father," she said.

"Oh yeah!" said Tyson. "He interrogated me once." And then his face went slightly purple from that particular foot in his mouth. Jodi's father was a high-ranking police deputy, which was a pretty dull job in this town. Usually.

"Didn't he talk to the Smartzes already?"

"Probably, but I'm sure he'd like to know of your interest in the case."

As I was still the prime suspect, talking to the police was not currently high on my list of fun activities. At least not until I had my own suspects. "Let's just leave this a private investigation," I told her.

"Yeah," said Tyson, grinning dumbly at her. "Kind of like 'intimate.' "

I went through a list of interrogation questions I had scrawled on my note pad: Were there any suspicious characters in the area? Have animals been stolen before? Blah blah blah. Every question was answered with a simple "No." When there were no questions left we said our good-byes, but before we headed back down the dirt road, I couldn't stop myself from turning to her and saying, "You know that I didn't do it, don't you?"

Jodi just shrugged. "Whatever you say." She adjusted her cap and went inside to finish tending to the rabbits.

"I think she likes me," said Tyson as we walked off.

I was about to say "Dream on," but stopped myself. Instead I said, "Maybe so." Because in all truth I couldn't tell what anyone was thinking anymore.

On Monday the school was plastered, and I mean *plastered* with campaign banners, spread like wallpaper so you couldn't see the color of the walls. **Vote for Tommy Nickols**, some of them said, **The thinking man's candidate** (which obviously wasn't true, because by choosing "thinking man's" rather than "thinking person's" he had thoughtlessly alienated the entire female vote). **Vote for Katrina Mendelson,** other banners proclaimed. **Isn't it time?** Cheryl had her share as well. Hers had no clever slogan but a practical and attractive list of the changes she planned to make. She included things like economic sanctions against old man Solerno until he changed the recipe of his god-awful pizza, and raising the temperature of the gym from subarctic conditions.

But by far the most banners, posters, fliers, and signs were for candidate Alec Emery Smartz Jr. I couldn't help but overhear a conversation between Alec and Cheryl near her locker.

"What did you do," she said, "hire elves to paint them for you?"

Alec laughed it off. "In a way," he said. "A lot of the seventh and eighth graders just volunteered."

"You know, that really shouldn't be allowed," said Cheryl. "I mean, they can't even vote in the ninth-grade election."

Alec sighed. "If it bothers you that much, I'll take them down."

But Cheryl, of course, backed off. "No, no," she said. "Anyway, it's quality not quantity, and after all, my banners say more than just my name." She smiled at him, he smiled back, and they toddled off to class together as if there were no tension between them. But I knew Cheryl better than that, and I was beginning to wonder which was more important to her now, their budding romance or the competition between them.

"I'm glad Alec has so much support," Cheryl told me the next day in science lab. "Especially being so new to town. He's made lots of friends very quickly."

"And lots of enemies."

She shrugged it off, but it clearly bothered her. "Kids that don't like him just don't know him." Then she quickly changed the subject. "Any more luck with the Shadow Club?" I put my eye to the microscope, where I caught several paramecia wandering around between the thin sheets of glass. "No," I answered. "I'm running my own investigation without them."

"Really," said Cheryl. "So is Alec. He still thinks you pulled the pranks and says he wants to prove to me what a sniveling waste of life you are. I told him I already knew that—but it doesn't mean you pulled those pranks." She gave me a smile that made her most biting comments go down smoothly. "Anyway," she said, "you don't have to worry, because I don't believe it was you."

"So convince him."

"I can't. Anytime we talk about you, we always start yelling at each other, so Alec and I have a rule that we are not allowed to discuss you anymore."

"Does that come before or after the rule that you're not allowed to be better than him in anything?"

Cheryl turned the microscope focus until the lens cracked the fragile glass slide.

"Oh, great." She reached to prepare another slide.

As I looked up I saw several kids around the lab quickly avert their eyes. They had been watching us, listening to us, and I got that feeling again. O. P. said it was just paranoia, but I don't know. One girl rolled her neck, as if she hadn't been looking at all. Another kid adjusted his baseball cap when I looked at him, as if he hadn't been motioning to his lab partner to look our way. Suddenly I began to feel like those paramecia beneath the microscope's eye, unable to squirm out of view.

I was late leaving school that day, and there weren't many people left in the halls. Usually those halls are so noisy, you can't hear your own thoughts, but with most of the school gone, even the slightest noises sounded as if they were blasted over the loudspeaker. The sound of tearing paper echoed down the locker-lined hallway, and I followed it to the first floor, where I found Austin Pace tearing down one of Cheryl's big campaign banners.

"What are you doing?"

He turned to me, then went back to his task. "Isn't it obvious?" He crumpled the banner down, so it would fit in a trash can. It wasn't like he was doing this in secret—I mean, there were still some kids and teachers wandering the halls, but he didn't care. It was as if he wanted to be caught. He was daring people to make him stop.

"What's the point?"

"The point is, after what you and Cheryl did, she doesn't deserve to run for class president, or anything else. You might have been the mastermind, but *she* was the one who broke my ankle." By now he had crumpled the banner down to the size of a basketball. He tossed it toward the Hefty-lined trash can. It dropped in without even touching the rim. "Three pointer," he said. "Nothing but bag."

He crossed the hallway, to tear down another of Cheryl's banners. I grabbed his wrist to stop him, but he shook me off. Then he shoved me. I shoved him back, and we both stood there, waiting to see if it would escalate. Instead of going for me again, he reached over and tore down the banner.

"Y'know, my mom invited Cheryl over for dinner, too," Austin said. "She was smarter than you, though. She refused." He wadded up the banner. "Hey, why don't you help me? You once asked what would make me happy, and right now you helping me tear down *her* banners would warm the bottom of my heart."

He waited, but I didn't move.

"No, I didn't think so. I'm sure you'll even tell her that it was me who tore them down. Well, good. I want you to tell her."

But I had already decided not to tell Cheryl about it. Resentment had more faces and more sideways glances than a deck of cards, and if this was how Austin wanted to play out his hand, I wasn't going to stop him, and I wasn't going to give him the satisfaction of tattling to Cheryl. Part of me even agreed with Austin. After what the Shadow Club had done, Cheryl should have stayed out of the election the way I resigned from the track team—but that was her decision to make, and I wasn't going to judge her for it. My judging days were over.

"Have fun with your anti-campaign," I told him, and left him alone to score whatever trash can baskets he felt he needed.

Austin's banner vandalism was just more evidence that the anger in our school was breeding like bacteria. I might not have been responsible for everyone's anger, but I had certainly been a carrier. I could only hope it wasn't about to become an epidemic.

By now the entire school was anxiously anticipating what would happen to Alec next. I knew that I was, and I was not looking forward to getting the blame, or the credit, as some kids at school would put it.

It happened after gym class—another class that Alec and I had together. We'd been doing tumbles and unimpressive moves on the parallel bars. I never minded gym, but I could tell Alec hated it. As he liked to enter any activity at the very top, he despised being forced to engage in sports in which he wasn't already the best—and though he claimed to be a whiz at any sport that involved a ball, he was an absolute klutz when it came to gymnastics. So when class was over and we hit the locker rooms, he wasn't in the best of moods. My gym locker was just a few feet away from his. Usually we faced in opposite directions when we dressed so we wouldn't have to deal with each other, but today he felt like striking up a conversation.

"You really must like that shirt," he said to me with a smirk on his face. "You wear it an awful lot."

It was the same shirt he had commented about once before. It was just a plain, old blue-buttoned shirt.

"So," I said. "It's comfortable."

"You should wash it once in a while," he suggested. "You might find it smells better."

"At least it doesn't smell like skunk," I said under my breath but loud enough for him to hear.

"You've got Cheryl fooled, but you haven't fooled me," he said. "And you'll get what you deserve sooner than you think."

I closed my locker. "Was that a threat?"

"Nope," he said, "because I won't sink down to your level."

He pulled out a hairbrush and a bottle of styling gel, then pumped some of the clear gel into his hand.

"You believe what you want," I told him, "but when the truth comes out, I'll be expecting a major apology from you."

He laughed at that, rubbing the gel between his hands, then brushing his hands through his perfect hair. Right about then I began to smell a chemical odor, like paint or varnish. Schools were filled with weird smells, so I didn't think about it at first, until I noticed the look on Alec's face. His hands were still moving through his hair, spreading the gel, but his hands weren't moving as freely as they should have been.

By now some other kids had begun to take notice.

"What the . . . what is this?"

His hands were still firmly pressed against the sides of his head. He tried to pull them away, but they weren't coming.

"This isn't my hair gel!"

As the smell around me grew stronger, I recognized it. My father and I had smelled it out in the garage when trying to glue back together some broken lawn furniture. It was the smell of Lunar Glue—a super-epoxy "so strong it could hold the moon in orbit," went the slogan—and right now it was spread across Alec Smartz's entire head. Lunar Glue was a prank as old as time, and although it was always funny in TV and in movies, the reality wasn't so funny. It was like watching a hummingbird caught on flypaper.

I found myself backing away, as if putting distance between me and the sabotaged bottle of gel would cast the guilt off of my shoulders.

"Don't look at *me*," I said, but that's exactly where Alec was looking.

"*What did you do to me!*" he shouted, beginning to go red in the face. He tried to pull his hands away from his hair, but his head just tilted with the motion of his hands, bonded there, like a pot. Shirtless and barefoot he stumbled out of the locker room with me and a dozen other kids behind him. The bell had rung and the hall was filled with kids. Someone bumped his elbow. "Ahh," he screamed, and he spun like a turnstile.

"You're going down for this, Mercer," he said. "You're going down in a major way."

Through the crowd I saw Cheryl, wondering what on earth was going on.

"Alec?"

By now the group of kids around us had expanded, and more people took notice of Alec's strange shirtless position. Now Alec was the center of attention—the place he always wanted to be, but not quite the way that he wanted it.

"Alec, what's wrong?" asked Cheryl, looking to him, to me, then back to him again.

"I've been Lunar Glued," he said with a whine in his voice.

And that's when someone laughed. I don't know who it was, but that laugh started it. It was just a snicker at first, and then another, and then another.

"Shut up!" said Alec. "It's not funny!"

And he was right. It wasn't, and yet I found a grin coming to my face as well. It had to do with the way that he was just standing there, his hands in a permanent pose on the sides of his head, like a fashion model. A hummingbird on flypaper, horrible and helpless—but the mob's laughter was contagious. I found myself beginning to giggle, just one among the rising chorus of laughter, as Cheryl reached up and tried to pull his hands away from his head.

"Oh, Alec," she said, and she, too, started laugning.

It became uncontrollable. As awful and as terrible as it was—as cruel as it was—a part of all of us just had to laugh and laugh and laugh, until tears came to our eyes. But it wasn't everyone's laughter that Alec heard. It was mine and Cheryl's.

I Am Not Now Nor Have I Ever Been a Waste of Life

SOMETIMES I HAVE to close my eyes and put myself back in the burning lighthouse. It's kind of like scratching at a scab; it itches, and you know that's because it's healing, but you can't stop scratching it. Pretty soon it begins to bleed, and you've got to start healing all over again. They put these cones around dogs' heads to keep them from scratching wounds. I wish someone could put some kind of cone around me, because on the day Alec's hand got glued to his head, I couldn't help but scratch. I went down to the beach where Tyson and I had washed ashore, that day back in October. There were still plenty of reminders—like the burned timbers half buried in the sand. The smell of charred wood had mingled with the salty aroma of decaying kelp. The sound of the sea was a constant reminder, too—the rumble of the breakers and the hiss of the spray—such a comfort to some people, so threatening to me.

I walked the beach all that afternoon, looking at the

burned driftwood, listening to the uneasy echoes of the world around me in seashells, picking the scab.

I was so lost in my own thoughts, I didn't notice that I wasn't alone on the beach, until I practically walked into two kids heading the other way.

"Oh, sorry," I said. It took me a moment to register who they were. It was none other than Brett Whatley and our resident large dude, Moose SanGiorgio. After my fight with Brett the other week, he was the last person I wanted to see. As for Moose, well, he was kind of like human flavor enhancer; he wasn't much by himself, but somehow his linebacker presence doubled the intensity of whomever he was with. In this case it turned Brett Whatley from a general nuisance into a four-star general nuisance.

"We got a message for you from Alec Smartz," Brett said, then he tried to deliver a punch to my gut. He must have seen too many action movies, however, because he sort of did it in slow motion. I caught his fist in my open palm and squeezed, cracking all of his knuckles. It sounded like a bag of microwave popcorn.

"Arrggg!"

He pulled back his hand, grimacing, and almost fell to his knees.

"That's gotta hurt," said Moose.

Moose was actually a pretty intelligent guy when he was around intelligent people, but today he was taking his lead from a guy with the mental capacity of a canned ham. Still, I tried to address Moose's more sensible side.

"So, Moose, what's the deal here? Did Alec really send you guys to beat me up?"

"He hired us as bodyguards," Moose said happily. "The beating-you-up part was Brett's idea."

Brett grunted, still shaking his aching hand.

"What's Alec paying you?" I asked Moose.

"He says he'll give us positions in his cabinet when he gets elected class president."

"Get cash," I told him.

"I'll consider it."

Brett, having recovered, glared at me. "We're here to tell you that you'd better lay off Alec, or we may have to take steps."

"Ooh—that's a tough one," I said, and did a quick search through my long-term movie memory. "Ah! I've got it! Michael Beihn said that in *The Abyss*. Am I right?"

"Shut up."

By now my moron-meter was in the red, and I couldn't stand much more. "Listen if you guys want to be Alec's personal Secret Service, that's fine with me—but until you catch me red-handed trying to mess with him, stay out of my airspace!"

"Fair enough," said Moose, and stepped aside.

I shouldered Brett out of my way, and although he threw

a clump of wet sand at my back, I refused to let him provoke me.

"It'll only be a matter of time, Mercer," he shouted after me. "The truth is out there!"

My father cornered me in the kitchen the next morning before I left for school. "I want to talk about the message I got from your vice principal yesterday."

"I thought we talked last night." Actually I got out of having to discuss it by asking him to help me with math. I did need the help, and he was so pleased that I had asked him for anything that he forgot about the phone message from Mr. Greene (which luckily didn't give a clue as to why he had called). We had a good time, believe it or not, doing algebra together. Then, when the work was done, I guess he didn't have the heart to talk to me about Greene. I did hear him and Mom worry-talking, though, later at night when they thought I was asleep.

Dad poured himself a bowl of cereal. "I plan to call him back as soon as I get into work."

"Good. He likes it when people are prompt." I burned my fingers as I pulled my waffle from the toaster, and grimaced, shaking the pain out of my hand. My mom had already left for work, so they couldn't double-team me, but Dad was doing fine on his own.

"Are you in some sort of trouble, Jared? What's going

on in school? Have you done something we should know about?"

In social studies, we'd been learning about McCarthyism—you know—how back in the fifties some senators whose shorts got too tight decided that everyone who picked their nose the wrong way was a Communist. They formed a committee and began to ask people all kinds of questions like, "Are you now, or have you ever been a Communist?" Sort of like the questions my dad was asking now. Some people got really good at not answering.

"Have you done something wrong, Jared?"

"Not that I recall."

"Is there a reason why Mr. Greene would be calling us?"

"Not that I know of."

"What about your friends? Have they been getting into any trouble?"

"You want me to name names?"

He stared at me, like he so often did, in that state of parental confusion. It was Tyson who saved me.

"Mr. Greene was probably calling about me," Tyson said as he came into the kitchen. "He said he would call to see how I was doing with my new foster family." Tyson took my waffle. "So how am I doing?"

Dad relaxed. He was much more at ease with Tyson lately than he was with me. "Aside from eating us out of house and home, you're doing fine." Then he said his standard good-bye, and left.

"I really don't like lying to my parents," I told Tyson after my father was gone.

"Hey, what use am I if I don't teach you some bad habits?" he said.

"Anyway," I reminded him, "it won't hold up very long. He'll call Greene back, and I'll get my butt kicked halfway to China."

"Naah," Tyson said. "Your dad's not a butt-kicker, and anyway, he's not going to punish you for something you didn't do."

I wasn't so sure about that. I knew I had broken my parents' trust before. Would they believe me now, or would the weight of everyone else's suspicion sway them? When the Shadow Club was brought to justice the first time, they had taken away all my privileges—TV, video games, time with friends, time *anywhere* unsupervised. Gradually they had begun to give those things back, but they still withheld the most important thing of all: their trust. I had always taken it for granted that a parent's trust was a right, not a privilege.

As I pondered my own parents' faith in me, there was a knock at the door. I opened the door to see a kid standing there. A kid with a crew cut. It took me a few seconds to realize that it was Alec. Then it occurred to me that his little run-in with the Lunar Glue would leave him like that. I took a step back, almost expecting him to sock me or something, but that's not what he had in mind. He had a new look on his face. Yes, I could see anger there, but now there was something else, too, on top of the anger and resentment. It was fear.

"I want to know what I have to do to get you to stop," he said.

Tyson came in from the kitchen, took a few moments to gauge the situation, and slipped out the back door, realizing this was between just me and Alec.

"Why don't you come in," I said to him.

"Why? Is there an anvil hanging over the door?"

I backed up and opened the door wide to show him there was nothing about to fall on his head. Then he stepped in. I hurried to the kitchen.

"Want a waffle?" I asked him, fumbling with the package of frozen waffles.

"Not hungry."

"The haircut kinda suits you," I said, and then grimaced, realizing how dumb it was to say it.

"No, it doesn't," he said. "My cheeks are too big. I look like a chipmunk with a crew cut. What is it going to take to make you stop?" he said again.

This was a white flag of surrender, and as much as his arrogant nature irked me, I was even more bothered to see him defeated.

"You've got it wrong, Alec," I told him. "I'm not the enemy."

"Then what are you?" he said. "Because you're definitely not a friend."

I put my hands in my pockets. He was right, I wasn't a friend, but that really wasn't my fault.

"You don't have friends, Alec," I told him. "You have subjects, and servants."

"You wish you had a tenth of the respect that I had, but you don't, and that's why you hate me, isn't it? That and Cheryl."

"Leave Cheryl out of this." Then I leaned against the counter and took a deep breath. He was trying to draw me in, to make me angry, but I wasn't falling for that.

"Listen," I said, "maybe this was the last prank. Maybe, just maybe, the person who did it has realized it's gone too far, and they feel sorry they did it."

Alec stared at me, his eyes cold, unbelieving.

"And maybe they don't."

No matter how hard I tried, I couldn't help but face his angry distrust with matching defiance. "I guess we'll just have to wait and see, won't we."

A Bitter Pill

WAS CALLED INTO Mr. Greene's office right after lunch.

There were several chairs in Mr. Greene's office: a plush comfortable one for setting kids' minds at ease, a beanbag for less formal counseling sessions . . . and then there was the old wooden chair; a worn-out, high-backed, dark monster with wide armrests. Kids called it the "Electric Chair." This was the chair he had positioned in front of his desk when I was escorted into his office that morning.

"Come in, Jared. Have a seat," he said.

I sat down in the uncomfortable chair, figuring I would hear the same old stuff about how he thought I was the center of all local evil, but all he said was: "I like your shirt."

I looked down to notice that this was the same shirt I had worn on the days when Alec had commented on my shirt as well.

"I like your tie," I said to him. "Have you spoken to my parents yet?"

"We've been missing each other's calls." And then he sat there and just stared at me.

"Listen, is this important, because I'm missing English class."

"I will ask you this once," he said, "and I expect an honest answer."

"Sure."

"Did you put a skunk in Alec Smartz's minivan?"

"No, I did not," I said as directly as I could.

He leaned back in his chair, with a slight look of satisfaction on his face. "You might want to think about your answer." And then he reached into his drawer, pulled out a tiny plastic bag, and tossed it on his desk. At first I thought the bag was empty, but then I saw something in it—something small—something round and blue. It was a shirt button that looked very familiar. I looked down at the shirt I was wearing—the button was identical to my shirt buttons, and when I reached up to my collar, I found that the top button was missing. Suddenly I felt the hardness of the Electric Chair, and I knew what Mr. Greene's look of satisfaction was all about. It was the look of an executioner preparing to throw the switch.

"Do you know where this button was found?" he asked.

I shook my head.

"It was found on Alec Smartz's driveway—right near the spot where his van was parked that night." He reached out and took the button away from me. "Maybe you'd like to re-consider your answer."

I could only stammer, because I knew that no matter what I said, it would sound like a lie.

"Don't you have anything to say for yourself?"

"It's not my button," I said weakly, but we both knew that it had to be mine. The question was, how had it gotten there? I had never *been* on Alec Smartz's driveway.

"I'm going to give you one final chance, Jared," he said with the patience of someone completely sure of himself. "I'd like to put an end to this situation by tomorrow. Other-wise, it might get ugly."

But I wasn't listening to him anymore. I was thinking about that button. There were only two possibilities: either Alec was lying about where he found the button . . . or some-one had intentionally put it there for Alec to find.

But who? I thought. Who could have gotten that button? Then it dawned on me, in growing disbelief, that there was only one person in this school who had access to my shirts.

When I got home that afternoon, Tyson was already there, sitting in the living room with his headphones on, blasting his ears with one of my CDs. I pulled his headphones off, and his eyes snapped open.

"Hey, what gives?" he asked.

I wanted to grab him and shake him. I wanted to accuse him right there and pass judgment on him the way Greene had passed judgment on me, but I had done that once before to Tyson, hadn't I? I had beaten him silly, convinced that he was the one pulling the deadly pranks last fall, but I had been dead wrong. Maybe Greene was ready to throw the switch on me, but I wasn't going to do that to Tyson. No matter what I suspected, he deserved the benefit of my doubt.

I took a deep breath to steady myself, and said, "How do you like my shirt?"

He looked at me like I was nuts. "It's OK," he said.

"Notice anything wrong with it?"

He looked at my chest and pointed to it. "You got some mustard there." I looked down, and he dragged his finger up across my face.

"Gets 'em every time!" he said. "Nyuk, nyuk, nyuk."

I pushed his hand away, and he finally realized that this wasn't a laughing matter. "What's your problem today, huh?"

"Remember when you said you hated me?"

He rolled his eyes. "Are we going to go through that again?"

"Do you hate me enough to get me suspended? Do you hate me enough to get me thrown out of school?"

He sat up, and answered me with the same directness I answered Mr. Greene.

"No," he said, "I don't. I hate you enough to take the extra hamburger at dinner, so you don't get seconds."

"Do you hate me enough to plant evidence on Alec's driveway?"

"Are you accusing me of something?" He started to get that red-in-the-face look he always got when someone lit his microscopic fuse.

"I'm just asking." I watched him closely, trying to gauge the truth in his answer.

"No. I didn't." He thought for a moment, then said, "There was a time when I hated you more than anything, and there are still times when I want to hate you, but I just can't—and unless you do something *really* stupid, I probably never will." Then he stormed across the room, and turned to face me again, but he kept his distance. "You're my best friend, OK? There, I said it. The guy who ruined my life is now my best friend. Pretty pathetic, huh?"

"No, it's not," I said, feeling like a total jerk. There was no doubting his honesty about it.

"It *is* pathetic," Tyson insisted, "because I know you're not really my friend at all."

"What?"

"You feel sorry for me . . . you feel *guilty* for what you did, but you really don't *like* me."

"That's not true!"

"Prove it," he said.

I opened my mouth to speak, but nothing came out. I couldn't prove to Tyson that I was his friend, any more than I could prove my innocence to Greene.

"We'll never be on equal ground," said Tyson, "unless I

ruin your life, and then turn around and save it, like you did to me. Then if you can tell me we're friends, that's when I'll believe you."

I don't know if Greene had spoken to my parents, because they didn't talk to me about it. That, I think, was as unsettling as if I had been punished for something I didn't do. Still, I tried to convince myself that this was over; that three dirty tricks was the charm that would break the spell, and whoever was doing it would slink back into whatever hole they crawled out of. But, like I said, something was set loose in our school, and Alec, simply by being Alec, kept making himself the target. But what he did next—his own little counterattack—was as unforgivable as any of the pranks pulled against him. It wasn't a prank that he pulled, but it was despicable nonetheless. It was as mean-spirited as it was self-serving, but all it served to do was feed the fires of resentment.

It happened on the day of the candidates' televised statements. About a year ago, our school had converted the audiovisual office into a television studio of sorts, and the school got wired for closed-circuit TV. This year, for the first time, each presidential candidate had recorded a five-minute campaign speech that would be televised throughout the entire ninth grade. I watched in social studies class—a class I didn't share with either Cheryl or Alec. Tommy Nickols came on first. The highlight of his rather dull speech was a top ten list—the top ten reasons why he should be voted in. It was supposed to be very funny, but was in fact so unfunny that people were laughing hysterically by the end of it. Unfortunately, they were laughing *at* Tommy and not *with* him. Next came Katrina's speech, which seemed like one long, rambling telephone conversation with herself. Cheryl's speech was masterful, as I knew it would be, and then came Alec's. No one, not even me, was prepared for what he did.

"Hello, friends and classmates," his speech began. "It is with great regret that I share with you some information I discovered just the other day. Something that every one of you has a right to know." We all listened closely, wondering what sort of bombshell Alec had to drop. Like everything else he did, it fell like a nuke.

"The video you are about to see was filmed a few days ago," he said on the TV. "I ask that you all watch closely." Suddenly the image of Alec changed to a handheld video shot of a place I recognized—a place filled with old, crumbling boats. *Oh no,* I said to myself, *he didn't . . .* but unfortunately he did. The video had been edited down to less than a minute, and within that minute, I saw Tyson and myself climb up in the hole of the tugboat, and then Abbie, Darren, O. P., Jason, and Randall. Finally the camera zoomed in to catch Cheryl, the image grainy and wobbly. She looked around, as if she was up to no good, and there the video ended. Alec came back on the screen. I slunk low in my chair.

"Several months ago," he said, "a group of seven kids terrorized this school, and they called themselves the Shadow Club. You thought they had been brought to justice. You thought they were sorry for what they had done, but you thought wrong. If that's the kind of person you want leading your class into high school, then vote for Cheryl whats-her-face. Otherwise you know where to cast your vote."

I didn't see it, but I hear their breakup was spectacular. Jodi Lattimer told me, and she was never one to gossip, so the source was reliable.

"Alec accused Cheryl of tearing down his posters," Jodi said, "and Cheryl called Alec more four-letter words than I knew existed. Some of them had, like, ten letters."

It was a breakup that could make record books, but this was about much more than that. Alec had incriminated us all with that video. Even though it showed nothing, really, it showed just enough to let everyone's imagination run rampant.

I went to the tugboat to be alone, to convince myself that there was a way to deal with this, and that I was strong enough to do it. I wasn't feeling strong at all, I was feeling weak, angry, and confused. That's when Cheryl showed up.

"Permission to come aboard?" she asked.

"Permission granted."

She climbed in through the hole in the hull, and we sat across from each other, as we had done so many times before in the old tree house. A winter storm had taken down that tree house this year, and most of its wood had been burned in her fireplace. Thinking about that bothered me more than I think it should have.

"Someone find me a bear so I can put it in Alec's minivan," she said.

"Careful—we might find ourselves on cable tonight."

She shook her head, furious at herself. "How could I have been so stupid to trust him? I'm never going to trust anyone ever again."

I laughed. "Now you sound like me." Then I took a long look at her. I could see how much she was hurting. "Don't worry," I told her, "he'll get his someday."

"Well, I hope he gets it soon." Then she drew up her knees, realizing what she was saying. There it was, that old resentment.

"You want him hurt as much as he hurt you," I said. "I mean, what he did was really nasty, it's OK to feel that way."

"Are you my guidance counselor now?"

I grinned. "Me, or Greene—take your pick."

Cheryl took a deep breath and let it out slowly. "Do you think he would have done it if he knew *why* we were all meeting . . . and if I hadn't laughed at him the other day?"

I fiddled with a nail that was sticking out of the hull. "Maybe, maybe not. You know him better than I do."

"That's what I thought." She considered it for a few moments and clenched her fists, still fighting her fury.

"I swore that I would never feel that way about anyone ever again," Cheryl said. "I swore I would never be so angry that I'd wish awful things on someone."

"Wishing and making it happen are two different things," I reminded her.

"Yeah, but sometimes wishes come true."

The Shadow Club might have been dead, but thanks to Alec Smartz it had risen from the grave. Everyone from Principal Diller to the cafeteria servers believed we were conspiring up a new reign of terror. Whether or not Alec realized what he did, he put the seven of us back in the center of attention.

I was in Greene's office first thing the next morning. I had expected it—he couldn't leave that incriminating video unanswered. Once I took my seat in the Electric Chair, he didn't waste any time beating around the bush.

"It was made very clear to you last October," he began, "that if the so-called Shadow Club was ever caught meeting again, it would be grounds for dismissal."

"You're going to expel us because we talked for five minutes? You don't even know what we talked about!"

"I have an idea."

"We were trying to figure out who's pulling tricks on Alec—ask the others—they'll tell you."

"I'm sure that's what they'll tell me," Greene said calmly, making it clear he wouldn't believe it, no matter who told him. "But the only thing I know for sure is that *you* called the meeting. That makes you the only one who's really in danger of being expelled."

"Fine! Then take me to Principal Diller! Maybe he'll listen to me!"

"No. I won't bother Principal Diller with you, because you're my problem, Jared. You've been my problem this entire school year, and I will make sure this is taken care of."

"Go ahead," I shouted. "Tell my parents I'm a delinquent. I'm sure you've told them already."

Greene sighed. "Your parents," he said, "are very defensive of you."

I wasn't expecting to hear that my parents would defend me in anything. While I grappled with what to make of that, there was a knock at the door, and a teacher poked her head inside. She stood with a girl who was upset about something that, mercifully, didn't involve me.

"Mr. Greene, could I have your help?" the teacher asked.

Reluctantly, Greene stood up from his desk. "I'm not done with you," Greene told me. "You wait right here, and think very carefully about your future in this school. When I get back I want to hear about your meeting, and about the pranks."

He strode out, closing the door behind him, leaving me with my thoughts . . . but when I looked at his desk, I realized he had left me alone with *his* thoughts, too. There, on his desk, was my file. For an instant I fought the urge to look at what he had written about me, but in the end, I reached over and flipped open the file with one finger, tilting my head to look at it, afraid he'd notice if I moved it. Although his handwriting was hard to read, one phrase in his latest report leaped out at me like a nasty jack-in-the-box—"deeply troubled," it said, "with sociopathic tendencies."

My first instinct was to laugh. Me? Troubled? I thought. I might have been *in trouble* from time to time. I might have done some pretty stupid things now and then, but it always seemed to me that my troubles were no deeper than a wading pool. My family life was okay, my frustrations were typical, I guess. Troubled? That was absolutely ridiculous. When I rebounded from my laughter, it was the second phrase that hit me hard—*sociopathic*. I wasn't quite certain what the word meant, but I had my suspicions. I found a fat dictionary on Mr. Greene's shelves, and pulled it down to look up the word.

"Sociopath," it said; "a person who lacks conscience, or moral responsibility."

I felt as if someone had just punched me in the stomach. I could feel the air squeeze out of my lungs, and I gasped to breathe it back in. "There's a word for people like you," Brett Whatley had said. Had he been sneaking a peek at my file, too? I sat back down in the Electric Chair, slamming the dictionary closed. Then I closed my eyes and reached down into myself—really deep down—to prove to myself that Greene was wrong, and just because he wrote it, it didn't make it so. I didn't have to go very deep at all to find the conscience Greene thought was so lacking in me. It was alive and well, but it was totally hidden from his view.

What Greene was doing to me was like a witch trial. Hundreds of years ago they used to try witches in a water test. They believed witches were made out of wood, and since wood floats, obviously a witch would float, too. If the person sank and drowned in the well, then obviously that person wasn't a witch. I felt myself sinking into the bottom of that well now—my life and everything I cared about slipping away. I wasn't about to let that happen. I was stronger than that—stronger than Greene—and it dawned on me exactly what I had to do.

Mr. Greene's supposed evidence of my crimes sat in a little plastic bag clipped to my file. The blue shirt button. I slipped it out of the bag and put it in my shirt pocket, then realized that it was easily found there. So, instead, I put it on my tongue and swallowed it. I could feel it going all the way down. The tips of my fingers and toes became numb, as if I had swallowed some pill instead of a button. Then I sat back down in the Electric Chair, just as Mr. Greene came back into the room and took his place across from me. I forced myself to stare him straight in the eye, unwavering, pretending to be in total control of myself, of the situation, and of him.

"I'm ready to listen, if you're ready to talk," he said.

"I have nothing to say to you." I forced a rudeness into my voice that I had never showed anyone before—much less an adult.

Greene was ready for this, as if he had been expecting it all along.

"How much longer do you think you can keep up the lies, Jared? It's only a matter of time before the truth surfaces. We already have your button and—"

"What button?"

He glanced down at the file, and the smug look on his face dissolved.

"All right, give it back."

Although I was feeling queasy—not from the button, but from the course I was choosing—I forced myself to grin.

"I don't know what you're talking about," I said very slowly, pretending to be in control, keeping my eyes locked onto his. I don't know, but maybe my own lurking discomfort coupled with that icy stare appeared suitably sociopathic to him, because he changed. He seemed a little bit smaller, and maybe even frightened.

"What are you trying to pull?" he asked.

But I kept that grin painted across my face, and suddenly

I realized that I was no longer *pretending* to be in control of the situation. I was.

"Maybe I did all of those things to Alec," I told Greene. "But you'll never prove it . . . because I'm too smart for you." Then I stood up, and strutted out of his office without looking back. If this was a witch trial, then I was not going to drown with a whimper, I would float in defiance. I would be the witch.

Shaditude

PLAYING THE BAD kid is hard work when it doesn't come naturally, but I was a quick study, and I was motivated. Tyson helped some. He was never really a bad kid himself—he was just kind of creepy—but he did understand what it took far better than I did. He treated it like a joke as he taught me the ins and outs of being unwholesome.

"This is the way you slouch in your chair," he said as we sat at the kitchen table. "You lean way far back from your desk."

I tried it.

"No," he said. "You're still too close. Your hands can still reach your schoolwork. You gotta slouch far enough away—maybe even tip your chair back a little bit—so that there is no way you can get to anything on your desk without major effort."

"Oh, I get it. It's kind of like your textbooks are repelling you."

"Exactly." He walked across the room and watched me

again. "Okay, the slouch is good. Now pretend I'm the teacher. What are you going to do?"

"I'm going to stare at you," I said. "Like I can see through you."

Tyson shook his head. Wrong answer.

"Naah. That might have worked for Greene, because he was trying to see through you first. With a teacher you want to look away."

So I tried looking away.

"No, not out of the window—then it seems like you're just daydreaming. You can't look down either. You have to pick a blank spot on the wall and look at it, so that it's very clear you're not looking at anything. Everyone has to know that you're doing it on purpose."

I took a deep breath and sighed. "Is all this really necessary?"

"Hey, you're the one who wants to look bad."

I went out before dark and bought some new clothes. "Bad" clothes. Shirts and pants that had the ragged and rude look of defiance. When I got home, I modeled them for Tyson. That's when he started to get worried.

"What's the matter?" I asked. "Did I get the wrong clothes?"

"No," Tyson answered. "It's just that . . . I don't know . . . You don't look like yourself, Jared."

I turned to look at the mirror on Tyson's closet door. He was right. I looked like my own evil twin.

"Well, this is how I look now."

He shifted his shoulders uncomfortably. "Why do you want to do this?" he asked.

But I didn't tell him. I had my reasons, but right now I couldn't share them with anyone.

When I left Tyson's room, I ran into my mom in the hallway. Mom, always to the point said, "I don't like when you dress that way, Jared."

I wasn't surprised that she didn't like it. What surprised me was the way she said it—like I had dressed this way before.

"It's what everyone's wearing."

"You're not everyone," she said, then added, "you want to dress like that, you wash those clothes yourself. I won't do it."

I wore the clothes to school the next day, and the effect was instantaneous. I got double takes from everyone in the hallway—kids and teachers alike. I raised eyebrows in every class as I slouched and looked off toward nothing, wearing my attitude like a heavy cologne that filled the air around me.

Shaditude, I called it—the attitude everyone thought the leader of the Shadow Club would have.

It really infuriated Greene—and as much as that scared me, there was some satisfaction in it as well. Suddenly *he* was the paranoid one instead of me. During passing that first day, Jodi Lattimer tried to give me some notes that I had missed while receiving Greene's third degree. Greene seemed to appear out of nowhere, staring at Jodi, like we were doing something illegal. "What's this all about?" he snapped. We both looked at him as if he was from Mars.

"Tell me about that hat, Miss Lattimer."

Jodi was wearing her denim baseball cap—this time it was forward instead of backward. On the front in bright orange were the letters "TSC."

"What's to tell?" she said calmly. "My father belongs to the Tennis and Squash Center. We have a bunch of them."

It took me a second to realize what Greene was thinking. That "TSC" could also stand for The Shadow Club.

"Are you going to expel her because of the hat?" I asked.

He threw me a gaze meant to chill me. I knew he had scheduled me a parent conference for the end of the week. He was making all these noises about suspension and expulsion, and yeah, it bothered me—an expulsion followed you wherever you went—but Greene's X-ray gaze didn't intimidate me anymore, because I knew it wasn't going to see through anything.

There must be some fourth law of thermodynamics. Along with the law of conservation of energy, there must be some kind of conservation of oddity, keeping the world in balance. It only figured that as I began to resemble a mother's worst nightmare, someone else's act began to clean up.

I came home from school during that first week of the

Shaditude to find some strange kid rummaging through my refrigerator for food. One of Tyson's friends, I figured, which was bizarre, because Tyson never brought home friends. I didn't know he had any. I was about to ask if I could help him find something, then I remembered my Shaditude, and said, "You take something, you pay for it, dude."

The kid turned around to reveal a familiar face in an entirely unfamiliar package.

"Hi, Jared."

It wasn't a friend of Tyson's at all. It was Tyson himself. His hair, which had always been long and stringy, was cut short, with a smooth line along the back of his neck. He had even shaved those goat hairs on his neck that might someday become a beard.

"Uh . . . nice 'do," I said, still reeling from the sight. What's the word for something that's a total logical inconsistency? An oxymoron. Yeah, that's what Tyson was. "Tyson McGaw" and "clean cut" did not go together in the same sentence without causing a major short circuit—like the one I had now as I gaped at him. Actually, oxy-moron was a better description of me at that moment—a *moron* whose brain wasn't getting enough *oxy*gen.

"You like it?" he asked, running his hand through what was left of his hair.

"Yeah, sure," I said, still wading through recovery. "It'll blow everyone away."

"Well," he said, "I figured if you could be your own evil

twin, I could be my own un-psycho twin." He grabbed his jacket and headed for the door.

"You're off in a hurry," I said, and laughed. "What, have you got a date or something?" I meant it as a joke, but Tyson wasn't laughing.

"As a matter of fact, I do."

Right about now, the signpost up ahead was beginning to read "The Twilight Zone," but I couldn't exactly say why. *Yes, you can say why,* my get-real voice told me. *It's because Tyson is Tyson and the earth spins out of orbit if he suddenly has friends and short hair and a girlfriend and—*

"Who's the lucky girl?"

"Jodi Lattimer."

"No way."

"Yeah—we're going out to Dairy Queen for some ice cream, and just to hang out, y'know."

"That's not exactly a date," I informed him, even though I knew it technically was.

He shrugged. "Call it whatever you want."

Then I noticed something else about him. He was wearing one of my shirts.

"Who gave you permission to put that on?" This time it wasn't Shaditude—it was all me.

"Well, you're not wearing your old stuff anymore."

"It doesn't fit you anyway, it just hangs on you on account of you don't have any pecs."

Tyson took it as an insult, which I suppose it was. "I got pecs!" he said, pushing out his chest. "I've been working out—I've got pecs up the wazoo!"

The fact that, yes, my shirt actually *did* fit him wasn't really the point. I wasn't exactly sure what the point was, only that I was truly annoyed.

Then something struck me, and suddenly Tyson looked all different to me again.

"How long have you been wearing my shirts?"

He shrugged. "I tried one on yester—" And his face changed again, like he was a regular chameleon, the minute he realized why I was asking. He thought for a moment, his face going granite hard, his lips pursing into a tight little hole in his face. "Well, of course, there was the time last week when I wore your shirt and popped a button on Alec Smartz's driveway. Nobody knew but me and the skunk."

Sometimes—not often, but sometimes my brain turns into Play-Doh, and I find my mouth opening and closing as I try to squeeze an intelligent thought through the doh-matic press.

"Duh . . . Are you serious? You're not serious, right? Are you kidding? Was that a confession? You're kidding, right?"

Tyson shook his head. "If you have to ask, then you don't deserve an answer."

And he left, leaving me on the doorstep to press my Play-Doh.

By the next day I had reached the inevitable conclusion that Tyson was just being Tyson, and probably had nothing to do with the button. At first I wondered how he even knew about it, but by now everyone knew about that button. Still some residual suspicion remained, like the smell of bug spray in the summer. One minute I was suspicious of him, and the next I felt all guilty about feeling that way.

Between classes, I found Jodi Lattimer at her locker. I approached her as though I was just making friendly conversation, but I had a reason for looking for her. Two reasons, actually.

"Hi, Jodi," I said.

"Hi, Jared."

"So . . . I hear you and Tyson went to the Dairy Queen."

"Yeah," she said as if it was nothing. "And next week we're going to the movies."

"Good," I said. "That's great. So you actually like him."

"Yeah. Is that so hard to believe?"

"No, not at all." Now this was getting awkward. "It's just . . . it's just that Tyson's been through a lot, y'know. I just don't want to see him hurt."

"Sounds like you're jealous."

Well, maybe I was and maybe I wasn't. I hadn't quite sorted that out yet, but I was pretty certain that jealousy—if there was any—was secondary to my genuine concern for Tyson. At least the concern I felt when I wasn't feeling suspicious of him. Anyway, the last thing Tyson needed was a game of hormonal tetherball with a girl who took it too lightly.

"Just don't toy with him, OK?"

"What, are you his father now?"

"He doesn't have a father—in case you didn't know."

"So I've heard."

This wasn't going well, but before we escalated into the "fine-be-that-way" mode, Jodi disarmed.

"Listen . . . Tyson can take care of himself," she said. "And he does it pretty well." Then she looked me over. "Nice clothes," she said, in a way that made it completely unclear whether she liked my new clothes, or whether she was just being sarcastic.

"Yeah, well, it's a look," I said. "Anyway, Tyson's not the reason why I wanted to talk to you. I wanted to see if I could get your hat."

"My hat?"

"Yeah," I said offhandedly, trying to hide how much I really wanted it. "It's kind of cool."

"Why don't you just go to the Tennis and Squash Center and get your own?"

I pulled a bill out of my pocket. "I'll give you ten dollars for it."

"Suit yourself." She took my money, pulled the hat from her head, and handed it to me. I suppose ten bucks warranted no questions asked. Or maybe she just didn't care.

Regardless, anyone who saw me wearing the hat, even if they knew where it really came from, would know what TSC meant for me. It was exactly what I needed to make my bad-kid illusion complete.

For lunch that day I didn't go out to Solerno's, I stayed in the cafeteria. I positioned my TSC hat just right, then I found a kid who wouldn't give me any trouble, and just pushed my way in front of him in line.

"Hey!" he complained.

I turned to him and stared. "You got a problem?"

He backed down and said nothing.

Quite a few kids noticed my behavior, and I took note of which kids were intimidated, which kids were annoyed, and which kids suddenly seemed to gravitate toward me, impressed by my new mean image. During the next couple of days, it was those impressed kids that I made a point of nodding to, and giving a friendly rap on the shoulder as I passed by, like they were all my new best friends.

Mitchell Bartok, a kid so tough he must have worn leather diapers as a baby, made a point of sitting at my lunch table on the third day of the Shaditude. We bad-mouthed teachers together and said some rude things about various girls we saw around the cafeteria. I pretended that I knew something about Harleys, and suddenly he was telling me his life story. Then, as the lunch bell rang, I turned to him and said: "Hey, Mitchell, all that stuff you did to Alec was pretty funny."

But he looked at me cluelessly. "I thought *you* did all that stuff."

"Yeah . . . yeah sure," I said. "Just kidding you."

When he was gone I opened my notebook and crossed him off my list of suspects.

Each day, when I got home, I went straight into the bathroom and peeled off my new self, like a full body mask. Then I stepped into a hot shower and scrubbed myself, feeling dirty, but knowing that the worst dirt wouldn't come off with soap. All those nasty things I said and did to build my new false image, all the tricks I was playing on kids like Mitch Bartok to ferret out the truth. I guess what bothered me most was that everyone seemed to believe my bad-kid act. I mean, I'm not a great actor, but in this case it wasn't hard to become what they made me. And it scared me . . . because part of me liked it—just as part of me had liked the secret power I wielded as the leader of the Shadow Club, back when we were at our worst. And so each day I didn't stop scrubbing until I could find myself underneath, and remembered that I liked my real self a whole lot more.

And then there were my parents, who seemed to have invoked a ten-foot-pole policy with me. Not physical distance, but emotional. I knew that Greene was preparing for a big meeting with them next week—and yet my parents said nothing to me about that, or any of the things Greene must have been telling them. That scared me more than their House un-American Activities questioning. It's like they were so worried, they chose to stick their heads in the ground, and broke off all communication with me. I mean, what if I really was up to something terrible? How could they not get after me for the way I was acting—even if it was just an act? I could forgive my parents for prying too much, but it was harder to forgive them for not prying at all.

Jodi showed up at our house that Friday—the end of my first week of Shaditude. She walked in the front door like she owned the place—serves me right for leaving it open. I was lying on my bed, trying not to think of anything in particular. I used to be very good at that, but in recent months my thoughts were way too focused much of the time—usually on things I didn't enjoy thinking about. I was tossing that seashell of mine up into the air, trying to see how high I could get it without actually hitting the ceiling. My mom once told me it was a very "Zen" thing to do—whatever that means. With my headphones blasting music, a freight train could have come through the house and I wouldn't have known. Naturally, when I looked up and saw Jodi there at my bedroom door I was startled, lost my concentration and the shell came down, hitting me in the face. I took the headphones off and the blaring music became tinny and distant.

"I'm looking for Tyson," she said.

"He's not here," I told her. "I'll tell him you came by."

But she didn't go just yet. She glanced at the ballistic seashell that had done its damage and now lay innocently on my bed. "You're supposed to do that with a baseball, aren't you?" she asked. "Y'know—toss it up and down."

I shrugged looking at the shell. "Baseballs don't break."

"Isn't that the point?"

"I don't know," I said. "Where's the challenge if nothing's at risk?"

"Wow," she said. "Deep."

She looked around, never stepping into the room. I felt like I was under a microscope again. "See anything interesting?"

"Your room's not what I expected."

I looked around. My desk was a mess of schoolwork, but otherwise, the room was pretty neat. There was a poster of Carl Lewis bursting through an Olympic finish line, because I'm a runner; a poster of a Ferrari Testarosa, because I like cars; and a poster of supermodel Lorna LeBlanc because . . . well, just because. All in all, my room was nothing out of the ordinary.

"What did you expect?" I asked. "Pipe bombs and hate literature?"

"Nah, you're too smart for that," she said, and then added far too seriously for my taste, "You'd keep that stuff much better hidden." She glanced at the shell, which had found its way back into my fidgety hands. "So what do you hear when you put that thing to your ear, the sea?"

"I hear the voices of all the kids I had to kill, because they saw my room." I thought she might laugh at that, but she didn't give me so much as a chuckle. "Yeah," I told her, "I do hear the sea and it reminds me of all the bad stuff that happened in October."

"If it were me," Jodi said, "I'd never put it to my ear."

"I like being reminded," I told her, "so I'll never do it again." I could sense that she didn't really believe me, but I didn't care who believed me anymore. "If you're dating Tyson, why are you so interested in me?"

Jodi shrugged. "A few months ago you almost got him killed, yet now he talks about you like you're God at fourteen, so I guess I was just curious." She backed out of the doorjamb, preparing to leave. "Tell Tyson I stopped by," she said, and she pointed at my eye, which was still aching from where the shell hit. "And you better get some ice on that, unless a black eye is part of your new look."

After she left, I put the shell in a drawer instead of back on the shelf.

If it were me, I'd never put it to my ear.

Maybe she was right. I had a world full of reminders already. There were enough people looking back at what I had done. That was one club I didn't need to be a part of anymore.

Alec
Blows Up

I SHOULD HAVE been the town hero for what happened next, but when you're pegged, you're pegged, and if people want to, they can see the worst of intentions in the best of acts. I spent the next lunch period alone in the library. It was one of those cold windy days when few kids would brave the walk to Solerno's. Most everyone was down in the cafeteria, and that's not where I wanted to be. I didn't want to see Alec, didn't want to think about him, so I sat studying world history, idly wondering if it could teach me anything about how to avoid bad situations. Unfortunately, all history taught me was that bad situations tended to get worse and worse until an awful lot of people were dead.

That's when O. P. sort of staggered into the library. The worried look was plastered as prominently across her face as the campaign fliers in the hallways. She sat down across from me, not saying anything, waiting for me to ask the obvious question.

"What's up, O. P.?"

"Somebody slipped this into my backpack," she said, and handed me a piece of paper. Scrawled on it, in a handwriting I could barely read, were the words:

We're on your side.

"Who's 'we'?" I asked.

She shook her head. "I don't know . . . but that's not all." She looked around, like a spy about to hand me some crucial microfilm, and then flipped the paper over to reveal that the note had been scribbled on a medical form—the kind that the school nurse kept in her office for every student. This one has been filled out, and the name on the form was Alec Smartz.

"Someone gave you Alec's medical info?" I asked, not quite getting it.

"I don't know what it means," she said, looking more worried than the time she forgot to study for a science exam. "But I'm beginning to think that maybe you were right about things starting all over again . . . and that maybe this note wasn't meant just for me—maybe it was meant for the whole Shadow Club.

"But what does it have to do with Alec's medical record?"

O. P. just shrugged.

I read through Alec's medical form three times—like I

said, I'm not that great with details—but on the third pass I caught it.

At first I refused to believe that anyone would stoop so low, but the more I thought about it, the more I realized that only one thing on that sheet of paper could be used against Alec. O. P. must have seen it in my face.

"What is it?"

I handed back the piece of paper, feeling the tiny hairs on my arms and legs begin to rise, even though the library was oppressively warm.

"Alec's allergic to penicillin."

I bolted out of there before I could see O. P.'s reaction, and raced down the hall, bursting down the stairwell, taking four steps at a time. I knocked a kid down as I crashed into the first-floor hallway. The cafeteria was at the far end, and as I ran toward it, putting all my speed and strength into my legs, I felt the same sense of futility I had four months earlier when I watched Austin Pace race barefoot toward a jagged pile of rocks lying in wait for him. Back then I knew I wasn't fast enough to catch up with him, to stop him. That's exactly how I felt now.

I ran into the cafeteria door with the full force of my body. Someone caught behind the door yelped, but I never saw him. Instead I scoured the crowded room for Alec. He was in the far corner, surrounded by his close friends and bodyguards: an unlikely inner circle that ranged from the brawny likes of Moose SanGiorgio, to the weaselly Calvin Horner, who was responsible for Alec's nomination, and was probably the spy who took that video. Then I saw Alec reach for a bottle of orange soda. He had given up Dr Pepper, and anything that reminded him of it, for obvious reasons. He probably assumed drinking from a bottle was safer than from a cup—after all, anyone can mess with a cup—but was he cautious enough to listen for that telltale hiss as the soda was opened to make sure it hadn't been tampered with?

I pushed my way through crowds, knocking over kids in my way. The sound of crashing trays gained everyone's attention, but I couldn't worry about that now. Weaving between tables and leaping over chairs like a hurdler, I finally reached him. I tried to slow down, but lost my balance, nailing my gut against the side of the table. Alec had his head tilted back guzzling the orange soda, and I reached out and slammed it out of his hands.

"Hey, what the . . ."

It splashed all over the kids around him before landing on the floor, spilling out on the green linoleum.

"Are you nuts?" Alec yelled. "Have you totally lost your mind?"

I didn't have time for stupid questions. *Was it flat?* I asked.

"Huh?"

"The soda—*was it flat when you opened it?*"

He just looked at me blankly, so I got down on my hands and knees, running my fingers through the sticky orange liquid. I wasn't sure what I was searching for . . . maybe undissolved granules within the soda that fizzed between my fingers.

I grabbed for the bottle that still spun on the floor. Nothing inside but a few drops of soda. I drank it. It tasted normal, untainted. I took a deep and welcomed breath of relief.

When I looked up, about a dozen kids were staring down at me. For a moment I locked eyes with Austin Pace, who was now a part of Alec's entourage. What's that old expression? My enemy's enemy is my friend? The two of them must have been getting along famously.

"He's insane!" said Austin. "He's gone completely off the deep end!"

"I don't think he was all there to begin with," said Alec.

My camouflage pants had now absorbed enough of the soda to be orange from the knees down, and my hands were still dripping the stuff. I came to the sudden realization that in my entire life I had never looked quite so stupid. I wished I could have been anywhere else in the world right then.

"Are you having fun?" Alec asked.

I stood up, trying to avoid eye contact with the kids around me, and reached into my pocket, pulling out a crumpled dollar bill. "Sorry," I said, handing him the dollar. "Buy yourself a new soda."

He threw the bill back at me. "I don't want your stupid money. I want to know what this is all about."

I opened my mouth to tell him, but quickly shut it again. I had overreacted—I knew that now. I had drawn the wrong conclusion from that medical report, and I looked silly enough without trying to explain the details of my stupidity. "I just thought there was something wrong with your soda, that's all."

"I don't like your mind games, Mercer."

"Yeah, get lost," said Austin.

"Yeah," echoed Brett Whatley, who stood with his arms crossed, trying to fill his role as bodyguard. Alec sat back down, dismissing me like a fly he had swatted away. "Better clean that up," he said, chowing down on his chili. But getting back down on all fours again was an indignity I wasn't going to endure. I turned, fully prepared to make my escape from this painful situation . . . until I heard something that stopped me dead in my tracks.

"Ugh!" Alex said. "What do they make this chili out of, anyway? Cigarette butts and coffee grounds?"

I turned back to see Moose take a taste of his own chili. "Mine tastes fine."

Alec took a second spoonful. "Barely edible," he said.

I moved toward them again, and this time dipped my finger into his chili, and tasted it.

Moose got up, ready to hurl me through the wall like a

nightclub bouncer. But Moose was the least of my concerns now . . . because Alec's chili had a distinctly bitter, chalky taste . . .

"Alec, how allergic are you to penicillin?"

Suddenly he began to take me far more seriously than he had a moment before. "Why?"

But I already could tell that he was starting to feel uncomfortable, as though he had a slight fever coming on. His face was beginning to flush.

"We've got to get you out of here! We've got to get you to the nurse's office!"

I could see in his face the moment that it clicked. His eyes were panicked and accusing.

"What did you do?"

There wasn't time to explain. His lips were beginning to get puffy. I knew what an allergic reaction was like. I was allergic to bees. I had been stung three times in my life, and each time my reaction got worse. Now they were more dangerous for me than a rattlesnake or black widow spider bite. There was an adrenaline injector in the office with my name on it. I didn't know if a shot of adrenaline worked on penicillin the way it worked on bee stings, but the nurse would have to know.

Alec began to walk toward the cafeteria door, his eyes swelling in tears of fear. He wasn't walking fast enough, so I grabbed his arm and pulled him. He didn't shake me off—he let me part the gawking onlookers, who were probably wondering what on earth that maniac Jared Mercer was up to.

By the time we got to the office, Alec's face was blotchy and he looked as though someone was slowly pumping him up with air. It wouldn't be long before his whole body became one huge, red, swollen hive. I could feel him quivering as I pulled him past the counter toward the nurse's office.

"You're not allowed back here," said the school secretary.

Ignoring her, we burst into the nurse's office, and miraculously, the nurse was actually there, in the middle of lunch. She looked up with linguini hanging out of her mouth.

"Allergic reaction!" I shouted. "Penicillin."

"My God." She was quick to react. She called out to the secretary to dial 911, and Alec settled into a chair, his knees shaky. I wasn't sure whether that was part of the reaction, or just his fear. "How much did he ingest? How long ago."

"A lot—just now. You need an adrenaline injector? Mine's here, somewhere."

I tried to find it, but ended up knocking over a shelf full of medical stuff.

"Go talk to the emergency operator. Tell them what you told me." Then she pushed me out the door.

It didn't take very long for word of this to get around school. Just about everyone knew about the "incident" by the time the ambulance arrived and took Alec away.

"Everyone knows you did it," taunted Brett Whatley,

who sat behind me in science. "Just because you chickened out at the last moment and tried to stop it doesn't mean you're not guilty." And I knew the whole school felt the same way. After all, who else but the person who did it could have known that his food was spiked with penicillin? And me, with my new set of clothes, and attitude—how could they draw any other conclusion? I couldn't find O. P. to get me off the hook with the note she had gotten, and I figured she was too scared to get anywhere near this now.

I kept looking around to see if there was anyone fidgeting—someone feeling the weight of the guilt for what they had done, or someone irritated that I got all the credit. I had compiled about fifteen possible suspects in my notebook. Half of them I had already crossed off, of the other half I was still uncertain.

There was nothing to do but run. I didn't want to talk to anybody, I didn't want to see anybody, and although I didn't want to be alone with my own thoughts either, I figured by running I could outdistance them a little bit. If I could focus my attention on the pounding of my feet and the rhythm of my breathing, maybe I could stop thinking for a few minutes. I cut class, ditching a math test, and took to the streets. I didn't know where I was going and didn't follow my usual path, I just ran. I ran down Pine Street, where there was nothing but winter-dead sycamores. I ran past Solerno's, empty at this off-hour of the afternoon. I ran to the marina toward the Ghosties, but didn't want to go into that old boat graveyard, so I turned around and doubled back, taking the road that wound around the jagged shoreline. I just kept weaving, for what seemed like hours.

I could take a lie-detector test, I thought, and prove to them I was telling the truth. But I had to face the fact that nothing I said would prove anything, because people beat lie-detector tests. Sociopaths could lie without a blip, so it wouldn't prove my innocence, it would only confirm what Greene already thought he knew about me. I began to wonder why we were made so people couldn't get into your head. Outside of your own thoughts, there was no such thing as truth, only what other people thought was true.

I was so wrapped up in my own thoughts I didn't even notice the car pulling up beside me, until the window rolled down and I heard the driver's voice.

"Get in."

It was so flat, so void of any familiar emotion, I didn't recognize it at first. I turned sharply, almost stumbling, and saw my father. I heard the power locks pop up. "Get in," he said again.

I stopped running, and the car slowed to a stop a few yards ahead of me. For a moment I considered turning around and running off in the other direction. I could ditch into the woods—he wouldn't be able to follow me then. And then I thought, How long has he been driving through town, looking for me? Our town is pretty big—the thought of my father driving for hours until finding me made me move toward the car, pull open the door, and get in.

I sat in the passenger seat without looking at him, closed the door, and we drove off. He started to wind through the outskirts of town, making turns without using his signal. It scared me, because my father wears a seat belt, goes the speed limit, and he always, *always* signals. His life is all safety and stability. That's probably why he got into selling homeowners' insurance. Everything has to be protected. He took the business with the Shadow Club pretty hard last October. I guess it drove him nuts that he couldn't protect me from me.

"Your mother and I have been called in to see your principal tomorrow," he finally said. "But I'm sure you already know that."

"I can explain—"

"BE QUIET!" he shouted. It caught me completely by surprise. He had raised his voice to me before, but never so suddenly—never with such rage behind his words. For an instant I thought he might hit me, even though he had never hit me before. *"You are not here to talk, you are here to listen. Do you understand me?"*

I nodded. "Yes, sir." I couldn't remember ever calling him "sir" before.

"Your mother and I know about what's been happening to that Alec kid. We know about the incident today, too."

I opened my mouth to say something, but he threw me a sharp gaze and I closed it again.

"The school is going to try to expel you—you know that, don't you? They might even bring you up on charges."

Although I hadn't wanted to think about it, yes, I knew.

"I want you to tell me what evidence they have that it was you."

I considered the question carefully. "Nothing, really. I mean, there was this button from my shirt on Alec's driveway, but I didn't put it—"

"Circumstantial," he said. "Is that all?"

"That, and the fact that I knew about the penicillin."

He weighed the thought. "Well, then, they don't have much of a case."

There was something off about this—something not just in the tone of his voice, but the pattern of his thoughts.

"If there are any witnesses," he said, "it will be your word against theirs."

The heater in the car was on full blast, but I shivered all the same. *He thinks I did it.* It wasn't just Greene, or the other kids at school. My father thought that I was the kind of kid who would spike an allergic kid's chili with penicillin. Tears welled up in my eyes. I didn't even think about holding them back, but I did turn away from him, for fear that he'd think they were tears of guilt.

"There are lawyers who specialize in this sort of thing," he went on. "They can't expel you—you're innocent until proven guilty, no matter what you've done."

"No matter what I've done?" I turned to him, my vision mercifully blurred, so I didn't have to see the way he looked at me. "Dad, how can you talk like this?"

Then his jaw hardened, and I could sense that rage inside him again, but also an intense sadness. Tears being contagious in my family, his eyes began to fill. "We're talking about your future here, Jared. We're talking about your life. You want to save it, you tell them you're innocent, and you stick to it like glue to the very end."

"But I *am* innocent."

He took a long look at me then. So long that I had to remind him to look back at the road. He hit the brakes, and his trusty antilock brake system ground us to a halt halfway through an empty intersection. He backed up and waited for the light to change.

"I didn't do any of those things," I said, trying so hard to be sincere, it sounded like a lie. "You know that, Dad, don't you? . . . Don't you?"

He sighed and nodded reluctantly. I couldn't tell whether he believed me, or whether he was just showing his approval for an earnest lie.

"Well," he said, "all the more reason to tough it out."

If anyone could sleep after a drive like that, he's a better man than me. I lay awake that night, my head caught in endless loops of conversations that I'd never have. All the things I could have said to my father that would have convinced him I was telling the truth. All the things I could say to Alec, to make him turn his investigation—and his hatred elsewhere. Then I started thinking about what would happen if Alec's allergic reaction was much worse than anyone thought. What if he didn't make it? What if he died because some stupid idiot poisoned his chili, and what if the whole world was convinced it was me? That's the type of thing they put on the news. The type of thing they put on the cover of a hundred magazines to show how very screwed up some kids are, and isn't it terrible, and isn't it all because of TV and movies and Barney the dinosaur, and parents who sell insurance. And then they turn off their TVs, and throw away the magazine, and go on with their lives, thinking everything is so simple. Except it's not. Because if your own parents can't see into your head and know that there's someone in there who might not be all that innocent, but at least is innocent most of the time . . . if my own parents can't see what's always been good in me, then nothing can ever be simple again.

Fire With Fire

ALEC DIDN'T DIE that day. In fact, he didn't even have to spend the night at the hospital. They pumped his stomach, shot him up with adrenaline, and gave him a Benadryl IV. He was home before dark.

Regardless of Alec's recovery, it was like a funeral when my parents drove me to school the next day for their meeting with the principal. Valentine's Day. Not much love went around today—in fact, my father said only one thing to me that morning. When I came out of my room, he took one look at me and said, "Change your clothes."

I looked at myself, realizing I was wearing my "bad" clothes. I had put them on without thinking. I changed silently into slacks and a plain shirt. One that had no missing buttons.

When we arrived, we suffered the indignation of sitting in the main office, in full view of everyone who passed by, until finally, ten minutes into first period, Principal Diller called us in. Only he didn't call all of us in. He had my parents go into his office. Me, he sent down the hall, to see Mr. Greene. Divide and conquer. I had learned about it in social studies.

A student escorted me to Mr. Greene's office. I recognized her as the girl from the chess team. The one who suggested that I teach Alec a lesson.

"For what it's worth, I think it was an excellent trick," she said to me.

I felt like lifting her up by her pigtails and screaming into her face. Instead I just said, "What if he died?"

She shook her head. "People don't die from allergic reactions. I'm allergic to cats, and it never killed me."

"Ever swallow a cat?" I asked. "Try it sometime, and we'll see if the allergic reaction kills you."

Mr. Greene was pacing outside of his office, waiting for me. Those last steps up to him felt like the thirteen steps up to the gallows, and no amount of denials would get me out of this.

"Good morning, Jared," Greene said as I approached him there in the hallway. "I suppose you know why you are here?"

There was no smug cockiness in his tone. Instead it was dead serious, and that was scary.

"How's Alec?" I asked.

"He's home today. We hope he'll be back by Friday." I took a deep, much needed breath of relief. "Understandably," said Mr. Greene, "his parents want to bring whoever did this up on criminal charges."

And one last time I looked Greene straight in the face. No attitude, no defenses, just the honest truth.

"I didn't do this, Mr. Greene."

And Mr. Greene said, "I know you didn't, Jared." Then he swung open the door to his office to reveal it was already full of people. Faces I knew—the Shadow Club.

I stepped in, wondering at first if I was the victim of some practical joke myself. The looks on everyone's faces made it clear that I wasn't. They were as scared, and worried as I was. Darren, Jason, O. P.—all of them, even Cheryl.

"They all came to my office right after school yesterday," Mr. Greene explained, "O. P. showed me this." He pulled from his desk the medical form O. P. had shown me, with the note on the back. **"We're on your side."**

"I told him why you were wearing that hat," Darren said. "Why you've been dressing that way. Going undercover and all."

"I told him exactly what happened at that meeting," said Jason.

"I didn't believe them at first," said Greene.

"Yeah," said Randall, "he thought it was some trick the Shadow Club had worked out to get ourselves off the hook."

"So what changed your mind?" I asked.

"I did," said a voice that I wasn't expecting to hear. As I moved deeper into the office, I saw that someone was sitting in the Electric Chair. Not a member of the Shadow Club, not even close—it was Austin Pace.

"Why don't the rest of you get back to class," Mr. Greene said.

The Shadow Club filed out and left me alone with Austin and Mr. Greene.

"It was you, Austin?" I said incredulously. "You pulled all those pranks? You poisoned Alec's lunch?"

Mr. Greene answered for him.

"No," Mr. Greene said, "but what he did wasn't much better."

Austin wouldn't look at me. Mr. Greene had to prompt him. "Why don't you tell him, Austin."

I sat down in one of the softer chairs reserved for kids who needed kindness instead of discipline.

"I put your button on Alec's driveway."

"What?!"

"I didn't think anyone would actually find it," said Austin, already getting defensive.

"But . . . but how did you get ahold of my button?"

"Dinner at my house, remember?" Austin said. "You lost it then."

"There's more," Mr. Greene said. "Go on, Austin." Austin threw me a quick glance, then looked down.

"I heard some noises outside the night that it happened. Alec lives across the street from me, and I looked out of my bedroom window that night. I saw somebody running away. I couldn't tell who it was, but I knew it wasn't you, because, believe me, I know the way you run. Jared."

He tried to say something else, but it seemed hard in coming. He looked at Mr. Greene, he looked at me, then he looked at his own fidgeting hands. "But even if I hadn't seen it, I would have known it wasn't you, because I knew you wouldn't do something like that again—not after what happened to me."

More than anything else, hearing that from Austin was like a pardon from prison. It suddenly struck me how strange it was that of all the people in school, the one who knew me well enough to know that my heart really was in the right place was my old adversary, Austin Pace.

"Why, Austin?" I asked. "If you knew it wasn't me, then why did you put the button there?"

Then he looked at me, his face twisted in conflicting emotions: guilt, anger, frustration.

"Because I wanted it to be you."

Mr. Greene dismissed Austin, who was happy to get out of there as quickly as possible. Then Mr. Greene sat on the edge of his desk and said, "I owe you an apology, Jared. For the way I've been treating you, for not believing you, for thinking the worst. For all that, I'm sorry."

They were words I thought I would never hear Mr. Greene utter. I had to admit I had him pegged, too, as the type of guy who would weasel out of an apology, even when he knew he was dead wrong. I guess we both had misjudged each other, because it took a lot of guts for someone like him to apologize to a fourteen-year-old kid.

"And my parents?"

"Principal Diller is letting them know that you're off the hook. He doesn't know the details yet, but we'll go down there in a bit to fill them all in."

"Good," I said. "Maybe you can apologize to them, too."

Mr. Greene grinned at that. "Fair enough. I owe you that."

I could literally feel the weight being lifted off my shoulders. My chest didn't feel so tight, and although my legs were sore from all the running I did yesterday, I felt like I could jump up and touch the ceiling. I could have just accepted that sense of vindication and left, but quitting while I was ahead was never one of my strong points.

"There's just one problem," I said. "We still don't know who's been pulling all these pranks."

"It's not your problem anymore," Mr. Greene said.

"Even so," I told him, "I'd like to finish what I've started, and flush out the creep."

Mr. Greene crossed his arms, looking at me no longer as a subject to study and dissect, but more like an equal—someone who had earned his respect. I never thought I would care about that.

"What do you have in mind?" he asked.

It was a fantastic plan if I do say so myself. Everyone would have to work together to pull off the scam of the century—

or at least the school year. It would take me, the members of the Shadow Club. It would take Principal Diller and school security, but it would also take Alec. He had the most crucial role to play. Although Alec hated me, I knew once Principal Diller sat him down and talked to him, he would play his part, because it would make him look real good.

I didn't see him, or speak to him about it, but Mr. Greene assured me that Principal Diller was taking care of it, and he'd be much more responsive to the principal than to me.

On Thursday night I wasn't good for much of anything. I was nervous, like an actor before the opening of a play. I sat at my desk staring at that blue denim cap with TSC in bright orange letters across the face.

Tyson came in, and I tried to hide the cap, but I was way too conspicuous about it. I wanted to tell him about our plan to flush out the rat in our school but somehow felt it would be wrong. He didn't need any more complications in his life.

"That's Jodi Lattimer's hat, isn't it?" he said.

I shrugged. "Tennis and Squash Center," I said. "Actually, lots of kids are wearing them now."

"But *that* one's Jodi's," he said.

"How can you tell?"

"The way the brim is curled. I notice things like that." He started to leave, probably assuming that Jodi and I had something between us. I stopped him.

"It's not what you think," I said.

"Who said I think anything?"

He went back to his room and closed the door. Not with a slam, but hard enough to mean business. I wondered if the morning would bring more of his fire sketches.

Alec was back in school on Friday, in time for the candidate debates. The day off had done wonders for him. There was no sign that he had had the allergic reaction at all. He and his parents supposedly were told by Principal Diller himself that I was not responsible for what happened, but Alec still avoided me that day. He wouldn't even make eye contact with me, and that was fine by me, because I wasn't quite ready to talk to him either.

The candidate debates went on as scheduled. Tommy Nickols tried to change his campaign slogan to "The thinking *person*'s candidate," but no spin doctor could patch up his earlier image. The final blow came when his girlfriend tried to dump him. Apparently she was more important than his quest for power, and he quit, putting his backing behind Katrina Mendelson. Alec's video ploy had rattled some votes away from Cheryl, according to the school poll, and since Katrina Mendelson was giving free, home-baked cookies to anyone who promised to vote for her, she was picking up steam. Still, Alec was way out in the lead. Although half the school couldn't stomach seeing him succeed again, the other half was ready to follow him into victory. And now the sympathy vote, which often went to Katrina in the past, was going to him, because he was the only candidate who had been glued, skunked, hair-balled, and poisoned.

By the time I arrived at school that day, everything was in place for the big show. Not the debate, but my big show. Although I was nervous, I knew I wasn't alone—each member of the Shadow Club was behind me, and so was Mr. Greene—even Principal Diller had a role to play. When I walked into the auditorium, the Shaditude had grown around me. It was no longer just an aura, it moved before me like a compression wave, and I rode the wave for the first time, allowing myself to really enjoy it, knowing it would be the last time I would feel the sense of head-turning power, even if it was just illusion. I could make a very successful creep, I thought, and although that should have bothered me, somehow it didn't. Perhaps because I knew I never would want to be one.

The debate questions were posed by people in the audience—people handpicked by their teachers, of course. I waited, not even hearing the questions or answers, just generating the nerve to do what I was there to do. I do remember one question, though. *What qualities make you the best candidate for the job?* Alec was asked. His answer was, *Because I'm not afraid to fight injustice, and I can tell the truth no matter how well the lies are concealed.* His words were directed at me, with that same cold stare he gave me before he knew I wasn't the one tormenting him. But I didn't have time to think about what was going on in Alec's head. I just assumed he was playing his part in the show, and I took it as my cue to stand. Principal Diller, the moderator, acknowledged me, and I came to the microphone to ask my question, feeling that compression wave of the Shaditude pushing around me, bringing me a chorus of whispers, then silencing the auditorium as I approached. It was so quiet you could hear the steam gently hissing through the radiator coils.

"I want to know," I said into the microphone, my voice larger than life, "I want to know how Alec can stand up there and say he has any self-respect whatsoever after I so completely humiliated him." The gasps and murmurs around the room rose in a wave, then silence fell again.

"Mr. Mercer," said Principal Diller, "exactly what are you saying?"

"You know what I'm saying," I answered. "How does it feel, Alec," I said, "to stand up there knowing that I'm out here, the one who glued your hands to your head, the one who skunked you, the one who gave you some chili-cillin and put a clump of my own hair in your soda? How does it feel to look at me and know that you can't do anything about it?"

I could see his face going red and was impressed by his acting ability—he was really playing this one for all that it was worth.

"There's something I can do about it, all right."

"I admit it," I said. "I did all those things. Me and the Shadow Club. So what are you going to do about it?"

"If you want to see the type of guy who'll lead you into the upper grades," he told the audience, "then watch me now."

By now Mr. Greene was heading toward me from the back of the auditorium with a security guard.

"Mr. Diller, it's time that the Shadow Club pays for what it's done. Their time is up." Mr. Diller came out from behind the moderator's podium. Slowly the growing murmur of the crowd became a roar. I felt as though I was in the middle of a courtroom and not a junior high school debate. I half expected Principal Diller to bang a gavel and tell everyone to come to order. Instead he said, "Mr. Greene, will you have Jared Mercer escorted out, along with all the other members of the Shadow Club."

The other members were in the audience as well, spread out in various locations, each of them wearing Tennis and Squash Center hats. It had been easy to get a hat for everyone—there were enough of them around school. It was just a matter of buying or borrowing them from other kids. Even Cheryl as she stood there behind her debate podium pulled out a TSC hat and proudly put it on, to the stunned amazement of everyone gathered. The result was perfect. We had everyone fooled! That's when the security guard, who was in on it, too, took handcuffs out from his back pocket and cuffed me.

"We have zero tolerance for the Shadow Club," Mr. Diller said. "Or for any gang, now or ever. All members of the Shadow Club are expelled from this school, effective immediately." And every last one of us was escorted out, with me in the lead with my hands cuffed behind my back. It was so realistic that for a few moments even I was scared as we walked down the hallway toward the main office.

"Okay," I said to the security guard, who was holding my arm a little too tightly, "you can take these off now."

"I don't think so," he said.

I looked at him in shock, and he looked at me with those hard dark eyes of his.

Then he cracked a smile. "Hah!" he said. "You should have seen the look on your face!"

"Very funny."

We were escorted into the teachers' lounge. Mr. Greene showed up a few minutes later after the bell had rung and kids were passing. The smoked glass on the teachers'-lounge door made it impossible for other kids to see all seven of us relaxing on the sofa, munching on chips, and enjoying the guilty pleasure of being in one of the few places that is completely off-limits to students.

"That was one heck of an act," Mr. Greene said. "You had me believing it."

"So what happens now?" asked Darren. "Now that we are EXPELLED." He laughed at the word.

"We wait," I told them.

"For what?" asked Jason.

"For someone to crack—right, Mr. Greene?"

Mr. Greene nodded. "The person who did this will crack one way or another. Either by cracking under the guilt at having gotten you all expelled or by bragging to friends, frustrated that you got all the credit."

I took off my TSC hat and looked at it, laughing.

"These things sure came in handy, didn't they?"

"Yeah," said Abbie. "Good thing for the Tennis and Squash Center."

And that's when Principal Diller stuck a pin in our swelled little balloon of a plan.

"What Tennis and Squash Center?" he asked.

"You know, *the* Tennis and Squash Center."

Principal Diller laughed. "I play squash—there's no Tennis and Squash Center in town. We've been trying to get one for years, but the nearest courts are twenty miles away."

The room fell silent, and I felt the way Alec must have felt when he peered into that cup and saw the hair ball. "Then . . . what does TSC stand for?" I kept looking at my hat, like it might answer me, then it finally began to dawn on me how wrong we'd been—all of us—about so many things. "Oh no . . ."

"How many of these hats have you seen around school?" Greene asked.

"I don't know," said Cheryl. "Ten . . . maybe twenty . . . maybe more."

And for one absurd little instant, a cartoon image of Mickey Mouse came to me. I saw him hacking apart an enchanted broom, only to find that when he wasn't looking, each splinter had grown arms and a will of its own. But instead of buckets in their hands, each of ours wore a hat on its head with the unmistakable insignia of "The Shadow Club."

Weekend Warriors

WHEN A STORM system is about to move through town, you can usually tell it's coming. The wind picks up, and the ocean starts churning. A storm came to town that long Presidents' Day weekend, but it didn't come by way of land or sea. It came by foot.

It began with Solerno's. Patrons sat there at lunchtime on Saturday, hoping against hope that their pizza might have a little less salt and garlic, when someone found something crunchy underneath the cheese. The story, which rumbled through town like thunder, hit me after who knows how many ears. Cheryl told me about it. "It wasn't exactly a sausage in the pizza," she said, "but you can say it was full of protein."

It was, in fact, a cockroach. Industrial-sized. As the story goes, Solerno then opened his storeroom to find everything from the flour to the Parmesan cheese infested with hundreds upon hundreds of roaches. It was too late to stop some of them from being baked into the pizza and lasagna. Although I can't be sure, I had a sneaking suspicion that one or more of his various part-time pizza makers wore a TSC hat.

I know tales get exaggerated in the telling, but I believe the part about Old Man Solerno bursting into tears, and swearing he'd never open his doors again.

Victim number two: Mrs. Hilda McBroom. More commonly known, even to our parents, as Broom Hilda, the Witch. Widowed since before I was born, it seemed her one remaining goal in life was to keep kids from getting anywhere near her beautiful rose garden. In the spring and summer, that garden was beautiful indeed. Her yard was full of trellises that sprouted roses in every color of the spectrum. She had recently cut them back in preparation for the growing season, but on this particular Sunday, she awoke to find that her rosebushes had been cut back a bit further. Like all the way to the roots. Every single rosebush had been beheaded like Marie Antoinette, never again to sprout another rose. Rumor was that she just stood outside in the middle of the thorny debris for an hour, until a neighbor led her back into her house.

Victim number three: Garson Underwood, a computer programmer who seemed to have been targeted for no other reason than the fact that he was amazingly fat. Me, I never had a problem with fat people unless they sat next to me on an airplane—but then, it's not their fault that airplane seats are so small—and it's not Garson's fault that his own body decided to be his enemy, refusing to burn off his fat. I knew he tried to slim down, because I often saw him running desperately. Anyway, Garson emerged from his house that Sunday morning to find his car had been spammed. I mean completely—there had to have been a dozen industrial-sized cans of Spam spread over every inch of his brand-new Caddy—but that was only the icing on the cake. After he cleaned off the Spam, and he tried to start the engine, it kept coughing and dying. What he didn't know was that the gas tank had been filled to the brim with molten Ben & Jerry's Chunky Monkey ice cream, the radiator was loaded with Mountain Dew, and several pounds of butter had been spread over the engine block.

After several attempts to start the engine, the spark plugs set the butter on fire, the car was soon engulfed in flames, and Mr. Underwood could do nothing but watch from the sidewalk as his new Cadillac went up in flames.

Victim number four: Ms. Regina Pfeiffer, children's librarian at our public library. She had become a friend of mine a few years back when she taught me, much to my surpirse, that there were tons of books I'd actually enjoy—even ones by dead writers. The attack on her began with a broken window in the library on Saturday night. In the morning the police found that almost all the books were gone from the kids' section. The only one left, right on a middle shelf, was *The Chocolate War*, which made sickeningly perfect sense, since the rest of the library was doused in Hershey's syrup. As for all the other books, they came washing up on the beach that day, the way jellyfish did in the summer.

More tales drifted in all weekend long, and what made it more frightening was that these stories all made the rounds by Sunday afternoon, which meant the culprits were actually bragging about what they had done. They couldn't wait for the stories to work their way down the grapevine.

Cheryl and I tried to track down the originators of the stories, knowing that the first person to tell the tale was probably involved in the crime, but by now everyone was suspect. Everyone *except* the original members of the Shadow Club.

We had gathered at Cheryl's house, and each member of the club was assigned the task of tracking down the person who had given them their TSC hat.

"What do we do when we find them?" O. P. asked. "Make a citizen's arrest?"

Jason chuckled nervously. "You want me to try to arrest Arliss Booth? He's not called the 'Pile Driver' for nothing. Even the football team's afraid of him."

"Besides, it's not like we have any proof," Abbie said.

"All we need is one confession," I told them.

"Yeah, right," said Randall. "They're just gonna swing open their door and spill their guts to us."

"Maybe so. Somebody's got to be feeling guilty."

"Don't be so sure," said Darren. "The more kids involved, the less guilty each one feels. We all know about that, don't we?"

Yes, we did know, and it made the situation that much graver. They left, leaving Cheryl and me alone.

"Do you remember who else was wearing those hats?" Cheryl asked.

I shook my head. I remembered the hats, but not a single face beneath them. "I'd better just start with Jodi."

"Do you know where she lives?"

"No, but I can find out."

Cheryl paused for a second. "Maybe you should ask Tyson. He'll know."

"I don't like the idea of bringing this up to Tyson. He'll think I'm accusing him."

"What if he's involved?"

"No—he's not violent like that."

"You don't call setting fires violent?"

"Yeah, but it was always a reaction to something someone else had done to him. It's like he's allergic to abuse from other kids and has a violent reaction to it. He wouldn't just go out and trash people's lives."

"But his girlfriend would."

"So did mine." It came out before I had the chance to hold back. Cheryl reeled as if I had slugged her in the face. "I'm sorry I said that."

"No," she said. "Never be sorry for telling the truth."

The next few moments were awkward and uncertain. Cheryl and I had never discussed Austin's broken ankle and the rocks she had spread out in the field. Although she made a full confession, I was the one who took the brunt of the blame. I didn't realize how much I had resented that, until now.

"I'm sorry about what happened to Austin," she said. "I still can't believe I could do something so horrible."

I took her hand and gently squeezed it. "You're not doing anything horrible now. But there are others who are."

She nodded, then she slipped her hand out from mine, and we got back to work.

"Did you hear about what happened down at the Gazilliaplex?" Jodi asked me when she answered her door not half an hour later. The Gazilliaplex was our local movie theater. It claimed the capacity to show more movies than were actually in release on any given day, but they usually just showed four or five movies on a gazillion different screens.

"When they opened today," she continued, "they found cows in the projection rooms chewing up the film and smashing all the equipment. Weird, huh?" Well, maybe not so weird, considering the fact that the owner of the Gazilliaplex was hated by kids because he ejected anyone who got caught trying to theater-surf and was fond of calling the people waiting in line "cattle."

"Tell me, Jodi, how could you know what happened when the theater only opened fifteen minutes ago?"

"Well, I just heard."

I paced a little bit on her porch, a bit unnerved by how calm she was.

"So why are you here?" she asked. "It's not like you can ask me to the movies now." She giggled. "Not unless they're showing *Steer Wars*."

I turned to her sharply. "I want names," I demanded. "I want to know who it is—every last one of them, and how many there are."

She twisted her lip in a disgusted snarl. "I don't know what you're talking about."

"Yeah, sure you don't. You're just as innocent as can be."

"You're acting too weird, Jared." The honesty in her expression was the most unnerving thing of all. How could she lie and lie and still not show it in her eyes? As for me, I couldn't imagine what my eyes must have been like by now.

"You're involved, and we both know it."

"I'm not involved in anything. I was at a sleepover with my friends last night."

"Swear it," I blurted.

"I swear."

"Still not good enough."

"OK, I swear on my grandmother's grave."

"Not good enough."

"Do you want me to put my hand on a Bible?"

"Yes," I said. "Yes, I do."

And she said without any hesitation, "Fine, I'll go get one." But before she went inside, she thought for a moment, and said, "Just because there're some people in town who are finally getting what they deserve, that doesn't mean me, or any of my friends are involved." Then she added, "Nobody wanted to see you expelled, Jared, but when you think about it, isn't it more likely that you and *your* friends did it?"

That left me speechless. "But . . . but the hats."

"They're just hats," she said, shrugging the whole thing off. "What does a hat prove?" Then she smiled at me. "I'll go get that Bible."

She went inside, but I left before she came back, because I knew that no matter what she had done, she *would* put her hand on that Bible, look me in the eye, and swear.

I went home after that. My mind was trying to roll into self-preservation mode by now, trying to convince me of all the things I'd rather be doing. Watching videos, playing computer games, net surfing, I'd even be happy to do homework now. But when I got home I couldn't bring myself to do much of anything at all. Tyson was gone, my parents were out, and I found myself just staring at the blinking light on the answering machine. I didn't want to hear any more bad news, so I just sat there, tossing that seashell of mine up and down, putting it to my ear, wishing I could hear a voice in there that might magically solve all my problems.

Finally I went to the answering machine and hit the button.

"Hi, Jared . . . this is Darren." I took a deep breath. Of all the ex-members of the Shadow Club, I figured Darren would be the least likely to call me. His voice sounded shaky. Scared. I hit the pause button, took a few deep breaths, then let the message continue.

"You gotta get down here," he said "It's Mr. Greene. See, I live on his block and . . . well . . . just get down here." And the message ended.

I left the house and made the long run alone to find out what had happened to Mr. Greene.

Silver Bullet Theory

IF THE OTHER things had been mean-spirited, what they did to Mr. Greene was downright evil. Darren was nowhere to be found when I got to his house. The curtains were drawn; no one answered the door. Clearly the only part he wanted in this was to be the messenger. He expected me to be the one to do something about it. Giving up on Darren, I made my way down the street toward Mr. Greene's home.

Sometimes houses are eerie. Their windows can be eyes, their door a mouth. Today Mr. Greene's house didn't just resemble a face; it looked like a corpse. The police had already come and gone, leaving behind the paint-splattered house, with broken windows. When I saw it I wanted to leave, but I knew I couldn't. I knew I had to go in there and see it for myself. Not the way you have to see an accident by the side of the road, but the way you sometimes have to sift through the wreckage of a storm to see if some part of your own life is lying there, too.

He was inside, slowly picking through the wreckage.

There was a lot of it. Anything breakable was broken, and the things that would not break had heavy dents that could only have come from a baseball bat.

Mr. Greene was being careful with the debris, gingerly picking up pieces of a broken plate, as though it still could be used, carefully placing it into a plastic trash bag. His motions were deliberate, respectful. He was so wrapped up in the task, he didn't notice me there.

"This looks worse than my room," I said.

He turned toward me, but didn't appear to be surprised to see me.

"And you thought you had no friends."

"What do you mean?"

Mr. Greene shook his head bitterly. "Don't you see? This was retaliation. Your plan worked, Jared; we convinced the whole school that you and the Shadow Club were expelled. So your secret admirers decided to retaliate."

Until that moment it hadn't occurred to me that any of this had been done for my benefit—as if it were something I wanted.

He returned to his task. Now he was trying to piece together the shredded fragments of a canvas. The empty frame lay in pieces on the exposed springs of an easy chair that wasn't so easy anymore.

I knelt down to help, as if anything we did could actually fix the painting.

"It's an original Thomas Kinkaid," he said. "We had always talked about getting one. My wife got it for our anniversary one year."

"I didn't know you were married."

"Was. My wife died some time ago."

I looked down. "I'm sorry."

But he just waved it off. "It was a long time ago—before I even moved here."

It's funny, but I never imagined my teachers having a life outside of school. I mean, sure I know that they did—but knowing and being able to imagine that life were two different things. I couldn't picture Mr. Greene doing anything but trying to get inside kids' heads to figure what made them tick. Knowing he had a past was an unexpected challenge to what Mr. Greene would call my "comfort zone."

I pieced two of the colorful strips close together and blurred my vision to make the rip go away, but that illusion didn't last long.

"I'm sure whoever did this didn't know," I said.

Mr. Greene only scoffed. "Do you think it would have stopped them if they *did* know?"

Mr. Greene took one more look at the fragmented landscape, and sighed. "What turns kids into monsters, Jared?" It was a strange thing to hear from a guidance counselor.

"Is this a multiple choice or an essay question?" I responded, holding up a strip of the torn canvas. "Because if it's an essay, I'm gonna need more paper."

He actually laughed at that. Not much of one, but at least it was something.

"I don't know," I said. "Maybe some kids are born that way." But even as I said it, I knew it wasn't that easy—because *I* had been a monster for a while. I wasn't born that way. I didn't stay that way either. So maybe I didn't know where the monsters came from, but I think I did know how to get rid of them.

"Silver bullets," I said before I even knew what I meant.

"Excuse me."

"You need a silver bullet to get rid of a monster. That, or a stake through the heart."

"Is this a joke?"

"No . . . What I mean is that it takes something really sharp and painful to kill that monster once it shows up in a kid—otherwise the monster will keep on going."

Mr. Greene nodded, realizing what I was saying. "Painful like almost drowning Tyson?" he reminded. "Like driving him to burn down his own home?"

I grimaced at the thought, and mimed pulling a stake out of my heart. "Yeah." Watching Tyson's house burn down was like receiving a silver bullet and stake at the same time. Living through that was more than enough to kill my nasty little monster.

Mr. Greene looked at me then in that vice-principalish sort of way. "One problem with your silver bullet theory," he said. "When Tyson almost died, it truly was your silver bullet. But this time, none of it stopped when Alec almost died. It only got worse." He didn't have to say anymore for me to know what he meant, and it was too awful to say aloud—as if mentioning it would make it so.

If this new armor-plated Shadow Club was resistant to silver bullets, it would take a mightier blow to kill it and make these kids see reason. Yes, someone had almost died, but for this new improved Shadow Club, almost wasn't good enough.

I didn't go home after that—Tyson might be back, and I couldn't face him. Did he have any clue that his girlfriend was a monster? Did it ever cross his mind that the girl of his dreams was at the heart of everyone else's nightmare, along with who knew how many others? I wanted to tell my parents, and have Jodi brought to justice, but my imagination began to twist all my thoughts. What if my parents didn't believe me? What if Jodi and her conspirators told better lies than I told the truth? I was the one acting shifty, not her. Who would *anyone* believe? Sure, my parents had been set straight by Principal Diller, but that didn't matter. They had been convinced I was capable of pure premeditated evil. That was different from what happened back in October. Back then, the evil snuck up on me—I never knew it was there until it ran its course and did all its damage. But I knew better now. To know better but to still follow that path would put me in a different class completely—a path my parents had believed I had chosen.

With so much hanging over my head at home, I decided to go to Cheryl's instead. I'm sure she had heard even more stories of cruelty racing through the well-worn gossip lines. She would be feeling much the same way I was. They say misery loves company, but I don't think that's true. I wasn't looking forward to sharing Mr. Greene's plight with Cheryl, I just felt I had no other choice.

I fought my instinct to run to her house. I was always running. Mostly I just ran in circles, but lately my pace had become erratic, my goal uncertain. I was no longer running a circuit, but a maze. So today I walked, forcing my feet to conform to the slower pace.

All the way to Cheryl's house, I kept having the uncanny feeling I was being watched. Paranoia, I told myself. So much unwanted attention had been thrown in my direction lately that I figured it was just my mind playing tricks on me. If I had listened to my intuition then, things might have come out a lot differently. I'm still not sure if that's good or bad. But the way it happened, I never saw it coming. I never felt the blow to my head before it was lights out.

There are a lot of things about being knocked unconscious that you can only learn from experience. Like that strange sense of disorientation when you come to, and losing the memory of how and where you got knocked out to begin with. That's how it was with me, when I woke up in a swiveling bucket seat in a van that stunk to high heaven.

"Welcome back, loser," said a voice that I only dimly recognized. "How was dreamland?"

I tried to move my arms and legs but couldn't. At first I thought it was me—that I had somehow been paralyzed—but then I realized my arms and legs were tied to the plush leather seat by safety belts that had been cut from the van. It was hard enough to get out of those things when they were just tangled—but tied, there was no hope of freeing myself.

My mouth tasted like blood, and the putrid smell in the air made me want to gag. It smelled of disinfectant and air freshener, but underneath it all was the unyielding stench of skunk. I thought it was dark outside, but then I realized the van was in a garage—Alec's *detached* garage, far enough from his house so even if I screamed no one would hear me.

"I gave you the best seat," Alec said. "The one that swivels." He kicked my seat, turning me sharply around to face him. He sat in the bench seat in the back. The moment I saw his eyes I knew something was horribly wrong.

"Of course, that's also the seat that the skunk sprayed, but only the best for Jared Mercer."

"Alec—what are you, nuts? What am I doing here? What do you want?"

He didn't answer. He only smiled, but it was more like a grimace. A leer. Suddenly I felt like I was being crushed under the wheels of the van rather than sitting in it.

"The school might think expelling you was punishment enough, but it's not enough for me," Alec said, kicking my chair again. I spun around and around until he caught the chair with his foot.

"Expelled? What are you talking about?" But one more look at his face and I knew. The pain throbbing in my head now beat a faster, heavier rhythm. "Principal Diller never told you?"

"Never told me what?" The contempt in his voice was proof of how bad the break in communication had been. It all made sense now—how well Alec had played his part during the debate, how his voice had quivered with anger, how his face had turned red. He hadn't been acting! He had thought it was real! It was widely known, even among the students, that Principal "Diller Do-Wrong" was an occasional screwup. But he never screwed up when it really mattered. Until now.

"It was all an act," I tried to explain. "It was an act to flush out the person who *really* did all those things to you! You were supposed to know. *How could you not know?*"

"You'd lie to get out of anything, wouldn't you? You're so pathetic."

I was light-years away from reaching him—he was so far

gone in his hatred and need for revenge that nothing I could say would convince him. I was scared now. As scared as I was in that burning lighthouse, because I knew that Alec was tipping over the edge.

"Alec," I said calmly, burying my fear as deep inside as I could, "you have to let me go. This is a misunderstanding. Whatever you're going to do, you'll be sorry you did it. So untie me, and let's just walk out of here."

"Forget it." He hopped up and grabbed something behind the seat. Something big. It was, of all things, a big empty water jug—a clear plastic twenty-gallon bottle, the kind they use for watercoolers. We used to use those things to bat tennis balls—grip the neck, swing away, and tennis balls would fly for a mile. But the neck had been sawed off this water jug, and the hole was covered with duct tape.

"How about a taste of your own medicine?" Alec held up the jug so I could see inside. Few things in the world could have frightened me more than I already was—but what I saw in that jug brought me to a new level of despair.

The jug was full of bees.

"How allergic are you to these things, Jared?" he asked cheerfully.

"A single sting . . . could kill me." I tried to show him my med-alert bracelet, but as usual I wasn't wearing it.

"A single sting, huh? What happens? Does your head swell up like a balloon and pop? Does your tongue turn purple and your eyes explode?"

I swallowed hard. "Something like that." Everything I said just goaded him further. He was loving this, and he didn't care. At this moment he didn't care how sorry he'd feel tomorrow, and by then it wouldn't matter to me either, because I'd be dead.

"Please, Alec," I begged. "Please, I'll do anything. ANY-THING you want. I'll leave town. I'll run away. You'll never have to see me again—just *please don't let the bees loose*."

"I wasn't planning to let the bees loose."

I breathed a shuddering sigh of relief, until he said, "If I let them loose, they might sting me, too." Then he pulled a single strip of duct tape from the opening, leaving a slit about eight inches long. "These bees are just for you." He lifted the jug in both hands, turned it upside down, and in a single swift motion, jammed it down over my head.

Instantly I was on the inside. A dozen bees swarmed around my head, bumping into my cheek, my neck, my eyebrows, as lethal as bullets. I wanted to scream but couldn't. I didn't dare open my mouth, because they'd fly inside and sting my throat. I would suffocate on my own swollen tonsils. I tugged my hands, but the bonds wouldn't give. I rolled my shoulders, but still the jug wouldn't come off. It just tilted left and right, forward and backward.

I could see Alec now through the plastic, as though I was looking out from a fishbowl. He wasn't laughing or even grinning anymore. The look on his face almost mirrored my own, but he was unable to stop himself.

A bee had rested on the rim of my ear. I could feel it spiral around until it was forcing itself into my ear canal, probing deeper as if my ear were the mouth of a flower. Finally I came to my own edge, and felt myself slipping off.

I screamed. I didn't care if the bees got in my mouth now, I didn't care about anything. All I cared about was the sound of my scream, echoing in the jug.

I barely noticed the light suddenly pouring into the garage, or the sliding door of the van opening. I barely saw Alec being pulled out, and when the jug was finally pulled off my head and I saw Jodi—wonderful, horrible Jodi—standing there, with Tyson right beside her, I still screamed. Even after the jug was gone, I still kept on screaming, believing, in my heart of hearts, that I would never stop.

Because of Alec.

Because of the bees.

And because Tyson was wearing a hat that said TSC.

Oxy-morons

ALEC HAD DISAPPEARED by the time Jodi and Tyson untied me, pulled away by kids whose faces I didn't see. "They're giving Alec what he deserves," Jodi said.

As soon as my arms were free, I felt all over my face and neck, still expecting the telltale swelling that would come from a lethal bee sting—but I had been lucky. Now the intense fear I had felt resolved into an aching head, and a weary sense of mental vagueness, like I was watching all this from a distance. Or maybe I just wished I was.

I followed them from Alec's house, downhill, wishing I could go home, but not feeling strong enough to do anything but follow.

"I'm really not a part of it," Tyson said on the way, when Jodi had gotten a few paces ahead and couldn't hear. "You've got to believe me."

"I believe you."

"I haven't done a thing, you've got to believe me."

"I believe you."

"She just told me today—I wouldn't be caught dead wearing this hat if Jodi and I weren't going out, you have to believe that."

"I believe it." But apparently Tyson had a harder time convincing himself than he did convincing me.

"Where did they take Alec?" I asked Jodi.

"Where do you think?" she said.

I followed them to the Ghosties, and to the tugboat, still resting in its cradle at the edge of the seawall. I climbed up through the hole in the hull to find them all there, crowding the hull of the old boat. Not seven or eight kids. Not a dozen, but thirty, maybe more. Kids from younger grades, maybe even a high schooler or two, all of them proudly wearing that terrible hat. It was late in the day now, and the weird upside-down attic space was lit by at least a dozen flashlights aimed at odd angles, casting jagged shadows that made Frankensteins out of everyone's faces.

And they all came to me when they saw me.

"Hey, Jared," they said. "Good to see you." They put their hands up for high fives, and when I didn't return them, they just clapped me on my shoulder or back as I passed, heading toward the front of the boat where their new leader awaited. It was Brett Whatley.

"I knew you'd end up with us sooner or later," said Brett, his arms crossed proudly as he stood toward the front, straddling the V-shaped hull. Moose SanGiorgio was also there, lurking large in the shadows. As always, his hulking presence enhanced the bitter flavor of the situation. Behind Brett was a wooden post supporting the deck up above. Tied to that post was Alec, or what was left of him.

Whatever they had done to him, they had done it quickly. His clothes were covered in mud, or at least I hoped it was mud. His face was swollen, bruised, and bleeding.

I turned to Moose. "You were supposed to be his body-guards!"

Moose raised his eyebrows. "We were double agents."

"It was my idea," Brett had to add.

My head was still pounding, my ears still buzzed with the memory of the bees. All I wanted to do was crawl up into a ball in the corner and let all this be someone else's problem, but I couldn't. The sight of Alec, battered as he was, brought my senses back into focus, and my thoughts back into clarity.

"What makes you think Alec won't tell who did this to him?"

"He won't tell," said Jodi, "because he knows if he does, it will only get worse."

"Yeah," echoed Brett. "Alec has paid his debt to society. After today, if he doesn't bother us, we don't bother him."

But somehow I found that hard to believe.

"As you can see, this is bigger than you now, Jared," Brett said.

"No sense fighting it," added Jodi as she took her place

beside Brett. So they were the ringleaders now, like Cheryl and I had been, but while Cheryl and I were fueled by resentment, these two were fueled by hate. You could feel it radiating from them like an aura. You could smell it as strongly as skunk.

"Alec thought it was you doing all that stuff to him!" Brett laughed. "He didn't have a clue."

"It was my hair in his soda," said Jackson Belmont.

"But I put it in," said J. J. Welsh, who worked the fair's food concession.

"I gave them the skunk," Jodi said.

"But *we* put it in the minivan," said the Rangley twins.

"I had some fun with Lunar Glue," said Angela Wyndham.

"I had some leftover penicillin," Wendy Gorman said.

I looked around me. All of them were guilty. And they were proud of it.

Brett gloated. "We are your last best defense against the scum of the universe."

I shook my head. "Tommy Lee Jones—*Men in Black*. You still can't come up with an original line, Brett."

Brett just shrugged.

"Keep dealing in hatred," I said, "and it'll bite you in the ass."

Still nothing. "Our hatred is justified," he said.

Justified hatred? "Oxymoron." I said.

That got a reaction from Brett. "What did you call me?"

Jodi grabbed him before he could lunge at me. "It means two things that don't make sense together. Like 'jumbo shrimp.'"

But I was also thinking of it the other way, because all that hatred was definitely keeping this pack of morons from getting enough oxygen to the brain. Unfortunately they needed something more than just fresh air, but I didn't know what it was.

I turned to Tyson. "You're okay with all of this?"

If his shoulders sank any lower they'd be dragging on the floor. "Not exactly . . ."

I knew I should have been pissed at him, but I wasn't, because I knew who he was, and what he had come from. He had gone from being the neighborhood outcast, to being accepted, and even dating the girl of his dreams. Today he was being asked to sell his soul to keep his new station in life. I knew it was tearing him apart. Still, I noticed he had taken off his TSC hat.

I looked at Alec. I'm sure he heard all of this. Even with swollen eyes I could see him watching, but when I approached him he turned away, unable to look me in the face. I knew what he was feeling now—hatred for the others, and guilt for what he had done to me. It wasn't just his face that was screwed up, it was his soul now, because he had been at the edge. He had tried to kill me, and the memory would be with him all his life.

I went up to Alec. I don't know what I felt for him—disgust, pity, anger—but regardless of how I felt, I knew one thing was true, and I knew Alec needed to hear it.

"I forgive you," I told him. He turned his head away. But I grabbed his chin and forced him to look at me. "Listen to me, you lousy SOB! I understand why you did what you did to me. I forgive you." I let go of his face, and this time he kept eye contact with me.

"I'm sorry," he said weakly.

I nodded. "Apology accepted." Then I turned toward Brett, speaking loudly enough so that everyone could hear.

"This ends here."

"I don't think so," said Brett. He was in his element now, the power going straight to that slab of meat loaf he called a brain.

"There are an awful lot of people in this town who need to be taught a lesson," Jodi chimed in.

"We've got lists," added Moose.

"Yeah," said Brett. "Lots of them—and everyone on those lists is gonna get what's coming to them."

The chess girl came up behind me. "It's a good thing, Jared—you'll see."

"Yeah," added Tommy Nickols. "People around here will start thinking twice before doing things that bug us."

"Who made you judge and jury?" I asked them all.

"*You* did, Jared," answered Jodi. "The whole thing was your idea, remember? That's why we trashed Greene's place for you. That's why we saved you from Alec today. That's why we brought you here."

Hearing her say that heated my blood to a boil. I had done some awful things, but I would not take the blame for all of this! I may have started the Shadow Club, but it took all of them to breathe new life into it. I reasoned that if I still held some mysterious power over this club, now was the time to wield it.

I went straight up to Brett. "I started the Shadow Club, and I ended it," I said. "Take that stupid hat off your head." I reached up and swatted off the hat, and in turn he hit me, knocking me across the boat. It rocked slightly in its cradle as I hit the side.

"We don't *really* need you," he said. He grabbed me again and threw me across to the other side of the boat. Everyone shifted out of the way of our fight. "Are you beginning to get the picture?"

My answer was a punch to his jaw. It stunned him, but not enough. He grabbed me again and hurled me to the other side of the boat.

Then the world began to move.

Metal fatigue. That's what they call it when a piece of hardware gives way and something big comes tumbling down, usually taking a whole lot of lives with it. With all those kids jammed into the hull of the old tugboat, something was bound to give. I heard the wood creak, and somewhere a piece of metal snapped, falling to the ground with a muted *clang*. Then the rusted steel cradle that held the tugboat gave way, and with a crash of metal, the entire ship fell to one side.

I've never been in an earthquake, but I imagine that's what it feels like, because thirty kids were hurled off their feet as the tugboat rocked to the right, then to the left, coming to rest. No one was screaming. People don't really scream in a real emergency—not unless they have a good long time to think about what is going to happen to them. There were just a few gasps and groans as kids hit the bulkhead. Funny thing about being in the hull of a ship that's tilted over on its side—you can't tell which way is down. It was strange enough with the floor tilting up like a V from the center, but now, with the ship fallen over on its side, my equilibrium was all thrown off. When I tried to stand up I just fell over as if I was drunk.

Everyone tried to gather themselves back together, wondering what had happened, but I already knew. The boat was resting in such a way that the hole in the hull—the one we all climbed through—*should* have been flat against the concrete now, leaving no way to get out. But instead there was light pouring through the hole—in fact, more light than before.

"Nobody move," I shouted, and for an instant everybody actually listened to me. We might have made it out had it not been for Brett. He was behind me, next to Alec, but he pushed me out of the way and made a beeline toward the hole in the hull, hurling kids out of the way in his panic to escape. When he finally reached the hole at the back of the boat, he jumped out and disappeared, falling like a paratrooper out of a plane. Then came his surprised distant yell, suddenly silenced by a *splash* that told me what I already suspected:

When the boat cradle gave way and the tug had fallen out, the tug's back end had slid over the edge of the seawall. There was no telling how close the entire tug was to slipping off the ledge and into the sea.

"Nobody move!" I screamed again, but Brett had already opened the door to panic. Now, having had enough time to think about their predicament, kids began to scream and jump over one another, racing for that little hole.

"Don't!" I yelled. "Don't you get it? We have to stay toward the front or—"

The boards creaked as the boat slid a little farther. Still they were crowding the hole, dropping through, one by one, into the water of the marina, figuring it was better than being trapped in the boat. It was like thirty people trying to escape from an elevator that was about to plunge.

I suppose I was in a panic, too, because I froze, not knowing what to do. But the thing about this I will always remember is that *Tyson* had the presence of mind to see the whole picture. He grabbed me by the shoulders to get my attention.

"Untie Alec," he said, looking me straight in the eye.

His look said everything. It gave me the whole picture, and the picture was this: with everyone shifting the weight of the precariously balanced tug, nothing we could do would stop it from going over the edge—which meant that things were about to get a whole lot worse. If we didn't untie Alec now, it might be the last chance we got.

And so, as the other kids crowded the hole, Tyson and I got behind Alec and worked the ropes. Luckily for us they weren't exactly seamen's knots. A little bit of tugging and they came undone. Alec didn't have much energy left, but he did dredge up enough to groan and complain at us all the while, still only seeing his own predicament and not the greater danger. Just about the instant the last knot came undone and Alec pulled his hands and feet free, the boat listed more on its side, giving off that sickly creaking of wood.

"Brace!" I said, grabbing onto the post that Alec had been tied to. The light through the hole changed, the world tilted, and gravity took over. My mind was filled with the strange surreal sight of twenty kids floating weightless in the hollow hull of a boat. Time seemed to dilate for that horrible instant, then everyone was smashed back down as the tug hit the water.

I was torn from the post. My shoulder hit a rib of the

hull, not hard enough to break, but hard enough to leave a deep bruise, assuming I survived to have a bruise. There was no light coming through the hole in the boat now, only water gushing in like a geyser. In seconds, the back end of the boat was filling up with water. The only light now came from various flashlights the kids had held, all of which were now scattered on the ground, aiming in random directions. I grabbed one and shone it into the faces scurrying up from the stern of the boat. How many kids could I count? How many had gotten out before the boat fell? What if someone was knocked unconscious by the fall and was still down there in the stern—or even worse, what if kids who were already out in the water were hit by the falling tugboat? There was no way to know.

A single ladder at the tugboat's widest point went up to a closed hatch, which I assumed led up to the main deck of the tug.

"This way," I shouted, pointing the light at the ladder. When I shone the flashlight back at them, the water level was higher. The entire stern was underwater now. Those kids farthest away were treading water and it was already beginning to pool around my feet, soaking through my sneakers. Then came that horrid creaking of wood again as the boat shifted from its side back to center, forcing the stern to sink even deeper. The few kids that hadn't screamed yet were screaming now.

The first kids reached the ladder and began scrambling up.

"One at a time," I yelled, but, of course, it was no use. When panic sets in, common sense is always the first casualty. They were on top of one another, tugging at each other, fighting to get up the ladder just as they had fought to get out of the hole before the boat fell. The first kid to the top of the ladder pushed on the hatch, but it didn't give.

"It won't open!" he screamed. "It's nailed shut. It's nailed shut and we're all going to drown!"

"Hit it again!" I told him. "Harder this time!"

When he hit it, the wood rattled enough for me to know that it wasn't nailed shut. It might have been locked from above, but like everything else in this old vessel, the lock would have rusted into nothing after years of salty air.

There were three kids up there now, all clinging to an edge of the ladder, pushing at the hatch with their arms and with their shoulders. Finally the hatch broke and flung open, letting in that wonderful light of day. The water was up to my knees now, and the flooding hull got dimmer and dimmer as more and more flashlights submerged and shorted out. Once it was open, those kids on the ladder didn't look back; they went out through the hole and the rest began to follow.

The water was up to my waist and rising fast—I could see it spilling in from between the weak, rotten boards of the hull, and still there were more than a dozen kids to get out.

None of them looked at me as they passed, they just kept their eyes fixed on that ladder and freedom. All the while, Tyson stood next to me, one hand on the ladder, the other grabbing floundering kids, helping them to the ladder. The last one to go was that chess-team girl—the one who had been so anxious for me "to get back at Alec."

"Checkmate" I wanted to say, but I didn't. Instead I just pushed her up toward the ladder, and she grabbed the rungs.

The water was up to my chest now, and that's when the cold really hit me. I could feel my muscles knotting, balling up in shock. I thought the ocean was cold in October when I had taken the plunge and saved Tyson, but that was nothing compared to this.

When all the others were gone, and Tyson and I were ready to go up the ladder, something occurred to me with a sense of dread that was sinking faster than the ship.

I hadn't seen Alec on the ladder.

I told Tyson, and he hesitated for a second. The water rose past my armpits.

"He must have gone up. Right? We got everybody out. He must have gone up."

"One of us would have seen him."

I wasted no time and did a surface dive, swimming as far down as I could go in that sunken hull, but even with the flashlight I couldn't see anything clearly in that murky water. I found nothing but loose timber, dead flashlights, hats—so many hats—then my own flashlight shorted out, leaving me in darkness.

I was at the end of my breath, and I realized I hadn't saved enough air to make it back to the ladder. With my chest aching and my head pounding, I swam forward, but when I got to where I thought the ladder was, I came up, bumping my head against a crossbeam, and I was still underwater.

The air is gone, I thought. The boat is entirely underwater now. How deep was the marina? How far down would the boat sink? And if I did find the hatch now, how far would I have to swim to reach the surface? Twenty feet? A hundred? With my lungs ready to explode, I propelled myself forward, my head still bumping against wood, then finally I surfaced into a pitch-black space. Coughing, sputtering, gasping deep breaths of air, I tried to get my bearings. I had no idea where I was, but as my breathing came under control, I heard just to my right someone else breathing.

"Alec?"

"Leave me alone!" His voice came through what must have been clenched teeth. I knew, because I was clenching my teeth to keep from shivering my fillings out. Now I had felt around enough to get a good idea where we were. We were in an air pocket at the very tip of the bow.

"Come on, the hatch is only about ten feet back," I told him. "We can make it, easy."

"Fine. You can go," Alec said.

Now, considering the fact that I was freezing and scared out of my mind, I was in no mood to deal with a pouting five-year-old, which was exactly how Alec sounded.

"Alec!"

"You wanna know why we moved here?" Alec said. "You wanna know why?"

"Alec, this really isn't the time for some deep, personal conversation, OK?"

"It's because they hated me there, too. We moved here so I could get a fresh start in a place where all the other kids didn't hate me."

"Not everyone hates you—just half of everyone." I couldn't believe I was being dragged into this. "Can't you just shut up long enough to save your own hide?"

"I hope they all drown," he said. "Every last one of them."

"No you don't—and don't even *think* it, because if any of them do drown, you'll never forgive yourself for thinking that."

"If *they* don't drown," Alec said, "maybe *I* should."

There was a splash next to me, I felt something brush past me, and for a bizarre moment my mind filled with the image of a shark—but instead someone surfaced and began taking deep breaths.

"Jared," said Tyson, struggling to clear the water from his

lungs. "I felt you swim past me before. You missed the hatch."

"Tell me something I don't know."

"I'm going to kill you for not teaching me how to swim underwater," Tyson said.

"I was going to get to it, eventually," I told him. "Alec's here, too." I moved over and bumped my head against an iron crossbeam that felt uneasily loose.

"So, are we just going to sit here and drown ourselves? Is that the plan?" Tyson asked.

"Alec's feeling sorry for himself," I informed Tyson. "Says he wants to die."

I could hear Tyson's teeth chattering now. "He might get his wish."

Just then I felt the boat hit bottom, shifting again. The jolt shook loose the crossbeam. It came plunging down, clipping my shoulder. I heard Alec yelp as he was struck and forced under by the weight of the beam. Suddenly the water that was just below my neck was up to my chin.

"Tyson!" I called.

"I'm OK," he said. "But Alec—"

"Alec!" I called. No answer. "Alec." But my voice was silenced as the last of the air emptied from the air pocket, and the old tugboat shuddered as it finally gave up the ghost.

Dead Reckoning

I WISH I could say that Tyson and I performed a heroic underwater rescue and saved Alec's life . . . but I can't.

As for the tugboat, its fall to the ocean deep wasn't exactly of *Titanic* proportions—in fact, the hatch was only a few feet underwater, and the tug's pilothouse still poked out of the bay like the conning tower of a submarine. But you see, it doesn't matter how much water there is; people can drown in one foot of water as easily as they can drown in a hundred feet.

I came up through the hatch, surprised by the short distance I had to rise until breaking the surface. My eyes quickly adjusted to the light, and when I looked around, I could see that the other kids had already made it to safety. Now they all clung to the edge of a dock no more than twenty yards away. They looked like a wet pack of stray dogs.

"We need help!" I screamed to them. "Alec's still underwater! He's pinned under a beam. I think . . . I think he might be dead."

Nobody moved—not a single one of them. I was furious, but not entirely surprised. Having just gotten off the tug with their lives, death had just been close enough without them having to haul it out from the depths.

Brett was the first to speak.

"The suction!" Brett yelled, clinging to a piling like a barnacle. "We got to stay away on account of the suction when it goes down."

"It's already sitting on the bottom, you idiot!"

Still we received no help, and Tyson—well, being the weak swimmer he was, it was all he could do just to tread water and stay afloat.

Cold as it was, I took a few deep breaths and went back down the hatch alone. My lungs held out as long as they needed to—a minute, maybe more. Then I surfaced, and the others watched as I came out from behind the pilothouse of the tug. Tyson, who had waited for me, labored to dog-paddle himself to the dock. I, on the other hand, had a much more grim task. With my arm across his chest, I pulled the limp, lifeless Alec in a slow, cross-chest carry toward the dock—just as I had done to Tyson four months before. Only this time, there was no fighting or kicking or struggling. Alec was a dead weight, putting up no fight at all. When I got halfway there, a few others jumped into the water to help me. We hauled him up onto the dock. I never knew a human body could be so heavy, so awkward. We let him go, and his head hit the wood with a *thud*. Water spilled from Alec's mouth. His lips were blue. His eyes half open. I don't know if any of the kids had ever seen a dead body before, but if they had, it was in much saner circumstances, in a funeral parlor surrounded by flowers and organ music. Half the kids there stared in disbelief; the other half looked away, unable to face what they saw. I labored to give him mouth-to-mouth, but nothing made any difference. Finally I stepped back from him and turned to the kids shivering around me.

"You got what you wanted," I said to the water-logged members of the new Shadow Club. "Alec Smartz won't be bothering anyone anymore."

No one said a thing. Brett looked as if he might pass out, stumbling for an instant, then he turned and he ran off the dock as fast as his legs could carry him, and kept on going.

"We're sorry," said Tommy Nickols. He'd been the ninth grade's best student until Alec came along. "We're so, so sorry—"

"Sorry?" I said. My voice growing louder as I spoke. "Tell his parents. Maybe it'll make them feel better, you think?" I couldn't tell whether the moistness in his eyes was tears, or just seawater. "You're gonna feel sorry for the rest of your life—all of you—and you know what? The feeling only gets worse."

Tommy finally burst into tears. "I'm sorry," he said. "Sorry, sorry, sorry."

By now Tyson had climbed up onto the dock as well and was catching his breath, his gaze fixed on Alec. "Someone ought to close his eyes," Tyson said. "It's not right leaving them open like that."

I looked around until I found the one girl who seemed to be trying to hide behind all the other kids, trying to be just a spectator and not a culprit.

"Jodi, you get yourself over here," I demanded. "Close his eyes."

"No," she said sheepishly. "You can do it."

"You owe it to him, Jodi," said Tyson, with more conviction in his voice than I had ever heard. "You do it, or nobody here will ever forgive you."

With that kind of pressure, Jodi finally came forward. The other kids parted for her, as if she had suddenly become an untouchable. With everyone watching, she knelt down in front of Alec's body. There were other kids crying now—some sobbing, others sniffling quietly. Jodi looked around one last time, hoping there was someone who would give her a last-minute reprieve from having to do this, but no one would. So, on her knees, she reached forward with two fingers spread like a peace sign toward Alec Smartz's half-opened eyes. Then, just as she was about to touch his lids, Alec said:

"Get out of my face."

If ever in the history of our town there was a Kodak moment, this was it. Jodi shrieked, and the skin on her face seemed to peel back as if she was under fighter-jet G-forces. She stumbled backward with the shock and fell on to the wet dock with a *splash* and a *thump*, receiving what I hoped was a whole constellation of splinters in her rear.

Like I said, I wish I could say that Tyson and I performed a heroic underwater rescue and saved Alec's life, but I can't. Because Alec didn't need saving. Like everything else, he was good at swimming. He had been hit by the falling cross-beam, but freed himself, and when the last of the air was forced from the air pocket, he was the first one out of the hatch. But I had a brainstorm on the way out—a brainstorm that turned Alec into a much-needed silver bullet; the very silver bullet we needed to deal a mortal blow to that monster called the Shadow Club. Alec was more than happy to play his part, because he got all the benefits of dying without actually having to go through with it.

He had hid in the tugboat's pilothouse when I went back down the hatch. The hardest part for him had to be not blinking and not flinching when his head hit the dock. I swear, for a moment there even I thought he was dead.

"That's not funny," said the chess-team girl, as Alec stood.

"It wasn't supposed to be funny," I told her.

Jodi got to her feet. "You're sick," Jodi said. "Both of you."

I had to laugh at that, but the laugh quickly faded. She actually thought *we* were the sick ones.

"You think your twisted little joke makes any difference?" she said. "The Shadow Club still has plenty of things left to do."

But I shook my head. "The Shadow Club is dead," I told her.

She looked around, unsure of her own support and, facing each other, we drew our lines in the sand as well as one could on a wooden dock.

"How many of you think the Shadow Club is dead?" I asked.

It was like a trick question in math class. Everyone looked to one another, no one wanted to make the first move, but Tommy Nickols, who was quite often the first to get any right answer, stepped forward. Then came another and another, until it became an entire mob moving over to stand beside Alec, Tyson, and me. I can't say Jodi was left alone—she wasn't. There were five or six kids who still stood beside her. I suppose there would always be those kids who found hate too tasty a flavor to give up. But the others— well, let's just say they lost their appetite.

Jodi broke off her cold eye contact with me and turned to Tyson, softening up a bit. "You don't owe him anything, Tyson," she told him. "You don't have to pretend to be on his side."

Tyson shrugged. "And just because we *were* going out doesn't mean I have to pretend to be on yours."

The police arrived quietly on the hill, no sirens, no rush. It was a single cruiser probably sent to investigate a call from a hillside neighbor who claimed boats were falling from the sky on this cold Presidents' Day. By the time they saw us, half the kids had run off—including Jodi—and the ones that remained were ready to confess whatever deeds they had done. These weren't the ones who needed to talk to the police, however. They needed to talk to their own parents. They needed to talk to Mr. Greene—to stand in his ruined house and confess to him. If we brought the police in now, we'd have nothing but hard feelings and headlines. Neither would do these kids any good.

I really did want to nail Jodi Lattimer to the wall for what she had done, but as the officers approached, I knew there was no chance of that.

"Jared Mercer," Deputy Lattimer said. "I should have known." He looked at the bunch of kids who were trying hard not to shiver. "What happened here?"

"The tugboat fell," I told him. "The wind blew it loose. We saw it fall."

"How come you're all wet?"

"Polar Bear Club," Alec quickly answered. "We read about them in the news—you know, people who go swimming in the middle of winter. We thought we'd try it."

"It sucked," added Tyson.

Deputy Lattimer studied Tyson for a moment. "Haven't I seen you with my daughter?"

"It won't happen again."

"Good."

He asked a few more questions, but in the end, he took the whole thing at face value. We were just a bunch of kids doing something stupid on Presidents' Day. I know I should have felt bad looking him in the eye and telling him something completely untrue, but I had been a good kid and I had been a bad kid, and both had taught me a thing or two. Such as "honesty is the best policy," except when it's best to lie. Having seen firsthand the lengths to which parents will go to protect their children, I knew this was not the time or place for the truth about his daughter.

He offered to shuttle us all home, but there were few takers, as it was better to be cold and wet than show up at home in a police car.

Once he had gone, the rest of us left for warmer places, no one talking as we made our separate ways home. I lingered with Tyson and Alec for a little, taking some shelter from the wind behind a boarded-up tackle shop.

"Did you really have to give me mouth-to-mouth?" Alec asked.

I cringed at the memory. "I had to make it look realistic. Believe me, it was no great pleasure."

Tyson held his arms across his chest as a gust of wind added to our chill. "You think your mom will have something good for dinner?" Tyson asked.

I laughed. To my mom even Thanksgiving came out of a box, and today was only Presidents' Day. "What do *you* think?"

Tyson sighed. "Probably pizza or takeout."

I turned to look at what was left of the tugboat. Its pilothouse was still above water, but I knew it would completely submerge, come high tide.

Then I looked at Alec, still swollen from the beating he had suffered. What do you say to a kid who, two hours ago tried to kill you, then almost got killed himself? "You wanna come home with us, Alec?" I asked. "Hang for a while?"

"Not really," he said. But he was soaked, the wind was still blowing, and as he looked up the road, I could tell he was thinking how much farther away his home was than mine.

"Sure, maybe for a while," he said.

Because sometimes it's like they say, "Any port in a storm."

Random Acts of Violets

MY ALARM WENT went off the next morning, chirping its evil shrill call, and after I hit the snooze button half a dozen times, Mom came to roust me out of bed. I rose to a typical morning—the only hint that anything out of the ordinary had happened were the bruises and muscle aches I had earned the day before.

Tyson was already at the breakfast table, inhaling a bowl of Corn Pops. Dad was mumbling to himself in his standard ritual of searching for his misplaced car keys.

After what happened, you'd think the world would just stop on its axis, but Tuesday came with such dull normality, it was enough to make a person sick. The sun, at least, had the common courtesy to hide its face behind a blanket of clouds for most of the day.

School wasn't much different; classes rolled at their typical snail's pace, and although I saw many of the kids who had been there the day before, none of us made eye contact.

I stopped by Mr. Greene's office before second period. I didn't know quite what to tell him. He deserved to know the whole story, but I wasn't up to reliving it. By the look of him, he wasn't up to it either. He looked older today. Well, maybe not older, but a bit more world-weary, as if his body and spirit no longer felt like fighting gravity. I wondered if I had that look, too.

"You'll be happy to know that the Shadow Club finally took a silver bullet, chased with a stake through the heart."

Mr. Greene eyed me with a suspicious mix of emotions. Then he said, "Brett Whatley has disappeared. Does that have anything to do with your silver bullet?"

"Yes, and no," I told him. "Brett ran off when he found out he had killed Alec Smartz."

Greene showed confusion, rather than shock. "But I just saw Alec a minute ago—"

"Exactly."

Greene stepped forward, about to ask something, but took a deep breath, reigning in his own curiosity. "Thank you," he said. "You'd better go, or you'll be late for class."

I turned and headed for the door, but just before I left he said, "Be vigilant, Jared."

I turned back to him. "Excuse me?"

"Stakes and silver bullets don't always take," he said. "Be vigilant."

I left, closing the door quietly, taking with me an uneasy vertigo left by Greene's advice.

The next day Brett Whatley stumbled out of the woods two towns away and headed straight for the nearest police department, where he tearfully confessed to having killed Alec Smartz.

When they called the Smartz home to inform the parents of this awful crime, Alec answered the phone, casting serious doubt on Brett's claim.

"Brett just kept sobbing and sobbing," Alec told me. "He couldn't believe I was alive. He didn't even ask how. 'You're the best, Alec,' he says, 'I love ya, man!'"

"He actually said 'I love ya, man'?"

"Swear to God—and then he tells me he's my slave for life."

"You gonna take him up on it?" I asked.

"I don't know. Maybe just long enough to have him clean out our garage."

Apparently our silver bullet had pierced Brett's brain and turned him into a repentant puppy. I knew it would set the mood for the other club members as well, but I wasn't satisfied. There was still more to do.

Mr. Greene had been right—killing the Shadow Club wasn't good enough—because then it would become legend, the way it had before. Its memory would loom larger than life, enticing others to invoke it again. No, the Shadow Club needed a different fate. That's why I went to the mall and ordered a whole bunch of denim caps to replace the ones lost at sea in the tugboat plunge. In school I found each of the kids who had been there and shoved a hat into their hands, telling them exactly what I expected them to do and exactly when I expected them to do it. And although none of them wanted any part of it, many of them reluctantly took the hats and agreed. That's how I found myself the leader of the Shadow Club again.

The following Saturday morning, the bitterly widowed and lately deflowered Hilda McBroom awoke to a commotion on her lawn. What she found was a whole bunch of kids wreaking havoc in her recently murdered garden. She stormed outside, cordless phone in hand, no doubt ready to call 911, which she probably had on auto dial.

"Who are you kids? What are you doing here? Haven't you made enough mischief yet? What else do you want from me, blood?"

I stepped forward. "That's a lot of questions, Mrs. Mc-Broom."

She wagged an arthritic finger at me. "I know you! You're that Mercer boy, aren't you? The one who caused all that trouble!" She turned to Cheryl. "And you! You're that Gannett girl—you're just as bad as him."

"We understand you've been having some problems with your garden," Cheryl said.

I pointed to my hat. Denim, with the letters TSC in bright orange across the face. "We're the Tree and Shrub Crew," I told her. "No garden goes unplanted. That's our motto."

Moose SanGiorgio rolled up with a wheelbarrow overloaded with winter-clipped rosebushes. "Hi, Old Lady. Where do you want these?"

"Leave my garden alone," she said. "I don't want any Tree and Shrub Crew!"

"Tough luck," shouted Brett Whatley from across the yard, "because you've got us, whether you like it or not." Brett's offer of perpetual servitude had apparently extended beyond just Alec. He didn't just turn over a new leaf, he flipped that sucker and pinned it for the count. Although he no longer dared to claim any leadership position, his take-my-help-and-love-it attitude helped to define us now.

There were more than twenty kids working away in Mrs. McBroom's garden. Many were members of the new Shadow Club—but the club's original members were there, too. Darren, Abbie, O. P., all of them. The new members showed up to redeem their guilt, and the originals showed up because I asked them. Of course the originals had complained.

"Why do *we* have to do it?" Jason had said. "We didn't do anything bad this time."

So I told them they didn't have to come, but I'd like it if they did. I guess I must still carry some clout, because they all showed up.

As for the rosebushes, they came from our own yards, along with other flowering shrubs that would bloom a full spectrum of color, come spring. If any of our parents were annoyed by it, once they knew where the plants were going, they kept their complaints and their questions to themselves.

Mrs. McBroom paced on her porch with a combination of disbelief and horror as she watched us replant her garden, threatening every five minutes to call the police, until finally she gave up and came out to direct us, telling us exactly where she wanted each plant to go.

Solerno's stayed closed for two weeks. According to Old Man Solerno, he would never set foot in the place again. His days as a restauranteur had come to an end. Naturally, when the place came back to life the next Sunday afternoon, Solerno was furious. Tipped off by an anonymous phone call, he arrived at his restaurant to find about two dozen kids making an absolute mess in his kitchen.

Like Mrs. McBroom, he threatened to call the police on us. Like Mrs. McBroom, he never actually dialed. Under protest, he sat down at one of his own tables, and we served him about fifteen different dishes—our parents' favorite

Italian recipes, which we had practiced cooking at home. "What's-a this all about?" Solerno asked, almost afraid to try the food.

"We're The Solerno Committee," I told him, pointing to the initials on my hat. "Your food stinks, so we thought we'd change your menu and convince you to open up again. After all, this town wouldn't be the same without Solerno's."

He called me a lousy rotten punk and crossed his arms as plate after plate was set before him. Finally the aroma of fresh garlic and basil weakened him, and he tried one dish. We must have done a good job, because he moved on from the first plate to the second to the third, sampling them all. Some of them he tried three and four times. Finally he separated them into two categories. He pointed to the ones to his left. "I add-a these to my menu, eh?" Then he pointed to the ones to his right. "These other ones, they make-a me puke."

He tasted the ones he liked once more. "Need-a more salt," he said.

The next Wednesday morning, five of the pudgier members of the Shadow Club went knocking on Garson Underwood's door just as he was about to leave for his morning jog. According to their report, here's how it went:

"We're here to go jogging with you," they told him.

He laughed, thinking it was some sort of joke, but when they didn't leave, he began to wonder what was going on.

"We want to get into shape," one of them said. "And since we knew you jog every day, we thought we could jog with you. Because, as you can see from our hats we're Tired of Sitting on the Couch."

From what I heard, he was distrustful of the whole thing—what with vandals in town destroying his car—but he must have sensed some sincerity in the kids, because he took them with him on his morning jog. At last report, he still jogs with them every morning, and has taken to wearing his own TSC hat, because he, too, is Tired of Sitting on the Couch.

Pretty soon word began to get out that some creepy bunch of juvenile philanthropists were making the rounds in town, striking when least expected. It was sort of good-deed terrorism, dumped on unsuspecting victims whether they wanted it or not. I figured if the Shadow Club was only capable of acts of aggression, why couldn't those acts be aggressively good? No one seemed to make the connection that these were the same kids who had caused the trouble a couple of weeks before. I guess it's true that once people see you in one light, it's hard for them to see you in another. This time it worked to our advantage.

"When is it going to stop?" Cheryl asked.

"I hope it doesn't," I told her.

There were still a hundred things left to do. Solerno's and Broom Hilda's garden were just drops in the bucket, but that was all right. Hatred and violence, I knew, could be habit forming—but so could acts of kindness—and just because the Shadow Club had its origins in small-town terrorism didn't mean it couldn't redefine itself. It took vision. It took *vigilance*, as Mr. Greene had said—never turning a blind eye, always being aware of the danger. Vigilance not just for today, but tomorrow, and every day after that. A long-term goal.

Me, I've always been a goal-oriented person, the finish line always in my sights. True, I had always been a sprinter, but perhaps it was time to become a distance runner. If I could pace myself, I knew I could pace all of them—all of *us*—who wore the hat. It wasn't exactly a Boy Scout hat, if you know what I mean—there was still quite a lot of Shaditude in the things we did—and that seemed to satisfy even the angriest outsiders who had gravitated to the group. But we couldn't reach everyone. And I knew that *those* were the ones to be careful of.

That's why I mailed the package.

I had wrapped the package, and it sat on my desk for days before I decided to actually mail it.

"What's that?" Tyson asked, stepping into my room. "A letter bomb?"

"Thermonuclear," I told him, handing it to him.

"Amazing how small those things are getting." He

looked it over, then tossed the small package back to me. "Do me a favor, don't detonate it tonight. I'm taking Marla Nixbok to the Gazilliaplex."

"Fine, I promise not to smash your atoms before *she* does." And then I laughed. "*Marla Nixbok Dates Tyson McGaw*—isn't that one of the biblical signs of the end of the world?"

"Ha-ha," he said. "You just can't stand that I'm not a freak anymore."

"You were never a freak," I told him with deep sincerity. "Just a loser." I thought he might curse me out, but instead he just smiled, and I smiled back. "Have a good time, Tyson," I told him, and added, "Don't kiss her with popcorn in your mouth. That grosses girls out."

He laughed. "Can I write that down? My first bit of brotherly advice."

Brotherly. Now, *there* was a thermonuclear word.

"So . . I guess my parents talked to you about it," I said cautiously. "They told me they would."

Tyson looked away. "They mentioned it. They said it's up to me."

"So, what do you think?"

Tyson shrugged, for a brief moment looking like the scared kid I once rescued from his own flames. "I'm not sure yet. I mean, my initials would be the same, right? But calling myself Tyson Mercer would be weird. Still, I wouldn't mind it, y'know? Being your brother?" He thought about it a moment more, then brightened. "Tell you what. When I decide, you'll be the first to know."

"Fair enough."

After he left, I returned my attention to the small package that still had no address. If it was a letter bomb, it wasn't much of one, but it wasn't a large-scale type of thing. It was more like a surgical strike. Carefully I wrote the address in block letters. Then I took a run down to the post office, getting there just before it closed.

There have been a lot of changes in my life over the past year—awful things I've seen and done, mistakes I've made. A person can grow from mistakes, or a person can deny them completely, letting their anger build up inside them until it blows. That's why I sent my little letter bomb.

And so, tomorrow or the next day, Jodi Lattimer will receive a package. It will have no return address, no hint of who sent it, but she'll know all the same. Because she will open it to find—wrapped in tissue paper—a shiny seashell, about the size of her fist. I don't know what she'll hear when she holds it up to her ear, but maybe, just maybe she'll hear the echoes of the world around her and finally feel the depth of the pain she helped to cause.

But if, in the end, all she can hear is the sea . . . then vigilance will have to be enough.

Woodland High School
800 N. Moseley Dr.
Stockbridge, GA 30281
770-389-2784

NOUVEAUX CLASSIQUES LAROUSSE

Collection fondée en 1933 par
FÉLIX GUIRAND

continuée par
LÉON LEJEALLE (1949 à 1968)   et   **JEAN-POL CAPUT** (1969 à 1972)
Agrégés des Lettres

LE
BOURGEOIS GENTILHOMME

comédie-ballet

Librairie Larousse (Canada) limitée, propriétaire pour le Canada des droits d'auteur
et des marques de commerce Larousse. — Distributeur exclusif au Canada : les
Éditions Françaises Inc., licencié quant aux droits d'auteur et usager inscrit des
marques pour le Canada.

Phot. Larousse.

M. JOURDAIN VU PAR GEFFROY (1804-1895), COMÉDIEN ET
PEINTRE

Bibliothèque de l'Arsenal. Fonds Rondel.

[Handwritten annotations:]

Monsieur Jourdain: vaniteux, crédule, dupe, bourgeois, prétentieux
gauche (rustre), immoral, infidèle

· Madame Jourdain:
raisonnable, sage,
elle a du bon sens, franche, directe

Nicole - raisonnable, bon sens, moqueuse, hypocrite
Dorante - noble, avec un train de vie luxeuse, trompeur, profiteur
Dorimène - marquise (noble) Aimée de Dorante et de M. Jourdain

Léonte aime la fille de M. Jourdain - Lucille
elle aime Nicole
d'excentrique amoureuse
Lucile a ignoré
Cléonte

IJ
veut un intellect
mais il ne s'efforce
pas pour son éducation
il est incapable de réfléchir
à un problème sérieux

aime le titre
il est victime de la flatterie des laquais
even fooles
part if something not his mitren
il est extrement prétentieux
(il veut être ce qu'il n'est pas)
will never be anything else except mann - wh is
ridiculous title

MOLIÈRE

LE BOURGEOIS
GENTILHOMME

comédie-ballet

avec une Notice biographique, une Notice historique et littéraire,
des Notes explicatives, une Documentation thématique, des Jugements,
un Questionnaire et des Sujets de devoirs,
par

YVES HUCHER
Professeur de Lettres
au Lycée Voltaire

LIBRAIRIE LAROUSSE
17, rue du Montparnasse, et boulevard Raspail, 114
Succursale : 58, rue des Écoles (Sorbonne)

RÉSUMÉ CHRONOLOGIQUE
DE LA VIE DE MOLIÈRE
1622-1673

1622 (15 janvier) — Baptême à **Paris**, à l'église Saint-Eustache, de Jean-Baptiste Poquelin, fils aîné du marchand tapissier Jean Poquelin et de Marie Cressé.

1632 (mai) — Mort de Marie Cressé.

1637 — Jean Poquelin assure à son fils Jean-Baptiste la survivance de sa charge de tapissier ordinaire du roi. (Cet office, transmissible par héritage ou par vente, assurait à son possesseur le privilège de fournir et d'entretenir une partie du mobilier royal; Jean Poquelin n'était évidemment pas le seul à posséder une telle charge.)

1639 (?) — Jean-Baptiste termine ses études secondaires au collège de Clermont (aujourd'hui lycée Louis-le-Grand), tenu par les Jésuites.

1642 — Il fait ses études de droit à Orléans et obtient sa licence. C'est peut-être à cette époque qu'il subit l'influence du philosophe épicurien Gassendi et lie connaissance avec les « libertins » Chapelle, Cyrano de Bergerac, d'Assoucy.

1643 (16 juin) — S'étant lié avec une comédienne, **Madeleine Béjart,** née en 1618, il constitue avec elle une troupe qui prend le nom d'**Illustre-Théâtre;** la troupe est dirigée par Madeleine Béjart.

1644 — Jean-Baptiste Poquelin prend le surnom de **Molière** et devient directeur de l'Illustre-Théâtre, qui, après des représentations en province, s'installe à Paris et joue dans des salles de jeu de paume désaffectées.

1645 — L'Illustre-Théâtre connaît des difficultés financières; Molière est emprisonné au Châtelet pour dettes pendant quelques jours.

1645 — Molière part pour la **province** avec sa troupe. Cette longue période
1658 de treize années est assez mal connue : on a pu repérer son passage à certaines dates dans telle ou telle région, mais on ne possède guère de renseignements sur le répertoire de son théâtre, il est vraisemblable qu'outre des tragédies d'auteurs contemporains (notamment Corneille) Molière donnait de courtes farces de sa composition, dont certaines n'étaient qu'un canevas sur lequel les acteurs improvisaient, à l'italienne.
1645-1653 — La troupe est protégée par le duc d'Epernon, gouverneur de Guyenne. Molière, qui a laissé d'abord la direction au comédien Dufresne, imposé par le duc, reprend lui-même (1650) la tête de la troupe : il joue dans les villes du Sud-Ouest (Albi, Carcassonne, Toulouse, Agen, Pézenas), mais aussi à Lyon (1650 et 1652).
1653-1657 — La troupe passe sous la protection du prince de Conti, gouverneur du Languedoc. Molière reste dans les mêmes régions : il joue le personnage de Mascarille dans deux comédies de lui (les premières dont nous ayons le texte) : l'**Étourdi,** donné à Lyon en **1655,** le **Dépit amoureux,** à Béziers en **1656.**
1657-1658 — Molière est maintenant protégé par le gouverneur de Normandie; il rencontre Corneille à Rouen; il joue aussi à Lyon et à Grenoble.

1658 — Retour à Paris de Molière et de sa troupe, qui devient « troupe de Monsieur »; le succès d'une représentation (Nicomède et une farce) donnée devant le roi (24 octobre) lui fait obtenir la **salle du Petit-Bourbon** (près du Louvre), où il joue en alternance avec les comédiens italiens.

1659 (18 novembre) — Première représentation des **Précieuses ridicules** (après Cinna) : grand succès.

1660 — Sganarelle (mai). Molière crée, à la manière des Italiens, le personnage de **Sganarelle,** qui reparaîtra, **toujours interprété par lui,** dans plusieurs comédies qui suivront. — Il reprend, son frère étant mort, la survivance de la charge paternelle (tapissier du roi) qu'il lui avait cédée en 1654.

© Librairie Larousse, 1970.   ISBN 2-03-034657-8

1661 — Molière, qui a dû abandonner le théâtre du Petit-Bourbon (démoli pour permettre la construction de la colonnade du Louvre), s'installe au **Palais-Royal**. *Dom Garcie de Navarre*, comédie héroïque : échec. *L'École des maris* (24 juin) : succès. *Les Fâcheux* (novembre), première comédie-ballet, jouée devant le roi, chez Fouquet, au château de Vaux-le-Vicomte.

1662 — **Mariage** de Molière avec **Armande Béjart** (sœur ou fille de Madeleine), de vingt ans plus jeune que lui. *L'École des femmes* (26 décembre) : grand succès.

1663 — Querelle à propos de l'*École des femmes*. Molière répond par *la Critique de l' « École des femmes »* (1er juin) et par l'*Impromptu de Versailles* (14 octobre).

1664 — Naissance et mort du premier enfant de Molière : Louis XIV en est le parrain. *Le Mariage forcé* (janvier), comédie-ballet. Du 8 au 13 mai, fêtes de l' « Ile enchantée » à Versailles : Molière, qui anime les divertissements, donne la *Princesse d'Élide* (8 mai) et les trois premiers actes du *Tartuffe* (12 mai) : **interdiction** de donner à Paris cette dernière pièce. Molière joue *la Thébaïde*, de Racine.

1665 — *Dom Juan* (15 février) : malgré le succès, Molière, toujours critiqué par les dévots, retire sa pièce après quinze représentations. Louis XIV donne à la troupe de Molière le titre de « troupe du Roi » avec une pension de 6 000 livres (somme assez faible, puisqu'une bonne représentation au Palais-Royal rapporte, d'après le registre de La Grange, couramment 1 500 livres et que la première du *Tartuffe*, en 1669, rapportera 2 860 livres). *L'Amour médecin* (15 septembre). Brouille avec Racine, qui retire à Molière son *Alexandre* pour le donner à l'Hôtel de Bourgogne.

1666 — Molière, malade, cesse de jouer pendant plus de deux mois ; il loue une maison à Auteuil. *Le Misanthrope* (4 juin). *Le Médecin malgré lui* (6 août), dernière pièce où apparaît Sganarelle. En décembre, fêtes du « Ballet des Muses » à Saint-Germain : *Mélicerte* (2 décembre).

1667 — Suite des fêtes de Saint-Germain : Molière y donne encore la *Pastorale comique* (5 janvier) et le *Sicilien ou l'Amour peintre* (14 février). **Nouvelle version du** *Tartuffe*, sous le titre de l'*Imposteur* (5 août) : la pièce est **interdite** le lendemain.

1668 — *Amphitryon* (13 janvier). *George Dandin* (18 juillet). *L'Avare* (9 septembre).

1669 — Troisième version du *Tartuffe* (5 février), enfin **autorisé** : immense succès. Mort du père de Molière (25 février). A Chambord, *Monsieur de Pourceaugnac* (6 octobre).

1670 — *Les Amants magnifiques*, comédie-ballet (30 janvier à Saint-Germain). *Le Bourgeois gentilhomme*, comédie-ballet (14 octobre à Chambord).

1671 — *Psyché*, tragédie-ballet avec Quinault, Corneille et Lully (17 janvier), aux Tuileries, puis au Palais-Royal, aménagé pour ce nouveau spectacle. *Les Fourberies de Scapin* (24 mai). *La Comtesse d'Escarbagnas* (2 décembre à Saint-Germain).

1672 — Mort de Madeleine Béjart (17 février). *Les Femmes savantes* (11 mars). Brouille avec Lully, qui a obtenu du roi le privilège de tous les spectacles avec musique et ballets.

1673 — *Le Malade imaginaire* (10 février). A la quatrième représentation (17 février), Molière, pris en scène d'un malaise, est transporté chez lui, rue de Richelieu, et **meurt** presque aussitôt. N'ayant pas renié sa vie de comédien devant un prêtre, il n'avait, selon la tradition, pas le droit d'être enseveli en terre chrétienne : après intervention du roi auprès de l'archevêque, on l'enterre sans grande cérémonie à 9 heures du soir au cimetière Saint-Joseph.

Molière avait seize ans de moins que Corneille, neuf ans de moins que La Rochefoucauld, un an de moins que La Fontaine.

Il avait un an de plus que Pascal, quatre ans de plus que Mme de Sévigné, cinq ans de plus que Bossuet, quatorze ans de plus que Boileau, dix-sept ans de plus que Racine.

MOLIÈRE ET SON TEMPS

	vie et œuvre de Molière	le mouvement intellectuel et artistique	les événements politiques
1622	Baptême à Paris de J.-B. Poquelin (15 janvier).	Succès dramatiques d'Alarcon, de Tirso de Molina en Espagne.	Paix de Montpellier, mettant fin à la guerre de religion en Béarn.
1639	Quitte le collège de Clermont, où il a fait ses études.	Mainard : Odes. Tragi-comédies de Boisrobert et de Scudéry. Naissance de Racine.	La guerre contre l'Espagne et les Impériaux, commencée en 1635, se poursuit.
1642	Obtient sa licence en droit.	Corneille : la Mort de Pompée (décembre). Du Ryer : Esther.	Prise de Perpignan. Mort de Richelieu (4 décembre).
1643	Constitue la troupe de l'Illustre-Théâtre avec Madeleine Béjart.	Corneille : le Menteur. Ouverture des petites écoles de Port-Royal-des-Champs. Arrivée à Paris de Lully.	Mort de Louis XIII (14 mai). Victoire de Rocroi (19 mai). Défaite française en Aragon.
1645	Faillite de l'Illustre-Théâtre.	Rotrou : Saint Genest. Corneille : Théodore, vierge et martyre.	Victoire française de Nördlingen sur les Impériaux (3 août).
1646	Reprend place avec Madeleine Béjart dans une troupe protégée par le duc d'Épernon. Va en province.	Cyrano de Bergerac : le Pédant joué. Saint-Amant : Poésies.	Prise de Dunkerque.
1650	Prend la direction de la troupe, qui sera protégée à partir de 1653 par le prince de Conti.	Saint-Évremond : la comédie des Académistes. Mort de Descartes.	Troubles de la Fronde : victoire provisoire de Mazarin sur Condé et les princes.
1655	Représentation à Lyon de l'Étourdi.	Pascal se retire à Port-Royal-des-Champs (janvier). Racine entre à l'école des Granges de Port-Royal.	Négociations avec Cromwell pour obtenir l'alliance anglaise contre l'Espagne.
1658	Arrive à Paris avec sa troupe, qui devient la « troupe de Monsieur » et occupe la salle du Petit-Bourbon.	Dorimond : le Festin de pierre.	Victoire des Dunes sur les Espagnols. Mort d'Olivier Cromwell.
1659	Représentation triomphale des Précieuses ridicules.	Villiers : le Festin de pierre. Retour de Corneille au théâtre avec Œdipe.	Paix des Pyrénées : l'Espagne cède l'Artois et le Roussillon à la France.
1660	Sganarelle ou le Cocu imaginaire.	Quinault : Stratonice (tragédie). Bossuet prêche le carême aux Minimes.	Mariage de Louis XIV et de Marie-Thérèse. Restauration des Stuarts.
1661	S'installe au Palais-Royal. Dom Garcie de Navarre. L'École des maris. Les Fâcheux.	La Fontaine : Élégie aux nymphes de Vaux.	Mort de Mazarin (8 mars). Arrestation de Fouquet (5 septembre).

1662	Se marie avec Armande Béjart. *L'École des femmes.*	Corneille : *Sertorius. La Rochefoucauld : Mémoires.* Mort de Pascal (19 août). Fondation de la manufacture des Gobelins.	Michel Le Tellier, Colbert et Hugues de Lionne deviennent ministres de Louis XIV.
1663	Querelle de l'*École des femmes. La Critique de « l'École des femmes ».*	Corneille : *Sophonisbe.* Racine : ode *Sur la convalescence du Roi.*	Invasion de l'Autriche par les Turcs.
1664	Le *Mariage forcé.* Interdiction du premier *Tartuffe.*	Racine : *la Thébaïde ou les Frères ennemis.*	Condamnation de Fouquet, après un procès de quatre ans.
1665	*Dom Juan. L'Amour médecin.*	La Fontaine : *Contes et Nouvelles.* Mort du peintre N. Poussin.	Peste de Londres.
1666	Le *Misanthrope.* Le *Médecin malgré lui.*	Boileau : *Satires* (I à VI). Furetière : le *Roman bourgeois.* Fondation de l'Académie des sciences.	Alliance franco-hollandaise contre l'Angleterre. Mort d'Anne d'Autriche. Incendie de Londres.
1667	*Mélicerte. La Pastorale comique. Le Sicilien.* Interdiction de la deuxième version du *Tartuffe : l'Imposteur.*	Corneille : *Attila.* Racine : *Andromaque.* Milton : le *Paradis perdu.* Naissance de Swift.	Conquête de la Flandre par les troupes françaises (guerre de Dévolution).
1668	*Amphitryon. George Dandin. L'Avare.*	La Fontaine : *Fables* (livres I à VI). Racine : les *Plaideurs.* Mort du peintre Nicolas Mignard.	Fin de la guerre de Dévolution : traités de Saint-Germain et d'Aix-la-Chapelle. Annexion de la Flandre.
1669	Représentation du *Tartuffe. Monsieur de Pourceaugnac.*	Racine : *Britannicus.* Fondation de l'Académie royale de musique et de danse.	
1670	Les *Amants magnifiques.* Le *Bourgeois gentilhomme.*	Racine : *Bérénice.* Corneille : *Tite et Bérénice.* Édition des *Pensées* de Pascal. Mariotte découvre la loi des gaz.	Mort de Madame. Les états de Hollande nomment Guillaume d'Orange capitaine général.
1671	*Psyché.* Les *Fourberies de Scapin. La Comtesse d'Escarbagnas.*	Débuts de la correspondance de Mme de Sévigné avec Mme de Grignan.	Louis XIV prépare la guerre contre la Hollande.
1672	Les *Femmes savantes.* Mort de Madeleine Béjart.	Racine : *Bajazet.* Th. Corneille : *Ariane.* P. Corneille : *Pulchérie.*	Déclaration de guerre à la Hollande. Passage du Rhin (juin).
1673	Le *Malade imaginaire.* Mort de Molière (17 février).	Racine : *Mithridate.* Séjour de Leibniz à Paris. Premier grand opéra de Lully : *Cadmus et Hermione.*	Conquête de la Hollande. Prise de Maestricht (29 juin).

BIBLIOGRAPHIE SOMMAIRE

OUVRAGES GÉNÉRAUX SUR MOLIÈRE :

Gustave Michaut, *la Jeunesse de Molière* (Paris, Hachette, 1922). — *Les Débuts de Molière à Paris* (Paris, Hachette, 1923). — *Les Luttes de Molière* (Paris, Hachette, 1925).

Ramon Fernandez, *la Vie de Molière* (Paris, Gallimard, 1930).

Daniel Mornet, *Molière, l'homme et l'œuvre* (Paris, Boivin, 1943).

René Bray, *Molière, homme de théâtre* (Paris, Mercure de France, 1954).

Antoine Adam, *Histoire de la littérature française au XVIIe siècle*, tome III (Paris, Domat, 1952).

Alfred Simon, *Molière par lui-même* (Paris, Éd. du Seuil, 1957).

SUR « LE BOURGEOIS GENTILHOMME » :

Sylvie Chevalley, *« le Bourgeois gentilhomme »* (Coll. Comédie-Française, Éd. S.I.P.E., Paris).

SUR LA LANGUE DE MOLIÈRE :

Jean-Pol Caput *la Langue française, histoire d'une institution*, tome I (842-1715) [Paris, Larousse, collection L, 1972].

Jean Dubois, René Lagane et A. Lerond *Dictionnaire du français classique* (Paris, Larousse, 1971).

Vaugelas *Remarques sur la langue française* (Paris, Larousse, « Nouveaux Classiques », 1969).

DISQUE :

Le Bourgeois gentilhomme a été enregistré par la troupe de la Comédie-Française le dimanche 22 mai 1955 (« l'Encyclopédie sonore », Paris, Hachette).

LE BOURGEOIS GENTILHOMME
1670

NOTICE

CE QUI SE PASSAIT EN 1670

■ **EN POLITIQUE** : *Louis XIV avait achevé, deux ans avant, la guerre de Dévolution par l'avantageux traité d'Aix-la-Chapelle (1668), et venait de conclure avec le roi d'Angleterre le traité secret de Douvres (1670), dirigé contre la Hollande. Les états de Hollande nomment capitaine général Guillaume, prince d'Orange. Rapports diplomatiques très tendus avec la Turquie : de 1667 à 1669, un corps expéditionnaire français combat l'avance turque en Crète. — 30 juin, mort subite à Saint-Cloud de Madame, Henriette d'Angleterre.*

■ **EN LITTÉRATURE** : *Zayde, roman de Mme de La Fayette. Port-Royal donne la première édition des Pensées de Pascal. La Rochefoucauld polit la troisième édition de ses Maximes. Bossuet prononce, le 21 août, l'Oraison funèbre de Madame, à Saint-Denis. Bourdaloue prêche l'Avent devant la Cour. — Au théâtre : En février, Molière fait représenter les Amants magnifiques, à Saint-Germain. En novembre, Racine fait jouer Bérénice, et Corneille, Tite et Bérénice.*

■ **DANS LES SCIENCES ET DANS LES ARTS** : *Le physicien français Mariotte découvre la loi des gaz. — Perrault achève la colonnade du Louvre. Mansard succède à Le Vau pour édifier le palais de Versailles. Colbert se fait construire son château de Sceaux. — Nanteuil, portrait de Colbert. Ruysdael, le Cimetière juif.*

LA COMÉDIE-BALLET EN FRANCE AVANT MOLIÈRE

Quoique l'occasion et les circonstances soient à l'origine des comédies-ballets que Molière nous a laissées, il n'est pas sans intérêt de rappeler les tentatives antérieures dans un genre auquel il a donné ses lettres de noblesse.

Dès le Moyen Age, le genre existait. Faut-il rappeler le *Jeu de Robin et de Marion*, dont Adam de la Halle fut, au XIIIe siècle, le poète et le musicien ? Est-ce à vrai dire autre chose qu'une comédie mêlée de chants et de danses, sur le canevas traditionnel de la pastorale, qui conte l'histoire d'une bergère aimée de « son » Robin et à qui un chevalier fait la cour sans succès ? Et l'œuvre ne fut pas écrite dans une autre intention que de divertir le prince Charles d'Anjou et sa cour, en exil à Naples (Noël 1283).

Trois siècles plus tard, en 1581, était représenté le *Ballet comique de la reine*, œuvre due à la collaboration de trois auteurs, Beaujoyeux, La Chesnaie et le sieur de Beaulieu; ici, à l'union des vers, du chant et de la danse, s'ajoutent l'éclat des costumes et le luxe des machines et des décors. En 1640, De Beys, sous le pseudonyme de Chillac, produit une *Comédie de chansons* dont le mérite, selon l'auteur lui-même, « consiste dans l'ingénieuse invention d'avoir enchaîné des airs de cour et de vaudeville d'une façon subtile ». Ce qui n'était là qu'ambition fort mal réalisée, nous le retrouvons dans l'*Andromède* de Corneille, représentée en 1650, sur le théâtre royal du Petit-Bourbon, avec la musique de Charles d'Assoucy et dans des « machines » inventées par Torelli. « Souffrez, disait Corneille dans l'Argument, que la beauté de la représentation supplée au manque des beaux vers, que vous n'y trouverez pas en si grande quantité que dans *Cinna* ou dans *Rodogune*, parce que mon principal but ici a été de satisfaire la vue par l'éclat et la diversité du spectacle, et non pas de toucher l'esprit par la force du raisonnement, ou le cœur par la délicatesse des passions. »

De son côté, le théâtre du Marais jouait en 1654 la *Comédie sans comédie*, de Quinault, « réunion de pièces détachées, qui ne sont reliées entre elles que par le prologue et quelques vers en tête du second acte et à la fin du dernier ». *L'Amour malade* (1657) est une sorte de comédie en musique, dont le souvenir ne s'est pas plus conservé que celui de bien des essais précédents. Si l'on ajoute que Perrin et Cambert ont connu un succès, réel sans doute mais sans lendemain, avec leur *Pastorale en musique*, que *les Rieurs du Beau Richard*, de La Fontaine, furent joués à Château-Thierry, la même année (1659), on comprendra combien l'auteur du *Bourgeois gentilhomme* doit peu à ses prédécesseurs.

Cependant, il faut dire encore un mot des « ballets de cour », composés d'entrées, de vers et de récits, pour lesquels on distribuait un programme, ou « livre », qui mettait les spectateurs au fait de ce que représentaient les danseurs et de ce qu'ils voulaient exprimer; le tout s'accompagnait de « madrigaux » à la louange de ceux qui devaient paraître dans divers rôles, et de « récits », tirades ou couplets, qui assuraient les enchaînements. Sur ces sortes d'ouvrages, contentons-nous de citer le jugement de l'abbé de Pure : « Il n'est tenu que de plaire aux yeux, de leur fournir des objets agréables et dont l'apparence et le dehors impriment de fortes et de belles images. » A cela, rien de surprenant : l'invention des ballets, le « dessein », n'était nullement le fait d'hommes de lettres, mais le privilège de seigneurs de la Cour; déjà, à l'époque d'Henri IV ou de Louis XIII, Sully, le duc de Guise, le duc de Nemours surtout, considérèrent cet office comme un privilège, avant même certains contemporains de Molière, le duc de Saint-Aignan, par exemple, qui a peut-être servi de modèle à l'auteur du *Misanthrope* pour son personnage d'Oronte. La magnificence était la seule qualité de ces productions, dont la monotonie, le manque d'unité et d'art, le seul souci de frapper les yeux expliquent le succès éphémère. Le jour où, le goût s'amendant, on aura l'idée de faire appel à un spécialiste pour établir un juste équilibre entre la poésie, la musique et la danse, où l'on ne verra plus alterner des scènes sans suite avec des danses sans signification, ce jour-là on assistera à la naissance d'un spectacle nouveau : ce sera l'œuvre de Molière.

LA COMÉDIE-BALLET DANS L'ŒUVRE DE MOLIÈRE

Ce genre occupe une part importante dans l'œuvre de Molière et alterne avec ce qu'on est convenu d'appeler les « farces » et les « grandes comédies ». Ce sont : *les Fâcheux* (1661), *le Mariage forcé* (1664), *la Princesse d'Élide* (1664), *l'Amour médecin* (1665), *Mélicerte, la Pastorale comique, le Sicilien ou l'Amour peintre* (déc. 1666-févr. 1667), *George Dandin* (1668), *Monsieur de Pourceaugnac* (1669), *les Amants magnifiques* (1670), *le Malade imaginaire* (1673).

Comme on le voit, la cadence de ces œuvres ne se ralentit pas au cours des années, ce qui dit assez le plaisir que Molière prenait à un genre qu'il avait abordé par hasard. En effet, le désir de Fouquet d'éblouir Louis XIV, lors des fêtes qu'il offrit au souverain en 1661 et qui devaient entraîner sa perte, la nécessité de réaliser en quinze jours une comédie « à tiroir », voilà ce qui dicta à Molière l'une des plus originales de ses idées. A ce sujet, l'Avertissement des *Fâcheux* est un document de première importance : « Comme il n'y avait, écrit Molière, qu'un petit nombre choisi de danseurs excellents, on fut contraint de séparer les entrées de ce ballet, et l'avis fut de les jeter dans les entractes de la comédie, afin que ces intervalles donnassent temps aux mêmes baladins de revenir sous d'autres habits; de sorte que, pour ne point rompre aussi le fil de la pièce par ces manières d'intermèdes, on s'avisa de les coudre au sujet du mieux que l'on put et de ne faire qu'une seule chose du ballet et de la comédie. » Ne faire « qu'une seule chose », n'est-ce pas tout justement mettre un trait d'union entre les deux termes, autrement dit créer la « comédie-ballet » ?

A vrai dire, « créer » n'est pas le terme exact. Sans être « grand Grec » et pour être plus proche de Plaute et de Térence que d'Aristophane, Molière n'ignorait pas la manière dont le grand comique d'Athènes unissait la musique, la danse et la poésie. Incorporer la danse à l'action, demander à la musique de fortifier l'expression du sentiment et l'intérêt des situations, voilà ce qu'emprunte à l'auteur des *Nuées* l'auteur des *Amants magnifiques,* qui ose même, dans cette dernière œuvre, recréer la pantomime. « Ne voudriez-vous pas, Madame, dit ici Cléonice à Ériphile, voir un petit essai de la disposition de ces gens admirables qui veulent se donner à vous? Ce sont des personnes qui, par leurs pas, leurs mouvements et leurs gestes, expriment aux yeux toutes choses; et on appelle cela pantomime.

J'ai tremblé à vous dire ce mot, et il y a des gens dans votre cour qui ne me le pardonneraient pas. »

La pantomime aura sa place dans toute l'œuvre de Molière, et surtout peut-être dans *le Bourgeois gentilhomme*. Mais si Molière se soucie du moindre détail des costumes et de la décoration, et si, à la faveur de la danse et de la musique, il traite toute une catégorie de sujets que, sans leur concours, il n'eût pu aborder, il a néanmoins toujours considéré comme admis et indiscutable qu'à son art propre revenait la première place. Relisons, à ce sujet, le Prologue de *l'Amour médecin* : la comédie seule y a la parole (au moins dans l'édition originale); la comédie-ballet s'intitule « comédie » tout court. Enfin, et surtout, c'est à la comédie que revient l'honneur de proposer à la musique et au ballet de cesser leurs querelles

> Pour donner du plaisir au plus grand roi du monde.

Si « tout le secret des armes ne consiste qu'en deux choses : à donner et à ne point recevoir », le secret de la comédie-ballet consiste, pour le poète, à donner encore plus qu'on ne reçoit; c'est ce secret qui inspira à Molière son *Bourgeois gentilhomme* et même son *Malade imaginaire*. Pour l'auteur du *Tartuffe* — il l'affirme dans la Préface —, « la comédie est un poème ingénieux qui, par des leçons agréables, tend à reprendre les défauts des hommes » : lorsqu'il a conçu un poème, encore plus « ingénieux », où l'agréable prend le pas sur la morale ou sur l'intention moralisante, alors Molière a réalisé le chef-d'œuvre de la comédie-ballet; sans doute même est-il le seul à avoir donné à ce genre hybride valeur d'œuvre d'art.

CIRCONSTANCES DE LA COMPOSITION ET DE LA REPRÉSENTATION DU « BOURGEOIS GENTILHOMME »

« Le roi ayant voulu faire un voyage à Chambord pour y prendre le divertissement de la chasse voulut donner à sa cour celui d'un ballet, et comme l'idée des Turcs, qu'on venait de voir à Paris, était encore toute récente, il crut qu'il serait bon de les faire paraître sur la scène. »

Ce que dit aussi le chevalier d'Arvieux en ses *Mémoires*, c'est que la visite à la Cour de l'envoyé de la Porte, en novembre 1669, avait laissé un souvenir assez cocasse. Pour impressionner l'homme du sérail, Louis XIV s'était présenté dans le plus grand faste : son brocart d'or était tellement couvert de diamants « qu'il semblait environné de lumière »; son chapeau était orné d'un « bouquet de plumes magnifiques ». Les gentilshommes étaient à l'image du maître, groupés dans la salle d'audience, où un trône d'argent avait été dressé sur une haute estrade. Or, à l'issue de la réception, le Turc, d'un ton froid et cinglant, d'affirmer que « lorsque le Grand Seigneur se montrait au peuple, son cheval était plus richement orné que l'habit qu'il venait de voir ».

Laurent d'Arvieux était mieux placé que quiconque pour connaître les impressions du Turc, puisqu'il jouait, dans cette farce vécue, le rôle de l'interprète, du « truchement », et, plus d'une fois sans doute, Louis XIV dut-il, avant Monsieur Jourdain, lui dire : « Où allez-vous donc ? Nous ne saurions rien dire sans vous ! »

Nous savons très précisément par les *Mémoires* de l'illustre voyageur dans quelles circonstances le divertissement fut commandé par le roi. « Sa Majesté m'ordonna, écrit d'Arvieux, de me joindre à MM. Molière et Lully pour composer une pièce de théâtre où l'on pût faire entrer quelque chose des habillements et des manières des Turcs. Je me rendis pour cet effet au village d'Auteuil, où M. Molière avait une maison fort jolie. Ce fut là que nous travaillâmes à cette pièce de théâtre que l'on voit dans les œuvres de Molière sous le titre de *Bourgeois gentilhomme*, qui se fait Turc pour épouser la fille du Grand Seigneur. Je fus chargé de tout ce qui regardait les habillements et les manières des Turcs. La pièce achevée, on la présenta au roi qui l'agréa, et je demeurai huit jours chez Baraillon, maître tailleur, pour faire faire les habits et les turbans à la turque. Tout fut transporté à Chambord, et la pièce fut représentée dans le mois avec un succès qui satisfit le roi et la Cour. »

Ce texte reste capital pour deux raisons. Tout d'abord, il contient cette curieuse précision au sujet de Monsieur Jourdain *qui se fait Turc pour épouser la fille du Grand Seigneur.* Certains commentateurs en ont déduit que d'Arvieux n'avait pas même lu la pièce. A cette explication peu vraisemblable, nous préférons une autre explication : c'était là le dénouement d'un canevas primitif sur lequel Molière a brodé et qu'il a considérablement modifié. D'autre part, certains ont prétendu que l'œuvre avait été improvisée en dix jours à Chambord ; ils s'appuient pour cela sur le titre primitif, « comédie-ballet *faite* à Chambord », et sur les dates connues du déplacement de la troupe, qui arriva le 3 octobre 1670 et joua le 14. Il est bien évident qu'il faut comprendre « représentée » et non « écrite, montée et représentée », comme le furent *les Fâcheux* en 1661. *Le Bourgeois gentilhomme* est donc une œuvre de circonstance, certes, non une œuvre hâtivement improvisée.

L'accueil fait à la création est douteux : Grimarest prétend que le roi se montra distant et froid. Ce ne serait qu'à la deuxième représentation qu'il aurait dit à Molière : « En vérité, vous n'avez encore rien fait qui m'ait plus diverti, et votre pièce est excellente. » Selon le gazetier Robinet, au contraire, la première représentation semble avoir été un succès. En tout état de cause, l'œuvre fut jouée quatre fois à Chambord, les 14, 16, 20 et 21 octobre, et plusieurs fois au début de novembre à Saint-Germain, pour le divertissement des nobles invités. Dès le 23 novembre, les spectateurs de la ville virent *le Bourgeois gentilhomme* au théâtre du Palais-Royal, et lui firent un franc succès, car on ne retrancha aucun des « agréments » — le terme est de Molière —, c'est-à-dire des danses, chants et autres divertissements de la comédie. De 1680 à 1967, *le Bourgeois gentilhomme* a été représenté 1 065 fois à la Comédie-Française, contre 2 762 représentations du *Tartuffe* et 1 656 du *Malade imaginaire*. En fait, pendant le XVIIIe et le XIXe siècle, la pièce fut relativement peu jouée : si le nombre des représentations a approché de 50 en 1690, 1720, 1860 et 1930, il a été inférieur à 10 en 1800 et en 1850. Le renouveau du *Bourgeois gentilhomme* à la Comédie-Française date de 1944, quand on fit appel à Raimu, plus connu alors du public comme acteur de cinéma, pour tenir le rôle de Monsieur Jourdain; mais le succès de la pièce s'est encore affirmé depuis 1951, c'est-à-dire depuis que Louis Seigner a pris possession du rôle du Bourgeois : 407 représentations de la comédie ont été données de 1951 à 1967. C'est le premier spectacle que la troupe du Théâtre-Français a présenté en Amérique et à Moscou, avec un égal succès. La qualité de cette interprétation, la beauté des décors et des costumes, la perfection des ensembles et de la mise en scène expliquent peut-être ce regain de succès. Mais sans doute faudrait-il en chercher les causes plus loin, dans l'œuvre elle-même, dans son mouvement et sa verve, et dans le goût d'un public que le cinéma a habitué aux « superproductions » et qui va volontiers vers les réalisations scéniques capables de rendre le théâtre à son état premier d'art de synthèse, où s'accordent la poésie, la musique, la danse et même les couleurs.

ANALYSE DE LA PIÈCE

(Les scènes principales sont indiquées entre parenthèses.)

L'œuvre comprend cinq actes, si l'on considère la « comédie »; mais si l'on s'en tient au livret du « ballet », elle se découpe en trois parties.

■ *ACTE PREMIER ET ACTE II.* **Monsieur Jourdain et ses maîtres.**

Le maître à danser et le maître de musique s'entretiennent de leur art et se moquent complaisamment du parvenu qui les paie. Monsieur Jourdain survient et, après avoir jugé « lugubre » une chanson qu'on lui fait entendre, estime « bien troussé » le premier divertissement qu'on lui présente, avant de voir le suivant, qui forme le premier intermède **(acte premier, scène II).**

Monsieur Jourdain commande alors un ballet pour un dîner qu'il doit offrir à des personnes de qualité. Il prend sa leçon de danse et s'instruit de la manière de faire la révérence à une marquise. Violente intrusion du maître d'armes, qui oppose sa science à celle des deux autres maîtres. On va en venir aux mains quand survient le maître de philosophie, qui prêche « la patience et la modération ». Interrogé sur la suprématie de l'un des trois arts, il soutient la prééminence de la philosophie, et fait l'unanimité contre lui. Une bataille, où Monsieur Jourdain refuse d'intervenir pour ne pas gâter sa belle robe de chambre, entraîne la sortie des combattants. De retour auprès de son élève, le maître de philosophie propose de lui enseigner la logique, la morale et la physique. Monsieur Jourdain préfère se limiter à l'orthographe; ayant pris leçon, il demande conseil pour la rédaction d'un billet galant destiné à une marquise (**acte II, scène IV**). Il reçoit ensuite son maître tailleur, qui lui apporte son habit. Mais « cela ne va pas sans cérémonie », et l'acte se termine par une entrée de ballet des garçons tailleurs, qui habillent Monsieur Jourdain, en cadence, après avoir reçu un généreux pourboire (**acte II, scène V**).

■ *ACTE III.* **Qui sera gendre de Monsieur Jourdain?**

Au moment d'aller en ville pour montrer son habit, Monsieur Jourdain essuie les moqueries de sa servante Nicole et les sarcasmes de sa femme, qui lui reproche de fréquenter les nobles, de négliger sa maison et de ne pas s'occuper du mariage de leur fille Lucile (**scène III**). Survient Dorante, ce seigneur qui parle de Monsieur Jourdain dans la chambre du roi, mais qui vit à ses dépens et se prépare à utiliser sa maison et sa bourse en abusant de sa crédulité. Au désespoir de sa femme, Monsieur Jourdain accepte encore de prêter de l'argent à Dorante, qui s'est chargé d'offrir une bague à cette fameuse marquise dont rêve le Bourgeois et dont on sait le nom : Dorimène (**scène IV**). Alors qu'il prépare la réception que Dorante veut offrir à Dorimène aux frais de son bienfaiteur, Monsieur Jourdain, à demi découvert par son épouse et sa servante, quitte la place (**scène VI**). Surviennent Cléonte, amoureux de Lucile, et son valet Covielle, qui courtise Nicole. Une scène de dépit amoureux éclate entre les deux amants, scène reprise en écho comique par les deux serviteurs (**scène X**). Mais tout finit par une double réconciliation, et Madame Jourdain, prête à défendre la candidature de Cléonte, conseille à celui-ci de profiter du retour de Monsieur Jourdain pour lui demander la main de Lucile. Le malheureux jeune homme se voit brutalement évincé parce qu'il a eu l'honnêteté de ne pas se faire passer pour gentilhomme (**scène XII**). Fureur de Madame Jourdain qui sort à la poursuite de son mari, tandis que Covielle propose à son jeune maître un stratagème dont il l'entretiendra mieux hors de la maison. Dorante reparaît en compagnie de Dorimène, qui s'inquiète de toutes les dépenses qu'à ses yeux Dorante fait pour elle. Monsieur Jourdain revient, se pavane devant Dorimène, qui ne comprend pas tout de ce manège, et les convives se mettent à table, tandis que les cuisiniers exécutent le troisième intermède (**scène XIX**).

■ *ACTES IV ET V.* **De la cérémonie turque au ballet des nations.**

A la fin du festin, Madame Jourdain surgit et interrompt les ridicules compliments dans lesquels s'empêtre Monsieur Jourdain, fort préoccupé de plaire à Dorimène; celle-ci, outrée, sort en compagnie de Dorante **(acte IV, scène II).** La dispute entre les deux époux est à peine terminée qu'on voit arriver Covielle, déguisé en Turc; Monsieur Jourdain, naturellement, ne le reconnaît pas. Covielle annonce au Bourgeois épanoui que le fils du Grand Turc a vu Lucile, s'est follement épris d'elle et veut l'épouser sur le champ. Il s'agit bien entendu de Cléonte, également déguisé en Turc. Mais cela nécessite une petite cérémonie : il faut que Monsieur Jourdain soit, de la main de son futur gendre, élevé à la dignité de « Mamamouchi » **(acte IV, scène V).** Monsieur Jourdain accepte, et la cérémonie a lieu en présence de Dorante, qui consent, dans son propre intérêt, à favoriser l'intrigue.

A peine remis des coups de sabre et des coups de bâton qu'il a reçus durant la cérémonie, mais fier de son titre et de son turban, Monsieur Jourdain voit revenir son épouse, de plus en plus outrée. Elle croit son mari devenu fou et veut l'empêcher de sortir **(acte V, scène première).** Pendant qu'elle se lance à sa poursuite, Dorimène reparaît et propose à Dorante de l'épouser... pour mettre un terme aux dépenses qu'elle lui voit faire pour elle! Cléonte et Covielle entrent pour procéder au contrat qui unira le prétendu fils du Grand Turc à la fille de Monsieur Jourdain. Monsieur Jourdain veut imposer le fils du Grand Turc à Lucile, qui ne refuse qu'un instant, le temps de reconnaître Cléonte et Covielle sous leur déguisement. Madame Jourdain, qui, elle, dans son entêtement, ne veut rien voir, est plus longue à découvrir la supercherie et à faire semblant de s'incliner **(acte V, scène VII).** L'action se termine donc par un triple mariage : le notaire viendra établir les contrats de Lucile et de Cléonte, de Dorimène et de Dorante, de Nicole et de Covielle. Monsieur Jourdain, que rien ne peut détromper, assistera, avec toute la compagnie, au fameux ballet qui avait été préparé.

LES SOURCES DU « BOURGEOIS GENTILHOMME »

Molière a, comme souvent, fait ici quelques emprunts. Le désir de s'instruire animait déjà Strepsiade, dans *les Nuées* d'Aristophane, et le vieillard s'émerveillait de la science de son maître Socrate, qui ne lui enseignait pourtant que des rudiments; il s'empressait ensuite de faire bien maladroitement étalage de sa science auprès de son fils Phidippide, comme le fera Monsieur Jourdain auprès de sa femme et de Nicole. Plaute a peut-être fourni à Molière l'idée de la scène du festin offert à Dorimène et troublé par l'arrivée inattendue de Madame Jourdain. Quant à la « turquerie », elle a été inspirée, on l'a vu, par des événements récents, mais cette première forme de l'exotisme oriental n'est pas unique dans la littérature du XVIIe siècle. Dès 1641, Scudéry et sa sœur avaient fait paraître un long roman, *Ibrahim ou l'Illustre Bassa,* qui se passait dans une Turquie de fantaisie. En 1645, Rotrou, dans sa comédie *la Sœur,* fait parler turc à l'un de ses personnages. Lully avait offert, en 1660, à la Cour un *Récit turquesque* qui avait enchanté Louis XIV. Toutes les œuvres grecques, latines ou modernes qu'on vient de citer ont pu suggérer à Molière des situations, des répliques, des détails, sans qu'il y ait d'imitation à proprement parler. L'essentiel du *Bourgeois gentilhomme* vient de Molière lui-même.

Non seulement les scènes de brouille et de réconciliation entre Cléonte et Lucile, Covielle et Nicole (acte III, scènes IX et X) rappellent la comédie du *Dépit amoureux,* mais il est possible que Molière ait consulté les notes de ce « magasin d'ébauches » dont parle Baron et où le « contemplateur » avait accumulé vingt bonnes années d'observations amusées ou amères. Ce qui est frappant surtout dans *le Bourgeois gentilhomme,* c'est que Molière a, beaucoup plus qu'ailleurs, façonné ses personnages en pensant aux interprètes auxquels il allait confier les différents rôles.

Le maître d'armes « grand cheval de carrosse », c'est de Brie. Lucile a les yeux et la taille d'Armande Béjart. Nicole a le rire de la Beauval, et le public de l'époque, connaissant la bêtise et le caractère acariâtre de celle-ci, devait bien rire en entendant Monsieur Jourdain dire à sa femme et à Nicole : « Vous parlez toutes deux comme des bêtes. » Madame Jourdain, c'est un rôle en or pour Hubert, qui avait l'art de jouer les femmes d'âge mûr. Enfin, Monsieur Jourdain, c'est un rôle que Molière se donne à lui-même, le plus complet et le plus haut en couleur, dans tous les sens de l'expression. Il aime chanter, et Monsieur Jourdain chante, comme Sganarelle, Argan et tant d'autres de ses personnages, parmi lesquels Alceste lui-même; il aime parodier et Monsieur Jourdain reproduit les jeux de physionomie de son maître de philosophie ou les gestes de son maître d'armes. Il est bilieux et entre en des colères d'enfant, qui ne durent pas et ne vont pas loin : Monsieur Jourdain s'emporte contre tout et contre tous. Il aime les déguisements et les couleurs chatoyantes : le rôle de Monsieur Jourdain est pour lui une occasion de déguisements variés, éclatants et... coûteux!

Ainsi, *le Bourgeois gentilhomme* reprend, par certains aspects, l'allure d'une comédie « à l'italienne », où les personnages semblent un peu faits pour leurs interprètes. Cette conception s'explique d'autant mieux dans une pièce qui est un divertissement et dans laquelle l'action est assez librement menée.

L'ACTION DANS « LE BOURGEOIS GENTILHOMME »

Toute la pièce tient entre la préparation et la représentation du ballet à offrir en « cadeau » à la marquise Dorimène. Aussi voit-on Monsieur Jourdain, en cette journée si importante pour sa vie sentimentale, donner toute son attention aux morceaux de musique qu'il a commandés (acte premier, scène II) et apprendre la révérence (acte II, scène première); s'il fait appel pour la première fois à un maître de philosophie, c'est pour apprendre à tourner un billet galant autant que pour s'initier à l'orthographe (acte II, scène IV). Mais, au troisième acte, l'opposition de Madame Jourdain aux folies de son mari la pousse non seulement à faire échec aux intrigues amoureuses de celui-ci, mais aussi à hâter le mariage de Lucile avec Cléonte, afin de tenir tête sur ce point également aux prétentions de Monsieur Jourdain. Ces deux plans de l'action se déroulent parallèlement : à peine Madame Jourdain a-t-elle mis fin par son arrivée inopinée au divertissement offert pour Dorimène que Covielle survient, mettant en œuvre le stratagème qui permettra le mariage de Cléonte et de Lucile; tout le monde, y compris Dorante et Dorimène, participe à ce jeu, dont le spectateur est aussi complice. Et puisque les vœux de tous sont satisfaits, on peut, dans la joie générale, assister au ballet qui avait été prévu à l'origine pour couronner la réception de Dorimène.

Infiniment moins ténue que dans les autres comédies-ballets, moins âpre que dans *George Dandin,* mais aussi beaucoup moins profonde, moins vraisemblable et moins « une » que dans *le Malade imaginaire,* l'action du *Bourgeois gentilhomme* est suffisamment étoffée, habilement conduite, et surtout supérieurement unie aux divertissements et aux intermèdes dont elle n'est que l'occasion. Si c'est là un prétexte, il demeure essentiel, et il fournit à Molière une riche peinture de caractère, une satire de mœurs hardie et un véritable feu d'artifice de comique et d'esprit.

LES PERSONNAGES ET LEURS CARACTÈRES

Comme à l'ordinaire, le couple des jeunes premiers est ici fort sacrifié. Si nous avons le temps de nous apercevoir que **Cléonte** est un charmant garçon, d'une parfaite droiture de caractère, qui ne se prête à la ruse que lui fournit son valet que par nécessité, **Lucile** est à peine esquissée et ne fait que bien jouer sa scène de dépit amoureux. Elle n'a pas même le temps de supplier son père, encore moins d'envisager « de se donner la mort si l'on me violente », comme Mariane dans *le Tartuffe.* Au reste, pas un instant nous ne craignons pour le bonheur de ce jeune couple, car pas un instant la comédie n'est au bord du drame.

Dorimène, marquise authentique, jeune veuve discrète et sincère, traverse l'action sans bien se rendre compte de ce que tout cela veut dire : elle ne soupçonne ni le double jeu de Dorante ni les intentions de Monsieur Jourdain, et ne comprend rien aux reproches de Madame Jourdain.

Covielle, issu de la comédie italienne — son nom l'indique assez —, est cousin de Scapin, comme **Nicole** est digne de Dorine et de Toinette. Toujours prêts à rire et heureux de jouer quelque bon tour qui serve les intérêts de leurs jeunes maîtres, ils ont aussi une scène bien à eux : celle du dépit amoureux, où ils doublent de façon plaisante les sentiments et les paroles de Lucile et de Cléonte.

Aidée et soutenue de cette servante qui n'o[...]
paysannes, **Madame Jourdain,** femme de te[...]
son bien, son foyer et surtout sa fille. Une rap[...]
son sujet, montre bien l'art de Molière pour mett[...]
« en situation ». Harpagon est veuf : la solitude où [...]
au dénouement de *l'Avare* en sera mieux marquée. Arg[...]
ce n'est pas la mère de Louison et d'Angélique qui che[...]
la main sur le bien du Malade imaginaire et guette sa m[...]
est aussi remarié, et la lutte d'Elmire contre Tartuffe, pour l[...]
de tous, n'en a que plus de grandeur et de noblesse. Il falla[...]
douce folie de Monsieur Jourdain s'opposât au bon sens d'une ép[...]
qui ne s'est jamais gênée pour contrecarrer les volontés de son m[...]
Si le langage de celle-ci paraît vulgaire et son idéal un peu bor[...]
c'est qu'elle tient aux traditions et même aux préjugés de cette bour[...]
geoisie que son mari veut renier. Par esprit de contradiction, elle
accentue encore, quand elle est en présence de Dorante, cette rudesse
qui est pour elle une forme de la résistance.

Personnages épisodiques et nullement secondaires, les **« maîtres »** :
le tailleur, intéressé, arrogant, incapable de cacher son mépris;
le bretteur, silhouette haute en couleur, qui ne s'embarrasse pas de
préambule; le musicien et le danseur, qui s'entendent et se complètent
si bien; le philosophe, avec des traits caricaturaux hérités du pédant
traditionnel de la farce, mais observé jusque dans le moindre détail.

Les « maîtres » ne sont pas seuls à profiter de Monsieur Jourdain,
car voici **Dorante.** Il s'agit en fait d'un personnage fort équivoque,
ancêtre de ceux qu'on appellera bientôt « chevaliers d'industrie ». Il
pratique sans scrupule l'abus de confiance, et on peut plaindre Dorimène, qui semble ne rien voir de sa duplicité. Est-il un noble authentique ou usurpe-t-il ses titres? Rien ne le précise. Il n'a point, en tout
cas, la dignité morale qui convient à son rang. Il est au centre de la
satire sociale dont nous parlerons.

Mais voici que paraît **Monsieur Jourdain,** et le rire fuse : en robe
de chambre, en habit aux « fleurs en en-bas », en Mamamouchi,
toujours il fera rire. D'abord, parce qu'il combine la sottise et la
vanité. Ensuite, parce que pas un instant, à la différence d'Harpagon,
d'Orgon et même d'Argan, il ne nous inquiète. Pour un peu, tant
il nous amuse, nous serions tentés de prendre sa défense. Au fond,
il n'a que le tort de se laisser aller trop tard à des prétentions, alors
fort communes; tous ses efforts sont ceux d'un pataud, lourdaud et
maladroit. Mais sa naïveté est désarmante tout comme sa maladresse.
Au reste, il n'est ni intéressé ni méchant : menace-t-il sa fille de la
faire marquise ou duchesse? Nous n'y croyons pas plus qu'à sa
colère contre son maître tailleur ou contre Nicole. Fait-il la cour à
Dorimène? C'est au titre, non à la femme, qu'il s'intéresse; ce n'est
pas « Dorimène » qui l'aveugle, c'est « une marquise ». Pour enve-
lopper ce rôle de notre dédain, de notre mépris et même de notre
dégoût, attendons de voir tous les personnages inquiétants, répu-

ccesseurs de Molière, et en par-
, auquel il faut sans cesse penser
i-ci n'est pas plus antipathique
Et nous dirions volontiers que
vait que de la sympathie pour
t de sa haine : les tartufes et
ut langage. On connaît ceux
Harpagon et Dandin, Orgon
Monsieur Jourdain, lui, n'est
ique d'un tapissier qui ven-
ui envoie son fils au collège,
fasse ses études de droit,
... ns ce que Monsieur Jourdain
me! Monsieur Jourdain est d'un ridicule
in instant il n'inspire répulsion ni dégoût. Dans
en lire la description dans la Documentation théma-
, la dominante est le vert, couleur préférée de Molière. C'est
aussi la couleur des rubans d'Alceste : toute la différence, c'est que,
sur toute la personne de Monsieur Jourdain, le vert se mélange au
rouge et au jaune, ce qui est normal pour ce perroquet de la noblesse,
un perroquet fort apprivoisé, aux colères sans gravité, et dont le
bec ne s'avance jamais de façon inquiétante!

LA SATIRE SOCIALE ET LA PORTÉE DE L'ŒUVRE

A rire de si bon cœur de Monsieur Jourdain, on en oublierait bien
volontiers que le Bourgeois gentilhomme comporte une satire sociale.
A vrai dire, on n'est point très sûr que Molière y ait beaucoup songé!
Mais d'autres y ont pensé pour lui, qui sont même allés jusqu'à voir
dans la cérémonie turque une parodie de la messe! Sans aller aussi
loin, on peut admettre que la discussion entre Cléonte et Monsieur
Jourdain (acte III, scène XII) est la preuve des préoccupations que
Molière n'a cessé de répandre dans son œuvre depuis Dom Juan
et le Tartuffe. En refusant de passer pour ce qu'il n'est pas, pour un
gentilhomme, Cléonte veut se distinguer de tous ceux qui s'arrogent
des titres auxquels ils n'ont pas droit. Cette usurpation de titres,
si fréquente alors, soulève un problème plus général et plus grave :
celui du recrutement des élites. Un italien, Primi Visconti, écrivait
à l'époque : « Il y a à Paris plus de vingt mille gentilshommes qui
n'ont pas un sou et qui subsistent pourtant par le jeu et par les
femmes et qui vivent d'industrie. Aujourd'hui, ils vont à pied et le
lendemain en carrosse. » Ce problème n'a pas été sans préoccuper
Colbert; Molière y fait allusion ici, mais c'est Lesage, avec son
Turcaret, qui l'abordera franchement, après que La Bruyère y aura
consacré maintes pages de ses Caractères, notamment dans le chapitre
des « Biens de fortune ».

L'évolution de la société n'a pas enlevé à Monsieur Jourdain son actualité : le Bourgeois préfigure en effet ceux qu'on a appelés au XXᵉ siècle les « nouveaux riches » et, en général, tous ceux qui, comblés d'argent par le hasard ou par des profits plus ou moins honnêtes, rêvent d'éblouir les autres par l'étalage d'un luxe auquel ni leur éducation ni leur goût ne les ont préparés. La folie des grandeurs s'empare d'eux, et ils ménagent à leurs enfants les beaux mariages qui leur permettront de porter des noms à particule. Ils sont même pires que Monsieur Jourdain : celui-ci fait effort pour s'instruire, regrette autant de ne pas avoir appris quand il était jeune que de ne pas avoir quatre quartiers de noblesse. Par-dessus tout, Monsieur Jourdain ne nous semble nullement « perdu »; on sent très bien que, gorgé de vanités, saturé de flatteries et de mondanités, il reviendra, comme un brave et honnête bourgeois qu'il n'a cessé d'être au fond, finir ses jours entre sa femme, sa fille, son gendre et ses petits-enfants.

LE COMIQUE

Infiniment plus importante nous paraît être la question du comique dans *le Bourgeois gentilhomme*. Utilisons, pour ne donner ici que des indications, le schéma suivant :

procédés	moyens mis en œuvre	sortes de comédies
GESTES	gifles, coups de bâton, etc. bataille, disputes, poursuites déguisements personnages cachés	
		FARCE
MOTS	calembours, mots déformés langages professionnels répétitions de termes	
SITUATION	quiproquos et malentendus de toutes sortes; poursuite vaine d'un objet ou d'un bien	COMÉDIE D'INTRIGUE
MŒURS ET CARACTÈRES	exagération } d'une époque dans la peinture } des manières d'être } d'un individu	GRANDE COMÉDIE

Ce schéma peut s'appliquer à toutes les œuvres comiques. Nous voulons seulement faire à son propos deux remarques :

Iº Il n'y a aucune séparation (aucun trait horizontal) dans ce tableau, car le secret du comique est justement l'union étroite, intime et naturelle, de ces différentes sources de comique. Or, tout le secret de la vitalité immortelle du rire de Molière vient de ce qu'il a su, mieux que n'importe quel autre auteur comique, créer, nourrir et entretenir cette union;

2° Cette union, qui existe dans toutes les œuvres de Molière, et jusque dans *le Misanthrope* (par la scène du valet Du Bois), c'est dans *le Bourgeois gentilhomme* qu'elle est la plus constante, la plus spontanée, la plus réussie.

LE STYLE ET LA MUSIQUE

Mais ce comique doit s'exprimer par des mots, par un langage, ou mieux par des langages. Là encore, Molière triomphe, car aucun des personnages du *Bourgeois gentilhomme* ne parle la même langue. On peut insister sur la simplicité, la familiarité, la vivacité et la portée directe de ce style; on peut relever les répétitions, les négligences et les incorrections de cette langue parlée; on peut inversement mettre en lumière tout autant de procédés savants de style : inversions, anacoluthes, asyndètes, syllepses, traits de préciosité, etc. Ce qui est essentiel, c'est qu'ici, autant et mieux peut-être que dans ses autres œuvres, Molière fait parler à chacun de ses personnages le langage de sa condition et « de son âme ». Un exemple : il suffira de comparer le langage des maîtres, et même celui des deux plus étroitement unis, le maître à danser et le maître de musique; l'un est plus intéressé, l'autre plus précieux, et, dans le style de Molière, toutes ces nuances sont indiquées : il suffit d'écouter, comme il suffit de voir pour rire.

Pourtant, il faut dire un mot encore d'une particularité : la prose du *Bourgeois gentilhomme* abonde en vers sans rimes : vers de douze pieds, décasyllabes et octosyllabes. Certes, il s'en trouvait dans *l'Avare*, *le Sicilien* et surtout *Dom Juan*. Il s'en trouve davantage dans *le Bourgeois gentilhomme,* œuvre pourtant écrite rapidement. Jalons pour une versification future? Langage naturel de l'acteur qui entend les rôles qu'il écrit? Sens inné et besoin de l'harmonie et du rythme? Thèse plus originale et hardie : la force des sentiments et des passions impose tout naturellement un rythme, et c'est parler en vers qui est naturel et spontané? Nous nous contentons d'énoncer ici ces quelques théories.

Mais notons surtout combien ce langage s'allie à la musique des divertissements. Si les vers mirlitonesques et précieux des « agréments » nous semblent aujourd'hui presque une parodie bouffonne de la poésie, il reste le charme de la partition de Lully, auquel celui-ci a pris certainement plaisir, jouant lui-même le rôle du Muphti, avant la brouille regrettable qui devait un peu plus tard surgir entre les deux collaborateurs et amis.

Il faut donc rendre justice à Lully, et ne jamais admettre une représentation du *Bourgeois gentilhomme* sans la danse et la musique. On doit seulement envisager des coupures et des allégements, la durée admise de nos jours pour un spectacle ne permettant pas l'exécution intégrale — à laquelle Molière lui-même avait dû renoncer — d'une partition qui demeure l'une des plus typiques de Lully et l'une des plus probantes de son génie, de son instinct dramatique et de son sens de la vie. Rendre hommage au talent de celui qui devait devenir « escuyer, surintendant et compositeur de la musique de la chambre, maître de la musique de la famille royale », c'est encore rendre hommage à Molière, qui sut lui communiquer sa *vis comica* et partager l'élan de son inspiration.

LA PLACE DU « BOURGEOIS GENTILHOMME » DANS L'ŒUVRE DE MOLIÈRE

Certes, *le Bourgeois gentilhomme* n'est pas la meilleure pièce de Molière : son action commence au troisième acte, et elle manque d'unité; elle n'a ni la profondeur ni la résonance humaine des grands chefs-d'œuvre. Mais elle demeure l'une des plus vivantes et la plus complète sans doute de toutes ses œuvres. Pourquoi?

Donner la réponse à cette question, c'est dire en même temps ce qu'est le génie de Molière, et pourquoi il a persévéré dans le genre de la comédie-ballet.

Dès son enfance, Molière a les dons de l'acteur comique : art de l'observation, art de l'imitation. Il se fait acteur par amour sans doute, mais aussi par vocation. A vingt-deux ans, il prend tout naturellement la direction d'une troupe qu'il mène en province durant quatorze ans, avant de la « présenter » au roi, un soir d'octobre 1658. A dater de ce jour, il s'attachera à faire rire le peuple et les bourgeois, mais aussi à satisfaire la Cour et le roi. Alors, tout naturellement, après des essais sur canevas, des ébauches, après douze farces dont nous ne connaissons que deux, l'acteur et le directeur de troupe vont s'unir pour dicter à l'auteur son œuvre, cette œuvre qui va de *l'Etourdi* au *Malade imaginaire*. Dans cette production abondante et riche, *le Bourgeois gentilhomme* n'est pas seulement la dernière œuvre parfaitement comique, gaie et heureuse, elle est aussi une anthologie, où toutes les situations, tous les effets comiques, tous les traits d'observation et de langage se retrouvent, fusent et fusionnent pour l'amusement des jeunes, la détente heureuse des plus grands. Cette comédie n'est pas « achevée » au sens de « parfaite », tant s'en faut; mais elle fait rire; elle demeure, sans un essoufflement, sans une ride, au travers des siècles, parce qu'elle contient et résume tout Molière; elle est le chef-d'œuvre de la comédie-ballet.

PERSONNAGES

MONSIEUR JOURDAIN   bourgeois.

MADAME JOURDAIN   sa femme.

LUCILE   fille de M. Jourdain.

NICOLE   servante.

CLÉONTE   amoureux de Lucile.

COVIELLE   valet de Cléonte.

DORANTE   comte, amant de Dorimène.

DORIMÈNE   marquise.

MAITRE DE MUSIQUE

ÉLÈVE DU MAITRE DE MUSIQUE

MAITRE À DANSER

MAITRE D'ARMES

MAITRE DE PHILOSOPHIE

MAITRE TAILLEUR

GARÇON TAILLEUR

DEUX LAQUAIS

PLUSIEURS MUSICIENS, MUSICIENNES, JOUEURS D'INSTRUMENTS,
DANSEURS, CUISINIERS, GARÇONS TAILLEURS,
ET AUTRES PERSONNAGES DES INTERMÈDES ET DU BALLET.

La scène est à Paris[1].

La distribution à la première représentation était la suivante : *Monsieur Jourdain,* Molière; *Madame Jourdain,* Hubert; *Lucile,* Armande Béjart; *Nicole,* Mlle Beauval; *Cléonte,* La Grange; *Dorante,* La Thorillière; *Dorimène,* Mlle de Brie; *Maitre d'armes,* de Brie.

---

1. Voir dans la Documentation thématique les indications données sur le décor et le costume de Monsieur Jourdain.

LE BOURGEOIS GENTILHOMME

ACTE PREMIER

L'ouverture se fait par un grand assemblage d'instruments ; et dans le milieu du théâtre on voit un élève du maître de musique qui compose sur une table un air que le Bourgeois a demandé pour une sérénade[1].

SCÈNE PREMIÈRE. — MAITRE DE MUSIQUE, MAITRE À DANSER, TROIS MUSICIENS, DEUX VIOLONS, QUATRE DANSEURS.

MAÎTRE DE MUSIQUE, *parlant à ses musiciens*. — Venez, entrez dans cette salle, et vous reposez là, en attendant qu'il[2] vienne.

MAÎTRE À DANSER, *parlant aux danseurs*. — Et vous aussi, de ce côté.

5   MAÎTRE DE MUSIQUE, *à l'élève*. — Est-ce fait ?

L'ÉLÈVE. — Oui.

MAÎTRE DE MUSIQUE. — Voyons... Voilà qui est bien.

MAÎTRE À DANSER. — Est-ce quelque chose de nouveau ?

MAÎTRE DE MUSIQUE. — Oui, c'est un air pour une sérénade
10 que je lui[3] ai fait composer ici, en attendant que notre homme
fût éveillé. **(1)**

MAÎTRE À DANSER. — Peut-on voir ce que c'est ?

MAÎTRE DE MUSIQUE. — Vous l'allez entendre, avec le dialogue[4], quand il viendra. Il ne tardera guère.

---

1. Il y a une ouverture en musique sur l'air : « Je languis nuit et jour », qu'on entendra à la scène II ; 2. *Il* : Monsieur Jourdain ; 3. *Lui* désigne l'élève que montre le maître de musique ; 4. *Dialogue* : ici composition musicale pour deux ou plusieurs voix ou instruments, qui se répondent alternativement.

QUESTIONS

1. A quel moment commence l'action ? Peut-on prévoir combien de temps elle durera ?

15 MAÎTRE À DANSER. — Nos occupations, à vous et à moi, ne sont pas petites maintenant.

MAÎTRE DE MUSIQUE. — Il est vrai. Nous avons trouvé ici un homme comme il nous le faut à tous deux. Ce nous est une douce rente[1] que ce monsieur Jourdain, avec les visions 20 de noblesse et de galanterie qu'il est allé se mettre en tête. Et votre danse et ma musique auraient à souhaiter que tout le monde lui ressemblât. **(2)**

MAÎTRE À DANSER. — Non pas entièrement; et je voudrais pour lui qu'il se connût mieux qu'il ne fait aux choses que 25 nous lui donnons.

MAÎTRE DE MUSIQUE. — Il est vrai qu'il les connaît mal, mais il les paye bien; et c'est de quoi maintenant nos arts ont plus besoin que de toute autre chose.

MAÎTRE À DANSER. — Pour moi, je vous l'avoue, je me repais 30 un peu de gloire. Les applaudissements me touchent; et je tiens que, dans tous les beaux-arts, c'est un supplice assez fâcheux que de se produire à des sots, que d'essuyer sur des compositions la barbarie d'un stupide[2]. Il y a plaisir, ne m'en parlez point, à travailler pour des personnes qui soient capables 35 de sentir les délicatesses d'un art; qui sachent faire un doux accueil aux beautés d'un ouvrage et, par de chatouillantes approbations, vous régaler de votre travail. Oui, la récompense la plus agréable qu'on puisse recevoir des choses que l'on fait, c'est de les voir connues, de les voir caressées[3] d'un applau- 40 dissement qui vous honore. Il n'y a rien, à mon avis, qui nous paye mieux que cela de toutes nos fatigues; et ce sont des douceurs exquises que des louanges éclairées[4].

MAÎTRE DE MUSIQUE. — J'en demeure d'accord, et je les goûte comme vous. Il n'y a rien assurément qui chatouille 45 davantage que les applaudissements que vous dites; mais cet encens ne fait pas vivre. Des louanges toutes pures ne mettent point un homme à son aise : il y faut mêler du solide; et la meilleure façon de louer, c'est de louer avec les mains[5]. C'est

---

1. Rente facile à gagner et bonne à prendre; 2. Subir, à propos d'œuvres qu'on a composées, le manque de goût et l'ignorance de celui qui les a commandées; 3. *Caressé :* flatté; 4. On peut comprendre que Molière remercie par la bouche de son personnage les spectateurs éclairés qui l'applaudissent et le roi en premier lieu; 5. En payant.

— **QUESTIONS** —————————

2. Comment se révèlent progressivement l'identité et le caractère du personnage principal? Que savez-vous déjà de lui?

un homme, à la vérité, dont les lumières sont petites, qui parle
à tort et à travers de toutes choses, et n'applaudit qu'à contre-
sens; mais son argent redresse les jugements de son esprit.
Il a du discernement dans sa bourse. Ses louanges sont mon-
nayées; et ce bourgeois ignorant nous vaut mieux, comme
vous voyez, que le grand seigneur éclairé (3) qui nous a
introduits ici. (4)

MAÎTRE À DANSER. — Il y a quelque chose de vrai dans ce
que vous dites; mais je trouve que vous appuyez un peu trop
sur l'argent; et l'intérêt est quelque chose de si bas qu'il ne
faut jamais qu'un honnête homme[1] montre pour lui de l'atta-
chement.

MAÎTRE DE MUSIQUE. — Vous recevez fort bien pourtant
l'argent que notre homme vous donne.

MAÎTRE À DANSER. — Assurément; mais je n'en fais pas
tout mon bonheur, et je voudrais qu'avec son bien il eût encore
quelque bon goût des choses.

MAÎTRE DE MUSIQUE. — Je le voudrais aussi, et c'est à quoi
nous travaillons tous deux autant que nous pouvons. Mais,
en tout cas, il nous donne moyen de nous faire connaître
dans le monde; et il payera pour les autres ce que les autres
loueront pour lui.

MAÎTRE À DANSER. — Le voilà qui vient. (5)

---

1. *Honnête homme :* homme cultivé et bien élevé.

QUESTIONS

3. Il s'agit de Dorante : pourquoi Molière est-il si pressé de présenter
ce personnage?

4. Étudiez la composition symétrique des deux premières tirades :
comment chacun des deux maîtres conçoit-il le rôle de l'artiste dans la
société?

5. SUR L'ENSEMBLE DE LA SCÈNE PREMIÈRE. — En quoi cette scène tend-
elle à l'exposition? Quels éléments permettent de situer l'action et les
personnages?

— La discussion entre le maître de musique et le maître à danser est-
elle une digression inutile? Résumez leurs arguments; cette discussion
garde-t-elle encore son actualité? Les conditions de vie de l'artiste ont-
elles changé dans la société d'aujourd'hui?

— Étudiez le langage des deux maîtres : en quoi révèle-t-il l'influence
de leur profession sur leur manière de vivre? Leur caractère : ressemblances et différences.

Phot. Lipnitzki.

Maître de musique. — Vous recevez fort bien pourtant l'argent que notre homme vous donne.
Maître à danser. — Assurément, mais je n'en fais pas tout mon bonheur. (Page 27.)

« LE BOURGEOIS GENTILHOMME »

« La jambe droite. La, la, la. » (Page 38.)

Phot. Lipnitzki.

Phot. Lipnitzki.

« En garde, monsieur, en garde! » (Page 39.)

À LA COMÉDIE-FRANÇAISE

Monsieur Jourdain. — Mon Dieu, arrêtez-vous. (Page 41.)

Phot. Lipnitzki.

Scène II. — MONSIEUR JOURDAIN,
en robe de chambre et bonnet de nuit,
DEUX LAQUAIS, MAITRE DE MUSIQUE,
MAITRE À DANSER, VIOLONS,
MUSICIENS ET DANSEURS.

MONSIEUR JOURDAIN. — Hé bien, messieurs? Qu'est-ce?
Me ferez-vous voir votre petite drôlerie?

MAÎTRE À DANSER. — Comment? Quelle petite drôlerie? (6)

MONSIEUR JOURDAIN. — Eh! là... Comment appelez-vous
5 cela? Votre prologue, ou dialogue de chansons et de danse.

MAÎTRE À DANSER. — Ah! ah!

MAÎTRE DE MUSIQUE. — Vous nous y voyez préparés.

MONSIEUR JOURDAIN. — Je vous ai fait un peu attendre,
mais c'est que je me fais habiller aujourd'hui comme les gens
10 de qualité[1], et mon tailleur m'a envoyé des bas de soie[2] que
j'ai pensé ne mettre jamais.

MAÎTRE DE MUSIQUE. — Nous ne sommes ici que pour attendre
votre loisir[3].

MONSIEUR JOURDAIN. — Je vous prie tous deux de ne vous
15 point en aller qu'on ne m'ait apporté[4] mon habit, afin que
vous me puissiez voir.

MAÎTRE À DANSER. — Tout ce qu'il vous plaira.

MONSIEUR JOURDAIN. — Vous me verrez équipé[5] comme
il faut, depuis les pieds jusqu'à la tête.

20 MAÎTRE DE MUSIQUE. — Nous n'en doutons point.

MONSIEUR JOURDAIN. — Je me suis fait faire cette indienne-ci[6].

MAÎTRE À DANSER. — Elle est fort belle.

---

1. *Gens de qualité* : personnes de noble condition. Les gens de qualité, dont Monsieur Jourdain ne cessera de se réclamer, s'habillaient de vêtements de couleur tandis que les bourgeois étaient vêtus de sombre (gris ou noir); 2. Grand luxe pour l'époque; il en est de même de la robe de chambre que Monsieur Jourdain fait admirer quelques instants plus tard; 3. Le moment où vous serez libre; 4. Avant qu'on ne m'ait apporté; 5. *Equipé* : habillé; 6. *Indienne* : étoffe exotique (venant des Indes) de grand prix.

QUESTIONS

6. L'entrée de Monsieur Jourdain: Importance du mot *drôlerie* : quelle indication donne-t-il immédiatement non seulement sur la culture, mais aussi sur le caractère de Monsieur Jourdain?

MONSIEUR JOURDAIN. — Mon tailleur m'a dit que les gens de qualité étaient comme cela le matin.

25 MAÎTRE DE MUSIQUE. — Cela vous sied à merveille.

MONSIEUR JOURDAIN. — Laquais, holà! mes deux laquais.

PREMIER LAQUAIS. — Que voulez-vous, monsieur?

MONSIEUR JOURDAIN. — Rien. C'est pour voir si vous m'entendez bien. *(Aux deux maîtres.)* Que dites-vous de mes livrées[1]?

30 MAÎTRE À DANSER. — Elles sont magnifiques.

MONSIEUR JOURDAIN. — *(Il entrouvre sa robe et fait voir un haut-de-chausses[2] étroit de velours rouge, et une camisole de velours vert, dont il est vêtu.)* Voici encore un petit déshabillé pour faire le matin mes exercices[3].

35 MAÎTRE DE MUSIQUE. — Il est galant[4].

MONSIEUR JOURDAIN. — Laquais!

PREMIER LAQUAIS. — Monsieur?

MONSIEUR JOURDAIN. — L'autre laquais!

SECOND LAQUAIS. — Monsieur?

40 MONSIEUR JOURDAIN, *ôtant sa robe de chambre.* — Tenez ma robe. *(Aux deux maîtres.)* Me trouvez-vous bien comme cela?

MAÎTRE À DANSER. — Fort bien. On ne peut pas mieux. **(7)**

MONSIEUR JOURDAIN. — Voyons un peu votre affaire[5].

MAÎTRE DE MUSIQUE. — Je voudrais bien auparavant vous
45 faire entendre un air *(montrant son élève)* qu'il vient de composer pour la sérénade que vous m'avez demandée. C'est un de mes écoliers qui a pour ces sortes de choses un talent admirable.

MONSIEUR JOURDAIN. — Oui, mais il ne fallait pas faire faire

---

1. *Livrées* : habits de couleur dont on habille les laquais. Tout le personnel d'une même maison portait la même livrée, à laquelle on le reconnaissait; sur ce point aussi, Monsieur Jourdain veut adopter les habitudes de la noblesse; 2. *Haut-de-chausses* : culotte; 3. Allusion à la venue prochaine du maître d'armes; 4. *Galant* : élégant; 5. *Affaire* : terme moins désobligeant que *drôlerie*, mais encore très maladroit.

—— **QUESTIONS** ——

7. Les effets comiques dans ce début de scène : de quoi Monsieur Jourdain est-il surtout fier? Sur quel ton les deux maîtres se prêtent-ils aux vanités du Bourgeois? Quel est leur sentiment profond?

50 cela par un écolier[1]; et vous n'étiez pas trop bon vous-même
pour cette besogne-là. **(8)**

MAÎTRE DE MUSIQUE. — Il ne faut pas, monsieur, que le nom
d'écolier vous abuse. Ces sortes d'écoliers en savent autant
que les plus grands maîtres, et l'air est aussi beau qu'il s'en
55 puisse faire. Écoutez seulement.

MONSIEUR JOURDAIN[2], *à ses laquais.* — Donnez-moi ma robe
pour mieux entendre... Attendez, je crois que je serai mieux
sans robe... Non, redonnez-la moi, cela ira mieux. **(9)**

MUSICIEN *chantant.*

Je languis nuit et jour, et mon mal est extrême,
60   Depuis qu'à vos rigueurs vos beaux yeux m'ont soumis :
    Si vous traitez ainsi, belle Iris, qui vous aime,
    Hélas! que pourriez-vous faire à vos ennemis?

MONSIEUR JOURDAIN. — Cette chanson me semble un peu
lugubre, elle endort, et je voudrais que vous la pussiez un peu
65 regaillardir par-ci par-là.

MAÎTRE DE MUSIQUE. — Il faut, monsieur, que l'air soit accom-
modé aux paroles[3].

MONSIEUR JOURDAIN. — On m'en apprit un tout à fait joli,
il y a quelque temps. Attendez... Là... Comment est-ce qu'il dit?

70 MAÎTRE À DANSER. — Par ma foi, je ne sais.

MONSIEUR JOURDAIN. — Il y a du mouton dedans.

MAÎTRE À DANSER. — Du mouton?

MONSIEUR JOURDAIN. — Oui. Ah! *(M. Jourdain chante.)*

    Je croyais Jeanneton
75   Aussi douce que belle;
    Je croyais Jeanneton
    Plus douce qu'un mouton.

---

1. *Écolier* est pris par le maître de musique au sens d' « élève »; mais Monsieur
Jourdain comprend qu'il s'agit d'un « apprenti »; **2.** Avant la réplique, et à chaque
série de points de suspension, le musicien commence à chanter : *Je languis...*,
mais il est interrompu par Monsieur Jourdain; **3.** Opposée aux Italiens qui n'ont
d'oreille que pour l'air, l'école française de musique attache quelque importance
aux paroles; c'est le début d'une querelle qui n'est pas près de s'éteindre.

QUESTIONS

8. Est-ce seulement l'ignorance de Monsieur Jourdain qui transparaît
ici? Quel autre trait, lié à sa condition, se révèle ici?
9. A quel genre de comique est-il fait appel ici?

> Hélas! Hélas!
> Elle est cent fois, mille fois plus cruelle
> 80   Que n'est le tigre aux bois. **(10)**

N'est-il pas joli?

MAÎTRE DE MUSIQUE. — Le plus joli du monde.

MAÎTRE À DANSER. — Et vous le chantez bien[1].

MONSIEUR JOURDAIN. — C'est sans avoir appris la musique[2].

85   MAÎTRE DE MUSIQUE. — Vous devriez l'apprendre, monsieur, comme vous faites la danse. Ce sont deux arts qui ont une étroite liaison ensemble.

MAÎTRE À DANSER. — Et qui ouvrent l'esprit d'un homme aux belles choses.

90   MONSIEUR JOURDAIN. — Est-ce que les gens de qualité apprennent aussi la musique?

MAÎTRE DE MUSIQUE. — Oui, monsieur.

MONSIEUR JOURDAIN. — Je l'apprendrai donc. Mais je ne sais quel temps je pourrai prendre : car, outre le maître d'armes
95   qui me montre, j'ai arrêté encore un maître de philosophie qui doit commencer ce matin.

MAÎTRE DE MUSIQUE. — La philosophie est quelque chose; mais la musique, monsieur, la musique...

MAÎTRE À DANSER. — La musique et la danse... La musique
100   et la danse, c'est là tout ce qu'il faut.

MAÎTRE DE MUSIQUE. — Il n'y a rien qui soit si utile dans un État que la musique[3].

---

1. Flatterie évidente, car il faut, bien entendu, que Monsieur Jourdain chante ses couplets d'une manière ridicule, avec une voix de fausset; 2. Dans *les Précieuses ridicules* (scène IX), Mascarille dit déjà : « Les gens de qualité savent tout sans avoir jamais rien appris »; 3. Idée qui se trouve déjà dans *la République* de Platon (livre IV) et que l'humanisme de la Renaissance avait remis à la mode.

——— QUESTIONS ———

10. Alceste dans *le Misanthrope* (I, II) préfère lui aussi la chanson populaire à l'art savant, le naturel à l'affectation. Comparez ces deux passages : l'effet est-il le même? Alceste est-il ridicule comme Monsieur Jourdain? Que peut-on conclure de cette comparaison sur l'opinion personnelle de Molière? Le personnage ridicule émet-il forcément sur toutes choses des points de vue ridicules?

MAÎTRE À DANSER. — Il n'y a rien qui soit si nécessaire aux hommes que la danse[1].

105 MAÎTRE DE MUSIQUE. — Sans la musique, un État ne peut subsister.

MAÎTRE À DANSER. — Sans la danse, un homme ne saurait rien faire.

MAÎTRE DE MUSIQUE. — Tous les désordres, toutes les guerres qu'on voit dans le monde n'arrivent que pour n'apprendre pas la musique.

MAÎTRE À DANSER. — Tous les malheurs des hommes, tous les revers funestes dont les histoires sont remplies, les bévues des politiques et les manquements des grands capitaines, tout cela n'est venu que faute de savoir danser.

MONSIEUR JOURDAIN. — Comment cela?

MAÎTRE DE MUSIQUE. — La guerre ne vient-elle pas d'un manque d'union entre les hommes?

MONSIEUR JOURDAIN. — Cela est vrai.

120 MAÎTRE DE MUSIQUE. — Et, si tous les hommes apprenaient la musique, ne serait-ce pas le moyen de s'accorder ensemble, et de voir dans le monde la paix universelle?

MONSIEUR JOURDAIN. — Vous avez raison. **(11)**

MAÎTRE À DANSER. — Lorsqu'un homme a commis un manquement dans sa conduite, soit aux affaires de sa famille, ou au gouvernement d'un État, ou au commandement d'une armée, ne dit-on pas toujours : « Un tel a fait un mauvais pas dans une telle affaire »?

MONSIEUR JOURDAIN. — Oui, on dit cela.

---

1. La question est d'actualité puisque l'établissement des « académies d'opéra » date de juin 1669; mais, dès 1661, on lisait dans les lettres patentes qui établissaient l'Académie de danse : « L'art de la danse a toujours été reconnu l'un des plus honnêtes et des plus nécessaires à former le corps et à lui donner les premières et les plus naturelles dispositions à toutes sortes d'exercices, et entre autres à ceux des armes, et par conséquent l'un des plus utiles à notre noblesse. »

━━━━━━━━ ■ QUESTIONS ■ ━━━━━━━━

11. Comment est composé ce dialogue sur l'utilité de la musique et de la danse? Les deux maîtres croient-ils sincèrement aux arguments qu'ils avancent? A travers leurs exagérations, quelles idées intéressantes se dégagent sur le rôle moral et social de leur art? — Le rôle du maître à danser dans la discussion : montrez qu'il est moins égoïste que son camarade. — L'attitude de Monsieur Jourdain; est-il sensible à l'idéal de ses interlocuteurs? Pourquoi approuve-t-il toujours?

130 MAÎTRE À DANSER. — Et faire un mauvais pas **(12)** peut-il procéder d'autre chose que de ne savoir pas danser?

MONSIEUR JOURDAIN. — Cela est vrai, et vous avez raison tous deux.

MAÎTRE À DANSER. — C'est pour vous faire voir l'excellence
135 et l'utilité de la danse et de la musique.

MONSIEUR JOURDAIN. — Je comprends cela, à cette heure.

MAÎTRE DE MUSIQUE. — Voulez-vous voir nos deux affaires?

MONSIEUR JOURDAIN. — Oui.

MAÎTRE DE MUSIQUE. — Je vous l'ai déjà dit, c'est un petit
140 essai que j'ai fait autrefois des diverses passions que peut exprimer la musique.

MONSIEUR JOURDAIN. — Fort bien.

MAÎTRE DE MUSIQUE, *aux musiciens.* — Allons, avancez.
(A M. Jourdain.) Il faut vous figurer qu'ils sont habillés en
145 bergers.

MONSIEUR JOURDAIN. — Pourquoi toujours des bergers[1]?
On ne voit que cela partout.

MAÎTRE À DANSER. — Lorsqu'on a des personnes à faire parler en musique, il faut bien que pour la vraisemblance
150 on donne dans la bergerie. Le chant a été de tout temps affecté aux bergers; et il n'est guère naturel en dialogue que des princes ou des bourgeois chantent leurs passions. **(13)**

MONSIEUR JOURDAIN. — Passe, passe. Voyons.

DIALOGUE EN MUSIQUE
UNE MUSICIENNE ET DEUX MUSICIENS

MUSICIENNE

Un cœur, dans l'amoureux empire,
155 De mille soins[2] est toujours agité :
On dit qu'avec plaisir on languit, on soupire;
Mais quoi qu'on puisse dire,
Il n'est rien de si doux que notre liberté.

---

1. Dans *le Malade imaginaire* (a. II, s. v), Molière reprendra la même question;
2. *Soins :* soucis.

--- **QUESTIONS** ---

12. Expliquez le jeu de mot sur le sens de « mauvais pas ».
13. Molière est-il d'accord sur la pastorale avec Monsieur Jourdain ou avec le maître à danser? Expliquez avec précision la réplique du maître à danser.

PREMIER MUSICIEN

160   Il n'est rien de si doux que les tendres ardeurs
Qui font vivre deux cœurs
Dans une même envie :
On ne peut être heureux sans amoureux désirs;
Otez l'amour de la vie,
Vous en ôtez les plaisirs.

SECOND MUSICIEN

165   Il serait doux d'entrer sous l'amoureuse loi,
Si l'on trouvait en amour de la foi,
Mais, hélas! ô rigueur cruelle!
On ne voit point de bergère fidèle;
Et ce sexe inconstant trop indigne du jour,
170   Doit faire pour jamais renoncer à l'amour.

PREMIER MUSICIEN

Aimable ardeur;

MUSICIENNE

Franchise[1] heureuse!

SECOND MUSICIEN

Sexe trompeur!

PREMIER MUSICIEN

Que tu m'es précieuse!

MUSICIENNE

175   Que tu plais à mon cœur!

SECOND MUSICIEN

Que tu me fais d'horreur!

PREMIER MUSICIEN

Ah! quitte, pour aimer,
Cette haine mortelle!

MUSICIENNE

On peut, on peut te montrer
180   Une bergère fidèle.

SECOND MUSICIEN

Hélas! où la rencontrer?

---

1. *Franchise* : liberté.

MUSICIENNE

Pour défendre notre gloire,
Je te veux offrir mon cœur.

SECOND MUSICIEN

Mais bergère, puis-je croire
185   Qu'il ne sera point trompeur?

MUSICIENNE

Voyons par expérience
Qui des deux aimera mieux.

SECOND MUSICIEN

Qui manquera de constance,
Le puissent perdre les dieux!

TOUS TROIS ENSEMBLE

190   A des ardeurs si belles
Laissons-nous enflammer;
Ah! qu'il est doux d'aimer,
Quand deux cœurs sont fidèles.

MONSIEUR JOURDAIN[1]. — Est-ce tout?

195 MAÎTRE DE MUSIQUE. — Oui.

MONSIEUR JOURDAIN. — Je trouve cela bien troussé; et il y a là-dedans de petits dictons assez jolis. **(14)**

MAÎTRE À DANSER. — Voici, pour mon affaire, un petit essai des plus beaux mouvements et des plus belles attitudes dont
200 une danse puisse être variée.

MONSIEUR JOURDAIN. — Sont-ce encore des bergers?

MAÎTRE À DANSER. — C'est ce qu'il vous plaira. *(Aux danseurs.)* Allons. **(15)**

---

1. Monsieur Jourdain applaudit : voyant qu'il est seul à le faire, intimidé, il s'arrête et se demande s'il n'a pas commis une bévue.

--- **QUESTIONS** ---

14. Relevez quelques-uns de ces *dictons*. (Le mot signifie ici « formule remarquable », « mots plaisants ».)

15. SUR L'ENSEMBLE DE LA SCÈNE II. — Le comique dans cette scène : par quels moyens Molière rend-il Monsieur Jourdain ridicule? Son vêtement, son caractère, son langage.

— L'attitude des deux maîtres en face de Monsieur Jourdain : comment s'y prennent-ils pour se moquer de lui sans qu'il s'en aperçoive?

ENTRÉE DE BALLET

(Quatre danseurs exécutent tous les mouvements différents et toutes les sortes de pas[1] que le maître à danser leur commande; et cette danse fait le premier intermède.) **(16)**

ACTE II

Scène première. — MONSIEUR JOURDAIN, MAITRE DE MUSIQUE, MAITRE À DANSER, LAQUAIS.

MONSIEUR JOURDAIN. — Voilà qui n'est point sot, et ces gens-là se trémoussent[2] bien.

MAÎTRE DE MUSIQUE. — Lorsque la danse sera mêlée avec la musique, cela fera plus d'effet encore, et vous verrez quelque
5 chose de galant[3] dans le petit ballet que nous avons ajusté[4] pour vous.

MONSIEUR JOURDAIN. — C'est pour tantôt au moins; et la personne pour qui j'ai fait faire tout cela me doit faire l'honneur de venir dîner céans[5].

10 MAÎTRE À DANSER. — Tout est prêt.

MAÎTRE DE MUSIQUE. — Au reste, monsieur, ce n'est pas assez, il faut qu'une personne comme vous, qui êtes magnifique[6] et qui avez de l'inclination pour les belles choses, ait un concert de musique chez soi tous les mercredis, ou tous
15 les jeudis.

MONSIEUR JOURDAIN. — Est-ce que les gens de qualité en ont?

---

1. Les danses lentes et rapides alternent selon le principe de la « suite ». On entend entre chacun des pas le maître de danse commander : « Allons, Messieurs, gravement — Messieurs, plus vite — Gravement ce mouvement de sarabande — Pressez bien cette bourrée », etc.; 2. *Se trémousser :* s'agiter d'un mouvement vif et saccadé; encore un terme maladroit qui révèle la vulgarité de Monsieur Jourdain; 3. *Galant :* voir page 29, note 4; 4. *Ajuster :* préparer, arranger; 5. *Céans :* ici, à la maison; 6. *Magnifique :* qui fait des dépenses somptueuses.

--- ■ QUESTIONS ■ ---

16. Sur l'ensemble de l'acte premier. — L'intrigue a-t-elle été nouée? Recherchez les indications qui permettent de prévoir certaines scènes dans la suite : sont-elles suffisantes pour intéresser le spectateur à l'action? Quel plaisir a-t-on pris alors à ce premier acte?
— Le personnage de Monsieur Jourdain : comment est-il déjà fortement dessiné? Est-il antipathique?

ignorant

MAÎTRE DE MUSIQUE. — Oui, monsieur.

MONSIEUR JOURDAIN. — J'en aurai donc. Cela sera-t-il beau?

MAÎTRE DE MUSIQUE. — Sans doute. Il vous faudra trois
20 voix, un dessus, une haute-contre et une basse, qui seront
accompagnées d'une basse de viole, d'un téorbe et d'un clavecin pour les basses continues, avec deux dessus de violon
pour jouer les ritournelles[1].

MONSIEUR JOURDAIN. — Il y faudra mettre aussi une trom-
25 pette marine[2]. La trompette marine est un instrument qui me
plaît, et qui est harmonieux.

let us do our

MAÎTRE DE MUSIQUE. — Laissez-nous gouverner les choses.

MONSIEUR JOURDAIN. — Au moins, n'oubliez pas tantôt de
m'envoyer des musiciens pour chanter à table.

30 MAÎTRE DE MUSIQUE. — Vous aurez tout ce qu'il vous faut.

MONSIEUR JOURDAIN. — Mais surtout que le ballet soit beau.

MAÎTRE DE MUSIQUE. — Vous en serez content, et, entre
autres choses, de certains menuets[3] que vous y verrez. **(1)**

MONSIEUR JOURDAIN. — Ah! les menuets sont ma danse.
35 et je veux que vous me les voyiez danser. Allons, mon maître.

MAÎTRE À DANSER[4]. — Un chapeau, monsieur, s'il vous plaît.
*(M. Jourdain va prendre le chapeau de son laquais et le met
par-dessus son bonnet de nuit. Son maître lui prend les mains
et le fait danser sur un air de menuet qu'il chante.)* La, la, la;
40 — La, la, la, la, la, la; — La, la, la, *bis;* — La, la, la; — La, la.

---

1. Suite de termes techniques, que Molière a pu apprendre de Lully et que l'on peut
transcrire ainsi : *un dessus*, un ténor; *une haute-contre*, un soprano; *basse de viole*,
grand violon à sept cordes et à archet; *téorbe*, sorte de luth à six cordes doubles
que l'on pinçait, plus la chanterelle; *clavecin*, instrument à clavier, ancêtre du piano;
basses continues, accompagnement d'arpèges et d'accords qui soutiennent le chant;
dessus de violon, violon au timbre plus aigu; *ritournelle*, prélude et intermède des
instruments entre les couplets chantés; 2. *Trompette marine :* sorte de mandoline
triangulaire monocorde, au son assez rude, fort à la mode au XVIIᵉ siècle, et même
au XVIIIᵉ (voir Lesage, *Turcaret*, IV, v); 3. Le *menuet*, d'origine populaire très ancienne
(Poitou) était ainsi appelé parce qu'on le dansait à petits pas; Pécour, maître à
danser de Louis XIV, contribua à mettre cette danse à la mode; il y a donc là un
trait d'actualité; 4. Des danseurs célèbres (Vestris au XVIIIᵉ siècle, Faure au XIXᵉ)
ont tenu à jouer ce rôle; l'air de Lully pouvant être allongé par des reprises, la
tirade a été elle-même développée. Voir dans la Documentation thématique le
texte de Faure, souvent utilisé encore aujourd'hui.

■■■■ **QUESTIONS** ■■■■

1. Appréciez l'habileté du maître de musique dans ce début de scène;
comment se confirment certains traits de son caractère qu'avait révélés
le premier acte? — L'élégance avec laquelle il cède la place au maître à
danser : pourquoi l'union de ces deux maîtres est-elle si étroite?

En cadence, s'il vous plaît. La, la, la, la. La jambe droite.
La, la, la. Ne remuez point tant les épaules. La, la, la, la, la;
— La, la, la, la, la. Vos deux bras sont estropiés. La, la, la,
la, la. Haussez la tête. Tournez la pointe du pied en dehors.
45 La, la, la. Dressez votre corps.

MONSIEUR JOURDAIN. — Euh? (2)

MAÎTRE DE MUSIQUE. — Voilà qui est le mieux du monde.

MONSIEUR JOURDAIN. — A propos. Apprenez-moi comme
il faut faire une révérence pour saluer une marquise; j'en
50 aurai besoin tantôt[1].

MAÎTRE À DANSER. — Une révérence pour saluer une marquise?

MONSIEUR JOURDAIN. — Oui, une marquise qui s'appelle
Dorimène. (3)

MAÎTRE À DANSER. — Donnez-moi la main.

55 MONSIEUR JOURDAIN. — Non. Vous n'avez qu'à faire, je le
retiendrai bien.

MAÎTRE À DANSER. — Si vous voulez la saluer avec beaucoup
de respect, il faut faire d'abord une révérence en arrière, puis
marcher vers elle avec trois révérences en avant, et à la dernière
60 vous baisser jusqu'à ses genoux.

MONSIEUR JOURDAIN. — Faites un peu. *(Après que le maître
à danser a fait trois révérences.)* Bon!

LE LAQUAIS. — Monsieur, voilà votre maître d'armes qui est là.

MONSIEUR JOURDAIN. — Dis-lui qu'il entre ici pour me donner
65 leçon. *(Au maître de musique et au maître à danser.)* Je veux
que vous me voyiez faire. (4) (5)

---

1. Monsieur Jourdain pense déjà à la visite de Dorimène; il semble croire que la
révérence réservée aux marquises est différente des révérences de cour ordinaires.
Le *A propos* du début de la réplique se justifie fort bien, la danse finissant sur une
révérence, chapeau à la main.

QUESTIONS

2. Comment interpréter ce *Euh?*
3. Comment les deux dernières répliques de Monsieur Jourdain sont-
elles habilement utilisées pour la conduite de l'action et pour la connaissance du caractère de Monsieur Jourdain?
4. Étudiez les trois dernières répliques de Monsieur Jourdain : quels
effets comiques contiennent-elles?
5. SUR L'ENSEMBLE DE LA SCÈNE PREMIÈRE. — Comment se fait la liaison
entre l'acte premier et l'acte II? En quoi cette scène prolonge-t-elle les
scènes précédentes?
— Monsieur Jourdain et les beaux-arts : comment se précise le motif
qui lui donne surtout envie de savoir danser et d'avoir chez lui un orchestre?

Scène II. — MAITRE D'ARMES,
MAITRE DE MUSIQUE, MAITRE À DANSER,
MONSIEUR JOURDAIN,
UN LAQUAIS, *tenant deux fleurets.*

MAÎTRE D'ARMES, *après avoir pris les deux fleurets de la main du laquais et en avoir présenté un à M. Jourdain.* — Allons, monsieur, la révérence[1]. Votre corps droit. Un peu penché sur la cuisse gauche. Les jambes point tant écartées. Vos pieds sur une même ligne. Votre poignet à l'opposite[2] de votre
5 hanche. La pointe de votre épée vis-à-vis de votre épaule. Le bras pas tout à fait si étendu. La main gauche à la hauteur de l'œil. L'épaule gauche plus quartée[3]. La tête droite. Le regard assuré. Avancez. Le corps ferme. Touchez-moi, l'épée de quarte[4], et achevez de même. Une, deux. Remettez-vous.
10 Redoublez de pied ferme. Une, deux. Un saut en arrière. Quand vous portez la botte[5], monsieur, il faut que l'épée parte la première, et que le corps soit bien effacé. Une, deux. Allons, touchez-moi, l'épée de tierce, et achevez de même. Avancez. Le corps ferme. Avancez. Partez de là. Une, deux. Remettez-
15 vous. Redoublez. Une, deux. Un saut en arrière. En garde, monsieur, en garde! (6)

(*Le maître d'armes lui pousse deux ou trois bottes en lui disant : « En garde! »*)

MONSIEUR JOURDAIN. — Euh? (7)

MAÎTRE DE MUSIQUE. — Vous faites des merveilles. (8)

MAÎTRE D'ARMES. — Je vous l'ai déjà dit; tout le secret des
20 armes ne consiste qu'en deux choses : à donner et à ne point recevoir; et, comme je vous fis voir l'autre jour par raison

---

1. C'est-à-dire le « salut des armes »; 2. *A l'opposite* : vis-à-vis de; 3. *Quarter* : tourner l'épaule à gauche, pour porter une botte de quarte; 4. La *quarte* et, plus loin, la *tierce* désignent, dans la technique de l'escrime, deux façons d'attaquer, différentes selon la position de la main sur le fleuret et selon la ligne de tir; 5. *Porter la botte* : porter un coup avec le fleuret.

--- **QUESTIONS** ---

6. Le langage professionnel du maître d'armes : quels en sont les caractères?

7. Comparez ce *Euh* à celui qui suivait la leçon de danse (p. 38); sa signification.

8. Pourquoi les compliments qui sont décernés à Monsieur Jourdain ne le sont-ils jamais par le spécialiste? Cherchez dans la scène II du premier acte des effets du même genre.

Chacun pense que son métier est le plus utile

démonstrative[1], il est impossible que vous receviez, si vous savez détourner l'épée de votre ennemi de la ligne de votre corps; ce qui ne dépend seulement que d'un petit mouvement
25 de poignet, ou en dedans ou en dehors.

MONSIEUR JOURDAIN. — De cette façon donc, un homme, sans avoir du cœur[2], est sûr de tuer son homme et de n'être point tué?

MAÎTRE D'ARMES. — Sans doute. N'en vîtes-vous pas la
30 démonstration?

MONSIEUR JOURDAIN. — Oui.

MAÎTRE D'ARMES. — Et c'est en quoi l'on voit de quelle considération, nous autres, nous devons être dans un État[3], et combien la science des armes l'emporte hautement sur
35 toutes les autres sciences inutiles, comme la danse, la musique, la... **(9)**

MAÎTRE À DANSER. — Tout beau[4], monsieur le tireur d'armes. Ne parlez de la danse qu'avec respect.

MAÎTRE DE MUSIQUE. — Apprenez, je vous prie, à mieux
40 traiter l'excellence de la musique.

MAÎTRE D'ARMES. — Vous êtes de plaisantes gens, de vouloir comparer vos sciences à la mienne!

MAÎTRE À DANSER. — Voyez un peu l'homme d'importance!

MAÎTRE DE MUSIQUE. — Voilà un plaisant animal avec son
45 plastron!

MAÎTRE D'ARMES. — Mon petit maître à danser, je vous ferais danser comme il faut. Et vous, mon petit musicien, je vous ferais chanter de la belle manière.

MAÎTRE À DANSER. — Monsieur le batteur de fer, je vous
50 apprendrai votre métier.

---

1. *Raison démonstrative :* terme de rhétorique assez inattendu de la part d'un maître d'armes; Monsieur Jourdain s'en souvient (voir page 41, ligne 54 et page 63, ligne 118); **2.** *Cœur :* courage; **3.** En 1656, des lettres patentes du roi avaient accordé, aux six plus anciens maîtres d'armes de Paris, la noblesse transmissible à leurs descendants; **4.** *Tout beau :* expression pour arrêter ou imposer silence; elle appartient au langage noble.

———— QUESTIONS ————

9. Que pensez-vous du profit que Monsieur Jourdain veut tirer de la pratique des armes. Comparez le maître d'armes à ses deux confrères : ressemblances et différences.

MONSIEUR JOURDAIN[1], *au maître à danser.* — Êtes-vous fou de l'aller quereller, lui qui entend la tierce et la quarte, et qui sait tuer un homme par raison démonstrative?

MAÎTRE À DANSER. — Je me moque de sa raison démons-
55 trative, et de sa tierce, et de sa quarte.

MONSIEUR JOURDAIN, *au maître à danser.* — Tout doux, vous dis-je.

MAÎTRE D'ARMES, *au maître à danser.* — Comment? petit impertinent!

60 MONSIEUR JOURDAIN. — Eh! mon maître d'armes.

MAÎTRE À DANSER, *au maître d'armes.* — Comment? grand cheval de carrosse[2]!

MONSIEUR JOURDAIN. — Eh! mon maître à danser.

MAÎTRE D'ARMES. — Si je me jette sur vous...

65 MONSIEUR JOURDAIN, *au maître d'armes.* — Doucement.

MAÎTRE À DANSER. — Si je mets sur vous la main...

MONSIEUR JOURDAIN, *au maître à danser.* — Tout beau.

MAÎTRE D'ARMES. — Je vous étrillerai d'un air...

MONSIEUR JOURDAIN, *au maître d'armes.* — De grâce...

70 MAÎTRE À DANSER. — Je vous rosserai d'une manière...

MONSIEUR JOURDAIN, *au maître à danser.* — Je vous prie...

MAÎTRE DE MUSIQUE. — Laissez-nous un peu lui apprendre à parler.

MONSIEUR JOURDAIN, *au maître de musique.* — Mon Dieu,
75 arrêtez-vous. **(10) (11)**

---

1. De nos jours, la tradition de la Comédie-Française est de reprendre ici et jusqu'à la fin de la dispute l'air du menuet pour accompagner la querelle, de même dans la scène suivante. Cela crée un plaisant effet de contraste; **2.** Brutal et stupide comme un cheval de trait; rappelons que de Brie, créateur du rôle, était de taille imposante.

=== **QUESTIONS** ===

10. Le développement de la querelle : son point de départ, sa progression : sur quels procédés comiques est fondée l'alternance des répliques? Le rôle de Monsieur Jourdain dans la dispute.

11. SUR L'ENSEMBLE DE LA SCÈNE II. — Est-ce seulement une scène divertissante? Quelle moralité s'en dégage?

Scène III. — MAITRE DE PHILOSOPHIE, MAITRE DE MUSIQUE, MAITRE À DANSER, MAITRE D'ARMES, MONSIEUR JOURDAIN, LAQUAIS.

MONSIEUR JOURDAIN. — Holà! monsieur le philosophe, vous arrivez tout à propos avec votre philosophie. Venez un peu mettre la paix entre ces personnes-ci. **(12)**

MAÎTRE DE PHILOSOPHIE. — Qu'est-ce donc? Qu'y a-t-il,
5 messieurs?

MONSIEUR JOURDAIN. — Ils se sont mis en colère pour la préférence[1] de leurs professions, jusqu'à se dire des injures et vouloir en venir aux mains.

MAÎTRE DE PHILOSOPHIE. — Hé quoi! messieurs, faut-il s'em-
10 porter de la sorte? et n'avez-vous point lu le docte traité que Sénèque[2] a composé de la colère? Y a-t-il rien de plus bas et de plus honteux que cette passion, qui fait d'un homme une bête féroce? Et la raison ne doit-elle pas être maîtresse de tous nos mouvements?

15 MAÎTRE À DANSER. — Comment! Monsieur, il vient nous dire des injures à tous deux, en méprisant la danse, que j'exerce, et la musique, dont il fait profession.

MAÎTRE DE PHILOSOPHIE. — Un homme sage est au-dessus de toutes les injures qu'on lui peut dire; et la grande réponse
20 qu'on doit faire aux outrages, c'est la modération et la patience.

MAÎTRE D'ARMES. — Ils ont tous deux l'audace de vouloir comparer leurs professions à la mienne.

MAÎTRE DE PHILOSOPHIE. — Faut-il que cela vous émeuve? Ce n'est pas de vaine gloire et de condition[3] que les hommes
25 doivent disputer[4] entre eux; et ce qui nous distingue parfaitement les uns des autres, c'est la sagesse et la vertu.

MAÎTRE À DANSER. — Je lui soutiens que la danse est une science à laquelle on ne peut faire assez d'honneur.

---

1. *Préférence :* supériorité, préséance; 2. Allusion au *De ira*, en trois livres;
3. *Condition :* rang que donne dans la société la naissance ou la profession; 4. *Disputer :* discuter.

──────── **QUESTIONS** ────────

12. L'accueil fait par Monsieur Jourdain au maître de philosophie est-il sur le même ton que celui qu'il a réservé à ses trois autres professeurs? Pourquoi cette déférence?

Ils se lancent des injures

MAÎTRE DE MUSIQUE. — Et moi, que la musique en est une
30 que tous les siècles ont révérée.

MAÎTRE D'ARMES. — Et moi, je leur soutiens à tous deux
que la science de tirer des armes est la plus belle et la plus
nécessaire de toutes les sciences.

MAÎTRE DE PHILOSOPHIE. — Et que sera donc la philosophie?
35 Je vous trouve tous trois bien impertinents de parler devant
moi avec cette arrogance, et de donner impudemment le nom
de science à des choses que l'on ne doit pas même honorer
du nom d'art (13), et qui ne peuvent être comprises que sous
le nom de métier misérable de gladiateur, de chanteur et de
40 baladin!

MAÎTRE D'ARMES. — Allez, philosophe de chien!

MAÎTRE DE MUSIQUE. — Allez, bélître¹ de pédant!

MAÎTRE À DANSER. — Allez, cuistre fieffé²!

MAÎTRE DE PHILOSOPHIE. — Comment! mârauds que vous
45 êtes...

(*Le philosophe se jette sur eux, et tous trois le chargent de
coups.*)

MONSIEUR JOURDAIN. — Monsieur le philosophe!

MAÎTRE DE PHILOSOPHIE. — Infâmes! coquins! insolents!

MONSIEUR JOURDAIN. — Monsieur le philosophe!

MAÎTRE D'ARMES. — La peste l'animal³!

50 MONSIEUR JOURDAIN. — Messieurs.

MAÎTRE DE PHILOSOPHIE. — Impudents!

MONSIEUR JOURDAIN. — Monsieur le philosophe!

MAÎTRE À DANSER. — Diantre soit de l'âne bâté!

MONSIEUR JOURDAIN. — Messieurs.

55 MAÎTRE DE PHILOSOPHIE. — Scélérats!

MONSIEUR JOURDAIN. — Monsieur le philosophe!

MAÎTRE DE MUSIQUE. — Au diable l'impertinent!

---

1. *Bélître* : coquin, gueux; **2.** *Fieffé* s'ajoute à un terme péjoratif pour indiquer
qu'on a un défaut au suprême degré, qu'on le possède aussi solidement qu'un fief;
3. Expression abrégée, couramment employée pour « la peste emporte l'animal ».

QUESTIONS

13. Expliquez l'opposition entre *science* et *art* en tenant bien compte
du sens qu'avait ce dernier mot dans la langue du XVIIe siècle.

MONSIEUR JOURDAIN. — Messieurs.

MAÎTRE DE PHILOSOPHIE. — Fripons! gueux! traîtres! impos-
60 teurs! **(14)**

MONSIEUR JOURDAIN. — Monsieur le philosophe, messieurs,
monsieur le philosophe, messieurs, monsieur le philosophe!...
(Ils sortent en se battant.) Oh! battez-vous tant qu'il vous
plaira, je n'y saurais que faire, et je n'irai pas gâter ma robe
65 pour vous séparer. Je serais bien fou de m'aller fourrer parmi
eux pour recevoir quelque coup qui me ferait mal. **(15) (16)**

SCÈNE IV. — MAITRE DE PHILOSOPHIE, MONSIEUR JOURDAIN, DEUX LAQUAIS.

MAÎTRE DE PHILOSOPHIE, *en raccommodant son collet*[1]. —
Venons à notre leçon.

MONSIEUR JOURDAIN. — Ah! monsieur, je suis fâché des
coups qu'ils vous ont donnés.

MAÎTRE DE PHILOSOPHIE. — Cela n'est rien. Un philosophe
5 sait recevoir comme il faut les choses, et je vais composer
contre eux une satire du style de Juvénal[2], qui les déchirera
de la belle façon. Laissons cela. Que voulez-vous apprendre?

MONSIEUR JOURDAIN. — Tout ce que je pourrai, car j'ai
toutes les envies du monde d'être savant, et j'enrage que mon
10 père et ma mère ne m'aient pas fait bien étudier dans toutes
les sciences, quand j'étais jeune.

---

1. En remettant en place son *collet* ou *rabat* (pièce de toile blanche que l'on met
autour du cou); **2.** *Juvénal :* poète satirique latin (vers 60 - vers 140 apr. J.-C.), à
qui Molière empruntera aussi certains traits pour sa peinture des *Femmes savantes*
(Satire VI).

■ QUESTIONS ■

14. Étudiez le développement de cette nouvelle querelle : se déroule-
t-elle sur le même rythme que la précédente? Pourquoi est-elle plus violente? Expliquez les insultes qui sont lancées par chacun des antagonistes :
en quoi correspondent-elles à leur condition et à leur caractère? Qui lance
les injures les plus violentes?

15. A quelle occasion Monsieur Jourdain avait-il déjà laissé deviner
qu'il n'était pas très brave?

16. SUR L'ENSEMBLE DE LA SCÈNE III. — Les deux langages du maître
de philosophie : étudiez son vocabulaire au début et à la fin de la scène.
Qu'en conclure sur son caractère?

— Les effets comiques dans cette scène : montrez qu'ils prennent toute
leur valeur par comparaison avec la scène précédente. Quel comique de
situation est notamment exploité ici?

Phot. Bernand.

LE MAÎTRE DE PHILOSOPHIE ET MONSIEUR JOURDAIN

Denis d'Inès et Louis Seigner (Comédie-Française).

Louis Seigner, qui tient depuis 1950 le rôle de Monsieur Jourdain à la Comédie-Française, explique ainsi son interprétation :
« Il faut surtout ne pas faire de Monsieur Jourdain un pitre. C'est un rôle tout de simplicité et d'humanité, une humanité touchante et vraie. Commerçant habile et très fortuné, il l'a été, mais il ne s'en souvient ici qu'un instant, lorsqu'il reconnaît du drap de son habit sur les épaules de son maître tailleur. Tout le reste du temps, il n'est qu'un grand enfant. Et remarquez bien que pas un instant il ne nous inquiète. »

MAÎTRE DE PHILOSOPHIE. — Ce sentiment est raisonnable. *Nam sine doctrina vita est quasi mortis imago*[1]. Vous entendez cela, et vous savez le latin sans doute?

15 MONSIEUR JOURDAIN. — Oui, mais faites comme si je ne le savais pas. Expliquez-moi ce que cela veut dire.

MAÎTRE DE PHILOSOPHIE. — Cela veut dire que sans la science la vie est presque une image de la mort.

MONSIEUR JOURDAIN. — Ce latin-là a raison.

20 MAÎTRE DE PHILOSOPHIE. — N'avez-vous point quelques principes, quelques commencements des sciences?

MONSIEUR JOURDAIN. — Oh! oui, je sais lire et écrire. (17)

MAÎTRE DE PHILOSOPHIE. — Par où vous plaît-il que nous commencions? Voulez-vous que je vous apprenne la logique[2]?

25 MONSIEUR JOURDAIN. — Qu'est-ce que c'est que cette logique?

MAÎTRE DE PHILOSOPHIE. — C'est elle qui enseigne les trois opérations de l'esprit.

MONSIEUR JOURDAIN. — Qui sont-elles, ces trois opérations de l'esprit?

30 MAÎTRE DE PHILOSOPHIE. — La première, la seconde et la troisième. La première est de bien concevoir par le moyen des universaux[3]; la seconde, de bien juger par le moyen des catégories[4]; et la troisième, de bien tirer une conséquence par le moyen des figures[5]. *Barbara, Celarent, Darii, Ferio,* 35 *Baralipton*[6], etc.

---

1. « Car sans la science, la vie est comme l'image de la mort. » Cette citation est empruntée à une pièce de Larivey, *le Fidèle* (II, XIV), qui date de 1611; 2. *Logique :* science qui apprend à raisonner. Un édit de 1600 faisait commencer par là le cours donné dans les classes terminales des collèges, d'où le nom de « logique » donné alors à cette classe. Le maître de philosophie propose d'ailleurs à Monsieur Jourdain le programme traditionnel des études; 3. *Universaux :* caractères communs à plusieurs choses; 4. *Catégories :* les dix classes selon lesquelles se répartissent les êtres; 5. *Figures :* dispositions des trois termes dont est formé le raisonnement appelé « syllogisme »; 6. Formules mnémotechniques destinées à retenir les principales formes de syllogismes. Ces formules étaient traditionnelles depuis la scolastique du Moyen Age.

--- **QUESTIONS** ---

17. Quel est le degré d'instruction de Monsieur Jourdain? Est-ce normal, étant donné sa condition? Molière veut-il le ridiculiser en le montrant désolé de n'avoir pas reçu d'instruction? Monsieur Jourdain a-t-il raison de dissimuler qu'il ne sait pas le latin?

MONSIEUR JOURDAIN. — Voilà des mots qui sont trop rébarbatifs. Cette logique-là ne me revient point. Apprenons autre chose qui soit plus joli. **(18)**

MAÎTRE DE PHILOSOPHIE. — Voulez-vous apprendre la morale?

40 MONSIEUR JOURDAIN. — La morale?

MAÎTRE DE PHILOSOPHIE. — Oui.

MONSIEUR JOURDAIN. — Qu'est-ce qu'elle dit, cette morale?

MAÎTRE DE PHILOSOPHIE. — Elle traite de la félicité, enseigne aux hommes à modérer leurs passions, et...

45 MONSIEUR JOURDAIN. — Non, laissons cela. Je suis bilieux comme tous les diables; et, il n'y a morale qui tienne, je me veux mettre en colère tout mon soûl, quand il m'en prend envie. **(19)**

MAÎTRE DE PHILOSOPHIE. — Est-ce la physique[1] que vous 50 voulez apprendre?

MONSIEUR JOURDAIN. — Qu'est-ce qu'elle chante, cette physique?

MAÎTRE DE PHILOSOPHIE. — La physique est celle qui explique les principes des choses naturelles et les propriétés du corps; 55 qui discourt de la nature des éléments, des métaux, des minéraux, des pierres, des plantes et des animaux, et nous enseigne les causes de tous les météores[2], l'arc-en-ciel, les feux volants[3], les comètes, les éclairs, le tonnerre, la foudre, la pluie, la neige, la grêle, les vents et les tourbillons[4].

_____

1. *Physique* : ensemble des sciences de la nature; au XVIIᵉ siècle, ce terme englobe la physique proprement dite, la chimie, l'astronomie, l'anatomie, la botanique, etc.; 2. *Météores* : tous les phénomènes qui se passent dans les parties supérieures de l'atmosphère; 3. *Feux volants* : feux follets; 4. *Tourbillons*. Il ne s'agit sans doute pas des tempêtes, mais des tourbillons que Descartes avait définis, dans son livre des *Météores* (1637), comme les mouvements d'une quantité de matière qui tourne autour d'un astre ou d'une planète. La théorie cartésienne des tourbillons était alors fort en vogue, et Molière y fait plusieurs fois allusion.

_____

————— **QUESTIONS** —————

18. La méthode du maître de philosophie : pense-t-il à adapter son enseignement au niveau de son élève? La réponse de Monsieur Jourdain, si comique soit-elle, est-elle pourtant absurde?

19. Relevez l'effet comique : 1º sur la définition de la morale par le maître de philosophie; 2º dans le refus de Monsieur Jourdain. Le trait de caractère qui se révèle ici ne se retrouve-t-il pas dans d'autres personnages de Molière? De quelle qualité nécessaire à la vie sociale manque celui qui *veut* pouvoir se mettre ainsi en colère?

60 MONSIEUR JOURDAIN. — Il y a trop de tintamarre là-dedans, trop de brouillamini. (20)

MAÎTRE DE PHILOSOPHIE. — Que voulez-vous donc que je vous apprenne ?

MONSIEUR JOURDAIN. — Apprenez-moi l'orthographe.

65 MAÎTRE DE PHILOSOPHIE. — Très volontiers.

MONSIEUR JOURDAIN. — Après, vous m'apprendrez l'almanach, pour savoir quand il y a de la lune et quand il n'y en a point. (21)

MAÎTRE DE PHILOSOPHIE. — Soit. Pour bien suivre votre
70 pensée et traiter cette matière en philosophe, il faut commencer, selon l'ordre des choses, par une exacte connaissance de la nature des lettres et de la différente manière de les prononcer toutes. Et là-dessus j'ai à vous dire que les lettres sont divisées en voyelles, ainsi dites voyelles parce qu'elles expriment
75 les voix ; et en consonnes, ainsi appelées consonnes parce qu'elles sonnent avec les voyelles, et ne font que marquer les diverses articulations des voix. Il y a cinq voyelles ou voix : A, E, I, O, U[1].

MONSIEUR JOURDAIN. — J'entends tout cela.

MAÎTRE DE PHILOSOPHIE. — La voix A se forme en ouvrant
80 fort la bouche : A.

MONSIEUR JOURDAIN. — A, A, oui.

MAÎTRE DE PHILOSOPHIE. — La voix E se forme en rapprochant la mâchoire d'en bas de celle d'en haut : A, E.

MONSIEUR JOURDAIN. — A, E ; A, E. Ma foi, oui. Ah ! que
85 cela est beau !

MAÎTRE DE PHILOSOPHIE. — Et la voix I, en rapprochant encore davantage les mâchoires l'une de l'autre, et écartant les deux coins de la bouche vers les oreilles : A, E, I.

MONSIEUR JOURDAIN. — A, E, I, I, I, I. Cela est vrai. Vive
90 la science !

---

1. Le cours de phonétique qui commence ici pourrait avoir été inspiré à Molière par la lecture d'un ouvrage récent : *Discours physique de la parole* (1668).

─────── **QUESTIONS** ───────

20. L'enseignement des sciences physiques et naturelles peut-il intéresser Monsieur Jourdain ? En prenant pour point de comparaison *les Femmes savantes*, rappelez quel est le niveau moyen des connaissances scientifiques que peut avoir un bourgeois de cette époque.

21. Les demandes de Monsieur Jourdain sont-elles toutes deux absurdes ?

MAÎTRE DE PHILOSOPHIE. — La voix O se forme en rouvrant les mâchoires et rapprochant les lèvres par les deux coins, le haut et le bas : O.

MONSIEUR JOURDAIN. — O, O. Il n'y a rien de plus juste.
95 A, E, I, O, I, O. Cela est admirable! I, O, I, O.

MAÎTRE DE PHILOSOPHIE. — L'ouverture de la bouche fait justement comme un petit rond qui représente un O.

MONSIEUR JOURDAIN. — O, O, O. Vous avez raison. O. Ah! la belle chose que de savoir quelque chose!

100 MAÎTRE DE PHILOSOPHIE. — La voix U se forme en rapprochant les dents sans les joindre entièrement, et allongeant les deux lèvres en dehors, les approchant aussi l'une de l'autre sans les joindre tout à fait : U.

MONSIEUR JOURDAIN. — U, U. Il n'y a rien de plus véri-
105 table, U.

MAÎTRE DE PHILOSOPHIE. — Vos deux lèvres s'allongent comme si vous faisiez la moue, d'où vient que, si vous la voulez faire à quelqu'un et vous moquer de lui, vous ne sauriez lui dire que U.

110 MONSIEUR JOURDAIN. — U, U. Cela est vrai. Ah! que n'ai-je étudié plus tôt pour savoir tout cela! (22)

MAÎTRE DE PHILOSOPHIE. — Demain nous verrons les autres lettres, qui sont les consonnes.

MONSIEUR JOURDAIN. — Est-ce qu'il y a des choses aussi
115 curieuses qu'à celles-ci?

MAÎTRE DE PHILOSOPHIE. — Sans doute. La consonne D, par exemple, se prononce en donnant du bout de la langue au-dessus des dents d'en haut : DA.

MONSIEUR JOURDAIN. — DA, DA. Oui. Ah! les belles choses!
120 les belles choses!

MAÎTRE DE PHILOSOPHIE. — L'F, en appuyant les dents d'en haut sur la lèvre de dessous : FA.

MONSIEUR JOURDAIN. — FA, FA. C'est la vérité. Ah! mon père et ma mère, que je vous veux de mal!

——————— QUESTIONS ———————

22. La pédagogie du maître de philosophie : est-il clair dans son enseignement? Mais ce qu'il enseigne a-t-il grande utilité? — A quel genre de comique se prête cette partie de la scène? Comment les réflexions de Monsieur Jourdain ajoutent-elles encore à ses grimaces?

125   MAÎTRE DE PHILOSOPHIE. — Et l'R, en portant le bout de la langue jusqu'au haut du palais; de sorte, qu'étant frôlée par l'air qui sort avec force, elle lui cède et revient toujours au même endroit, faisant une manière de tremblement : R, ra.

    MONSIEUR JOURDAIN. — R, r, ra; R, r, r, r, r, ra. Cela est
130 vrai. Ah! l'habile homme que vous êtes! et que j'ai perdu de temps! R, r, r, ra.

    MAÎTRE DE PHILOSOPHIE. — Je vous expliquerai à fond toutes ces curiosités. **(23)**

    MONSIEUR JOURDAIN. — Je vous en prie. Au reste, il faut
135 que je vous fasse une confidence. Je suis amoureux d'une personne de grande qualité, et je souhaiterais que vous m'aidassiez à lui écrire[1] quelque chose dans un petit billet que je veux laisser tomber à ses pieds.

    MAÎTRE DE PHILOSOPHIE. — Fort bien.

140   MONSIEUR JOURDAIN. — Cela sera galant, oui.

    MAÎTRE DE PHILOSOPHIE. — Sans doute. Sont-ce des vers que vous lui voulez écrire?

    MONSIEUR JOURDAIN. — Non, non, point de vers.

    MAÎTRE DE PHILOSOPHIE. — Vous ne voulez que de la prose?

145   MONSIEUR JOURDAIN. — Non, je ne veux ni prose ni vers.

    MAÎTRE DE PHILOSOPHIE. — Il faut bien que ce soit l'un ou l'autre.

    MONSIEUR JOURDAIN. — Pourquoi?

    MAÎTRE DE PHILOSOPHIE. — Par la raison, monsieur, qu'il n'y
150 a pour s'exprimer que la prose ou les vers.

    MONSIEUR JOURDAIN. — Il n'y a que la prose ou les vers?

    MAÎTRE DE PHILOSOPHIE. — Non, monsieur[2] : tout ce qui n'est point prose est vers; et tout ce qui n'est point vers est prose.

---

    1. Cette demande n'a rien de surprenant; même des gens plus cultivés que Monsieur Jourdain avaient recours à des poètes ou à des écrivains de profession pour rédiger leur correspondance galante; 2. La réponse de Monsieur Jourdain appelait une réponse affirmative; le maître de philosophie répond à une question qui serait ainsi formulée : « N'y a-t-il rien d'autre que la prose ou les vers? » Mais ce *non* annonce le mouvement négatif de la phrase qui suit.

■■ QUESTIONS ■■

    23. Pourquoi le désir d'en savoir davantage est-il à la fois louable et ridicule ici? Les expressions *choses curieuses*, *curiosités*, employées tour à tour par chacun des personnages, conviennent-elles bien au sujet étudié?

155 MONSIEUR JOURDAIN. — Et comme l'on parle, qu'est-ce que c'est donc que cela?

MAÎTRE DE PHILOSOPHIE. — De la prose.

MONSIEUR JOURDAIN. — Quoi! quand je dis : « Nicole, apportez-moi mes pantoufles, et me donnez mon bonnet
160 de nuit », c'est de la prose?

MAÎTRE DE PHILOSOPHIE. — Oui, monsieur.

MONSIEUR JOURDAIN. — Par ma foi! il y a plus de quarante ans que je dis de la prose sans que j'en susse rien[1]; et je vous suis le plus obligé du monde de m'avoir appris cela. **(24)** Je
165 voudrais donc lui mettre dans un billet : « Belle marquise, vos beaux yeux me font mourir d'amour[2] », mais je voudrais que cela fût mis d'une manière galante, que ce fût tourné gentiment.

MAÎTRE DE PHILOSOPHIE. — Mettre que les feux de ses yeux
170 réduisent votre cœur en cendres; que vous souffrez nuit et jour pour elle les violences d'un...

MONSIEUR JOURDAIN. — Non, non, non, je ne veux point tout cela; je ne veux que ce que je vous ai dit : « Belle marquise, vos beaux yeux me font mourir d'amour. »

175 MAÎTRE DE PHILOSOPHIE. — Il faut bien étendre un peu la chose.

MONSIEUR JOURDAIN. — Non, vous dis-je, je ne veux que ces seules paroles-là dans le billet, mais tournées à la mode, bien arrangées comme il faut. Je vous prie de me dire un peu,
180 pour voir, les diverses manières dont on les peut mettre.

MAÎTRE DE PHILOSOPHIE. — On les peut mettre premièrement comme vous avez dit : « Belle marquise, vos beaux yeux me font mourir d'amour. » Ou bien : « D'amour mourir me font, belle marquise, vos beaux yeux. » Ou bien : « Vos yeux beaux
185 d'amour me font, belle marquise, mourir. » Ou bien : « Mourir

---

1. Naïveté attribuée au comte de Soissons (cf. Lettre de Mme de Sévigné, 12 juin 1681); 2. Ce que souhaite sans doute Monsieur Jourdain, sans pouvoir l'exprimer en termes propres, c'est adresser un madrigal. Le madrigal, court poème d'amour, était alors fort à la mode.

────── **QUESTIONS** ──────

24. Étudiez, depuis « la confidence » de Monsieur Jourdain, les répliques du maître : son agacement, puis la solennité avec laquelle il révèle à son élève une vérité première. — Monsieur Jourdain est-il effrayé de sa propre ignorance?

vos beaux yeux, belle marquise, d'amour me font. » Ou bien :
« Me font vos yeux beaux mourir, belle marquise, d'amour. »

MONSIEUR JOURDAIN. — Mais, de toutes ces façons-là, laquelle
est la meilleure?

190 MAÎTRE DE PHILOSOPHIE. — Celle que vous avez dite : « Belle
marquise, vos beaux yeux me font mourir d'amour. »

MONSIEUR JOURDAIN. — Cependant je n'ai point étudié, et
j'ai fait cela tout du premier coup. Je vous remercie de tout
mon cœur, et vous prie de venir demain de bonne heure. **(25)**

195 MAÎTRE DE PHILOSOPHIE. — Je n'y manquerai pas[1]. *(Il sort.)*

MONSIEUR JOURDAIN, *à son laquais.* — Comment, mon habit
n'est point encore arrivé?

LE LAQUAIS. — Non, monsieur.

MONSIEUR JOURDAIN. — Ce maudit tailleur me fait bien
200 attendre pour un jour où j'ai tant d'affaires! J'enrage. Que
la fièvre quartaine puisse serrer[2] bien fort le bourreau de
tailleur! Au diable le tailleur! La peste étouffe le tailleur!
Si je le tenais maintenant, ce tailleur détestable, ce chien de
tailleur-là, ce traître de tailleur, je... **(26) (27)**

---

1. Au théâtre, on ajoute quelquefois : « Souvenez-vous bien de FA, FA », ce qui rend plus comique la sortie du maître de philosophie; 2. Que la fièvre quarte (fièvre intermittente dont les accès reviennent après trois jours) puisse éteindre...

--- **QUESTIONS** ---

25. Monsieur Jourdain et le beau langage : ses prétentions au style élégant ont-elles obscurci totalement son bon sens? Pourquoi refuse-t-il les développements et les images proposés par le maître de philosophie? — La conclusion du débat : quelle idée chère à Molière transparaît à travers cet épisode comique?

26. Cette colère subite contre le tailleur étonne-t-elle de la part de Monsieur Jourdain?

27. SUR L'ENSEMBLE DE LA SCÈNE IV. — La composition de cette scène : montrez-en les différents moments; les effets comiques sont-ils de plusieurs sortes?

— L'attitude de Monsieur Jourdain : son respect de la science l'empêche-t-il d'imposer au maître sa volonté? Tout en reconnaissant son ignorance, a-t-il perdu sa vanité?

— Molière pense-t-il qu'il est inutile de s'instruire à l'âge de Monsieur Jourdain?

— Le personnage du pédant : quels sont les ridicules du maître de philosophie? Comparez-le à Métaphraste dans *le Dépit amoureux*, à Pancrace et Marphurius dans *le Mariage forcé*, à Robinet dans *la Comtesse d'Escarbagnas*, à Vadius dans *les Femmes savantes*. Résumez les griefs de Molière contre toutes les formes de pédantisme.

Scène V. — MAITRE TAILLEUR,
GARÇON TAILLEUR, *portant l'habit de Monsieur Jourdain,*
MONSIEUR JOURDAIN, LAQUAIS.

MONSIEUR JOURDAIN. — Ah! vous voilà? Je m'allais mettre en colère contre vous.

MAÎTRE TAILLEUR. — Je n'ai pas pu venir plus tôt, et j'ai mis vingt garçons après votre habit.

5 MONSIEUR JOURDAIN. — Vous m'avez envoyé des bas de soie si étroits que j'ai eu toutes les peines du monde à les mettre, et il y a déjà deux mailles de rompues.

MAÎTRE TAILLEUR. — Ils ne s'élargiront que trop.

MONSIEUR JOURDAIN. — Oui, si je romps toujours des mailles.
10 Vous m'avez aussi fait faire des souliers qui me blessent furieusement[1].

MAÎTRE TAILLEUR. — Point du tout, monsieur.

MONSIEUR JOURDAIN. — Comment, point du tout!

MAÎTRE TAILLEUR. — Non, ils ne vous blessent point.

15 MONSIEUR JOURDAIN. — Je vous dis qu'ils me blessent, moi.

MAÎTRE TAILLEUR. — Vous vous imaginez cela.

MONSIEUR JOURDAIN. — Je me l'imagine parce que je le sens. Voyez la belle raison! **(28)**

MAÎTRE TAILLEUR. — Tenez, voilà le plus bel habit de la
20 cour, et le mieux assorti[2]. C'est un chef-d'œuvre que d'avoir inventé un habit sérieux qui ne fût pas noir; et je le donne en six coups[3] aux tailleurs les plus éclairés.

MONSIEUR JOURDAIN. — Qu'est-ce que c'est que ceci? Vous avez mis les fleurs en enbas[4].

25 MAÎTRE TAILLEUR. — Vous ne m'avez pas dit que vous les vouliez en enhaut?

---

1. *Furieusement :* fortement. Exagération d'expression semblable à celle qu'on retrouve aujourd'hui dans « énormément », « terriblement », etc.; **2.** *Assorti :* dont l'ensemble est arrangé d'une heureuse façon; **3.** Je défie de faire en six coups ce que j'ai fait d'un seul coup (terme de jeu); **4.** La tête en bas. *En enbas* et *en enhaut* forment des expressions adverbiales.

■ QUESTIONS ■

28. Sur quel ton s'engage le dialogue? Pourquoi Monsieur Jourdain traite-t-il le tailleur beaucoup plus rudement que ses maîtres? Quelle est l'attitude du tailleur?

MONSIEUR JOURDAIN. — Est-ce qu'il faut dire cela?

MAÎTRE TAILLEUR. — Oui, vraiment. Toutes les personnes de qualité les portent de la sorte.

30 MONSIEUR JOURDAIN. — Les personnes de qualité portent les fleurs en enbas?

MAÎTRE TAILLEUR. — Oui, monsieur.

MONSIEUR JOURDAIN. — Oh! voilà qui est donc bien.

MAÎTRE TAILLEUR. — Si vous voulez, je les mettrai en enhaut.

35 MONSIEUR JOURDAIN. — Non, non.

MAÎTRE TAILLEUR. — Vous n'avez qu'à dire.

MONSIEUR JOURDAIN. — Non, vous dis-je, vous avez bien fait. Croyez-vous que l'habit m'aille bien?

MAÎTRE TAILLEUR. — Belle demande! Je défie un peintre 40 avec son pinceau de vous faire rien de plus juste. J'ai chez moi un garçon qui, pour monter une ringrave[1], est le plus grand génie du monde; et un autre qui, pour assembler un pourpoint[2], est le héros de notre temps.

MONSIEUR JOURDAIN. — La perruque et les plumes sont-elles 45 comme il faut?

MAÎTRE TAILLEUR. — Tout est bien. **(29)**

MONSIEUR JOURDAIN, *en regardant l'habit du tailleur.* — Ah! ah! monsieur le tailleur, voilà de mon étoffe du dernier habit que vous m'avez fait. Je la reconnais bien.

50 MAÎTRE TAILLEUR. — C'est que l'étoffe me sembla si belle que j'en ai voulu lever[3] un habit pour moi.

MONSIEUR JOURDAIN. — Oui, mais il ne fallait pas le lever avec le mien. **(30)**

---

1. *Ringrave* ou *rhingrave* : culotte de cheval fort large, dont la mode avait été apportée en France au milieu du siècle par un comte du Rhin (Rheingraf); 2. *Pourpoint* : partie du vêtement qui couvre le haut du corps; 3. *Lever* : prendre et couper sur une pièce d'étoffe.

——— QUESTIONS ———

29. Quelles sont les deux qualités qui révèlent chez le maître tailleur un commerçant habile? Monsieur Jourdain est-il un client aussi difficile qu'on pouvait le croire?

30. En quoi ce petit incident montre-t-il que Monsieur Jourdain est resté bien bourgeois? Le tailleur a-t-il du mal à se justifier?

MAÎTRE TAILLEUR. — Voulez-vous mettre votre habit?

55 MONSIEUR JOURDAIN. — Oui, donnez-le moi.

MAÎTRE TAILLEUR. — Attendez. Cela ne va pas comme cela. J'ai amené des gens pour vous habiller en cadence, et ces sortes d'habits se mettent avec cérémonie. Holà! entrez, vous autres. Mettez cet habit à monsieur de la manière que vous
60 faites aux personnes de qualité.

(Quatre garçons tailleurs entrent, dont deux lui arrachent le haut-de-chausses[1] de ses exercices, et deux autres la camisole, puis ils lui mettent son habit neuf; et Monsieur Jourdain se promène entre eux et leur montre son habit pour voir s'il est bien. Le tout à la cadence de toute la symphonie[2].)

GARÇON TAILLEUR. — Mon gentilhomme, donnez, s'il vous plaît, aux garçons quelque chose pour boire.

MONSIEUR JOURDAIN. — Comment m'appelez-vous?

GARÇON TAILLEUR. — Mon gentilhomme.

65 MONSIEUR JOURDAIN. — « Mon gentilhomme! » Voilà ce que c'est de se mettre en personne de qualité! Allez-vous-en demeurer toujours habillé en bourgeois, on ne vous dira point : « Mon gentilhomme. » *(Donnant de l'argent.)* Tenez, voilà pour « Mon gentilhomme ».

70 GARÇON TAILLEUR. — Monseigneur[3], nous vous sommes bien obligés.

MONSIEUR JOURDAIN. — « Monseigneur! » oh! oh! « Monseigneur! » Attendez, mon ami. « Monseigneur » mérite quelque chose, et ce n'est pas une petite parole que « Monseigneur ».
75 Tenez, voilà ce que monseigneur vous donne.

GARÇON TAILLEUR. — Monseigneur, nous allons boire tous à la santé de Votre Grandeur[4].

MONSIEUR JOURDAIN. — « Votre Grandeur! » oh! oh! oh! Attendez, ne vous en allez pas. A moi « Votre Grandeur »!
80 *(Bas, à part.)* Ma foi, s'il va jusqu'à l'Altesse[5], il aura toute la bourse. *(Haut.)* Tenez, voilà pour ma Grandeur.

GARÇON TAILLEUR. — Monseigneur, nous la remercions très humblement de ses libéralités.

---

1. Voir page 29, note 2; 2. *Symphonie* : concert d'instruments; 3. *Monseigneur* : titre qui ne se donnait qu'aux gentilshommes de la noblesse; 4. *Votre Grandeur* : titre réservé aux évêques et à quelques rares seigneurs; 5. *Altesse* est le titre des princes ou des ducs souverains.

MONSIEUR JOURDAIN. — Il a bien fait, je lui allais tout don-
85 ner (31).

(*Les quatre garçons tailleurs se réjouissent par une danse,
qui fait le second intermède.*) [32] [33]

ACTE III

SCÈNE PREMIÈRE. — MONSIEUR JOURDAIN, DEUX LAQUAIS.

MONSIEUR JOURDAIN. — Suivez-moi, que j'aille un peu montrer mon habit par la ville ; et surtout ayez soin tous deux de
marcher immédiatement sur mes pas, afin qu'on voie bien
que vous êtes à moi.

5 LAQUAIS. — Oui, monsieur.

MONSIEUR JOURDAIN. — Appelez-moi Nicole, que je lui
donne quelques ordres. Ne bougez, la voilà. (1)

──────── QUESTIONS ────────

31. L'effet comique de progression dans cette fin de scène. Étudiez en
particulier les trois dernières répliques : pourquoi le garçon tailleur ne
va-t-il pas jusqu'à l'Altesse ? Est-ce une déconvenue ou une satisfaction
pour Monsieur Jourdain ?

32. SUR L'ENSEMBLE DE LA SCÈNE V. — Le maître tailleur : relevez les
principaux traits de caractère. Comment Molière réussit-il à donner une
personnalité même aux personnages secondaires ? Se conduirait-il avec
un authentique grand seigneur comme avec le Bourgeois ? En quoi le
garçon tailleur est-il, à un échelon inférieur, la réplique de son patron ?
— L'attitude de Monsieur Jourdain : si on se rappelle qu'il a, en tant
que marchand drapier, eu bien des maîtres tailleurs dans sa clientèle,
comprend-on mieux son attitude ?

33. SUR L'ENSEMBLE DE L'ACTE II. — En quoi cet acte est-il le complément du premier ? N'est-il pas cependant plus comique ?
— L'action est-elle engagée ? Comment s'est précisée la préparation
d'épisodes ultérieurs ?
— Monsieur Jourdain, homme de qualité : comment conçoit-il sa for-
mation intellectuelle et artistique ? Quel profit pense-t-il tirer de l'escrime ?
Quelle part est accordée par lui au luxe du vêtement ?
— Les personnages épisodiques de cet acte : sont-ils de simples
silhouettes ? Sont-ce des caractères ? En quoi donnent-ils une image de
certains milieux sociaux ?

1. Cette simple scène de transition ne manque pas d'intérêt ; pourquoi ?

Scène II. — NICOLE, MONSIEUR JOURDAIN, DEUX LAQUAIS.

MONSIEUR JOURDAIN. — Nicole!

NICOLE. — Plaît-il?

MONSIEUR JOURDAIN. — Écoutez.

NICOLE. — Hi, hi, hi, hi, hi!

5 MONSIEUR JOURDAIN. — Qu'as-tu à rire?

NICOLE. — Hi, hi, hi, hi, hi, hi!

MONSIEUR JOURDAIN. — Que veut dire cette coquine-là?

NICOLE. — Hi, hi, hi! Comme vous voilà bâti[1]! Hi, hi, hi!

MONSIEUR JOURDAIN. — Comment donc?

10 NICOLE. — Ah! ah! mon Dieu! Hi, hi, hi, hi, hi!

MONSIEUR JOURDAIN. — Quelle friponne est-ce là? Te moques-tu de moi?

NICOLE. — Nenni, monsieur, j'en serais bien fâchée. Hi, hi, hi, hi, hi, hi!

15 MONSIEUR JOURDAIN. — Je te baillerai[2] sur le nez, si tu ris davantage.

NICOLE. — Monsieur, je ne puis pas m'en empêcher. Hi, hi, hi, hi, hi, hi!

MONSIEUR JOURDAIN. — Tu ne t'arrêteras pas?

20 NICOLE. — Monsieur, je vous demande pardon; mais vous êtes si plaisant que je ne saurais me tenir[3] de rire. Hi, hi, hi!

MONSIEUR JOURDAIN. — Mais voyez quelle insolence!

NICOLE. — Vous êtes tout à fait drôle comme cela. Hi, hi!

MONSIEUR JOURDAIN. — Je te...

25 NICOLE. — Je vous prie de m'excuser. Hi, hi, hi, hi!

MONSIEUR JOURDAIN. — Tiens, si tu ris encore le moins du monde, je te jure que je t'appliquerai sur la joue le plus grand soufflet qui se soit jamais donné.

NICOLE. — Hé bien, monsieur, voilà qui est fait, je ne rirai 30 plus.

---

1. *Bâti* : équipé, habillé (langage populaire); 2. *Bailler* : donner. Le mot est alors déjà vieilli et ne s'emploie plus dans la bonne société; 3. *Tenir* : retenir.

MONSIEUR JOURDAIN. — Prends-y bien garde. Il faut que pour tantôt tu nettoies...

NICOLE. — Hi, hi!

MONSIEUR JOURDAIN. — Que tu nettoies comme il faut...

35 NICOLE. — Hi, hi!

MONSIEUR JOURDAIN. — Il faut, dis-je, que tu nettoies la salle, et...

NICOLE. — Hi, hi!

MONSIEUR JOURDAIN. — Encore?

40 NICOLE, *tombant à force de rire*. — Tenez, monsieur, battez-moi plutôt, et me laissez rire tout mon soûl, cela me fera plus de bien. Hi, hi, hi, hi, hi!

MONSIEUR JOURDAIN. — J'enrage!

NICOLE. — De grâce, monsieur, je vous prie de me laisser 45 rire. Hi, hi, hi!

MONSIEUR JOURDAIN. — Si je te prends...

NICOLE. — Monsieur... eur, je crèverai... ai, si je ne ris. Hi, hi, hi!

MONSIEUR JOURDAIN. — Mais a-t-on jamais vu une pendarde 50 comme celle-là, qui me vient rire insolemment au nez, au lieu de recevoir mes ordres?

NICOLE. — Que voulez-vous que je fasse, monsieur?

MONSIEUR JOURDAIN. — Que tu songes, coquine, à préparer ma maison pour la compagnie qui doit venir tantôt.

55 NICOLE, *se relevant*. — Ah! par ma foi, je n'ai plus envie de rire; et toutes vos compagnies font tant de désordre céans que ce mot est assez pour me mettre en mauvaise humeur.

MONSIEUR JOURDAIN. — Ne dois-je point pour toi fermer ma porte à tout le monde?

60 NICOLE. — Vous devriez au moins la fermer à certaines gens. (2)

───────── QUESTIONS ─────────

2. SUR LA SCÈNE II. — Composition de cette scène : quels en sont les deux mouvements? Comment Molière met-il fin au rire de Nicole?
— Les sources du comique : pourquoi ce rire irrépressible de Nicole? Le procédé n'est-il pas un peu élémentaire?
— Le contraste de cette scène avec les deux premiers actes? Monsieur Jourdain fait-il ici aussi grande figure qu'en présence de ses maîtres? Est-il étonnant qu'une servante de comédie soit si irrévérencieuse?

Phot. Bernand.

GASTON VACCHIA DANS LE RÔLE DE M. JOURDAIN
Théâtre Sarah-Bernhardt, 1963.

MADAME JOURDAIN (Mathilde Casadesus) et NICOLE (Nicole Vassel).
Théâtre Sarah-Bernhardt, 1963.

Scène III. — MADAME JOURDAIN,
MONSIEUR JOURDAIN, NICOLE, DEUX LAQUAIS.

MADAME JOURDAIN. — Ah! ah! voici une nouvelle histoire. Qu'est-ce que c'est donc, mon mari, que cet équipage-là? Vous moquez-vous du monde de vous être fait enharnacher[1] de la sorte? et avez-vous envie qu'on se raille partout de vous? (3)

5 MONSIEUR JOURDAIN. — Il n'y a que des sots et des sottes, ma femme, qui se railleront de moi.

MADAME JOURDAIN. — Vraiment, on n'a pas attendu jusqu'à cette heure, et il y a longtemps que vos façons de faire donnent à rire à tout le monde.

10 MONSIEUR JOURDAIN. — Qui est donc tout ce monde-là, s'il vous plaît?

MADAME JOURDAIN. — Tout ce monde-là est un monde qui a raison et qui est plus sage que vous. Pour moi, je suis scandalisée de la vie que vous menez. Je ne sais plus ce que c'est que 15 notre maison. On dirait qu'il est céans[2] carême-prenant[3] tous les jours; et dès le matin, de peur d'y manquer, on y entend des vacarmes de violons ou de chanteurs dont tout le voisinage se trouve incommodé.

NICOLE. — Madame parle bien. Je ne saurais plus voir mon 20 ménage propre avec cet attirail de gens que vous faites venir chez vous. Ils ont des pieds qui vont chercher de la boue dans tous les quartiers de la ville pour l'apporter ici; et la pauvre Françoise est presque sur les dents à frotter les planchers que vos biaux maîtres viennent crotter régulièrement tous les 25 jours. (4)

MONSIEUR JOURDAIN. — Ouais, notre servante Nicole, vous avez le caquet bien affilé[4] pour une paysanne.

---

1. *Enharnacher* : accoutrer d'une façon grotesque, comme si on portait un harnais de cheval; 2. *Céans* : ici, dans la maison; 3. *Carême-prenant* (c'est-à-dire « quand le carême commence ») : le mardi gras, le carnaval. Le mot désigne aussi un homme déguisé comme au temps du carnaval; 4. *Affilé*. Avoir la langue affilée signifie « bavarder à tort et à travers »; le qualificatif passe ici au bavardage lui-même.

━━━━━━ QUESTIONS ━━━━━━

3. L'entrée de Madame Jourdain : relevez dans le ton et le vocabulaire ce qui la caractérise immédiatement.
4. Pourquoi la maîtresse et la servante sont-elles d'accord? Ont-elles les mêmes motifs de se plaindre?

MADAME JOURDAIN. — Nicole a raison, et son sens est meilleur que le vôtre. Je voudrais bien savoir ce que vous pensez
30 faire d'un maître à danser, à l'âge que vous avez?

NICOLE. — Et d'un grand maître tireur d'armes qui vient, avec ses battements de pieds, ébranler toute la maison, et nous déraciner tous les carríaux de notre salle.

MONSIEUR JOURDAIN. — Taisez-vous, ma servante, et ma
35 femme.

MADAME JOURDAIN. — Est-ce que vous voulez apprendre à danser pour quand vous n'aurez plus de jambes?

NICOLE. — Est-ce que vous avez envie de tuer quelqu'un?

MONSIEUR JOURDAIN. — Taisez-vous, vous dis-je; vous êtes
40 des ignorantes l'une et l'autre, et vous ne savez pas les préro-gatives[1] de tout cela.

MADAME JOURDAIN. — Vous devriez bien plutôt songer à marier votre fille, qui est en âge d'être pourvue.

MONSIEUR JOURDAIN. — Je songerai à marier ma fille quand
45 il se présentera un parti pour elle; mais je veux songer aussi à apprendre les belles choses.

NICOLE. — J'ai encore ouï dire, madame, qu'il a pris aujour-d'hui, pour renfort de potage, un maître de philosophie.

MONSIEUR JOURDAIN. — Fort bien. Je veux avoir de l'esprit,
50 et savoir raisonner des choses parmi les honnêtes gens.

MADAME JOURDAIN. — N'irez-vous point l'un de ces jours au collège vous faire donner le fouet, à votre âge?

MONSIEUR JOURDAIN. — Pourquoi non? Plût à Dieu l'avoir tout à l'heure[2], le fouet, devant tout le monde, et savoir ce
55 qu'on apprend au collège.

NICOLE. — Oui, ma foi, cela vous rendrait la jambe bien mieux faite[3].

MONSIEUR JOURDAIN. — Sans doute.

---

1. *Prérogatives :* avantages. Mot rare que Monsieur Jourdain a dû entendre dire par quelque personne de qualité; 2. *Tout à l'heure :* tout de suite; 3. Expression populaire pour signifier ironiquement qu'une chose est inutile. « Cela vous fait une belle jambe », dirait aujourd'hui Nicole.

les vers / la prose
un quiproquo

MADAME JOURDAIN. — Tout cela est fort nécessaire pour
60 conduire votre maison. **(5)**

MONSIEUR JOURDAIN. — Assurément. Vous parlez toutes
deux comme des bêtes, et j'ai honte de votre ignorance.
(A Madame Jourdain.) Par exemple, savez-vous, vous, ce que
c'est que vous dites à cette heure?

65 MADAME JOURDAIN. — Oui, je sais que ce que je dis est fort
bien dit et que vous devriez songer à vivre d'autre sorte.

MONSIEUR JOURDAIN. — Je ne parle pas de cela. Je vous
demande ce que c'est que les paroles que vous dites ici?

MADAME JOURDAIN. — Ce sont des paroles bien sensées, et
70 votre conduite ne l'est guère.

MONSIEUR JOURDAIN. — Je ne parle pas de cela, vous dis-je.
Je vous demande : Ce que je parle avec vous, ce que je vous
dis à cette heure, qu'est-ce que c'est?

MADAME JOURDAIN. — Des chansons[1].

75 MONSIEUR JOURDAIN. — Hé non, ce n'est pas cela. Ce que
nous disons tous deux, le langage que nous parlons à cette
heure?

MADAME JOURDAIN. — Hé bien?

MONSIEUR JOURDAIN. — Comment est-ce que cela s'appelle?

80 MADAME JOURDAIN. — Cela s'appelle comme on veut l'appeler.

MONSIEUR JOURDAIN. — C'est de la prose, ignorante.

MADAME JOURDAIN. — De la prose?

MONSIEUR JOURDAIN. — Oui, de la prose. Tout ce qui est
prose n'est point vers; et tout ce qui n'est point vers n'est

---

1. *Chansons :* sornettes, propos sans intérêt.

──────── **QUESTIONS** ────────

5. Montrez que les deux femmes choisissent à dessein les critiques qui
peuvent provoquer la mauvaise humeur de Monsieur Jourdain. Pourquoi
Nicole se joint-elle encore ici à sa maîtresse, dans un domaine qui ne la
concerne pas directement? Qu'est-ce qui l'autorise à tenir tête à son
maître? — La conception de la vie familiale selon Madame Jourdain;
savions-nous jusqu'ici que Monsieur Jourdain est père de famille? —
Comment Monsieur Jourdain justifie-t-il la présence des maîtres qui
l'enseignent? Ses arguments sont-ils mauvais?

il veut l'impressioner

85 point prose **(6)**. Heu! voilà ce que c'est d'étudier. *(A Nicole.)* Et toi, sais-tu bien comment il faut faire pour dire un U?

NICOLE. — Comment?

MONSIEUR JOURDAIN. — Oui. Qu'est-ce que tu fais quand tu dis un U?

90 NICOLE. — Quoi?

MONSIEUR JOURDAIN. — Dis un peu U, pour voir.

NICOLE. — Hé bien, U.

MONSIEUR JOURDAIN. — Qu'est-ce que tu fais?

NICOLE. — Je dis U.

95 MONSIEUR JOURDAIN. — Oui; mais, quand tu dis U, qu'est-ce que tu fais?

NICOLE. — Je fais ce que vous me dites.

MONSIEUR JOURDAIN. — O l'étrange chose que d'avoir affaire à des bêtes! Tu allonges les lèvres en dehors, et approches 100 la mâchoire d'en haut de celle d'en bas : U, vois-tu? Je fais la moue : U.

NICOLE. — Oui, cela est biau.

MADAME JOURDAIN. — Voilà qui est admirable.

MONSIEUR JOURDAIN. — C'est bien autre chose, si vous aviez 105 vu O, et DA, DA, et FA, FA. **(7)**

MADAME JOURDAIN. — Qu'est-ce que c'est donc que tout ce galimatias-là?

NICOLE. — De quoi est-ce que tout cela guérit?

MONSIEUR JOURDAIN. — J'enrage quand je vois des femmes 110 ignorantes.

MADAME JOURDAIN. — Allez, vous devriez envoyer promener tous ces gens-là avec leurs fariboles.

─────── **QUESTIONS** ───────

6. L'effet comique de cette première leçon donnée par Monsieur Jourdain : pourquoi les deux femmes ne comprennent-elles pas la question? Mauvaise volonté de leur part? stupidité? ou maladresse du « professeur »? — Que devient, dans la bouche de Monsieur Jourdain, la définition de la prose et des vers qu'il a apprise? Comparez l'effet comique avec la réplique d'Harpagon (« Il faut vivre pour manger », *l'Avare*, III, 1).

7. Que pensez-vous de ce choix parmi les souvenirs qu'a gardés Monsieur Jourdain de sa leçon de phonétique?

NICOLE. — Et surtout ce grand escogriffe[1] de maître d'armes, qui remplit de poudre[2] tout mon ménage.

15 MONSIEUR JOURDAIN. — Ouais! ce maître d'armes vous tient fort au cœur. Je te veux faire voir ton impertinence tout à l'heure. *(Il fait apporter les fleurets et en donne un à Nicole.)* Tiens. Raison démonstrative. La ligne du corps. Quand on pousse en quarte, on n'a qu'à faire cela; et quand on pousse 120 en tierce, on n'a qu'à faire cela. Voilà le moyen de n'être jamais tué; et cela n'est-il pas beau d'être assuré de son fait, quand on se bat contre quelqu'un? Là, pousse-moi un peu pour voir.

NICOLE. — Hé bien, quoi? *(Nicole lui pousse plusieurs coups.)*

125 MONSIEUR JOURDAIN. — Tout beau[3]! Holà! oh! doucement! Diantre soit la coquine!

NICOLE. — Vous me dites de pousser.

MONSIEUR JOURDAIN. — Oui; mais tu me pousses en tierce avant que de pousser en quarte, et tu n'as pas la patience 130 que je pare. (8)

MADAME JOURDAIN. — Vous êtes fou, mon mari, avec toutes vos fantaisies, et cela vous est venu depuis que vous vous mêlez de hanter la noblesse.

MONSIEUR JOURDAIN. — Lorsque je hante la noblesse, je 135 fais paraître mon jugement : et cela est plus beau que de hanter votre bourgeoisie. (9)

MADAME JOURDAIN. — Çamon[4] vraiment! Il y a fort à gagner à fréquenter vos nobles, et vous avez bien opéré avec ce beau monsieur le comte dont vous vous êtes embéguiné[5]...

140 MONSIEUR JOURDAIN. — Paix! Songez à ce que vous dites. Savez-vous bien, ma femme, que vous ne savez pas de qui vous parlez, quand vous parlez de lui? C'est une personne d'importance plus que vous ne pensez; un seigneur que l'on

---

1. *Escogriffe :* terme injurieux appliqué à des gens de grande taille et de mauvaise mine; 2. *Poudre :* poussière; 3. *Tout beau :* voir page 40, note 4; 4. *Çamon :* certainement (mot d'origine douteuse, peut être contraction et abrègement de « cela est mon avis »); 5. *S'embéguiner :* se mettre dans la tête. On dit aussi « être coiffé » de quelqu'un (voir *le Tartuffe,* vers 178).

■ QUESTIONS ■

8. Monsieur Jourdain a-t-il mieux tiré profit des leçons d'escrime que des leçons de grammaire? Quel genre de comique est ici employé?
9. Importance de ces deux dernières répliques pour la moralité de la comédie.

considère à la cour, et qui parle au roi tout comme je vous
145 parle. N'est-ce pas une chose qui m'est tout à fait honorable
que l'on voie venir chez moi si souvent une personne de cette
qualité qui m'appelle son cher ami et me traite comme si
j'étais son égal? Il a pour moi des bontés qu'on ne devinerait
jamais; et, devant tout le monde, il me fait des caresses[1] dont
150 je suis moi-même confus.

MADAME JOURDAIN. — Oui, il a des bontés pour vous et
vous fait des caresses, mais il vous emprunte votre argent.

MONSIEUR JOURDAIN. — Hé bien! ne m'est-ce pas de l'honneur de prêter de l'argent à un homme de cette condition-là[2]?
155 Et puis-je faire moins pour un seigneur qui m'appelle son
cher ami?

MADAME JOURDAIN. — Et ce seigneur, que fait-il pour vous?

MONSIEUR JOURDAIN. — Des choses dont on serait étonné
si on les savait. (10)

160 MADAME JOURDAIN. — Et quoi?

MONSIEUR JOURDAIN. — Baste[3], je ne puis pas m'expliquer.
Il suffit que, si je lui ai prêté de l'argent, il me le rendra bien,
et avant qu'il soit peu.

MADAME JOURDAIN. — Oui. Attendez-vous à cela.

165 MONSIEUR JOURDAIN. — Assurément. Ne me l'a-t-il pas dit?

MADAME JOURDAIN. — Oui, oui, il ne manquera pas d'y
faillir[4].

MONSIEUR JOURDAIN. — Il m'a juré sa foi de gentilhomme.

MADAME JOURDAIN. — Chansons!

170 MONSIEUR JOURDAIN. — Ouais! vous êtes bien obstinée, ma
femme; je vous dis qu'il me tiendra parole, j'en suis sûr.

MADAME JOURDAIN. — Et moi, je suis sûre que non, et que
toutes les caresses qu'il vous fait ne sont que pour vous enjôler.

MONSIEUR JOURDAIN. — Taisez-vous. Le voici.

---

1. *Caresses :* flatteries; **2.** Le mot *condition* évoque le rang social et moral, tandis
que *homme de qualité* ne précise que la noblesse de naissance; **3.** *Baste :* suffit (mot
du langage populaire); **4.** Il ne manquera pas d'y ... manquer, ce qui forme un
dicton ironique.

——— QUESTIONS ———

10. Le portrait de Dorante : que savait-on déjà de lui? Qu'en sait-on
maintenant? Comparez l'attitude de Monsieur Jourdain à celle d'Orgon
à l'égard de Tartuffe.

175 MADAME JOURDAIN. — Il ne nous faut plus que cela. Il vient peut-être encore vous faire quelque emprunt; et il me semble que j'ai dîné[1], quand je le vois.

MONSIEUR JOURDAIN. — Taisez-vous, vous dis-je. (11) (12)

Scène IV. — DORANTE, MONSIEUR JOURDAIN, MADAME JOURDAIN, NICOLE.

DORANTE. — Mon cher ami, monsieur Jourdain[2], comment vous portez-vous?

MONSIEUR JOURDAIN. — Fort bien, monsieur, pour vous rendre mes petits services.

5 DORANTE. — Et madame Jourdain que voilà, comment se porte-t-elle?

MADAME JOURDAIN. — Madame Jourdain se porte comme elle peut.

DORANTE. — Comment! monsieur Jourdain, vous voilà le 10 plus propre[3] du monde!

MONSIEUR JOURDAIN. — Vous voyez.

DORANTE. — Vous avez tout à fait bon air avec cet habit, et nous n'avons point de jeunes gens à la cour qui soient mieux faits que vous.

15 MONSIEUR JOURDAIN. — Hai! Hai!

MADAME JOURDAIN, *à part*. — Il le gratte par où il se démange.

---

1. Expression populaire : sa vue me coupe l'appétit; **2.** Il n'est pas poli d'appeler les gens par leur nom, sauf si on est d'une condition supérieure à la leur; Dorante marque ainsi la distance entre Monsieur Jourdain et lui; **3.** *Propre :* bien mis.

———— QUESTIONS ————

11. L'effet comique de cette fin de scène : quel pari est engagé entre le mari et la femme? Comment est mis en éveil l'intérêt du spectateur?

12. SUR L'ENSEMBLE DE LA SCÈNE III. — Composition de cette scène : sous quel jour nouveau fait-elle apparaître tout ce qu'on a vu jusqu'ici dans les actes précédents?

— Si Monsieur Jourdain a des motifs légitimes de vouloir se cultiver et s'instruire, peut-on dire qu'il tire grand profit des leçons qu'il reçoit? Qu'en conclure?

— Faites le portrait de Madame Jourdain : son caractère, son langage.

— Le rôle de Nicole : comparez-le à celui de Dorine dans *le Tartuffe*, de Martine dans *les Femmes savantes* et de Toinette dans *le Malade imaginaire*. Quels sont ses sentiments à l'égard de Monsieur Jourdain? de Madame Jourdain? Étudiez son langage : y reste-t-il beaucoup de traces de son passé paysan?

DORANTE. — Tournez-vous. Cela est tout à fait galant.

MADAME JOURDAIN, *à part*. — Oui, aussi sot par derrière que par devant. (13)

20 DORANTE. — Ma foi, monsieur Jourdain, j'avais une impatience étrange de vous voir. Vous êtes l'homme du monde que j'estime le plus, et je parlais de vous encore ce matin dans la chambre du roi.

MONSIEUR JOURDAIN. — Vous me faites beaucoup d'honneur,
25 monsieur. *(A Madame Jourdain.)* Dans la chambre du roi!

DORANTE. — Allons, mettez[1]...

MONSIEUR JOURDAIN. — Monsieur, je sais le respect que je vous dois.

DORANTE. — Mon Dieu, mettez; point de cérémonie entre
30 nous, je vous prie.

MONSIEUR JOURDAIN. — Monsieur...

DORANTE. — Mettez, vous dis-je, monsieur Jourdain; vous êtes mon ami.

MONSIEUR JOURDAIN. — Monsieur, je suis votre serviteur.

35 DORANTE. — Je ne me couvrirai point, si vous ne vous couvrez.

MONSIEUR JOURDAIN, *se couvrant*. — J'aime mieux être incivil qu'importun[2]. (14)

DORANTE. — Je suis votre débiteur, comme vous le savez.

MADAME JOURDAIN, *à part*. — Oui, nous ne le savons que trop.

40 DORANTE. — Vous m'avez généreusement prêté de l'argent en plusieurs occasions, et vous m'avez obligé de la meilleure grâce du monde, assurément.

MONSIEUR JOURDAIN. — Monsieur, vous vous moquez.

DORANTE. — Mais je sais rendre ce qu'on me prête, et reconn-
45 naître les plaisirs qu'on me fait.

---

1. Mettez votre chapeau; 2. Formule de politesse bourgeoise dont la forme banale et traditionnelle doit choquer Dorante.

───── QUESTIONS ─────

13. L'entrée de Dorante : sa civilité n'est-elle pas équivoque? Un « honnête homme » se mettrait-il dans le cas de reparaître chez quelqu'un où il est ainsi reçu par la maîtresse de maison?
14. Y a-t-il seulement un comique de geste dans cet assaut de courtoisie? Où réside la satire sociale?

Ils vont calculer la dette de Dorante

MONSIEUR JOURDAIN. — Je n'en doute point, monsieur.

DORANTE. — Je veux sortir d'affaire[1] avec vous, et je viens ici pour faire nos comptes ensemble.

50 MONSIEUR JOURDAIN, *bas à Mme Jourdain*. — Hé bien! vous voyez votre impertinence, ma femme.

DORANTE. — Je suis homme qui aime à m'acquitter le plus tôt que je puis.

MONSIEUR JOURDAIN, *bas à Mme Jourdain*. — Je vous le disais bien.

55 DORANTE. — Voyons un peu ce que je vous dois.

MONSIEUR JOURDAIN, *bas à Mme Jourdain*. — Vous voilà, avec vos soupçons ridicules.

DORANTE. — Vous souvenez-vous bien de tout l'argent que vous m'avez prêté?

60 MONSIEUR JOURDAIN. — Je crois que oui. J'en ai fait un petit mémoire. Le voici. Donné à vous une fois deux cents louis[2].

DORANTE. — Cela est vrai.

MONSIEUR JOURDAIN. — Une autre fois, six-vingts[3].

65 DORANTE. — Oui.

MONSIEUR JOURDAIN. — Et une fois, cent quarante.

DORANTE. — Vous avez raison.

MONSIEUR JOURDAIN. — Ces trois articles font quatre cent soixante louis, qui valent cinq mille soixante livres.

70 DORANTE. — Le compte est fort bon. Cinq mille soixante livres.

MONSIEUR JOURDAIN. — Mille huit cent trente-deux livres à votre plumassier.

DORANTE. — Justement.

75 MONSIEUR JOURDAIN. — Deux mille sept cent quatre-vingts livres à votre tailleur.

DORANTE. — Il est vrai.

---

1. *Sortir d'affaire* : régler les comptes; 2. *Louis* : monnaie d'or qui valait onze livres; 3. *Six-vingts* : cent vingt (vestige de la numération par vingtième qui ne subsiste plus aujourd'hui que dans « quatre-vingts »).

MONSIEUR JOURDAIN. — Quatre mille trois cent septante-neuf livres douze sols huit deniers[1] à votre marchand[2].

80 DORANTE. — Fort bien. Douze sols huit deniers; le compte est juste.

MONSIEUR JOURDAIN. — Et mille sept cent quarante-huit livres sept sols quatre deniers à votre sellier.

DORANTE. — Tout cela est véritable. Qu'est-ce que cela fait?

85 MONSIEUR JOURDAIN. — Somme totale, quinze mille huit cents livres. **(15)**

DORANTE. — Somme totale est juste : quinze mille huit cents livres. Mettez encore deux cents pistoles que vous m'allez donner, cela fera justement dix-huit mille francs, que je vous 90 payerai au premier jour. **(16)**

MADAME JOURDAIN, *bas à M. Jourdain*. — Hé bien, ne l'avais-je pas bien deviné?

MONSIEUR JOURDAIN, *bas à Mᵐᵉ Jourdain*. — Paix!

DORANTE. — Cela vous incommodera-t-il de me donner ce 95 que je vous dis?

MONSIEUR JOURDAIN. — Eh, non!

MADAME JOURDAIN, *bas à M. Jourdain*. — Cet homme-là fait de vous une vache à lait.

MONSIEUR JOURDAIN, *bas à Mᵐᵉ Jourdain*. — Taisez-vous!

100 DORANTE. — Si cela vous incommode, j'en[3] irai chercher ailleurs.

MONSIEUR JOURDAIN. — Non, monsieur.

MADAME JOURDAIN, *bas à M. Jourdain*. — Il ne sera pas content qu'il ne vous ait ruiné.

---

1. Le *sol* ou *sou* est la vingtième partie du franc, le *denier*, la douzième partie du sol. Quant au *franc*, il est équivalent de la livre, puisqu'il valait vingt sols comme elle; 2. *Marchand :* sans doute marchand de drap. Les marchands drapiers constituaient une des corporations les plus actives et les plus importantes, d'où l'habitude de les désigner par ce terme général. Dans *Dom Juan*, Monsieur Dimanche est aussi un « marchand »; 3. J'irai chercher de l'argent; emploi plus souple qu'aujourd'hui du pronom *en*.

——— **QUESTIONS** ———

15. La double personnalité de Monsieur Jourdain : comment le marchand reparaît-il très vite sous le « gentilhomme »? Dans quelle réplique apparaît cette dualité?
16. L'effet produit par cette courte réplique : quel contraste fait-elle avec l'énumération précédente? En quoi est-ce un tournant dans la scène?

105 MONSIEUR JOURDAIN, *bas à Mme Jourdain*. — Taisez-vous, vous dis-je.

DORANTE. — Vous n'avez qu'à me dire si cela vous embarrasse.

MONSIEUR JOURDAIN. — Point, monsieur.

MADAME JOURDAIN, *bas à M. Jourdain*. — C'est un vrai
110 enjôleux[1].

MONSIEUR JOURDAIN, *bas à Mme Jourdain*. — Taisez-vous donc.

MADAME JOURDAIN, *bas à M. Jourdain*. — Il vous sucera jusqu'au dernier sou.

115 MONSIEUR JOURDAIN, *bas à Mme Jourdain*. — Vous tairez-vous?

DORANTE. — J'ai force gens qui m'en prêteraient avec joie; mais, comme vous êtes mon meilleur ami, j'ai cru que je vous ferais tort si j'en demandais à quelque autre.

120 MONSIEUR JOURDAIN. — C'est trop d'honneur, monsieur, que vous me faites. Je vais querir[2] votre affaire. (**17**)

MADAME JOURDAIN, *bas à M. Jourdain*. — Quoi! vous allez encore lui donner cela?

MONSIEUR JOURDAIN, *bas à Mme Jourdain*. — Que faire?
125 Voulez-vous que je refuse un homme de cette condition-là, qui a parlé de moi ce matin dans la chambre du roi? (**18**)

MADAME JOURDAIN, *bas à M. Jourdain*. — Allez, vous êtes une vraie dupe. (**19**)

---

1. *Enjôleux* ou *enjôleur* : celui qui trompe par des paroles flatteuses; 2. Je vais chercher votre argent. Le langage du commerçant transparaît à travers l'expression.

──────── **QUESTIONS** ────────

17. Comparez l'attitude des trois personnages à ce qu'elle était dans la première partie de la scène : quel changement s'est produit? Étudiez en particulier le rôle de Dorante : soupçonne-t-il la déconvenue de Monsieur Jourdain et l'hostilité de sa femme? De quelle menace use-t-il?

18. Cet argument peut-il convaincre Madame Jourdain? N'est-ce pas aussi pour Monsieur Jourdain un moyen de se convaincre lui-même?

19. SUR L'ENSEMBLE DE LA SCÈNE IV. — Composition de la scène : étudiez le mécanisme qui permet le renversement de l'action. En tenant compte de la curiosité du spectateur au début de la scène, par quels sentiments celui-ci passe-t-il successivement?

— Le personnage de Dorante : son habileté. Comparez son attitude à celle de Dom Juan face à Monsieur Dimanche (*Dom Juan*, IV, III). Les contemporains de Molière étaient-ils surpris de voir un « comte » — à supposer qu'il soit authentique — criblé de dettes?

Scène V. — DORANTE, MADAME JOURDAIN, NICOLE.

DORANTE. — Vous me semblez toute mélancolique[1]. Qu'avez-vous, madame Jourdain?

MADAME JOURDAIN. — J'ai la tête plus grosse que le poing, et si[2] elle n'est pas enflée.

5 DORANTE. — Mademoiselle votre fille, où est-elle, que je ne la vois point?

MADAME JOURDAIN. — Mademoiselle ma fille est bien où elle est.

DORANTE. — Comment se porte-t-elle?

10 MADAME JOURDAIN. — Elle se porte sur ses deux jambes.

DORANTE. — Ne voulez-vous point un de ces jours venir voir avec elle le ballet et la comédie que l'on fait chez le roi?

MADAME JOURDAIN. — Oui vraiment, nous avons fort envie de rire, fort envie de rire nous avons.

15 DORANTE. — Je pense, madame Jourdain, que vous avez eu bien des amants[3] dans votre jeune âge, belle et d'agréable humeur comme vous étiez.

MADAME JOURDAIN. — Tredame[4]! monsieur, est-ce que madame Jourdain est décrépite, et la tête lui grouille[5]-t-elle 20 déjà?

DORANTE. — Ah! ma foi, madame Jourdain, je vous demande pardon. Je ne songeais pas que vous êtes jeune, et je rêve[6] le plus souvent. Je vous prie d'excuser mon impertinence. **(20)**

---

1. *Mélancolique* : d'humeur sombre; 2. *Et si* : et pourtant; 3. *Amants* : soupirants; 4. *Tredame* : renforcement de *dame* par l'adverbe *très*. L'expression est très familière; 5. *Grouiller* : se remuer, trembler; le mot est également populaire; 6. *Rêver* : être distrait.

─────── **QUESTIONS** ───────

20. Sur la scène V. — Comment Molière tire-t-il parti de cette scène de transition? La « gaffe » de Dorante : est-elle due vraiment à sa distraction? ou à la gêne que provoque en lui l'attitude rébarbative de Madame Jourdain? Ne pourrait-elle aussi être volontaire? — Le ton de Madame Jourdain : quelle influence sa mauvaise humeur a-t-elle sur son langage?

Scène VI. — MONSIEUR JOURDAIN, MADAME JOURDAIN, DORANTE, NICOLE.

MONSIEUR JOURDAIN, *à Dorante.* — Voilà deux cents louis bien comptés.

DORANTE. — Je vous assure, monsieur Jourdain, que je suis tout à vous, et que je brûle de vous rendre un service
5 à la cour.

MONSIEUR JOURDAIN. — Je vous suis trop obligé.

DORANTE. — Si madame Jourdain veut voir le divertissement royal[1], je lui ferai donner les meilleures places de la salle.

MADAME JOURDAIN. — Madame Jourdain vous baise les
10 mains[2]. **(21)**

DORANTE, *bas à M. Jourdain.* — Notre belle marquise, comme je vous ai mandé par mon billet, viendra tantôt ici pour le ballet et le repas; et je l'ai fait consentir enfin au cadeau[3] que vous lui voulez donner.

15 MONSIEUR JOURDAIN. — Tirons-nous un peu plus loin, pour cause.

DORANTE. — Il y a huit jours que je ne vous ai vu, et je ne vous ai point mandé de nouvelles du diamant que vous me mîtes entre les mains pour lui en faire présent de votre part :
20 mais c'est que j'ai eu toutes les peines du monde à vaincre son scrupule, et ce n'est que d'aujourd'hui qu'elle s'est résolue à l'accepter.

MONSIEUR JOURDAIN. — Comment l'a-t-elle trouvé?

DORANTE. — Merveilleux; et je me trompe fort, ou la beauté
25 de ce diamant fera pour vous sur son esprit un effet admirable.

MONSIEUR JOURDAIN. — Plût au ciel!

MADAME JOURDAIN, *à Nicole.* — Quand il est une fois avec lui, il ne peut le quitter.

DORANTE. — Je lui ai fait valoir comme il faut la richesse
30 de ce présent et la grandeur de votre amour.

---

1. C'est le titre même du *Bourgeois gentilhomme;* **2.** Formule qui permet de prendre congé, mais aussi d'exprimer un remerciement ou, ironiquement, un refus (cf. : « Je suis votre serviteur »); **3.** *Cadeau :* collation, fête ou divertissement offert à des dames.

— QUESTIONS —

21. Dorante s'engage-t-il beaucoup à l'égard de Monsieur Jourdain? Pourquoi renouvelle-t-il son invitation à Madame Jourdain?

MONSIEUR JOURDAIN. — Ce sont, monsieur, des bontés qui m'accablent; et je suis dans une confusion la plus grande du monde de voir une personne de votre qualité s'abaisser pour moi à ce que vous faites.

35 DORANTE. — Vous moquez-vous? Est-ce qu'entre amis on s'arrête à ces sortes de scrupules? Et ne feriez-vous pas pour moi la même chose, si l'occasion s'en offrait?

MONSIEUR JOURDAIN. — Oh! assurément, et de très grand cœur.

40 MADAME JOURDAIN, *à Nicole.* — Que sa présence me pèse sur les épaules!

DORANTE. — Pour moi, je ne regarde rien, quand il faut servir un ami; et, lorsque vous me fîtes confidence de l'ardeur que vous aviez prise pour cette marquise agréable chez qui 45 j'avais commerce[1], vous vîtes que d'abord je m'offris de moi-même à servir votre amour.

MONSIEUR JOURDAIN. — Il est vrai, ce sont des bontés qui me confondent.

MADAME JOURDAIN, *à Nicole.* — Est-ce qu'il ne s'en ira point!

50 NICOLE. — Ils se trouvent bien ensemble.

DORANTE. — Vous avez pris le bon biais pour toucher son cœur. Les femmes aiment surtout les dépenses qu'on fait pour elles; et vos fréquentes sérénades, et vos bouquets continuels, ce superbe feu d'artifice qu'elle trouva sur l'eau, le diamant 55 qu'elle a reçu de votre part, et le cadeau que vous lui préparez, tout cela lui parle bien mieux en faveur de votre amour que toutes les paroles que vous auriez pu lui dire vous-même. **(22)**

MONSIEUR JOURDAIN. — Il n'y a point de dépenses que je ne fisse, si par là je pouvais trouver le chemin de son cœur. 60 Une femme de qualité a pour moi des charmes ravissants, et c'est un honneur que j'achèterais au prix de toute chose. **(23)**

---

1. J'étais en relation.

────────── **QUESTIONS** ──────────

22. Sur quel personnage l'attention du spectateur est-elle maintenant attirée? Avions-nous jusqu'ici beaucoup de renseignements sur la marquise? Comment Molière complète-t-il adroitement l'exposition sur ce point?

23. Étudiez cette réplique de Monsieur Jourdain : à quoi reconnaît-on le marchand? Est-ce par amour qu'il courtise Dorimène?

MADAME JOURDAIN, *à Nicole*. — Que peuvent-ils tant dire ensemble? Va-t'en un peu tout doucement prêter l'oreille.

DORANTE. — Ce sera tantôt que vous jouirez à votre aise
65 du plaisir de sa vue, et vos yeux auront tout le temps de se satisfaire.

MONSIEUR JOURDAIN. — Pour être en pleine liberté, j'ai fait en sorte que ma femme ira dîner chez ma sœur, où elle passera toute l'après-dînée.

70 DORANTE. — Vous avez fait prudemment, et votre femme aurait pu nous embarrasser. J'ai donné pour vous l'ordre qu'il faut au cuisinier, et à toutes les choses[1] qui sont nécessaires pour le ballet. Il est de mon invention, et, pourvu que l'exécution puisse répondre à l'idée, je suis sûr qu'il sera trouvé...

75 MONSIEUR JOURDAIN *s'aperçoit que Nicole écoute, et lui donne un soufflet*. — Ouais! vous êtes bien impertinente! *(A Dorante.)* Sortons, s'il vous plaît. **(24) (25)**

Scène VII. — MADAME JOURDAIN, NICOLE.

NICOLE. — Ma foi, madame, la curiosité m'a coûté quelque chose; mais je crois qu'il y a quelque anguille sous roche, et ils parlent de quelque affaire où ils ne veulent pas que vous soyez.

5 MADAME JOURDAIN. — Ce n'est pas d'aujourd'hui, Nicole, que j'ai conçu des soupçons de mon mari. Je suis la plus trompée du monde[2], ou il y a quelque amour en campagne, et je travaille à découvrir ce que ce peut être. Mais songeons à ma fille. Tu sais l'amour que Cléonte a pour elle. C'est un homme
10 qui me revient, et je veux aider sa recherche[3], et lui donner Lucile, si je puis.

---

1. Et pour toutes les choses. Les deux compléments (de personne et de chose) introduits par la préposition *à* n'ont pas la même valeur; 2. Je me trompe fort; 3. *Recherche :* le fait pour un jeune homme de rechercher une jeune fille en mariage.

QUESTIONS
---

24. Comprend-on maintenant pourquoi Nicole et Madame Jourdain sont restées en scène?

25. SUR L'ENSEMBLE DE LA SCÈNE VI. — Le comique de situation : imaginez les jeux de scène et les attitudes des quatre personnages, deux par deux, pendant tout ce dialogue.

— Quelle partie de l'intrigue progresse ici? Comment le rôle d'intermédiaire joué par Dorante peut-il se justifier?

— Monsieur Jourdain amoureux : semble-t-il accorder beaucoup d'importance à la personne même de la marquise?

NICOLE. — En vérité, madame, je suis la plus ravie du monde de vous voir dans ces sentiments : car, si le maître vous revient, le valet ne me revient pas moins, et je souhaiterais que notre 15 mariage se pût faire à l'ombre du leur.

MADAME JOURDAIN. — Va-t'en lui parler de ma part, et lui dire que tout à l'heure[1] il me vienne trouver pour faire ensemble à mon mari la demande de ma fille.

NICOLE. — J'y cours, madame, avec joie, et je ne pouvais 20 recevoir une commission plus agréable. *(Seule.)* Je vais, je pense, bien réjouir[2] les gens. **(26)**

Scène VIII. — CLÉONTE, COVIELLE, NICOLE.

NICOLE, *à Cléonte.* — Ah! vous voilà tout à propos. Je suis ambassadrice de joie, et je viens...

CLÉONTE. — Retire-toi, perfide, et ne me viens point amuser avec tes traîtresses paroles.

5 NICOLE. — Est-ce ainsi que vous recevez...

CLÉONTE. — Retire-toi, te dis-je, et va-t'en dire de ce pas à ton infidèle maîtresse qu'elle n'abusera de sa vie le trop simple Cléonte.

NICOLE. — Quel vertigo[3] est-ce donc là? Mon pauvre Covielle, 10 dis-moi un peu ce que cela veut dire.

COVIELLE. — Ton pauvre Covielle, petite scélérate! Allons, vite, ôte-toi de mes yeux, vilaine, et me laisse en repos.

NICOLE. — Quoi! tu me viens aussi...

COVIELLE. — Ote-toi de mes yeux, te dis-je, et ne me parle 15 de ta vie.

NICOLE, *à part.* — Ouais! Quelle mouche les a piqués tous deux? Allons de cette belle histoire informer ma maîtresse. **(27)**

---

1. *Tout à l'heure :* voir page 60, note 2; 2. *Réjouir :* donner de la joie à; 3. *Vertigo :* folie, caprice. Le mot est du langage burlesque.

─────── **QUESTIONS** ───────

26. SUR LA SCÈNE VII. — Quel nouveau problème surgit ici? A-t-on beaucoup parlé jusqu'ici du mariage de Nicole? Pourquoi le moment est-il bien choisi pour nous montrer Madame Jourdain se décider brusquement à hâter le mariage de sa fille avec Cléonte? Dans quel cadre traditionnel s'intègre ici l'action de la comédie?

27. SUR LA SCÈNE VIII. — Une péripétie imprévue : le spectateur est-il très inquiet de voir déjà en danger un projet de mariage qui lui semblait sympathique?

Scène IX. — CLÉONTE, COVIELLE.

CLÉONTE. — Quoi! traiter un amant de la sorte? et un amant le plus fidèle et le plus passionné de tous les amants?

COVIELLE. — C'est une chose épouvantable que ce qu'on nous fait à tous deux.

5 CLÉONTE. — Je fais voir pour une personne toute l'ardeur et toute la tendresse qu'on peut imaginer; je n'aime rien au monde qu'elle, et je n'ai qu'elle dans l'esprit; elle fait tous mes soins, tous mes désirs, toute ma joie; je ne parle que d'elle, je ne pense qu'à elle, je ne fais des songes que d'elle, je ne respire 10 que par elle, mon cœur vit tout en elle : et voilà de tant d'amitié[1] la digne récompense! Je suis deux jours sans la voir, qui sont pour moi deux siècles effroyables; je la rencontre par hasard; mon cœur à cette vue se sent tout transporté, ma joie éclate sur mon visage; je vole avec ravissement vers elle; et 15 l'infidèle détourne de moi ses regards et passe brusquement comme si de sa vie elle ne m'avait vu! **(28)**

COVIELLE. — Je dis les mêmes choses que vous.

CLÉONTE. — Peut-on rien voir d'égal, Covielle, à cette perfidie de l'ingrate Lucile?

20 COVIELLE. — Et à celle, monsieur, de la pendarde de Nicole?

CLÉONTE. — Après tant de sacrifices ardents, de soupirs et de vœux que j'ai faits à ses charmes!

COVIELLE. — Après tant d'assidus hommages, de soins et de services que je lui ai rendus dans sa cuisine!

25 CLÉONTE. — Tant de larmes que j'ai versées à ses genoux!

COVIELLE. — Tant de seaux d'eau que j'ai tirés au puits pour elle!

CLÉONTE. — Tant d'ardeur que j'ai fait paraître à la chérir plus que moi-même!

30 COVIELLE. — Tant de chaleur que j'ai soufferte à tourner la broche à sa place!

CLÉONTE. — Elle me fuit avec mépris!

---

1. *Amitié* : amour, affection.

● QUESTIONS ●

28. Étudiez le vocabulaire et le style de Cléonte; ses exagérations nuisent-elles à la sincérité de son sentiment? Quel contraste fait ce langage après celui qu'on a entendu jusqu'ici? Y a-t-il un motif grave à son dépit?

COVIELLE. — Elle me tourne le dos avec effronterie!

CLÉONTE. — C'est une perfidie digne des plus grands châti-
35 ments.

COVIELLE. — C'est une trahison à mériter mille soufflets. (29)

CLÉONTE. — Ne t'avise point, je te prie, de me parler jamais
pour elle.

COVIELLE. — Moi, monsieur? Dieu m'en garde!

40 CLÉONTE. — Ne viens point m'excuser l'action de cette infidèle.

COVIELLE. — N'ayez pas peur.

CLÉONTE. — Non, vois-tu, tous tes discours pour la défendre
ne serviront de rien.

COVIELLE. — Qui songe à cela?

45 CLÉONTE. — Je veux contre elle conserver mon ressentiment
et rompre ensemble[1] tout commerce.

COVIELLE. — J'y consens.

CLÉONTE. — Ce monsieur le comte qui va chez elle lui donne
peut-être dans la vue; et son esprit, je le vois bien, se laisse
50 éblouir à la qualité. Mais il me faut, pour mon honneur, pré-
venir l'éclat[2] de son inconstance. Je veux faire autant de pas
qu'elle au changement où je la vois courir et ne lui laisser
pas toute la gloire de me quitter.

COVIELLE. — C'est fort bien dit, et j'entre pour mon compte
55 dans tous vos sentiments.

CLÉONTE. — Donne la main[3] à mon dépit, et soutiens ma
résolution contre tous les restes d'amour qui me pourraient
parler pour elle. Dis-m'en, je t'en conjure, tout le mal que
tu pourras. Fais-moi de sa personne une peinture qui me la
60 rende méprisable; et marque-moi bien, pour m'en dégoûter,
tous les défauts que tu peux voir en elle. (30)

COVIELLE. — Elle, monsieur? Voilà une belle mijaurée[4],

_____

1. *Ensemble* : l'un avec l'autre; 2. *Eclat* : scandale; 3. *Donner la main* : aider,
favoriser; 4. *Mijaurée* : femme sotte et vaniteuse.

━━━━━━━ QUESTIONS ━━━━━━━

29. L'effet comique développé ici : sur quel plan les répliques de
Covielle transposent-elles chacune des remarques de Cléonte?

30. Cléonte est-il très sûr d'avoir une bonne raison de garder rancune à
Lucile? Comment son imagination vient-elle au secours de son dépit?
Covielle prend-il l'attitude que Cléonte souhaitait lui voir prendre?

une pimpesouée[1] bien bâtie, pour vous donner tant d'amour!
Je ne lui vois rien que de très médiocre, et vous trouverez
65 cent personnes qui seront plus dignes de vous. Premièrement,
elle a les yeux petits.

CLÉONTE. — Cela est vrai, elle a les yeux petits, mais elle
les a pleins de feu, les plus brillants, les plus perçants du monde,
les plus touchants qu'on puisse voir.

70 COVIELLE. — Elle a la bouche grande.

CLÉONTE. — Oui; mais on y voit des grâces qu'on ne voit
point aux autres bouches; et cette bouche, en la voyant, inspire
des désirs, est la plus attrayante, la plus amoureuse du monde.

COVIELLE. — Pour sa taille, elle n'est pas grande.

75 CLÉONTE. — Non; mais elle est aisée et bien prise.

COVIELLE. — Elle affecte une nonchalance dans son parler
et dans ses actions.

CLÉONTE. — Il est vrai; mais elle a grâce à tout cela, et ses
manières sont engageantes, ont je ne sais quel charme à s'insi-
80 nuer dans les cœurs.

COVIELLE. — Pour de l'esprit...

CLÉONTE. — Ah! elle en a, Covielle, du plus fin, du plus
délicat.

COVIELLE. — Sa conversation...

85 CLÉONTE. — Sa conversation est charmante.

COVIELLE. — Elle est toujours sérieuse...

CLÉONTE. — Veux-tu de ces enjouements épanouis, de ces
joies toujours ouvertes? et vois-tu rien de plus impertinent
que des femmes qui rient à tout propos?

90 COVIELLE. — Mais enfin elle est capricieuse autant que personne au monde.

CLÉONTE. — Oui, elle est capricieuse, j'en demeure d'accord,
mais tout sied bien aux belles, on souffre tout des belles. **(31)**

---

1. *Pimpesouée* : coquette et doucereuse (terme familier aujourd'hui disparu).

─────── QUESTIONS ───────

31. Le nouvel effet comique utilisé ici : pourquoi Cléonte refuse-t-il
toutes les critiques présentées par Covielle? Comparez ce passage à la
tirade d'Éliante dans *le Misanthrope* (vers 711-730); quelle est la vérité
commune exprimée dans ces deux textes? D'après le portrait authentique
fait par Covielle à Cléonte, comment imaginez-vous Lucile?

COVIELLE. — Puisque cela va comme cela, je vois bien que
95 vous avez envie de l'aimer toujours.

CLÉONTE. — Moi, j'aimerais mieux mourir; et je vais la haïr
autant que je l'ai aimée.

COVIELLE. — Le moyen, si vous la trouvez si parfaite?

CLÉONTE. — C'est en quoi ma vengeance sera plus éclatante,
100 en quoi je veux faire mieux voir la force de mon cœur, à la
haïr, à la quitter, toute belle, toute pleine d'attraits, toute
aimable que je la trouve. La voici. **(32) (33)**

SCÈNE X. — CLÉONTE, LUCILE, COVIELLE, NICOLE.

NICOLE, *à Lucile.* — Pour moi, j'en ai été toute scandalisée.

LUCILE. — Ce ne peut être, Nicole, que ce que je te dis.
Mais le voilà.

CLÉONTE, *à Covielle.* — Je ne veux pas seulement lui parler.

5 COVIELLE. — Je veux vous imiter.

LUCILE. — Qu'est-ce donc, Cléonte? qu'avez-vous?

NICOLE. — Qu'as-tu donc, Covielle?

LUCILE. — Quel chagrin vous possède?

NICOLE. — Quelle mauvaise humeur te tient?

10 LUCILE. — Êtes-vous muet, Cléonte?

NICOLE. — As-tu perdu la parole, Covielle?

CLÉONTE. — Que voilà qui est scélérat!

COVIELLE. — Que cela est Judas[1]!

LUCILE. — Je vois bien que la rencontre de tantôt a troublé
15 votre esprit.

CLÉONTE, *à Covielle.* — Ah! ah! on voit ce qu'on a fait.

---

1. *Judas :* traître et hypocrite. Allusion à Judas, qui trahit Jésus.

--------- **QUESTIONS** ---------

32. Croit-on aux tragiques déterminations de Cléonte ou au bon sens
de Covielle?

33. SUR L'ENSEMBLE DE LA SCÈNE IX. — Composition de cette scène :
quel rôle joue Covielle aux différents moments du dialogue?
— Prend-on au sérieux le dépit des deux personnages? Montrez que
sous son apparence de légèreté et d'inutilité, cette scène retient le spectateur par sa vérité psychologique.

Cléonte est très jaloux de Dorante

NICOLE. — Notre accueil de ce matin t'a fait prendre la chèvre[1].

COVIELLE, *à Cléonte*. — On a deviné l'enclouure[2].

20   LUCILE. — N'est-il pas vrai, Cléonte, que c'est là le sujet de votre dépit? (34)

CLÉONTE. — Oui, perfide, ce l'est, puisqu'il faut parler; et j'ai à vous dire que vous ne triompherez pas comme vous pensez de votre infidélité, que je veux être le premier à rompre
25   avec vous, et que vous n'aurez pas l'avantage de me chasser. J'aurai de la peine sans doute à vaincre l'amour que j'ai pour vous; cela me causera des chagrins. Je souffrirai un temps; mais j'en viendrai à bout, et je me percerai plutôt le cœur que d'avoir la faiblesse de retourner à vous.

30   COVIELLE, *à Nicole*. — Queussi queumi[3].

LUCILE. — Voilà bien du bruit pour un rien. Je veux vous dire, Cléonte, le sujet qui m'a fait ce matin éviter votre abord. (35)

CLÉONTE, *voulant s'en aller pour éviter Lucile*. — Non, je ne
35   veux rien écouter.

NICOLE, *à Covielle*. — Je te veux apprendre la cause qui nous a fait passer si vite.

COVIELLE, *voulant aussi s'en aller pour éviter Nicole*. — Je ne veux rien entendre...

40   LUCILE, *suivant Cléonte*. — Sachez que ce matin...

CLÉONTE, *marchant toujours sans regarder Lucile*. — Non, vous dis-je.

NICOLE, *suivant Covielle*. — Apprends que...

COVIELLE, *marchant aussi sans regarder Nicole*. — Non,
45   traîtresse.

---

1. *Prendre la chèvre* : se cabrer, se fâcher; **2.** *Enclouure* : blessure faite au pied d'un cheval par le clou d'un fer mal placé, d'où, au figuré : empêchement, difficulté; **3.** *Queussi queumi* (quel soi, quel moi) : tel lui, tel moi (expression picarde).

--- QUESTIONS ---

34. Attendait-on cette arrivée de Lucile accompagnée de Nicole? Les deux femmes sont-elles, au début de la scène, tout à fait sûres que la rencontre du matin soit la cause de la mauvaise humeur de Cléonte et de Covielle? En quoi prennent-elles l'avantage quand leurs deux amoureux leur donnent la certitude qu'elles avaient deviné juste?

35. La différence de ton entre Cléonte et Lucile : que révèle-t-elle de leur caractère?

LUCILE. — Écoutez.

CLÉONTE. — Point d'affaire.

NICOLE. — Laisse-moi dire.

COVIELLE. — Je suis sourd.

50   LUCILE. — Cléonte!

CLÉONTE. — Non.

NICOLE. — Covielle!

COVIELLE. — Point.

LUCILE. — Arrêtez.

55   CLÉONTE. — Chansons!

NICOLE. — Entends-moi.

COVIELLE. — Bagatelles!

LUCILE. — Un moment.

CLÉONTE. — Point du tout.

60   NICOLE. — Un peu de patience.

COVIELLE. — Tarare[1].

LUCILE. — Deux paroles.

CLÉONTE. — Non, c'en est fait.

NICOLE. — Un mot.

65   COVIELLE. — Plus de commerce. **(36)**

LUCILE, *s'arrêtant*. — Hé bien, puisque vous ne voulez pas m'écouter, demeurez dans votre pensée, et faites ce qu'il vous plaira.

NICOLE, *s'arrêtant aussi*. — Puisque tu fais comme cela, 70   prends-le tout comme tu voudras.

CLÉONTE, *se tournant vers Lucile*. — Sachons donc le sujet d'un si bel accueil.

LUCILE, *s'en allant à son tour pour éviter Cléonte*. — Il ne me plaît plus de le dire.

---

1. *Tarare* : point du tout (expression d'origine obscure, peut-être empruntée au refrain d'une chanson).

QUESTIONS
---

36. Pourquoi Cléonte et Covielle s'obstinent-ils dans leur bouderie, alors que Lucile allait tout expliquer? Quel aspect du dépit se révèle ici? Étudiez l'effet comique tiré du parallélisme dans les répliques des personnages pris deux par deux et dans les jeux de scène?

75   COVIELLE, *se tournant vers Nicole.* — Apprends-nous un peu cette histoire.

NICOLE, *s'en allant aussi pour éviter Covielle.* — Je ne veux plus, moi, te l'apprendre.

CLÉONTE, *suivant Lucile.* — Dites-moi...

80   LUCILE, *marchant toujours sans regarder Cléonte.* — Non, je ne veux rien dire.

COVIELLE, *suivant Nicole.* — Conte-moi...

NICOLE, *marchant aussi sans regarder Covielle.* — Non, je ne conte rien.

85   CLÉONTE. — De grâce...

LUCILE. — Non, vous dis-je.

COVIELLE. — Par charité.

NICOLE. — Point d'affaire.

CLÉONTE. — Je vous en prie.

90   LUCILE. — Laissez-moi.

COVIELLE. — Je t'en conjure.

NICOLE. — Ote-toi de là.

CLÉONTE. — Lucile!

LUCILE. — Non.

95   COVIELLE. — Nicole!

NICOLE. — Point.

CLÉONTE. — Au nom des dieux!...

LUCILE. — Je ne veux pas.

COVIELLE. — Parle-moi.

100   NICOLE. — Point du tout.

CLÉONTE. — Éclaircissez mes doutes.

LUCILE. — Non, je n'en ferai rien.

COVIELLE. — Guéris-moi l'esprit.

NICOLE. — Non, il ne me plaît pas. **(37)**

105   CLÉONTE. — Hé bien, puisque vous vous souciez si peu de me tirer de peine et de vous justifier du traitement indigne

———— **QUESTIONS** ————

37. Comment la situation se retourne-t-elle? D'où vient l'effet comique par rapport au moment précédent?

que vous avez fait à ma flamme, vous me voyez, ingrate, pour la dernière fois, et je vais loin de vous mourir de douleur et d'amour.

110 COVIELLE, *à Nicole*. — Et moi, je vais suivre ses pas.

LUCILE, *à Cléonte, qui veut sortir*. — Cléonte!

NICOLE, *à Covielle, qui veut sortir*. — Covielle!

CLÉONTE, *s'arrêtant*. — Eh?

COVIELLE, *s'arrêtant aussi*. — Plaît-il?

115 LUCILE. — Où allez-vous?

CLÉONTE. — Où je vous ai dit.

COVIELLE. — Nous allons mourir.

LUCILE. — Vous allez mourir, Cléonte?

CLÉONTE. — Oui, cruelle, puisque vous le voulez.

120 LUCILE. — Moi, je veux que vous mouriez?

CLÉONTE. — Oui, vous le voulez.

LUCILE. — Qui vous le dit?

CLÉONTE, *s'approchant de Lucile*. — N'est-ce pas le vouloir que de ne vouloir pas éclaircir mes soupçons?

125 LUCILE. — Est-ce ma faute? Et, si vous aviez voulu m'écouter, ne vous aurais-je pas dit que l'aventure dont vous vous plaignez a été causée ce matin par la présence d'une vieille tante qui veut, à toute force, que la seule approche d'un homme déshonore une fille? qui perpétuellement nous sermonne sur
130 ce chapitre, et nous figure[1] tous les hommes comme des diables qu'il faut fuir?

NICOLE, *à Covielle*. — Voilà le secret de l'affaire.

CLÉONTE. — Ne me trompez-vous point, Lucile?

COVIELLE, *à Nicole*. — Ne m'en donnes-tu point à garder[2]?

135 LUCILE, *à Cléonte*. — Il n'est rien de plus vrai.

NICOLE, *à Covielle*. — C'est la chose comme elle est.

COVIELLE, *à Cléonte*. — Nous rendrons-nous à cela?

CLÉONTE. — Ah! Lucile, qu'avec un mot de votre bouche vous savez apaiser de choses dans mon cœur, et que facilement
140 on se laisse persuader aux personnes qu'on aime!

---

1. *Figurer* : représenter; 2. Ne m'en fais-tu pas accroire?

COVIELLE. — Qu'on est aisément amadoué par ces diantres d'animaux-là[1]! (38) (39)

Scène XI. — MADAME JOURDAIN, CLÉONTE, LUCILE, COVIELLE, NICOLE.

MADAME JOURDAIN. — Je suis bien aise de vous voir, Cléonte, et vous voilà tout à propos. Mon mari vient, prenez vite votre temps[2] pour lui demander Lucile en mariage.

CLÉONTE. — Ah! madame, que cette parole m'est douce et
5 qu'elle flatte mes désirs! Pouvais-je recevoir un ordre plus charmant, une faveur plus précieuse? (40)

Scène XII. — MONSIEUR JOURDAIN, MADAME JOURDAIN, CLÉONTE, LUCILE, COVIELLE, NICOLE.

CLÉONTE. — Monsieur, je n'ai voulu prendre personne pour vous faire une demande que je médite il y a longtemps. Elle me touche assez pour m'en charger moi-même; et, sans autre détour, je vous dirai que l'honneur d'être votre gendre est
5 une faveur glorieuse que je vous prie de m'accorder. (41)

MONSIEUR JOURDAIN. — Avant que de vous rendre réponse, monsieur, je vous prie de me dire si vous êtes gentilhomme.

---

1. C'est l'expression déjà utilisée par Arnolphe dans *l'École des femmes* (vers 1579);
2. Saisissez vite le moment.

——— QUESTIONS ———

38. Comment Cléonte et Covielle reprennent-ils l'avantage? Les deux femmes ont-elles vraiment peur qu'ils mettent à exécution leur menace d'aller mourir? Quelle est cependant leur appréhension?

39. SUR L'ENSEMBLE DE LA SCÈNE X. — Étudiez le mécanisme de la situation appelée « dépit amoureux ». Comment Molière la développe-t-il ici en plusieurs phases successives?

— Comparez cette scène à la scène IV de l'acte II du *Tartuffe* et dites ce qui la rend beaucoup plus comique?

— Cette scène n'est pas plus utile à l'action que la scène parallèle du *Tartuffe*; pourquoi Molière l'introduit-il cependant? Quel intérêt y trouve le spectateur?

40. SUR LA SCÈNE XI. — Appréciez le ton et la franchise de langage des deux personnages : Madame Jourdain n'est-elle pas bien différente ici de ce qu'elle est devant Dorante ou devant son mari?

41. Cléonte connaît les travers de Monsieur Jourdain : prouvez-le et montrez son habileté.

— LE BOURGEOIS GENTILHOMME

Molière's view of ppl. in the court

CLÉONTE. — Monsieur, la plupart des gens sur cette question n'hésitent pas beaucoup. On tranche le mot[1] aisément. Ce nom
10 ne fait aucun scrupule à prendre, et l'usage aujourd'hui semble en autoriser le vol. Pour moi, je vous l'avoue, j'ai les sentiments sur cette matière un peu plus délicats. Je trouve que toute imposture est indigne d'un honnête homme, et qu'il y a de la lâcheté[2] à déguiser ce que le Ciel nous a fait naître, à se
15 parer aux yeux du monde d'un titre dérobé, à se vouloir donner pour ce qu'on n'est pas. Je suis né de parents, sans doute, qui ont tenu des charges honorables[3]. Je me suis acquis dans les armes l'honneur de six ans de services, et je me trouve assez de bien pour tenir dans le monde un rang assez passable;
20 mais avec tout cela je ne veux point me donner un nom où d'autres en ma place croiraient pouvoir prétendre, et je vous dirai franchement que je ne suis point gentilhomme. (42) *I don't have noble blood*

MONSIEUR JOURDAIN. — Touchez là[4], monsieur. Ma fille n'est pas pour vous. (43) *If not gentleman no girl*

25 CLÉONTE. — Comment?

MONSIEUR JOURDAIN. — Vous n'êtes point gentilhomme, vous n'aurez pas ma fille.

MADAME JOURDAIN. — Que voulez-vous dire avec votre gentilhomme? Est-ce que nous sommes, nous autres, de la
30 côte de saint Louis[5]? *what is this do you have any royal blood in you?*

MONSIEUR JOURDAIN. — Taisez-vous, ma femme, je vous vois venir.

MADAME JOURDAIN. — Descendons-nous tous deux que de bonne bourgeoisie?

35 MONSIEUR JOURDAIN. — Voilà pas le coup de langue[6]!

MADAME JOURDAIN. — Et votre père n'était-il pas marchand aussi bien que le mien?

---

1. On décide hardiment de la question; 2. On commet en effet une *lâcheté* en trompant les autres et en se trahissant soi-même; 3. Cléonte semble donc appartenir à la bourgeoisie des fonctionnaires; 4. *Toucher là :* mettre sa main dans la main d'un autre pour conclure un accord; 5. De la plus vieille noblesse, descendante directe de Saint Louis; 6. *Le coup de langue :* la médisance.

QUESTIONS

42. Importance de cette tirade : la profonde maxime morale qui y est contenue. Pourquoi Molière attaque-t-il ceux qui usurpent des titres de noblesse?
43. Le comique de cette réplique : le ridicule de Monsieur Jourdain, surtout après la tirade précédente.

Phot. Harcourt.

RAIMU dans le rôle de Monsieur Jourdain, en 1944.

MONSIEUR JOURDAIN. — Peste soit de la femme! Elle n'y a
jamais manqué. Si votre père a été marchand, tant pis pour
40 lui; mais, pour le mien, ce sont des malavisés qui disent cela.
Tout ce que j'ai à vous dire, moi, c'est que je veux avoir un
gendre gentilhomme. **(44)**

MADAME JOURDAIN. — Il faut à votre fille un mari qui lui
soit propre[1], et il vaut mieux pour elle un honnête homme
45 riche et bien fait qu'un gentilhomme gueux et mal bâti. **(45)**

NICOLE. — Cela est vrai. Nous avons le fils du gentilhomme
de notre village qui est le plus grand malitorne[2] et le plus sot
dadais que j'aie jamais vu.

MONSIEUR JOURDAIN, *à Nicole.* — Taisez-vous, impertinente!
50 vous vous fourrez toujours dans la conversation. J'ai du bien
assez pour ma fille, je n'ai besoin que d'honneur, et je la veux
faire marquise.

MADAME JOURDAIN. — Marquise!

MONSIEUR JOURDAIN. — Oui, marquise.

55 MADAME JOURDAIN. — Hélas! Dieu m'en garde!

MONSIEUR JOURDAIN. — C'est une chose que j'ai résolue.

MADAME JOURDAIN. — C'est une chose, moi, où je ne consentirai point. Les alliances avec plus grand que soi sont sujettes
toujours à de fâcheux inconvénients. Je ne veux point qu'un
60 gendre puisse à ma fille reprocher ses parents, et qu'elle ait
des enfants qui aient honte de m'appeler leur grand'maman.
S'il fallait qu'elle me vînt visiter en équipage[3] de grand'dame,
et qu'elle manquât par mégarde à saluer quelqu'un du quartier, on ne manquerait pas aussitôt de dire cent sottises. « Voyez-
65 vous, dirait-on, cette madame la marquise qui fait tant la glorieuse? C'est la fille de monsieur Jourdain, qui était trop
heureuse, étant petite, de jouer à la madame avec nous : elle
n'a pas toujours été si relevée que la voilà; et ses deux grands-
pères vendaient du drap auprès de la porte Saint-Innocent[4].

---

1. Qui lui convient; **2.** *Malitorne :* mal tourné; **3.** *Équipage :* habillement, accou-
trement; **4.** La porte du cimetière des Saints-Innocents, situé dans le quartier des
Halles, à Paris, où Molière est né.

——— QUESTIONS ———

44. D'où naît la mauvaise humeur de Monsieur Jourdain? N'est-il pas
en train de commettre la tromperie qu'a condamnée justement Cléonte?

45. Le gendre idéal pour Madame Jourdain : ses trois qualités nécessaires. Comparez cette réplique à Dom Luis disant à son fils Dom Juan :
« Je ferai plus d'état du fils d'un crocheteur qui serait honnête homme
que du fils d'un monarque qui vivrait comme vous » (*Dom Juan*, IV, VI).

70 Ils ont amassé du bien à leurs enfants, qu'ils payent maintenant
peut-être bien cher en l'autre monde, et l'on ne devient guère
si riches à être honnêtes gens. » Je ne veux point tous ces caquets
et je veux un homme, en un mot, qui m'ait obligation de ma
fille, et à qui je puisse dire : « Mettez-vous là, mon gendre,
75 et dînez avec moi. » **(46)**

MONSIEUR JOURDAIN. — Voilà bien les sentiments d'un petit
esprit, de vouloir demeurer toujours dans la bassesse[1]. Ne me
répliquez pas davantage : ma fille sera marquise en dépit de
tout le monde; et, si vous me mettez en colère, je la ferai
80 duchesse. **(47)**

Scène XIII. — MADAME JOURDAIN, CLÉONTE, LUCILE, NICOLE, COVIELLE.

MADAME JOURDAIN. — Cléonte, ne perdez point courage
encore. *(A Lucile.)* Suivez-moi, ma fille, et venez dire résolu-
ment à votre père que, si vous ne l'avez, vous ne voulez épouser
personne. **(48)**

Scène XIV. — CLÉONTE, COVIELLE.

COVIELLE. — Vous avez fait de belles affaires, avec vos beaux
sentiments.

CLÉONTE. — Que veux-tu? J'ai un scrupule là-dessus que
l'exemple ne saurait vaincre.

5 COVIELLE. — Vous moquez-vous, de le prendre sérieusement
avec un homme comme cela? Ne voyez-vous pas qu'il est fou?
et vous coûtait-il quelque chose de vous accommoder à ses
chimères?

---

1. *Bassesse :* basse condition.

QUESTIONS
---

46. Les idées de Madame Jourdain sur le mariage : quelle est sa maxime
fondamentale? Son caractère : montrez que son bon sens est un peu
borné. Quelles précisions sont données ici sur le passé de la famille?

47. SUR L'ENSEMBLE DE LA SCÈNE XII. — Importance de cette scène pour
l'action; à quelle situation assez traditionnelle arrive-t-on? Est-on vraiment inquiet des menaces de Monsieur Jourdain comme on l'est de celles
d'Harpagon ou d'Orgon?

— Le désaccord entre Monsieur Jourdain et sa femme : en quoi s'op-
posent leurs conceptions de la vie sociale?

48. SUR LA SCÈNE XIII. — Comment se manifeste l'énergie de Madame
Jourdain?

CLÉONTE. — Tu as raison; mais je ne croyais pas qu'il fallût
10 faire preuve de noblesse pour être gendre de monsieur Jourdain.

COVIELLE, *riant*. — Ah! ah! ah!

CLÉONTE. — De quoi ris-tu?

COVIELLE. — D'une pensée qui me vient pour jouer notre homme et vous faire obtenir ce que vous souhaitez.

15 CLÉONTE. — Comment?

COVIELLE. — L'idée est tout à fait plaisante.

CLÉONTE. — Quoi donc?

COVIELLE. — Il s'est fait depuis peu une certaine mascarade[1]
qui vient le mieux du monde ici, et que je prétends faire entrer
20 dans une bourle[2] que je veux faire à notre ridicule. Tout cela
sent un peu sa comédie; mais, avec lui, on peut hasarder toute
chose, il n'y faut point chercher tant de façons, et il est homme
à y jouer son rôle à merveille, à donner aisément dans toutes
les fariboles qu'on s'avisera de lui dire. J'ai les acteurs, j'ai
25 les habits tout prêts, laissez-moi faire seulement.

CLÉONTE. — Mais apprends-moi...

COVIELLE. — Je vais vous instruire de tout; retirons-nous,
le voilà qui revient. **(49)**

SCÈNE XV. — MONSIEUR JOURDAIN, *seul*.

MONSIEUR JOURDAIN. — Que diable est-ce là? Ils[3] n'ont rien
que les grands seigneurs à me reprocher, et moi je ne vois rien
de si beau que de hanter les grands seigneurs; il n'y a qu'honneur et que civilité avec eux, et je voudrais qu'il m'eût coûté
5 deux doigts de la main et être né comte ou marquis.

SCÈNE XVI. — MONSIEUR JOURDAIN, UN LAQUAIS.

LAQUAIS. — Monsieur, voici monsieur le comte, et une dame
qu'il mène par la main.

---

1. Ceci est peut-être une allusion à *Monsieur de Pourceaugnac* (octobre 1669);
2. *Bourle* (de l'ital. *burla*) : plaisanterie (mot d'où est venu l'adjectif « burlesque »);
3. Monsieur Jourdain désigne sa femme et sa fille, peut-être aussi Cléonte.

— QUESTIONS —

49. SUR LA SCÈNE XIV. — Importance de cette scène pour l'action;
quel rôle traditionnel Covielle joue-t-il ici auprès de son maître déconfit?
— Le projet de Covielle n'est-il pas inattendu? Comment Molière
justifie-t-il, à l'usage du spectateur, la manière dont il fait évoluer l'action?

MONSIEUR JOURDAIN. — Hé! mon Dieu, j'ai quelques ordres à donner. Dis-leur que je vais venir ici tout à l'heure[1].

Scène XVII. — DORIMÈNE, DORANTE, LAQUAIS.

LAQUAIS. — Monsieur dit comme cela qu'il va venir ici tout à l'heure.

DORANTE. — Voilà qui est bien. (**50**)

Scène XVIII. — DORIMÈNE, DORANTE.

DORIMÈNE. — Je ne sais pas, Dorante; je fais encore ici[2] une étrange démarche de me laisser amener par vous dans une maison où je ne connais personne. (**51**)

5 DORANTE. — Quel lieu voulez-vous donc, madame, que mon amour choisisse pour vous régaler, puisque, pour fuir l'éclat, vous ne voulez ni votre maison, ni la mienne?

DORIMÈNE. — Mais vous ne dites pas que je m'engage insensiblement chaque jour à recevoir de trop grands témoignages de votre passion? J'ai beau me défendre des choses, vous 10 fatiguez ma résistance et vous avez une civile opiniâtreté qui me fait venir doucement à tout ce qu'il vous plaît. Les visites fréquentes ont commencé; les déclarations sont venues ensuite, qui après elles ont traîné[3] les sérénades et les cadeaux[4], que les présents ont suivi. Je me suis opposée à tout cela, mais 15 vous ne vous rebutez point, et pied à pied vous gagnez mes résolutions[5]. Pour moi, je ne puis plus répondre de rien, et je crois qu'à la fin vous me feriez venir au mariage, dont je me suis tant éloignée.

DORANTE. — Ma foi, madame, vous y devriez déjà être. 20 Vous êtes veuve, et ne dépendez que de vous. Je suis maître de moi et vous aime plus que ma vie. A quoi tient-il que dès aujourd'hui vous ne fassiez tout mon bonheur?

---

1. *Tout à l'heure* : voir page 60, note 2; 2. *Ici* : en ce moment; 3. *Traîner* : ici, entraîner; 4. *Cadeau* : voir page 71, note 3; 5. Vous l'emportez sur mes résolutions.

■■■ QUESTIONS ■■■

50. SUR LES SCÈNES XV, XVI ET XVII. — Pourquoi Molière fait-il revenir Monsieur Jourdain après l'avoir fait sortir à la fin de la scène XIV? et pourquoi le fait-il sortir de nouveau? Quel artifice apparaît ici dans le mécanisme de l'action?

51. La première impression produite par Dorimène : quel est alors le sentiment du spectateur?

DORIMÈNE. — Mon Dieu, Dorante, il faut des deux parts
bien des qualités pour vivre heureusement ensemble; et les deux
25 plus raisonnables personnes du monde ont souvent peine à
composer une union dont ils soient satisfaits.

DORANTE. — Vous vous moquez, madame, de vous y figurer
tant de difficultés; et l'expérience que vous avez faite ne conclut
rien pour tous les autres.

30 DORIMÈNE. — Enfin j'en reviens toujours là. Les dépenses
que je vous vois faire pour moi m'inquiètent par deux raisons :
l'une, qu'elles m'engagent plus que je ne voudrais; et l'autre,
que je suis sûre, sans vous déplaire, que vous ne les faites point
que vous ne vous incommodiez; et je ne veux point cela.

35 DORANTE. — Ah! madame, ce sont des bagatelles, et ce n'est
pas par là...

DORIMÈNE. — Je sais ce que je dis; et entre autres le diamant
que vous m'avez forcé à prendre est d'un prix...

DORANTE. — Eh! madame, de grâce, ne faites point tant
40 valoir une chose que mon amour trouve indigne de vous,
et souffrez... Voici le maître du logis. **(52)**

Scène XIX. — MONSIEUR JOURDAIN,
DORIMÈNE, DORANTE.

MONSIEUR JOURDAIN, *après avoir fait deux révérences, se
trouvant trop près de Dorimène.* — Un peu plus loin, madame.

DORIMÈNE. — Comment?

MONSIEUR JOURDAIN. — Un pas, s'il vous plaît.

45 DORIMÈNE. — Quoi donc?

MONSIEUR JOURDAIN. — Reculez un peu pour la troisième.

DORANTE. — Madame, monsieur Jourdain sait son monde.

──────── **QUESTIONS** ────────

52. SUR L'ENSEMBLE DE LA SCÈNE XVIII. — Les révélations inattendues
de cette scène : rappelez-vous l'entretien confidentiel de Dorante et de
Monsieur Jourdain à la scène VI de ce même acte III. A quel jeu se livre
Dorante? Qu'y a-t-il d'inquiétant dans le personnage? Son amour pour
Dorimène semble-t-il sincère?

— Le caractère de Dorimène : montrez que chacune de ses répliques
met en évidence un aspect de sa personnalité. Est-elle sympathique?
Connaissez-vous dans le théâtre de Molière d'autres caractères féminins
du même genre?

MONSIEUR JOURDAIN. — Madame, ce m'est une gloire bien
grande de me voir assez fortuné pour être si heureux que
10 d'avoir le bonheur que vous ayez eu la bonté de m'accorder
la grâce de me faire l'honneur de m'honorer de la faveur
de votre présence ; et, si j'avais aussi le mérite pour mériter
un mérite comme le vôtre, et que le ciel... envieux de mon
bien... m'eût accordé... l'avantage de me voir digne... des... **(53)**

15 DORANTE. — Monsieur Jourdain, en voilà assez ; madame
n'aime pas les grands compliments, et elle sait que vous êtes
homme d'esprit. *(Bas à Dorimène.)* C'est un bon bourgeois
assez ridicule, comme vous voyez, dans toutes ses manières.

DORIMÈNE, *de même.* — Il n'est pas malaisé de s'en apercevoir.

20 DORANTE, *haut.* — Madame, voilà le meilleur de mes amis.

MONSIEUR JOURDAIN. — C'est trop d'honneur que vous me
faites.

DORANTE. — Galant homme tout à fait.

DORIMÈNE. — J'ai beaucoup d'estime pour lui.

25 MONSIEUR JOURDAIN. — Je n'ai rien fait encore, madame,
pour mériter cette grâce.

DORANTE, *bas à M. Jourdain.* — Prenez bien garde, au moins,
à ne lui point parler du diamant que vous lui avez donné.

MONSIEUR JOURDAIN, *bas à Dorante.* — Ne pourrais-je pas
30 seulement lui demander comment elle le trouve ?

DORANTE, *bas à M. Jourdain.* — Comment ? gardez-vous-en
bien. Cela serait vilain[1] à vous ; et, pour agir en galant homme,
il faut que vous fassiez comme si ce n'était pas vous qui lui
eussiez fait ce présent. *(Haut.)* Monsieur Jourdain, madame,
35 dit qu'il est ravi de vous voir chez lui.

DORIMÈNE. — Il m'honore beaucoup.

MONSIEUR JOURDAIN, *bas à Dorante.* — Que je vous suis
obligé, monsieur, de lui parler ainsi pour moi !

---

1. *Vilain :* vulgaire, digne d'un roturier (s'oppose à *galant homme*).

--- **QUESTIONS** ---

53. Par comparaison avec la scène précédente, quel effet produit la
rentrée de Monsieur Jourdain ? Pourquoi est-il plus grotesque encore
qu'à l'accoutumée ? Comment se sert-il des leçons de savoir-vivre qu'il a
prises le matin même ? Comparez cette réception à celle de Mariane pour
Harpagon dans *l'Avare* (III, v) : qu'y a-t-il de commun entre les deux
situations ?

DORANTE, *bas à M. Jourdain*. — J'ai eu une peine effroyable
40 à la faire venir ici.

MONSIEUR JOURDAIN, *bas à Dorante*. — Je ne sais quelles
grâces vous en rendre.

DORANTE. — Il dit madame, qu'il vous trouve la plus belle
personne du monde.

45 DORIMÈNE. — C'est bien de la grâce qu'il me fait.

MONSIEUR JOURDAIN. — Madame, c'est vous qui faites les
grâces, et... **(54)**

DORANTE. — Songeons à manger. **(55)**

Scène XX. — MONSIEUR JOURDAIN, DORIMÈNE, DORANTE, UN LAQUAIS.

LAQUAIS, *à M. Jourdain*. — Tout est prêt, monsieur.

DORANTE. — Allons donc nous mettre à table, et qu'on
fasse venir les musiciens.

*(Six cuisiniers qui ont préparé le festin dansent ensemble
et font le troisième intermède ; après quoi ils apportent une
table couverte de plusieurs mets.)* **(56)**

――――― **QUESTIONS** ―――――

54. Le comique de situation : comment Dorante doit-il mener son jeu
à l'égard de Dorimène ? à l'égard de Monsieur Jourdain ? Montrez que
la stupidité de Monsieur Jourdain ne rend pas à Dorante la tâche trop
difficile. Quelle est la réplique qui révèle le mieux la sotte naïveté de
Monsieur Jourdain ?

55. SUR L'ENSEMBLE DE LA SCÈNE XIX. — Importance de cette scène pour
l'action ; attendait-on depuis longtemps cette rencontre entre Monsieur
Jourdain et la « belle marquise » ? Pourquoi est-elle plus comique encore
qu'on ne pouvait l'imaginer ?

— Monsieur Jourdain amoureux : comment Molière adapte-t-il à son
personnage certains traits traditionnels du barbon amoureux ?

56. SUR L'ENSEMBLE DE L'ACTE III. — Composition de cet acte : la
progression de l'action ; le développement parallèle de deux problèmes
(l'intrigue de Monsieur Jourdain avec Dorimène, le mariage de Lucile).

— La comédie du dépit amoureux (scènes VIII et X) est-elle tout à fait
inutile ? Comment connaîtrait-on Cléonte et Covielle si Molière n'avait
pas étoffé ainsi un peu leurs rôles ?

— Monsieur Jourdain en famille : fait-il aussi bonne figure à l'acte III
qu'aux deux premiers actes ? Comment ses ridicules s'accentuent-ils en
présence de ceux qui le narguent (Madame Jourdain, Nicole) ou qui le
dupent (Dorante) ?

— Étudiez les personnages de Dorante et de Madame Jourdain.

ACTE IV

Scène première. — DORANTE, DORIMÈNE,
MONSIEUR JOURDAIN, DEUX MUSICIENS,
UNE MUSICIENNE, LAQUAIS.

DORIMÈNE. — Comment, Dorante, voilà un repas tout à fait magnifique[1]!

MONSIEUR JOURDAIN. — Vous vous moquez, madame, et je voudrais qu'il fût plus digne de vous être offert. (*Tous se mettent à table.*)

DORANTE. — Monsieur Jourdain a raison, madame, de parler de la sorte, et il m'oblige de vous faire si bien les honneurs de chez lui. Je demeure d'accord avec lui que le repas n'est pas digne de vous. Comme c'est moi qui l'ai ordonné, et que je n'ai pas sur cette matière les lumières de nos amis, vous n'avez pas ici un repas fort savant, et vous y trouverez des incongruités[2] de bonne chère et des barbarismes[3] de bon goût. Si Damis s'en était mêlé, tout serait dans les règles; il y aurait partout de l'élégance et de l'érudition, et il ne manquerait pas de vous exagérer lui-même toutes les pièces du repas qu'il vous donnerait, et de vous faire tomber d'accord de sa haute capacité dans la science des bons morceaux; de vous parler d'un pain de rive[4], à biseau doré, relevé de croûte partout, croquant tendrement sous la dent; d'un vin à sève veloutée, armé d'un vert qui n'est point trop commandant[5], d'un carré de mouton gourmandé de persil[6]; d'une longe de veau de rivière[7] longue comme cela, blanche, délicate, et qui sous les dents est une vraie pâte d'amande, de perdrix relevées d'un fumet surprenant; et, pour son opéra[8], d'une soupe à bouillon perlé[9] soutenue d'un jeune gros dindon cantonné[10] de pigeonneaux et couronné d'oignons blancs mariés avec la

---

1. *Magnifique* : somptueux; 2. *Incongruité* : au propre, faute contre la grammaire; l'application de termes de grammaire à la cuisine faisait partie du jargon précieux; 3. *Barbarisme* : faute contre la pureté de la langue; 4. *Pain de rive* : pain cuit sur le bord du four, donc également de tous côtés; 5. Ayant un goût de vin nouveau (le vert) qui ne soit pas trop prononcé; 6. Deux sens possibles : dont le goût est corrigé par celui du persil, ou rendu appétissant par le persil; 7. Veau de Normandie, élevé dans les prairies qui bordent la Seine ou d'autres rivières; 8. Comme chef-d'œuvre; 9. *Soupe à bouillon perlé* : bouillon de viande avec des tranches de pain (soupe) et qui, jeté dans l'eau froide, y forme comme des perles; 10. *Cantonné* : garni aux quatre coins (terme de blason).

chicorée[1]. Mais, pour moi, je vous avoue mon ignorance; et, comme monsieur Jourdain a fort bien dit, je voudrais que le repas fût plus digne de vous être offert. **(1)**

30 DORIMÈNE. — Je ne réponds à ce compliment qu'en mangeant comme je fais.

MONSIEUR JOURDAIN. — Ah! que voilà de belles mains!

DORIMÈNE. — Les mains sont médiocres, monsieur Jourdain; mais vous voulez parler du diamant, qui est fort beau.

35 MONSIEUR JOURDAIN. — Moi, madame! Dieu me garde d'en vouloir parler : ce ne serait pas agir en galant homme, et le diamant est fort peu de chose.

DORIMÈNE. — Vous êtes bien dégoûté.

MONSIEUR JOURDAIN. — Vous avez trop de bonté... **(2)**

40 DORANTE, *après avoir fait signe à M. Jourdain*. — Allons, qu'on donne du vin à monsieur Jourdain et à ces messieurs, qui nous feront la grâce de nous chanter un air à boire.

DORIMÈNE. — C'est merveilleusement assaisonner la bonne chère que d'y mêler la musique, et je me vois ici admirable-
45 ment régalée.

MONSIEUR JOURDAIN. — Madame, ce n'est pas...

DORANTE. — Monsieur Jourdain, prêtons silence à ces messieurs; ce qu'ils nous diront vaudra mieux que tout ce que nous pourrions dire. **(3)**

(Les musiciens et la musicienne prennent des verres, chantent deux chansons à boire, et sont soutenus de toute la symphonie[2].)

---

1. L'oignon, qui était alors un mets aristocratique, se servait farci avec de la chicorée; 2. *Symphonie :* voir page 55, note 2.

■■■■■■ **QUESTIONS** ■■■■■■

1. Pourquoi cette longue digression sur les raffinements culinaires? On propose pour explication la nécessité pour Dorante d'empêcher le plus possible Monsieur Jourdain de parler, le désir de Molière de glisser ici un tableau de mœurs, ou simplement l'idée de donner un aperçu du menu servi le jour même à la table du roi. Ces explications sont-elles d'ailleurs incompatibles?

2. Analysez les cinq dernières répliques en montrant quelles sont, à chacune d'elles, les intentions de Dorimène et de Monsieur Jourdain. Pourquoi cette situation est-elle un moment du plus haut comique pour le spectateur? Serait-il possible que Monsieur Jourdain et Dorimène découvrent la vérité sur le diamant? Comment le malentendu se prolonge-t-il?

3. Les divertissements musicaux sont adroitement liés à l'action. Pourquoi?

PREMIÈRE CHANSON À BOIRE

(1ᵉʳ et 2ᵉ musicien ensemble, un verre à la main.)

50 Un petit doigt, Philis, pour commencer le tour;
Ah! qu'un verre en vos mains a d'agréables charmes!
Vous et le vin, vous vous prêtez des armes,
Et je sens pour tous deux redoubler mon amour :
55 Entre lui, vous et moi, jurons, jurons, ma belle,
Une ardeur éternelle.

Qu'en mouillant votre bouche il en reçoit d'attraits,
Et que l'on voit par lui votre bouche embellie!
Ah! l'un de l'autre ils me donnent envie,
Et de vous et de lui je m'enivre à longs traits :
60 Entre lui, vous, et moi, jurons, jurons, ma belle,
Une ardeur éternelle.

SECONDE CHANSON À BOIRE
(2ᵉ et 3ᵉ musicien ensemble.)

Buvons, chers amis, buvons.
Le temps qui fuit nous y convie;
Profitons de la vie
65 Autant que nous pouvons :
Quand on a passé l'onde noire[1]
Adieu le bon vin, nos amours;
Dépêchons-nous de boire,
On ne boit pas toujours.

70 Laissons raisonner les sots
Sur le vrai bonheur de la vie;
Notre philosophie
Le met parmi les pots :
Les biens, le savoir et la gloire
75 N'ôtent point les soucis fâcheux.
Et ce n'est qu'à bien boire
Que l'on peut être heureux.

(Tous trois ensemble.)

Sus, sus, du vin, partout versez, garçons, versez,
Versez, versez toujours tant qu[2]'on vous dise assez.

80 DORIMÈNE. — Je ne crois pas qu'on puisse mieux chanter,
et cela est tout à fait beau.

_____

1. *L'onde noire* du Styx, fleuve des Enfers; 2. *Tant que :* jusqu'à ce que.

MONSIEUR JOURDAIN. — Je vois encore ici, madame, quelque chose de plus beau.

85 DORIMÈNE. — Ouais[1]! monsieur Jourdain est galant plus que je ne pensais. *MS is a little more galant than I thought*

DORANTE. — Comment! madame, pour qui prenez-vous monsieur Jourdain?

MONSIEUR JOURDAIN. — Je voudrais bien qu'elle me prît pour ce que je dirais.

90 DORIMÈNE. — Encore!

DORANTE, *à Dorimène*. — Vous ne le connaissez pas.

MONSIEUR JOURDAIN. — Elle me connaîtra quand il lui plaira. **(4)**

DORIMÈNE. — Oh! je le quitte[2].

95 DORANTE. — Il est homme qui a toujours la riposte en main. Mais vous ne voyez pas que monsieur Jourdain, madame, mange tous les morceaux que vous touchez[3]?

DORIMÈNE. — Monsieur Jourdain est un homme qui me ravit...

100 MONSIEUR JOURDAIN. — Si je pouvais ravir votre cœur, je serais... **(5)**

SCÈNE II. — MADAME JOURDAIN, MONSIEUR JOURDAIN, DORIMÈNE, DORANTE, MUSICIENS, MUSICIENNE, LAQUAIS.

au milieu de la fête

fervente

MADAME JOURDAIN. — Ah! ah! je trouve ici bonne compagnie, et je vois bien qu'on ne m'y attendait pas. C'est donc pour cette belle affaire-ci, monsieur mon mari, que vous avez eu tant d'empressement à m'envoyer dîner chez ma sœur?

---

1. Exclamation qui peut marquer l'étonnement ou l'inquiétude, mais qui n'a rien de trivial; **2.** J'y renonce; **3.** Dorimène se sert évidemment la première et peut, selon les usages du temps, choisir ses morceaux; ce sont ceux qu'elle a laissés que mangera Monsieur Jourdain.

--- **QUESTIONS** ---

4. Appréciez la galanterie de Monsieur Jourdain lorsqu'il se met en peine de faire de lui-même des compliments.

5. SUR L'ENSEMBLE DE LA SCÈNE PREMIÈRE. — Montrez que cette scène prolonge la dernière scène de l'acte précédent : quel est l'effet comique qui en fait toute la saveur?

— Le jeu de Dorante : comment empêche-t-il aussi bien Dorimène que Monsieur Jourdain de découvrir la vérité? Quel effet de comique de répétition est ici utilisé?

5 Je viens de voir un théâtre là-bas[1], et je vois ici un banquet
à faire noces[2]. Voilà comme vous dépensez votre bien, et
c'est ainsi que vous festinez les dames en mon absence, et
que vous leur donnez la musique et la comédie tandis que
vous m'envoyez promener. **(6)**

10 DORANTE. — Que voulez-vous dire, madame Jourdain? et
quelles fantaisies[3] sont les vôtres de vous aller mettre en tête
que votre mari dépense son bien, et que c'est lui qui donne
ce régale[4] à madame? Apprenez que c'est moi, je vous prie;
qu'il ne fait seulement que me prêter sa maison, et que vous
15 devriez un peu mieux regarder aux choses que vous dites.

MONSIEUR JOURDAIN. — Oui, impertinente, c'est monsieur
le comte qui donne tout ceci à madame, qui est une personne
de qualité. Il me fait l'honneur de prendre ma maison, et de
vouloir que je sois avec lui.

20 MADAME JOURDAIN. — Ce sont des chansons que cela; je sais
ce que je sais.

DORANTE. — Prenez, madame Jourdain, prenez de meilleures
lunettes.

MADAME JOURDAIN. — Je n'ai que faire de lunettes, monsieur,
25 et je vois assez clair; il y a longtemps que je sens les choses,
et je ne suis pas une bête. Cela est fort vilain[5] à vous pour un
grand seigneur, de prêter la main, comme vous faites, aux
sottises de mon mari. Et vous, madame, pour une grand'dame,
cela n'est ni beau ni honnête à vous de mettre de la dissension
30 dans un ménage et de souffrir que mon mari soit amoureux
de vous. **(7)**

---

1. *Là-bas* : en bas. Il s'agit du théâtre dressé pour le ballet; 2. Propre à célébrer
des noces; 3. *Fantaisies* : vaines imaginations; 4. *Régale* : orthographe alors courante
pour « régal »; 5. *Vilain* : voir page 91, note 1.

───────── QUESTIONS ─────────

6. La scène précédente pouvait-elle encore se poursuivre longtemps
sans que Dorante soit en situation difficile? Cette intervention de Madame
Jourdain est-elle un véritable coup de théâtre (voir la fin de la scène VI
de l'acte III)? — Quels traits de caractère de Madame Jourdain reparaissent
ici? Bien que ses reproches soient justifiés, faut-il l'approuver de venir
faire ainsi un scandale? Quel contraste y a-t-il entre sa façon d'agir et
le savoir-vivre que veulent adopter son mari?

7. C'est Dorante, et non Monsieur Jourdain, qui réplique immédiatement à Madame Jourdain : pourquoi cette hâte? Comment tire-t-il parti
d'une situation gênante? Pourquoi Monsieur Jourdain ne peut-il que lui
faire écho?

DORIMÈNE. — Que veut donc dire tout ceci? Allez, Dorante, vous vous moquez, de m'exposer aux sottes visions[1] de cette extravagante.

35 DORANTE, *suivant Dorimène qui sort.* — Madame, holà! madame, où courez-vous?

MONSIEUR JOURDAIN. — Madame! monsieur le comte, faites-lui excuses, et tâchez de la ramener. (8)

SCÈNE III. — MADAME JOURDAIN, MONSIEUR JOURDAIN, UN LAQUAIS.

MONSIEUR JOURDAIN. — Ah! impertinente que vous êtes, voilà de vos beaux faits; vous me venez faire des affronts devant tout le monde, et vous chassez de chez moi des personnes de qualité.

5 MADAME JOURDAIN. — Je me moque de leur qualité.

MONSIEUR JOURDAIN. — Je ne sais qui[2] me tient, maudite, que je ne vous fende la tête avec les pièces du repas que vous êtes venu troubler. *(On ôte la table.)*

MADAME JOURDAIN, *sortant.* — Je me moque de cela. Ce
10 sont mes droits que je défends, et j'aurai pour moi toutes les femmes.

MONSIEUR JOURDAIN. — Vous faites bien d'éviter ma colère. (9)

SCÈNE IV. — MONSIEUR JOURDAIN, *seul.*

MONSIEUR JOURDAIN. — Elle est arrivée là bien malheureusement. J'étais en humeur de dire de jolies choses et jamais je ne m'étais senti tant d'esprit. Qu'est-ce que c'est que cela? (10)

---

1. *Visions :* idées folles ou suppositions ridicules; 2. *Qui :* ce qui. *Qui* pronom interrogatif peut, dans la langue du XVIIᵉ siècle, s'appliquer aux choses.

———— QUESTIONS ————

8. SUR L'ENSEMBLE DE LA SCÈNE II. — Une situation traditionnelle (une femme découvre son mari en galante compagnie) : comment Molière donne-t-il un relief nouveau à une telle scène?

— Que peut penser Dorimène de l'aventure? Dorante s'est-il déconsidéré à ses yeux?

9. SUR LA SCÈNE III. — Aurait-il été amusant de développer davantage cette scène de ménage?

10. SUR LA SCÈNE IV. — La colère de Monsieur Jourdain dure-t-elle longtemps? Montrez que sa vanité le console de ses déboires.

FRONTISPICE DE L'ÉDITION DE 1682

Phot. Larousse.

DÉCOR DE
SUZANNE
LALIQUE
À LA
COMÉDIE-
FRANÇAISE
(1955)

Phot. Bernand.

Scène V. — COVIELLE, *déguisé,*
MONSIEUR JOURDAIN, LAQUAIS.

COVIELLE. — Monsieur, je ne sais pas si j'ai l'honneur d'être connu de vous?

MONSIEUR JOURDAIN. — Non, monsieur.

COVIELLE, *étendant la main à un pied de terre.* — Je vous ai
5 vu que vous n'étiez pas plus grand que cela.

MONSIEUR JOURDAIN. — Moi?

COVIELLE. — Oui. Vous étiez le plus bel enfant du monde, et toutes les dames vous prenaient dans leurs bras pour vous baiser.

10 MONSIEUR JOURDAIN. — Pour me baiser?

COVIELLE. — Oui. J'étais grand ami de feu monsieur votre père[1].

MONSIEUR JOURDAIN. — De feu monsieur mon père?

COVIELLE. — Oui. C'était un fort honnête gentilhomme.

15 MONSIEUR JOURDAIN. — Comment dites-vous?

COVIELLE. — Je dis que c'était un fort honnête gentilhomme.

MONSIEUR JOURDAIN. — Mon père?

COVIELLE. — Oui.

MONSIEUR JOURDAIN. — Vous l'avez fort connu?

20 COVIELLE. — Assurément.

MONSIEUR JOURDAIN. — Et vous l'avez connu pour gentilhomme?

COVIELLE. — Sans doute.

MONSIEUR JOURDAIN. — Je ne sais donc pas comment le
25 monde est fait.

COVIELLE. — Comment?

MONSIEUR JOURDAIN. — Il y a de sottes gens qui me veulent dire qu'il a été marchand.

COVIELLE. — Lui, marchand! C'est pure médisance, il ne
30 l'a jamais été. Tout ce qu'il faisait, c'est qu'il était fort obligeant, fort officieux[2], et, comme il se connaissait fort bien

---

1. Dans *Monsieur de Pourceaugnac*, Sbrigani emploie une ruse comparable; **2.** *Officieux :* qui aime à rendre service.

en étoffes, il en allait choisir de tous les côtés, les faisait apporter chez lui, et en donnait à ses amis pour de l'argent.

MONSIEUR JOURDAIN. — Je suis ravi de vous connaître, afin
35 que vous rendiez ce témoignage-là que mon père était gentilhomme.

COVIELLE. — Je le soutiendrai devant tout le monde. **(11)** *I will stand to his being noble not a merchant*

MONSIEUR JOURDAIN. — Vous m'obligerez. Quel sujet vous amène?

40 COVIELLE. — Depuis avoir connu feu monsieur votre père, honnête gentilhomme, comme je vous ai dit, j'ai voyagé par tout le monde.

MONSIEUR JOURDAIN. — Par tout le monde!

COVIELLE. — Oui.

45 MONSIEUR JOURDAIN. — Je pense qu'il y a bien loin en ce pays-là.

COVIELLE. — Assurément. Je ne suis revenu de tous mes longs voyages que depuis quatre jours; et, par l'intérêt que je prends à tout ce qui vous touche, je viens vous annoncer
50 la meilleure nouvelle du monde.

MONSIEUR JOURDAIN. — Quelle?

COVIELLE. — Vous savez que le fils du Grand Turc est ici?

MONSIEUR JOURDAIN. — Moi? non.

COVIELLE. — Comment! Il a un train[1] tout à fait magnifique :
55 tout le monde le va voir, et il a été reçu en ce pays comme un seigneur d'importance.

MONSIEUR JOURDAIN. — Par ma foi, je ne savais pas cela.

COVIELLE. — Ce qu'il y a d'avantageux pour vous, c'est qu'il est amoureux de votre fille.

60 MONSIEUR JOURDAIN. — Le fils du Grand Turc?

COVIELLE. — Oui; et il veut être votre gendre.

MONSIEUR JOURDAIN. — Mon gendre, le fils du Grand Turc?

wants to be son in law

1. *Un train :* un cortège, une escorte.

———————— QUESTIONS ————————

11. Comparez cette entrée en matière de Covielle avec la façon dont Éraste aborde Monsieur de Pourceaugnac (*Monsieur de Pourceaugnac*, I, IV). Pourquoi Monsieur Jourdain est-il pris au piège encore plus vite que Pourceaugnac?

COVIELLE. — Le fils du Grand Turc votre gendre. Comme
je le fus voir, et que j'entends parfaitement sa langue, il s'entre-
65 tint avec moi; et, après quelques autres discours, il me dit :
*Acciam croc soler ouch alla moustaph gidelum amanahem varahini
oussere carbulath*[1]. C'est-à-dire : « N'as-tu point vu une jeune
belle personne qui est la fille de monsieur Jourdain, gentilhomme parisien? »

70 MONSIEUR JOURDAIN. — Le fils du Grand Turc dit cela de
moi? **(12)**

COVIELLE. — Oui. Comme je lui eus répondu que je vous
connaissais particulièrement et que j'avais vu votre fille : « Ah!
me dit-il, *Marababa sahem* »; c'est-à-dire : « Ah! que je suis
75 amoureux d'elle! »

MONSIEUR JOURDAIN. — *Marababa sahem* veut dire : Ah!
que je suis amoureux d'elle?

COVIELLE. — Oui.

MONSIEUR JOURDAIN. — Par ma foi, vous faites bien de me
80 le dire, car, pour moi, je n'aurais jamais cru que ce *Marababa
sahem* eût voulu dire : Ah! que je suis amoureux d'elle! Voilà
une langue admirable que ce turc!

COVIELLE. — Plus admirable qu'on ne peut croire. Savez-
vous bien ce que veut dire *Cacaracamouchen?*

85 MONSIEUR JOURDAIN. — *Cacaracamouchen?* Non.

COVIELLE. — C'est-à-dire : Ma chère âme.

MONSIEUR JOURDAIN. — *Cacaracamouchen* veut dire : Ma
chère âme?

COVIELLE. — Oui.

90 MONSIEUR JOURDAIN. — Voilà qui est merveilleux! *Cacaracamouchen*, ma chère âme : dirait-on jamais cela? Voilà qui me
confond. **(13)**

COVIELLE. — Enfin, pour achever mon ambassade, il vient

1. Molière emprunte la plupart des mots de ce jargon à une comédie de Rotrou,
la Sœur (III, v et vi); à quelques exceptions près, ils n'ont aucun sens.

─────── QUESTIONS ───────

12. Monsieur Jourdain songe-t-il beaucoup à ce que pourrait penser
sa fille de ce mariage? Est-ce la première fois qu'on voit cet égoïsme,
conséquence de sa vanité?
13. Les étonnements de Monsieur Jourdain : comparez ce passage à la
scène iv de l'acte II.

vous demander votre fille en mariage; et pour avoir un beau-
95 père qui soit digne de lui, il veut vous faire *Mamamouchi*,
qui est une certaine grande dignité de son pays.

MONSIEUR JOURDAIN. — *Mamamouchi*[1]?

COVIELLE. — Oui, *Mamamouchi*; c'est-à-dire, en notre langue,
paladin. Paladin[2], ce sont de ces anciens... Paladin enfin!
100 Il n'y a rien de plus noble que cela dans le monde; et vous
irez de pair avec les plus grands seigneurs de la terre.

MONSIEUR JOURDAIN. — Le fils du Grand Turc m'honore
beaucoup, et je vous prie de me mener chez lui pour lui en
faire mes remerciements.

105 COVIELLE. — Comment! le voilà qui va venir ici.

MONSIEUR JOURDAIN. — Il va venir ici?

COVIELLE. — Oui; et il amène toutes choses pour la cérémonie
de votre dignité.

MONSIEUR JOURDAIN. — Voilà qui est bien prompt. **(14)**

110 COVIELLE. — Son amour ne peut souffrir aucun retardement[3].

MONSIEUR JOURDAIN. — Tout ce qui m'embarrasse ici, c'est
que ma fille est une opiniâtre qui s'est allé mettre dans la tête
un certain Cléonte, et elle jure de n'épouser personne que
celui-là.

115 COVIELLE. — Elle changera de sentiment quand elle verra
le fils du Grand Turc; et puis il se rencontre ici une aventure
merveilleuse : c'est que le fils du Grand Turc ressemble à ce
Cléonte, à peu de chose près. Je viens de le voir, on me l'a
montré; et l'amour qu'elle a pour l'un pourra passer aisément
120 à l'autre, et... Je l'entends venir; le voilà. **(15)**

---

1. Littré prétend que ce mot, forgé par Molière sur l'arabe *mà menou schi* (non
chose bonne), signifie « propre à rien ». Cette intention n'est pas évidente; 2. *Paladin :* seigneur de la cour de Charlemagne; 3. *Retardement* est couramment employé
pour « retard » au XVIIe siècle.

────── **QUESTIONS** ──────

14. Montrez que cette réplique devance une objection du spectateur.

15. SUR L'ENSEMBLE DE LA SCÈNE V. — Les sources du comique dans
cette scène : montrez que celle-ci sert de transition pour passer de la
comédie à la farce.

— Admet-on aisément que la sottise et la naïveté de Monsieur Jourdain soient telles qu'il ne voie nulle malice aux propositions surprenantes
de ce personnage de carnaval?

— Le sentiment du spectateur : a-t-il été prévenu (voir acte III,
scène XIII)? Prévoyait-il un tour aussi original?

Scène VI. — CLÉONTE, *en turc,*
avec trois pages portant sa veste,
MONSIEUR JOURDAIN, COVIELLE, *déguisé.*

CLÉONTE. — *Ambousahim oqui boraf, Jordina, salamalequi*[1].

COVIELLE, *à M. Jourdain.* — C'est-à-dire : « Monsieur Jourdain, votre cœur soit toute l'année comme un rosier fleuri. » Ce sont façons de parler obligeantes de ces pays-là.

5 MONSIEUR JOURDAIN. — Je suis très humble serviteur de Son Altesse Turque.

COVIELLE. — *Carigar camboto oustin moraf.*

CLÉONTE. — *Oustin yoc catamalequi basum base alla moran.*

COVIELLE. — Il dit que le ciel vous donne la force des lions
10 et la prudence des serpents. *parle des images d'animaux*

MONSIEUR JOURDAIN. — Son Altesse Turque m'honore trop, et je lui souhaite toutes sortes de prospérités.

COVIELLE. — *Ossa binamen sadoc babally oracaf ouram.*

CLÉONTE. — *Bel-men*[2].

15 COVIELLE. — Il dit que vous alliez vite avec lui vous préparer pour la cérémonie, afin de voir ensuite votre fille et de conclure le mariage.

MONSIEUR JOURDAIN. — Tant de choses en deux mots?

COVIELLE. — Oui; la langue turque est comme cela, elle dit
20 beaucoup en peu de paroles. Allez vite où il souhaite. **(16)**

Scène VII. — COVIELLE, *seul.*

COVIELLE. — Ha! ha! ha! Ma foi, cela est tout à fait drôle. Quelle dupe! Quand il aurait appris son rôle par cœur, il ne pourrait pas le mieux jouer. Ah! ah!

complètement dupe

1. *Salamalequi :* expression de salutation turque (« que la paix soit sur ta tête »), dont on a fait *salamalec,* profonde révérence; 2. Du turc *bil men :* « je ne sais pas ».

━━━━━━━ **QUESTIONS** ━━━━━━━

16. Sur la scène VI. — Comment cette scène complète-t-elle la précédente?
— Le comique de mots : est-ce seulement le caractère burlesque du jargon qui fait rire? La parodie de la politesse orientale.

Scène VIII. — DORANTE, COVIELLE.

COVIELLE. — Je vous prie, monsieur, de nous vouloir aider céans[1] dans une affaire qui s'y passe.

DORANTE. — Ah! ah! Covielle, qui t'aurait reconnu? Comme te voilà ajusté!

5 COVIELLE. — Vous voyez. Ah! ah!

DORANTE. — De quoi ris-tu?

COVIELLE. — D'une chose, monsieur, qui le mérite bien.

DORANTE. — Comment?

COVIELLE. — Je vous le donnerais en bien des fois[2], monsieur,
10 à deviner le stratagème dont nous nous servons auprès de monsieur Jourdain pour porter son esprit à donner sa fille à mon maître.

DORANTE. — Je ne devine point le stratagème, mais je devine qu'il ne manquera pas de faire son effet, puisque tu l'entre-
15 prends.

COVIELLE. — Je sais, monsieur, que la bête vous est connue[3].

DORANTE. — Apprends-moi ce que c'est.

COVIELLE. — Prenez la peine de vous tirer un peu plus loin pour faire place à ce que j'aperçois venir. Vous pourrez voir
20 une partie de l'histoire, tandis que je vous conterai le reste. (17)

(La cérémonie turque pour ennoblir le Bourgeois se fait en danse et en musique, et compose le quatrième intermède.)

1. *Céans* : voir page 36, note 5; 2. Pour cette expression, voir page 53, note 3;
3. Je vois que vous me connaissez bien (expression populaire).

——— QUESTIONS ———

17. SUR LA SCÈNE VIII. — Était-il indispensable que Dorante soit mis au courant du stratagème?

LA CÉRÉMONIE TURQUE

LE MUFTI[1], TURCS, DERVIS[2], *chantant et dansant,*
MONSIEUR JOURDAIN, *vêtu à la turque, la tête rasée,*
sans turban et sans sabre.

PREMIÈRE ENTRÉE DE BALLET

Six Turcs entrent gravement, deux à deux, au son des instruments.
Ils portent trois tapis, qu'ils lèvent fort haut, après en avoir fait, en
dansant, plusieurs figures. Les Turcs chantant passent par-dessous ces
tapis, pour s'aller ranger aux deux côtés du théâtre. Le Mufti, accom-
pagné des Dervis, ferme cette marche.
Les Turcs étendent les tapis par terre et se mettent dessus à genoux.
Le Mufti et les Dervis restent debout au milieu d'eux ; et pendant que
le Mufti invoque Mahomet, en faisant beaucoup de contorsions et de
grimaces, sans proférer une seule parole, les Turcs assistants se pros-
ternent jusqu'à terre, chantant Alli, lèvent les bras au ciel en chantant
Alla ; ce qu'ils continuent jusqu'à la fin de l'évocation. Alors ils se
relèvent tous chantant Alla eckber («Dieu est grand») ; et deux Dervis
vont chercher Monsieur Jourdain.

Texte	**Traduction**
LE MUFTI, *à Monsieur Jourdain*	LE MUFTI
Se ti sabir[3],	*Si toi savoir,*
Ti respondir ;	*Toi répondre ;*
Se non sabir,	*Si ne pas savoir,*
Tazir, tazir.	*Te taire, te taire.*
Mi star mufti.	*Moi être mufti.*
Ti qui star, ti?	*Toi, qui être, toi?*
Non intendir?	*Pas entendre?*
Tazir, Tazir.	*Te taire, te taire.*

5

(Deux Dervis font retirer Monsieur Jourdain.)

LE MUFTI	LE MUFTI
Dice, Turque, qui star quista?	*Dis, Turc, qui être celui-là?*
Anabatista? Anabatista?	*Anabaptiste[4]? Anabaptiste?*

10

---

1. *Mufti* : dignitaire de la religion musulmane, spécialement chargé d'interpréter la loi coranique. Le rôle du mufti était tenu par Lully, qui, dans le livret du ballet, a pris le nom de « Chiacheron » (ital. *chiacchierone*, le bavard, le babillard) ; 2. *Dervis* : religieux musulmans ; 3. Ces couplets sont écrits en un jargon qu'on appelle justement *sabir*, mélange de français, d'italien, d'espagnol et d'arabe, qu'on parlait dans les ports méditerranéens d'Afrique du Nord et du Levant ; 4 *Anabaptiste* : une des sectes de la religion réformée ; elle prit naissance en Allemagne dès le temps de Luther.

LES TURCS

Ioc.

LE MUFTI

Zuinglista?

LES TURCS

Ioc.

LE MUFTI

Coffita?

LES TURCS

15 Ioc.

LE MUFTI

Hussita? Morista? Fronista?

LES TURCS

Ioc, ioc, ioc!

LE MUFTI

Ioc, ioc, ioc! Star Pagana?

LES TURCS

Ioc.

LE MUFTI

20 Luterana?

LES TURCS

Ioc.

LE MUFTI

Puritana?

LES TURCS

Ioc.

LE MUFTI

Bramina? Moffina? Zurina⁶?

LES TURCS

25 Ioc, ioc, ioc!

LE MUFTI

Ioc, ioc, ioc! Mahametana?
[Mahametana?

LES TURCS

Hi Valla. Hi Valla.

LES TURCS

Non.

LE MUFTI

Zwinglien¹?

LES TURCS

Non.

LE MUFTI

Cophte²?

LES TURCS

Non.

LE MUFTI

Hussite³? More? Phrontiste⁴?

LES TURCS

Non, non, non!

LE MUFTI

Non, non, non! Être païen?

LES TURCS

Non.

LE MUFTI

Luthérien?

LES TURCS

Non.

LE MUFTI

Puritain⁵?

LES TURCS

Non.

LE MUFTI

Bramine⁷? ...? ...?

LES TURCS

Non, non, non!

LE MUFTI

Non, non, non! Mahométan?
[*Mahométan?*

LES TURCS

Oui, par Dieu. Oui, par Dieu.

---

1. *Zwinglien* : membre de la secte réformée fondée par le Suisse Zwingle (1484-1531); 2. *Cophte* ou *copte* : chrétien d'Égypte ou d'Éthiopie; 3. *Hussite* : sectateur de Jean Huss (1369-1415), réformateur et patriote tchèque; 4. Ces deux termes semblent sans signification précise : le premier évoque sans doute les Mores musulmans; le second pourrait être une transcription approximative du mot grec *phrontistês*, qui signifie « penseur »; 5. *Puritain* : membre des sectes presbytériennes qui s'opposaient en Angleterre à la haute Église; 6. Ces deux derniers termes sont du jargon burlesque; 7. *Bramine* : de la religion hindoue (brahmanisme).

Phot. Lipnitzki.

LA CÉRÉMONIE TURQUE

Mise en scène de la Comédie-Française.

LE MUFTI
Como chamara? *(bis)*

LE MUFTI
Comment s'appelle-t-il? (bis)

LES TURCS
Giourdina. *(bis)*

LES TURCS
Jourdain. (bis)

LE MUFTI, *sautant et regardant de coté et d'autre.*

30 Giourdina? *(ter)*

Jourdain? (ter)

LES TURCS
Giourdina. *(ter)*

LES TURCS
Jourdain. (ter)

LE MUFTI
Mahameta, per Giourdina,
Mi pregar sera e matina.
Voler far un paladina
35 De Giourdina, de Giourdina.

LE MUFTI
Mahomet, pour Jourdain,
Moi prier soir et matin.
Vouloir faire un paladin
De Jourdain, de Jourdain.

Dar turbanta é dar scarcina,
Con galera é brigantina,
Per deffender Palestina.
Mahameta, per Giourdina
40 Mi pregar sera e matina.
(*Aux Turcs.*)
Star bon Turca, Giourdina?

Donner turban et donner sabre,
Avec galère et brigantine[1],
Pour défendre la Palestine.
Mahomet, pour Jourdain
Moi prier soir et matin.

Est-il bon Turc, Jourdain?

LES TURCS
Hi Valla; Hi Valla!

LES TURCS
Oui, par Dieu. Oui, par Dieu!

LE MUFTI, *chantant et dansant.*

Ha, la, ba, ba, la, chou,
ba, la, ba, ba, la, da.

(On peut comprendre :)
Dieu, mon père, mon père, Dieu.

LES TURCS
45 Ha, la, ba, ba, la, chou, ba, la, ba, ba, la, da.

DEUXIÈME ENTRÉE DE BALLET

Le Mufti revient coiffé avec son turban de cérémonie, qui est d'une grosseur démesurée, et garni de bougies allumées à quatre ou cinq rangs; il est accompagné de deux Dervis qui portent l'Alcoran[2] et qui ont des bonnets pointus, garnis aussi de bougies allumées.

Les deux autres Dervis amènent le Bourgeois, qui est tout épouvanté de cette cérémonie, et le font mettre à genoux, les mains par terre, de façon que son dos, sur lequel est mis l'Alcoran, serve de pupitre au Mufti. Le Mufti fait une seconde invocation burlesque, fronçant les sourcils et ouvrant la bouche, sans dire mot; puis parlant avec véhémence, tantôt radoucissant sa voix, tantôt la poussant d'un enthousiasme

---

1. *Brigantine* ou *brigantin* : navire à deux mâts, plus léger que la galère; ces deux sortes de bâtiments étaient employés surtout en Méditerranée; **2.** *Alcoran* ou *Coran* : livre sacré de la religion musulmane.

à faire trembler, se tenant les côtes avec les mains comme pour faire sortir les paroles, frappant de temps en temps sur l'Alcoran, et tournant les feuillets avec précipitation. Après quoi, en levant les bras au ciel, le Mufti crie à haute voix : Hou!

Pendant cette seconde invocation, les Turcs assistants s'inclinent trois fois et trois fois se relèvent, en chantant aussi : Hou, hou, hou.

MONSIEUR JOURDAIN, *après qu'on lui a ôté l'Alcoran de dessus le dos.*

Ouf!

danse ridicule

Texte	Traduction
LE MUFTI, *à Monsieur Jourdain.*	LE MUFTI
Ti non star furba?	*Toi, n'être pas fourbe?*
LES TURCS	LES TURCS
No, no, no!	*Non, non, non!*
LE MUFTI	LE MUFTI
Non star forfanta?	*N'être pas imposteur?*
LES TURCS	LES TURCS
No, no, no!	*Non, non, non!*
LE MUFTI	LE MUFTI
Donar turbanta. *(bis)*	*Donner turban.* (bis)
LES TURCS	LES TURCS
Ti non star furba?	*Toi, n'être pas fourbe?*
No, no, no.	*Non, non, non!*
Non star forfanta?	*N'être pas imposteur?*
No, no, no.	*Non, non, non!*
Donar turbanta. *(bis)*	*Donner turban.* (bis)

50

55

TROISIÈME ENTRÉE DE BALLET

Les Turcs, dansant et chantant, mettent le turban sur la tête de Monsieur Jourdain au son des instruments.

LE MUFTI, *donnent le sabre à Monsieur Jourdain.*

Ti star nobile, non star fabbola.　　*Toi être noble, ce n'est pas une*
　　　　Pigliar schiabbola.　　　　　　　　　　　　　*[fable.*
　　　　　　　　　　　　　　　　　　　Prends le sabre.

LES TURCS, *mettant tous le sabre à la main, reprennent ces paroles.*

QUATRIÈME ENTRÉE DE BALLET

Les Turcs, dansant, donnent en cadence plusieurs coups de sabre à Monsieur Jourdain.

LE MUFTI

Dara, dara.　　　　　　　　　　　*Donnez, donnez.*

60 Bastonnara. *(ter)*   Bastonnade. (ter)

LES TURCS *reprennent ces paroles.*

CINQUIÈME ENTRÉE DE BALLET

Les Turcs, dansant, donnent à Monsieur Jourdain des coups de bâton en cadence.

LE MUFTI

Non tener honta ;   *N'avoir pas honte ?*
Questa star l'ultima affronta.   *Ceci être le dernier affront.*

Le Mufti commence une troisième invocation. Les Dervis le soutiennent par-dessous le bras avec respect ; après quoi les Turcs chantant et dansant, sautant autour du Mufti, se retirent avec lui et emmènent Monsieur Jourdain. (18) (19)

ACTE V

SCÈNE PREMIÈRE. — MADAME JOURDAIN,
MONSIEUR JOURDAIN.

MADAME JOURDAIN. — Ah ! mon Dieu ! miséricorde ! Qu'est-ce que c'est donc que cela ? Quelle figure ! Est-ce un momon[1] que vous allez porter, et est-il temps d'aller en masque ? Parlez donc, qu'est-ce que c'est que ceci ? Qui vous a fagoté comme cela ?

5 MONSIEUR JOURDAIN. — Voyez l'impertinente, de parler de la sorte à un *Mamamouchi* !

MADAME JOURDAIN. — Comment donc ?

---

1. *Momon :* défi que se portent au jeu de dés des personnages masqués ; c'est un terme de carnaval. Ce passage semble bien être un souvenir de Rotrou (*la Veuve*, III, III) :

        « A quoi bon ces habits turcs ? Dansez-vous un ballet ?
        Portez-vous un momon ?... »

——— QUESTIONS ———

18. SUR LA CÉRÉMONIE TURQUE. — Le comique de cette cérémonie : comparez-la à la cérémonie du *Malade imaginaire.*

19. SUR L'ENSEMBLE DE L'ACTE IV. — L'évolution de l'action : qu'est devenue l'intrigue avec Dorimène ? Que devient le projet de mariage de Cléonte avec Lucile ?

— Les différentes sources du comique : comment Molière passe-t-il de la comédie de mœurs à la farce ? En quoi la stupidité de Monsieur Jourdain aide-t-elle à la transition ?

MONSIEUR JOURDAIN. — Oui, il me faut porter du
10 maintenant, et l'on vient de me faire *Mamamouchi*.

MADAME JOURDAIN. — Que voulez-vous dire avec vo.
Mamamouchi?

MONSIEUR JOURDAIN. — *Mamamouchi*, vous dis-je. Je suis
Mamamouchi.

15 MADAME JOURDAIN. — Quelle bête est-ce là?

MONSIEUR JOURDAIN. — *Mamamouchi*, c'est-à-dire, en notre
langue, paladin.

MADAME JOURDAIN. — Baladin! Êtes-vous en âge de danser
des ballets?

20 MONSIEUR JOURDAIN. — Quelle ignorante! Je dis paladin;
c'est une dignité dont on vient de me faire la cérémonie.

MADAME JOURDAIN. — Quelle cérémonie donc?

MONSIEUR JOURDAIN. — *Mahametta per Jordina*[1].

MADAME JOURDAIN. — Qu'est-ce que cela veut dire?

25 MONSIEUR JOURDAIN. — *Jordina*, c'est-à-dire Jourdain.

MADAME JOURDAIN. — Hé bien quoi, Jourdain?

MONSIEUR JOURDAIN. — *Voler far un paladina dé Jordina.*

MADAME JOURDAIN. — Comment?

MONSIEUR JOURDAIN. — *Dar turbanta con galera.*

30 MADAME JOURDAIN. — Qu'est-ce à dire cela?

MONSIEUR JOURDAIN. — *Per deffender Palestina.*

MADAME JOURDAIN. — Que voulez-vous donc dire?

MONSIEUR JOURDAIN. — *Dara, dara, bastonnara.*

MADAME JOURDAIN. — Qu'est-ce donc que ce jargon-là?

35 MONSIEUR JOURDAIN. — *Non tener honta, questa star l'ultima
affronta.*

MADAME JOURDAIN. — Qu'est-ce que c'est donc que tout cela?

MONSIEUR JOURDAIN, *danse et chante.* — *Hou la ba, ba la
chou, ba la ba, ba la da. (Il tombe par terre.)*

40 MADAME JOURDAIN. — Hélas! mon Dieu, mon mari est
devenu fou.

---

1. Monsieur Jourdain répète et chante les répliques de la cérémonie précédente.

AIN, *se relevant et sortant.* — Paix, insolente!

onsieur le *Mamamouchi.*

N, *seule.* — Où est-ce qu'il a donc perdu

empêcher de sortir. *(Apercevant Dorimène*

h! voici justement le reste de notre écu[1]!

vois que chagrin de tous les côtés. **(1)**

(Elle sort.)

Scène II. — DORANTE, DORIMÈNE.

DORANTE. — Oui, madame, vous verrez la plus plaisante
chose qu'on puisse voir; et je ne crois pas que dans tout le
monde il soit possible de trouver encore un homme aussi
fou que celui-là; et puis, madame, il faut tâcher de servir
5 l'amour de Cléonte et d'appuyer toute sa mascarade. C'est
un fort galant homme et qui mérite que l'on s'intéresse pour lui.

DORIMÈNE. — J'en fais beaucoup de cas, et il est digne d'une
bonne fortune[2].

DORANTE. — Outre cela, nous avons ici, madame, un ballet
10 qui nous revient, que nous ne devons pas laisser perdre, et il
faut bien voir si mon idée pourra réussir.

DORIMÈNE. — J'ai vu là des apprêts magnifiques, et ce sont
des choses, Dorante, que je ne puis plus souffrir. Oui, je veux
enfin vous empêcher vos profusions; et, pour rompre le cours
15 à toutes les dépenses que je vous vois faire pour moi, j'ai
résolu de me marier promptement avec vous. C'en est le vrai
secret, et toutes ces choses finissent avec le mariage.

DORANTE. — Ah! madame, est-il possible que vous ayez
pu prendre pour moi une si douce résolution?

20 DORIMÈNE. — Ce n'est que pour vous empêcher de vous
ruiner; et sans cela je vois bien qu'avant qu'il fût peu vous
n'auriez pas un sou.

_____

1. Voilà qui complète notre infortune, il ne nous manquait plus que cela. Expression qui vient peut-être du vocabulaire des changeurs de monnaie; 2. *Une bonne fortune* : un heureux sort.

____ **QUESTIONS** ____

1. SUR LA SCÈNE PREMIÈRE. — Comparez cette scène à la scène III de
l'acte III : qu'y a-t-il de semblable dans le mouvement et la situation des
deux scènes? Jusqu'où est poussée ici la bouffonnerie?

DORANTE. — Que j'ai d'obligation, madame, aux soins que
vous avez de conserver mon bien! Il est entièrement à vous,
25 aussi bien que mon cœur, et vous en userez de la façon qu'il
vous plaira.

DORIMÈNE. — J'userai bien de tous les deux. Mais voici votre
homme : la figure[1] en est admirable. **(2)**

Scène III. — MONSIEUR JOURDAIN, DORANTE, DORIMÈNE.

DORANTE. — Monsieur, nous venons rendre hommage,
madame et moi, à votre nouvelle dignité, et nous réjouir avec
vous du mariage que vous faites de votre fille avec le fils du
Grand Turc.

5 MONSIEUR JOURDAIN, *après avoir fait les révérences à la turque.*
— Monsieur, je vous souhaite la force des serpents et la prudence des lions **(3)**.

DORIMÈNE. — J'ai été bien aise d'être des premières, monsieur,
à venir vous féliciter du haut degré de gloire où vous êtes monté.

10 MONSIEUR JOURDAIN. — Madame, je vous souhaite toute
l'année votre rosier fleuri; je vous suis infiniment obligé de
prendre part aux honneurs qui m'arrivent, et j'ai beaucoup
de joie de vous voir revenue ici, pour vous faire les très humbles
excuses de l'extravagance de ma femme.

15 DORIMÈNE. — Cela n'est rien; j'excuse en elle un pareil
mouvement : votre cœur lui doit être précieux, et il n'est pas
étrange que la possession d'un homme comme vous puisse
inspirer quelques alarmes. **(4)**

---

1. *La figure :* l'apparence extérieure de toute la personne.

————— **QUESTIONS** —————

2. Sur la scène ii. — N'est-il pas surprenant que Dorimène revienne
dans une maison où elle a subi un affront? A-t-elle d'autre part découvert
les supercheries de Dorante?
— Dorante est devenu sympathique : pourquoi? Faut-il s'indigner avec
J.-J. Rousseau (voir Jugements) qu'il fasse figure d' « honnête homme »
et reçoive la récompense de ses escroqueries? Est-ce tellement au point
de vue moral qu'il faut se placer pour juger cette scène?
3. Cherchez dans la scène iii de l'acte III une bévue du même genre :
quel trait de Monsieur Jourdain se précise ici?
4. Cette réplique est à la fois profonde et comique : étudiez-la en
détail.

MONSIEUR JOURDAIN. — La possession de mon cœur est une
20 chose qui vous est tout acquise.

DORANTE. — Vous voyez, madame, que monsieur Jourdain
n'est pas de ces gens que les prospérités aveuglent, et qu'il sait,
dans sa gloire, connaître encore ses amis.

DORIMÈNE. — C'est la marque d'une âme tout à fait généreuse.

25 DORANTE. — Où est donc son Altesse Turque? Nous vou-
drions bien, comme[1] vos amis, lui rendre nos devoirs.

MONSIEUR JOURDAIN. — Le voilà qui vient, et j'ai envoyé
quérir ma fille pour lui donner la main[2]. **(5)**

SCÈNE IV. — CLÉONTE, *habillé en turc*, COVIELLE,
MONSIEUR JOURDAIN, ETC.

DORANTE, *à Cléonte*. — Monsieur, nous venons faire la révérence à Votre Altesse comme amis de monsieur votre beau-
père, et l'assurer avec respect de nos très humbles services.

MONSIEUR JOURDAIN. — Où est le truchement pour lui dire
5 qui vous êtes et lui faire entendre ce que vous dites? Vous
verrez qu'il vous répondra; et il parle turc à merveille. Holà!
où diantre est-il allé? *(A Cléonte.) Strouf, strif, strof, straf.*
Monsieur est un *grande segnore, grande segnore, grande segnore*;
et, madame, une *granda dama, granda dama. (Voyant qu'il ne*
10 *se fait point entendre.) Ahi! (A Cléonte, montrant Dorante.)*
Lui monsieur, lui *Mamamouchi* français et madame, *Mama-*
mouchie française. Je ne puis pas parler plus clairement. Bon!
voici l'interprète. **(6)**

---

1. *Comme* : au titre de; **2.** *Donner la main* : geste qui consacrera la promesse de
mariage entre Lucile et Cléonte.

———— QUESTIONS ————

5. SUR L'ENSEMBLE DE LA SCÈNE III. — Monsieur Jourdain « Mamamouchi » : à quoi reconnaît-on que sa vanité est satisfaite? Quel ridicule
nouveau ajoute-t-il à ses ridicules anciens?
— L'attitude de Dorimène et de Dorante : montrez comment ils savent
flatter la folie des grandeurs.

6. SUR LA SCÈNE IV. — L'intérêt de cette courte scène : comment elle
souligne l'habileté de Dorante; la naïveté de Monsieur Jourdain. Cherchez dans cette scène des éléments qui prouvent que celui-ci n'est sensible
à aucun ridicule, si énorme soit-il.

Scène V. — MONSIEUR JOURDAIN, DORIMÈNE, DORANTE, CLÉONTE, *en turc,* COVIELLE, *déguisé.*

MONSIEUR JOURDAIN. — Où allez-vous donc? Nous ne saurions rien dire sans vous. *(Montrant Cléonte.)* Dites-lui un peu que monsieur et madame sont des personnes de grande qualité qui lui viennent faire la révérence comme mes amis,
5 et l'assurer de leurs services. *(A Dorimène et à Dorante.)* Vous allez voir comme il va répondre.

COVIELLE. — *Alabala crociam acci boram alabamen.*

CLÉONTE. — *Catalequi tubal ourin soter amalouchan.*

MONSIEUR JOURDAIN, *à Dorimène et à Dorante.* — Voyez-
10 vous?

COVIELLE. — Il dit que la pluie des prospérités arrose en tout temps le jardin de votre famille.

MONSIEUR JOURDAIN. — Je vous l'avais bien dit, qu'il parle turc!

15 DORANTE. — Cela est admirable. **(7)**

Scène VI. — LUCILE, MONSIEUR JOURDAIN, DORANTE, DORIMÈNE, CLÉONTE, COVIELLE.

MONSIEUR JOURDAIN. — Venez, ma fille; approchez-vous, et venez donner votre main à monsieur, qui vous fait l'honneur de vous demander en mariage.

LUCILE. — Comment! mon père, comme vous voilà fait!
5 Est-ce une comédie que vous jouez?

MONSIEUR JOURDAIN. — Non, non, ce n'est pas une comédie, c'est une affaire fort sérieuse, et la plus pleine d'honneur pour vous qui se peut souhaiter. *(Montrant Cléonte.)* Voilà le mari que je vous donne.

10 LUCILE. — A moi, mon père?

MONSIEUR JOURDAIN. — Oui, à vous. Allons, touchez-lui dans la main[1], et rendez grâces au ciel de votre bonheur.

---

1. *Touchez-lui dans la main :* voir page 84, note 4.

━━━ **QUESTIONS** ━━━

7. SUR LA SCÈNE V. — Devant Cléonte impassible et digne, quel effet comique produit l'agitation de Monsieur Jourdain? Comparez son attitude à celle de la fin de la scène IV de l'acte II.

e veux point me marier.

RDAIN. — Je le veux, moi, qui suis votre père.

e n'en ferai rien.

JOURDAIN. — Ah! que de bruit! Allons, vous
dis-je   otre main.

LUCILE. — Non, mon père, je vous l'ai dit, il n'est point
de pouvoir qui me puisse obliger à prendre un autre mari
20 que Cléonte; et je me résoudrai plutôt à toutes les extrémités
que de (8)... *(Reconnaissant Cléonte.)* Il est vrai que vous
êtes mon père, je vous dois entière obéissance; et c'est à vous
à disposer de moi selon vos volontés.

MONSIEUR JOURDAIN. — Ah! je suis ravi de vous voir si
25 promptement revenue dans votre devoir; et voilà qui me plaît
d'avoir une fille obéissante. (9)

SCÈNE VII. — MADAME JOURDAIN, MONSIEUR JOURDAIN, CLÉONTE, LUCILE, DORANTE, DORIMÈNE, COVIELLE.

MADAME JOURDAIN. — Comment donc? qu'est-ce que c'est
que ceci? On dit que vous voulez donner votre fille en mariage
à un carême-prenant[1]?

MONSIEUR JOURDAIN. — Voulez-vous vous taire, impertinente?
5 Vous venez toujours mêler vos extravagances à toutes choses,
et il n'y a pas moyen de vous apprendre à être raisonnable.

MADAME JOURDAIN. — C'est vous qu'il n'y a pas moyen
de rendre sage, et vous allez de folie en folie. Quel est votre
dessein, et que voulez-vous faire avec cet assemblage?
10 MONSIEUR JOURDAIN. — Je veux marier notre fille avec le fils
du Grand Turc.

MADAME JOURDAIN. — Avec le fils du Grand Turc?

---

1. *Carême-prenant* : voir page 59, note 3.

──────── **QUESTIONS** ────────

8. L'égoïsme autoritaire de Monsieur Jourdain : comment s'est-il précisé depuis qu'il est « Mamamouchi »? — L'attitude et le ton de Lucile : cherchez dans d'autres comédies de Molière des situations semblables.
9. SUR LA SCÈNE VI. — L'effet comique de cette scène : pourquoi Monsieur Jourdain n'est-il pas surpris du brusque revirement de Lucile?

MONSIEUR JOURDAIN, *montrant Covielle.* — Oui. Faites-lui faire vos compliments par le truchement que voilà.

15 MADAME JOURDAIN. — Je n'ai que faire de truchement, et je lui dirai bien moi-même, à son nez, qu'il n'aura point ma fille. **(10)**

MONSIEUR JOURDAIN. — Voulez-vous vous taire, encore une fois? **(11)**

20 DORANTE. — Comment! madame Jourdain, vous vous opposez à un honneur comme celui-là? Vous refusez Son Altesse Turque pour gendre?

MADAME JOURDAIN. — Mon Dieu, monsieur, mêlez-vous de vos affaires.

25 DORIMÈNE. — C'est une grande gloire, qui n'est pas à rejeter.

MADAME JOURDAIN. — Madame, je vous prie aussi de ne vous point embarrasser de ce qui ne vous touche pas.

DORANTE. — C'est l'amitié que nous avons pour vous qui nous fait intéresser dans vos avantages.

30 MADAME JOURDAIN. — Je me passerai bien de votre amitié.

DORANTE. — Voilà votre fille qui consent aux volontés de son père.

MADAME JOURDAIN. — Ma fille consent à épouser un Turc?

DORANTE. — Sans doute.

35 MADAME JOURDAIN. — Elle peut oublier Cléonte?

DORANTE. — Que ne fait-on pas pour être grand'dame?

MADAME JOURDAIN. — Je l'étranglerais de mes mains, si elle avait fait un coup comme celui-là.

MONSIEUR JOURDAIN. — Voilà bien du caquet. Je vous dis 40 que ce mariage-là se fera.

MADAME JOURDAIN. — Je vous dis, moi, qu'il ne se fera point.

MONSIEUR JOURDAIN. — Ah! que de bruit!

LUCILE. — Ma mère!

MADAME JOURDAIN. — Allez, vous êtes une coquine.

───── QUESTIONS ─────

10. Pourquoi Molière n'a-t-il pas mis Madame Jourdain dans la confidence de toute cette mascarade? Depuis quand est-elle hors de l'action?
11. Recherchez combien de fois depuis le début de la pièce Monsieur Jourdain a ordonné à sa femme de se taire. Y a-t-il réussi?

45 MONSIEUR JOURDAIN, *à Mme Jourdain*. — Quoi! vous la querellez de ce qu'elle m'obéit?

MADAME JOURDAIN. — Oui, elle est à moi aussi bien qu'à vous.

COVIELLE, *à Mme Jourdain*. — Madame!

MADAME JOURDAIN. — Que me voulez-vous conter, vous?

50 COVIELLE. — Un mot.

MADAME JOURDAIN. — Je n'ai que faire de votre mot.

COVIELLE, *à M. Jourdain*. — Monsieur, si elle veut écouter une parole en particulier, je vous promets de la faire consentir à ce que vous voulez.

55 MADAME JOURDAIN. — Je n'y consentirai point.

COVIELLE. — Écoutez-moi seulement.

MADAME JOURDAIN. — Non.

MONSIEUR JOURDAIN, *à Mme Jourdain*. — Écoutez-le.

MADAME JOURDAIN. — Non, je ne veux pas écouter.

60 MONSIEUR JOURDAIN. — Il vous dira...

MADAME JOURDAIN. — Je ne veux point qu'il me dise rien.

MONSIEUR JOURDAIN. — Voilà une grande obstination de femme! Cela vous fera-t-il mal de l'entendre? **(12)**

COVIELLE. — Ne faites que m'écouter, vous ferez après ce 65 qu'il vous plaira.

MADAME JOURDAIN. — Hé bien, quoi?

COVIELLE, *à part à Mme Jourdain*. — Il y a une heure, madame, que nous vous faisons signe. Ne voyez-vous pas bien que tout ceci n'est fait que pour nous ajuster aux visions[1] de votre mari, 70 que nous l'abusons sous ce déguisement, et que c'est Cléonte lui-même qui est le fils du Grand Turc?

MADAME JOURDAIN, *bas à Coville*. — Ah! ah!

1. *Visions* : voir page 98, note 1.

────────── **QUESTIONS** ──────────

12. La situation comique dans ce passage : est-on très inquiet des résultats possibles de l'obstination de Madame Jourdain? Le rôle ridicule de Monsieur Jourdain : comment soutient-il, surtout devant témoins, son autorité de chef de famille? Que peut-on penser de l'intervention de Dorante et de Dorimène dans cette querelle?

COVIELLE, *bas à Mme Jourdain.* — Et moi, Covielle, qui suis le truchement.

75 MADAME JOURDAIN, *bas à Covielle.* — Ah! comme cela je me rends.

COVIELLE, *bas à Mme Jourdain.* — Ne faites pas semblant de rien[1].

MADAME JOURDAIN, *haut.* — Oui, voilà qui est fait, je consens
80 au mariage.

MONSIEUR JOURDAIN. — Ah! voilà tout le monde raison-nable. *(A Mme Jourdain.)* Vous ne vouliez pas l'écouter. Je savais bien qu'il vous expliquerait ce que c'est que le fils du Grand Turc.

85 MADAME JOURDAIN. — Il me l'a expliqué comme il faut, et j'en suis satisfaite. Envoyons querir un notaire. **(13)**

DORANTE. — C'est fort bien dit. Et afin, madame Jourdain, que vous puissiez avoir l'esprit tout à fait content, et que vous perdiez aujourd'hui toute la jalousie que vous pourriez avoir
90 conçue de monsieur votre mari, c'est que nous nous servirons du même notaire pour nous marier, madame et moi.

MADAME JOURDAIN. — Je consens aussi à cela.

MONSIEUR JOURDAIN, *bas à Dorante.* — C'est pour lui faire accroire?

95 DORANTE, *bas à M. Jourdain.* — Il faut bien l'amuser avec cette feinte.

MONSIEUR JOURDAIN, *bas.* — Bon, bon! *(Haut.)* Qu'on aille vite querir le notaire. **(14)**

DORANTE. — Tandis qu'il viendra et qu'il dressera les contrats,
100 voyons notre ballet, et donnons-en le divertissement à Son Altesse Turque.

---

1. Pléonasme encore admis dans la langue familière au XVIIe siècle, incorrect aujourd'hui.

QUESTIONS

13. Madame Jourdain a-t-elle souvent été d'accord avec son mari? L'effet comique de ce moment.
14. Dorante laisse à Monsieur Jourdain ses illusions sur Dorimène : souhaiterait-on qu'il dise la vérité? Quelle serait la conséquence de cet aveu?

MONSIEUR JOURDAIN. — C'est fort bien avisé. Allons prendre nos places.

MADAME JOURDAIN. — Et Nicole?

105   MONSIEUR JOURDAIN. — Je la donne au truchement; et ma femme, à qui la voudra. *[whoever wants her can have her – still in pret w/wife – preserve rights]*

COVIELLE. — Monsieur, je vous remercie. *(A part.)* Si l'on en peut voir un plus fou, je l'irai dire à Rome[1]. (15) (16)

(La comédie finit par un ballet qui avait été préparé.)

[handwritten notes: la fin heureuse / Nicole/Covielle / Dorante/Dorimène / Cléonte/Lucile]

[handwritten notes: hard to find / agore as gullible as MJ.]

---

1. Cette dernière réplique est peut-être un souvenir d'une comédie de Boisrobert, *la Folle gageure* (1651), où un personnage disait, à propos de l'habileté d'un valet : « Si quelqu'un fourbe mieux, je l'irai dire à Rome. »

──────── **QUESTIONS** ────────

15. SUR L'ENSEMBLE DE LA SCÈNE VII. — L'opposition de Madame Jourdain met-elle en péril le dénouement? Pourquoi Molière a-t-il inventé ce dernier rebondissement?

— L'entêtement produit toujours un effet comique : étudiez celui de Madame Jourdain; comparez-le à celui de Madame Pernelle (*le Tartuffe*, V, III).

16. SUR L'ENSEMBLE DE L'ACTE V. — Le rythme de l'action comparé à celui des autres actes, notamment de l'acte III. Montrez qu'on est passé dans le domaine de la farce. Faut-il en conclure que cet acte est plus faible que les précédents? Comment le ballet vient-il couronner cet acte?

— Le dénouement : pouvait-on prévoir un heureux dénouement pour Cléonte-Lucile et Covielle-Nicole? En quoi le mariage de Dorante et de Dorimène peut-il satisfaire le spectateur, malgré le caractère un peu équivoque de Dorante?

— La moralité de la pièce. Monsieur Jourdain est-il guéri de ses prétentions nobiliaires? Comparez de ce point de vue la fin du *Bourgeois gentilhomme* à celle d'autres pièces de Molière que vous connaissez.

LE GRAND
SEIGNEUR
DE
CONSTAN-
TINOPLE

D'après
Bonnart,
dessinateur
de la
fin du
XVIIe
siècle.

Phot. Larousse.

Hosa Ki ou officier que le Grand seigneur employe pour porter ses ordres

Holuagi ou confiturier du serrail

vn Agiamoglan

Le CHIAOU BACKI, ou chef des Huissiers du Diuan.

vn DELI, ou vn des gardes du premier Visir.

Phot. Larousse.

COSTUMES TURCS DU XVIIᵉ SIÈCLE

Bibliothèque des Arts décoratifs.

BALLET DES NATIONS
PREMIÈRE ENTRÉE

Un homme vient donner les livres du ballet, qui d'abord est fatigué
par une multitude de gens de provinces différentes qui crient en musique
pour en avoir, et par trois importuns qu'il trouve toujours sur ses pas.

DIALOGUE DES GENS
qui, en musique, demandent des livres.

TOUS

A moi, monsieur, à moi, de grâce, à moi, monsieur :
Un livre, s'il vous plaît, à votre serviteur.

HOMME DU BEL AIR[1]

Monsieur, distinguez-nous parmi les gens qui crient.
Quelques livres ici; les dames vous en prient.

AUTRE HOMME DU BEL AIR

5   Holà, monsieur! Monsieur, ayez la charité
        D'en jeter de notre côté.

FEMME DU BEL AIR

    Mon Dieu, qu'aux personnes bien faites
    On sait peu rendre honneur céans[2]!

AUTRE FEMME DU BEL AIR

    Ils n'ont des livres et des bancs
10   Que pour mesdames les grisettes[3].

GASCON

Aho! l'homme aux livres, qu'on m'en vaille[4].
    J'ay déjà le poumon usé;
    Bous voyez qué chacun mé raille,
    Et je suis escandalisé
15   De boir ès mains de la canaille
    Ce qui m'est par bous refusé.

AUTRE GASCON

Eh! cadédis, monseu, boyez qui l'on put être;
Un libret, je bous prie, au varon d'Asbarat.
    Jé pensé, mordi! que le fat
20   N'a pas l'honnur dé mé connaître.

---

1. *Homme du bel air* : homme de manières élégantes et raffinées, sans nuance péjorative ici; 2. *Céans* : voir page 36, note 5; 3. *Grisette* : nom d'une étoffe dont s'habillent les femmes de condition médiocre; puis ces personnes mêmes; 4. *Vaille* : baille. Molière parodie la prononciation gasconne du temps, dont la particularité est de permuter les lettres *b* et *v*.

LE SUISSE

Mon'siur le donneur de papieir,
Que veul dire sti façon de fifre?
Moi l'écorchair tout mon gosieir
            A crieir,
25   Sans que je pouvre afoir ein lifre;
Pardi, mon foi, Mon'siur, je pense fous l'être ifre.

*Le donneur de livres, fatigué par les importuns qu'il trouve toujours
sur ses pas, se retire en colère.*

VIEUX BOURGEOIS BABILLARD

De tout ceci, franc et net,
Je suis mal satisfait;
Et cela sans doute est laid
30   Que notre fille,
Si bien faite et si gentille,
De tant d'amoureux l'objet,
        N'ait pas à son souhait
        Un livre de ballet,
35   Pour lire le sujet
Du divertissement qu'on fait,
Et que toute notre famille
        Si proprement s'habille,
Pour être placée au sommet
40   De la salle, où l'on met
Les gens de Lantriguet[1] :
De tout ceci, franc et net,
Je suis mal satisfait,
Et cela sans doute est laid.

VIEILLE BOURGEOISE BABILLARDE

45   Il est vrai que c'est une honte,
Le sang au visage me monte,
Et ce jeteur de vers qui manque au capital[2],
        L'entend fort mal;
        C'est un brutal,
50   Un vrai cheval
        Franc animal,
De faire si peu de compte
D'une fille qui fait l'ornement principal
Du quartier du Palais-Royal,
55   Et que ces jours passés un comte
Fut prendre la première au bal.

---

1. Nom breton de Tréguier. Les gens de Lantriguet représentent, pour le bourgeois parisien, les provinciaux, les gens du commun; 2. Qui manque à l'essentiel
de sa tâche.

Il l'entend mal,
C'est un brutal,
Un vrai cheval,
60 Franc animal.

HOMMES ET FEMMES DU BEL AIR

Ah! quel bruit!
Quel fracas!
Quel chaos!
Quel mélange!
Quelle confusion!
Quelle cohue étrange!
Quel désordre!
Quel embarras!
On y sèche.
L'on n'y tient pas.

GASCON

65 Bentre! je suis à vout.

AUTRE GASCON

J'enragé, Diou mé damne.

SUISSE

Ah! que l'y faire saif dans sti sal de cians.

GASCON

Jé murs.

AUTRE GASCON

Jé perds la tramontane[1].

SUISSE

Mon foi, moi, je foudrais être hors de dedans.

VIEUX BOURGEOIS BABILLARD

Allons, ma mie,
70 Suivez mes pas,
Je vous en prie.
Et ne me quittez pas,
On fait de nous trop peu de cas,
Et je suis las
75 De ce tracas :
Tout ce fatras,
Cet embarras,
Me pèse par trop sur les bras.
S'il me prend jamais envie
80 De retourner de ma vie
A ballet ni comédie,

---

1. *La tramontane* : l'étoile polaire. Cf. l'expression populaire contemporaine : « Je perds le nord, la boussole. »

Je veux bien qu'on m'estropie.
Allons, ma mie,
Suivez mes pas,
85   Je vous en prie,
Et ne me quittez pas,
On fait de nous trop peu de cas.

VIEILLE BOURGEOISE BABILLARDE

Allons, mon mignon, mon fils,
Regagnons notre logis,
90   Et sortons de ce taudis
Où l'on ne peut être assis;
Ils seront bien ébaubis
Quand ils nous verront partis.
Trop de confusion règne dans cette salle,
95   Et j'aimerais mieux être au milieu de la halle;
Si jamais je reviens à semblable régale[1],
Je veux bien recevoir des soufflets plus de six.
Allons, mon mignon, mon fils,
Regagnons notre logis,
100   Et sortons de ce taudis
Où l'on ne peut être assis.

TOUS

A moi, monsieur, à moi, de grâce, à moi, monsieur :
Un livre, s'il vous plaît, à votre serviteur.

———————

DEUXIÈME ENTRÉE

Les trois importuns dansent.

TROISIÈME ENTRÉE

Trois Espagnols chantent.

PREMIER ESPAGNOL, *chantant.*

Texte	**Traduction**
Sé que me muero de amor,	*Je sais que je meurs d'amour,*
Y solicito el dolor.	*Et je recherche la douleur.*
A un muriendo de querer,	*Quoique mourant de désir,*
De tan buen ayre adolezco,	*Je dépéris de si bon air*
5 Que es mas de lo que padezco	*Que ce que je désire souffrir,*
Lo que quiero padecer,	*Est plus que ce que je souffre;*

———————

1. *Régale :* voir page 97, note 4.

Y no pudiento exceder	*Et la rigueur de mon mal*
A mi deseo el rigor.	*Ne peut excéder mon désir.*

	Sé que me muero de amor	*Je sais que je meurs d'amour,*
10	Y solicito el dolor.	*Et je recherche la douleur.*

Lisonxeame la suerte	*Le sort me flatte*
Con piedad tan advertida,	*Avec une pitié si attentive*
Que me assegura la vida	*Qu'il m'assure la vie*
En el riesgo de la muerte.	*Dans le danger et dans la mort.*

15	Vivir de su golpe fuerte	*Vivre d'un coup si fort*
	Es de mi salud primor,	*Est le prodige de mon salut.*

Sé que me muero de amor,	*Je sais que je meurs d'amour,*
Y solicito el dolor.	*Et je recherche la douleur.*

Danse de six Espagnols,
après laquelle deux autres Espagnols dansent encore ensemble.

PREMIER ESPAGNOL, *chantant.*

	Ay! que locura, con tanto rigor	*Ah! Quelle folie de se plaindre*
20	Quexarce de Amor,	*Si fort de l'Amour ;*
	Del nino bonito	*De l'enfant gentil*
	Que todo es dulçura	*Qui est la douceur même!*
	Ay! que locura!	*Ah! Quelle folie!*
	Ay! que locura!	*Ah! Quelle folie!*

DEUXIÈME ESPAGNOL, *chantant.*

25	El dolor solicita,	*La douleur tourmente*
	El que al dolor se da,	*Celui qui s'abandonne à la dou-*
	Y nadie de amor muere	[*leur ;*
	Sino quien no save amar.	*Et personne ne meurt d'amour,*
		Si ce n'est celui qui ne sait pas
		[*aimer.*

PREMIER ET DEUXIÈME ESPAGNOLS, *chantant.*

	Duelce muerte es el amor	*L'amour est une douce mort,*
30	Con correspondencia igual,	*Quand on est payé de retour ;*
	Y si esta gozamos hoy	*Et nous en jouissons aujourd'hui,*
	Porque la quieres turbar?	*Pourquoi la veux-tu troubler?*

PREMIER ESPAGNOL, *chantant.*

	Alegrese enamorado	*Que l'amant se réjouisse*
	Y tome mi parecer,	*Et adopte mon avis ;*
35	Que en esto de querer	*Car, lorsqu'on désire,*
	Todo es hallar el vado.	*Tout est de trouver le moyen.*

TOUS TROIS ENSEMBLE

Vaya, vaya de fiestas!	*Allons! Allons! Des fêtes!*
Vaya de vayle!	*Allons! De la danse!*
Alegria, alegria, alegria!	*Gai, gai, gai!*
40 Que esto de dolor es fantasia!	*La douleur n'est qu'imagination!*

TROISIEME ENTRÉE

ITALIENS

UNE MUSICIENNE ITALIENNE *fait le premier récit dont voici les paroles.*

Di rigori armata il seno	*Ayant armé mon sein de rigueurs,*
Contro Amor mi ribellai,	*En un clin d'œil je me révoltai*
	[contre l'Amour;
Ma fui vinta in un baleno	*Mais je fus vaincue*
In mirar due vaghi rai.	*En regardant deux beaux yeux.*
5 Ahi! che resiste puoco	*Ah! Qu'un cœur de glace*
Cor di gelo a stral di fuoco!	*Résiste peu à une flèche de feu.*
Ma si caro è 'l mio tormento,	*Cependant mon tourment m'est*
	[si cher,
Dolce è si la piaga mia,	*Et ma plaie m'est si douce,*
Ch' il penare è 'l mio contento,	*Que ma peine fait mon bonheur,*
10 E 'l sanarmi è tirannia.	*Et que me guérir serait une*
	[tyrannie.
Ahi! che più giova e piace	*Ah! Plus l'amour est vif,*
Quanto amor è più vivace!	*Plus il y a de joie et de plaisir.*

Après l'air que la musicienne a chanté, deux Scaramouches, deux Trivelins et un Arlequin représentent une nuit à la manière des comédiens italiens, en cadence.

Un musicien italien se joint à la musicienne italienne et chante avec elle les paroles qui suivent:

Texte	**Traduction**

LE MUSICIEN ITALIEN

Bel tempo che vola	*Le beau temps qui s'envole*
Rapisce il contento;	*Emporte le plaisir;*
15 D'Amor ne la scola	*A l'école d'Amour*
Si coglie il momento.	*On apprend à profiter du moment.*

LA MUSICIENNE

Insin che florida	*Tant que rit l'âge fleuri,*
Ride l' età	*Qui trop promptement, hélas!*
Che pur tropp' horrida	*S'éloigne de nous.*
20 Da noi sen và.	

TOUS DEUX

Sù cantiamo,	*Chantons,*
Sù godiamo,	*Jouissons,*
Ne' bei di di gioventù :	*Dans les beaux jours de la jeu-*
	[*nesse.*
Perduto ben non si racquista più.	*Un bien perdu ne se recouvre plus.*

LE MUSICIEN

25

Pupilla ch'e vaga	*Un bel œil*
Mill' alm incatena,	*Enchaîne mille cœurs ;*
Fà dolce la piaga,	*Ses blessures sont douces ;*
Felice la pena.	*Le mal qu'il cause*
	Est un bonheur.

LA MUSICIENNE

Ma poiche frigida	*Mais quand languit*
30 Langue l'età	*L'âge glacé,*
Più l'alma rigida	*L'âme engourdie*
Fiamme non hà.	*N'a plus de feux.*

TOUS DEUX

Sù cantiamo,	*Chantons,*
Sù godiamo,	*Jouissons*
35 Ne' bei di di gioventù :	*Dans les beaux jours de la jeu-*
	[*nesse :*
Perduto ben non si racquista più.	*Un bien perdu ne se recouvre plus.*

Après le dialogue italien,
les Scaramouches et Trivelins dansent une réjouissance.

CINQUIÈME ENTRÉE

FRANÇAIS

Deux musiciens poitevins dansent et chantent les paroles qui suivent.

PREMIER MENUET

PREMIER MUSICIEN

Ah! qu'il fait beau dans ces bocages!
Ah! que le ciel donne un beau jour!

AUTRE MUSICIEN

Le rossignol, sous ces tendres feuillages,
Chante aux échos son doux retour.

5
Ce beau séjour,
Ces doux ramages,
Ce beau séjour,
Nous invite à l'amour.

DEUXIÈME MENUET

TOUS DEUX ENSEMBLE

Vois ma Climène,
10
Vois, sous ce chêne
S'entrebaiser ces oiseaux amoureux.
Ils n'ont rien dans leurs vœux
Qui les gêne,
De leurs doux feux
15
Leur âme est pleine.
Qu'ils sont heureux!
Nous pouvons tous deux,
Si tu le veux,
Être comme eux.

Six autres Français viennent après, vêtus galamment à la poitevine, trois en hommes et trois en femmes, accompagnés de huit flûtes et de hautbois, et dansent les menuets.

SIXIÈME ENTRÉE

Tout cela finit par le mélange des trois nations et les applaudissements en danse et en musique de toute l'assistance, qui chante les deux vers qui suivent :

Quels spectacles charmants, quels plaisirs goûtons-nous!
Les dieux mêmes, les dieux n'en ont point de plus doux[1].

---

1. A la fin du ballet des nations, l'édition de 1734 donne les noms des personnes qui ont chanté et dansé dans *le Bourgeois gentilhomme*. Rappelons que la partition de Lully avec des indications techniques sur les intermèdes nous est parvenue grâce à un exemplaire de 185 pages copié par le musicien Philidor et portant le titre suivant : « *Le Bourgeois gentilhomme*, comédie-ballet; donné par le roi à toute sa cour dans le château de Chambord au mois d'octobre 1670; fait par M. de Lully, surintendant de la musique du Roy, et par le sieur Molière. » Cet ouvrage reproduit le texte de Molière (conforme à l'édition de 1674) et les divers morceaux de musique insérés à la place que leur assignait la représentation de la comédie-ballet.

DOCUMENTATION THÉMATIQUE

réunie par la Rédaction des Nouveaux Classiques Larousse.

1. MONSIEUR JOURDAIN, PERSONNAGE COMIQUE

1.1. LES INTERPRÉTATIONS

Si certains acteurs ont marqué de leur personnalité les personnages de Molière qu'ils ont interprétés (ainsi de Louis Jouvet ou de Fernand Ledoux pour Tartuffe), aucun n'a incarné Monsieur Jourdain au point de laisser un souvenir ineffaçable dans ce rôle. Voici un rapide panorama des acteurs qui, de Molière à nos jours, jouèrent le Bourgeois, d'après M. Descotes, *les Grands Rôles du théâtre de Molière.*

C'est, tout d'abord, Molière : « Un Jourdain *bilieux,* et non sanguin, tel fut celui de Molière, un rôle encore d'homme emporté, trop vif, sans cesse en mouvement ; un rôle qui, en dépit des apparences, rejoint celui d'Arnolphe. »

On passe au siècle suivant avec Préville : « Le plus célèbre Jourdain du XVIIIe siècle fut Préville. Le rôle revenait encore à un comédien qui faisait merveille dans les valets, les Crispins en particulier : c'était la tradition de Paul Poisson continuée. Mais l'esprit du siècle imprégnait Préville et sa gaîté était plus leste, plus incisive que celle de son prédécesseur. Aussi atteignait-il à un haut point d'équilibre comique : dans le rôle, il était gauche de corps et d'esprit, d'un bout à l'autre, mais gauche à faire plaisir, et voilà le difficile. (Cailhava, *Etudes sur Molière.*)

On relèvera l'allusion à la gaucherie *de corps :* le côté mimique était bien mis en valeur.

Dugazon, appartenant aux XVIIIe et XIXe siècles, était d'un autre tempérament : « Avec un tempérament comme le sien, porté aux extrêmes de la bouffonnerie, il ne pouvait se satisfaire des nombreux lazzis prévus par Molière. Et, sans se préoccuper des exigences du bon goût, il en rajoutait. C'est Dugazon qui entreprit de corser encore la colère de M. Jourdain envers sa femme, lorsque celle-ci vient troubler le repas : saisissant les pièces du repas, il chassait l'importune en lui jetant des petits pâtés. C'était dépasser l'intention de Molière. »

Rien d'étonnant qu'il ait usé de mimiques expressives : « Dugazon mettait à profit d'autre part les ressources du rôle en grimaces. Son don naturel de mobiliser sa physionomie le servait alors admirablement. [...] Les effets comiques obtenus par Dugazon, même lorsqu'ils étaient dus à des moyens contestables, avaient le mérite d'être l'expression naturelle d'une personnalité exubérante. »

Et l'on aboutit au xx° siècle avec Maurice de Féraudy :
« Comédien « de réflexion et non de complexion », Féraudy
se trouva gêné par les parties franchement burlesques du
rôle et il donna, en quelque sorte, la « réhabilitation » du personnage. Avec lui, Jourdain devenait sympathique : après
tout, fit-on observer, mieux vaut être volé que voleur. »
« Il y met, écrivait Souday, un excès de finesse ou plutôt de
discrétion. Sa niaiserie est trop douce et point assez délirante
pour un homme qui consent à être sacré mamamouchi. »
Il ne faut donc pas s'étonner si *le Bourgeois* fut une des comédies de Molière choisies par ceux qui, à la même époque,
entendaient rendre à ce répertoire toute sa puissance comique.

Montpreux, directeur de l'Odéon, explique pourquoi Molière
passe à Bobino : « En jouant une œuvre de Molière, Bobino
ne croit pas manquer au respect que l'on doit à l'un des plus
grands génies dont s'honore notre littérature. Il estime que
son public populaire est plus près qu'aucun autre du génie de
Molière, et qu'en jouant Molière au peuple il renoue la tradition... Débarrassons-nous des traditions étroites et arbitraires
des écoles, des superstitions de certains lettrés qu'un amour
trop exclusif du maître aveugle, et jouons Molière au peuple
sans d'autre souci que d'être sincères et gais. »

Pour M. Descotes, c'est à Léon Bernard que l'on devrait la
meilleure interprétation du Bourgeois : « En fin de compte,
un des plus estimables Jourdains qu'ait connus l'époque
moderne reste celui que le Théâtre-Français présenta en 1925 :
Léon Bernard, l'Arnolphe qui fut opposé à celui de Guitry.
Cette fois, Léon Bernard n'avait pas à souffrir d'une comparaison trop lourde. Moins fin, moins subtil que Féraudy, il possé-
dait le « don de sympathie », c'est-à-dire la rondeur, le visage
épanoui. Il était jovial, candide, rubicond, plaisamment
« gonflé d'importance comme un dindon » [Catulle-Mendès];
mais son comique restait sagement mesuré : « plaisant et même
ridicule, jamais grotesque » [Mas]; « il ne tombe jamais dans
le burlesque » [Nozière].

Nous lui laisserons également le soin de conclure : « On en
arrive ainsi à cette conclusion qu'aucun comédien ne s'est
vraiment imposé dans le rôle de M. Jourdain au point d'atta-
cher son nom de façon définitive au personnage. [...] Les
acteurs à très forte personnalité (Molé, Guitry, Jouvet par
exemple) l'ont négligé; par contre Jourdain a permis d'excel-
lentes créations à des interprètes de style plus classique et
de moyens moins puissants. C'est que le rôle est d'un comique
traditionnel, qu'il ne permet pas de grandes variations, qu'il
ne met en jeu qu'un travers bénin (la vanité) et non pas un
vice ou une grande passion : un rôle de demi-caractère en

quelque sorte. Un Thiron, acteur honorable, y réussit mieux qu'un Coquelin ou qu'un Raimu. C'est enfin que, en dépit de sa position de protagoniste, M. Jourdain n'était, dans l'esprit de Molière, qu'une pièce dans un ensemble qui faisait la place essentielle aux ressources vocales, musicales et chorégraphiques du spectacle. »

En effet, la pièce n'est pas une comédie de caractère, essentiellement : « Quoi qu'il en soit, *le Bourgeois gentilhomme* présente dès l'abord aux comédiens un problème fondamental, qui porte sur la place à réserver au spectacle. On peut concevoir une représentation qui, selon les vœux de Sarcey, ne porte que sur la partie de comédie. On peut essayer d'élargir les dimensions de l'œuvre : c'est ce que tentait en 1913 l'Odéon en donnant à la pièce un décor somptueusement oriental (ce qui est un non-sens, car pourquoi M. Jourdain habiterait-il un appartement à la turque?). C'est ce qu'a réalisé, tout récemment, la Comédie-Française, sous la direction de M. P.-A. Touchard, d'abord pour le festival d'été de Strasbourg. Selon l'administrateur, « les divertissements avaient la splendeur d'un rêve des mille et une nuits ». (Id., *Ibid.*)

1.2. LE SPECTACLE

Le Bourgeois gentilhomme, comme le souligne M. Descotes, est une pièce où le spectacle a une place importante :

Ce caractère original de *spectacle* a pourtant laissé des traces dans le texte lui-même. On a bien souvent observé la faiblesse de l'intrigue, sa banalité même, la structure très lâche de l'action (à la fin du 1er acte aucun nœud dramatique n'est posé). Beaucoup plus que *l'Avare, le Bourgeois* se présente en fait comme une suite de sketches, ce qui laisse aux interprètes une certaine latitude pour broder, développer les jeux de scène : au début du XIXe siècle, Faure, danseur à l'Opéra, qui tenait le rôle du Maître à danser, s'en donnait à cœur joie pour multiplier le nombre des révérences (II, 1, fin de la scène) et les accompagnait même d'un texte de son cru.

Trois témoignages vont nous le faire sentir :

◆ *Le décor.* — On peut lire dans le *Mémoire* de Mahelot : « Le théâtre est une chambre. Une ferme. Il faut des sièges, une table pour le festin et une pour le buffet. Les ustensiles pour la cérémonie. » La *ferme,* en terme de théâtre, est, selon le *Dictionnaire de l'Académie* de 1694, « une décoration montée sur un châssis, qui se détache en avant de la toile de fond, telle qu'une colonnade ». On peut comprendre qu'il s'agissait ici d'un premier fond avec une porte praticable donnant sur un vestibule d'où pouvaient paraître les cortèges du troisième intermède et de la cérémonie turque.

◆ *Le costume de Monsieur Jourdain*. — L'inventaire fait au décès de Molière a permis de connaître assez exactement le costume des divers rôles que jouait l'acteur-auteur. En particulier, il est dit pour celui de Monsieur Jourdain :

Un habit pour la représentation du *Bourgeois gentilhomme*, consistant en une robe de chambre rayée, doublée de taffetas aurore et vert, un haut-de-chausses de panne rouge, une camisole de panne bleue [*ce doit être une erreur de l'huissier-priseur et sans doute faut-il lire « vert »*], un bonnet de nuit et une coiffe, des chausses et une écharpe de toile peinte à l'indienne [*cette écharpe servait sans doute de ceinture à la robe de chambre*].

Après cette description de ce qu'était le « déshabillé » dont il est question à l'acte premier, scène II, voici le costume de la cérémonie turque : *Une veste à la turque et un turban, un sabre*. Pour l'habit dont Monsieur Jourdain est revêtu à la fin du deuxième acte, voici ce qui en est dit : « Des chausses de brocard aussi garnies de rubans vert et aurore, et deux points de Sedan. Le pourpoint de taffetas garni de dentelle d'argent faux. Le ceinturon, des bas de soie verts et des gants, avec un chapeau garni de plumes aurore et vert. »

◆ *Une interprétation de la leçon de danse*. — On peut logiquement supposer que la tirade écrite par Molière pour la leçon de danse était amplifiée, du vivant même de l'auteur. Voici le texte, souvent choisi pour la représentation, dû à un certain Faure, danseur à l'Opéra avant la Révolution, et qui entra en 1808 à la Comédie-Française, où il triompha souvent dans le rôle du maître à danser.

Le maître à danser, à Monsieur Jourdain. — Placez-vous, Monsieur, le corps droit, la tête haute, le sourire aux lèvres. Bien. — Troisième position : le talon à la rosette du soulier. Effacez vos épaules... Un peu plus... Soutenez vos coudes... sans raideur. La poitrine en avant... Un peu moins... Écartez le petit doigt. — C'est ce que nous appelons de la grâce. Souriez. Bon. — Nous saluons du bras droit. (*Il salue.*) Un, deux, trois et quatre. — Pour le bras gauche : le coude à la hauteur de l'épaule. En passant la main devant vous, déployez le bras dans toute sa longueur pour présenter, en souriant, la main à la dame. Ainsi (*galamment*) : Madame ! Moi seul, une fois, pour la mémoire. (*Il danse en chantant.*) La, la, la, la, la, etc. A vous, Monsieur. (*Pendant que Monsieur Jourdain danse, le maître à danser chante.*) La, la, la, la, la ; la jambe droite. La, la, la. Bien.

Ensemble maintenant, Monsieur. Vous, par ici, moi, par là. (*Chantant et dansant.*) La, la, la, la, la, la, etc. Bien. Tenez-vous droit, Monsieur. Le corps sur la jambe qui est derrière.

Le menton à l'épaule ; regardez-moi ; souriez. Nous partons. Deux pas en avant ; en cadence (*il danse avec Monsieur Jourdain*) la, la, la. Ne remuez point tant les épaules. Donnez-moi la main. La, la, la. Regardez-moi, Monsieur, sous le bras, gracieusement. Là ; vos deux bras sont estropiés... Nous continuons, Monsieur. Rendons les saignées. Ne cassez point vos poignets. Deux pas en avant. En cadence (*il chante et danse*) : la, la, la, la, la, la... Tournez la pointe du pied en dehors. La, la, la. Dressez votre corps. Bien. Assemblé soutenu en tournant. Des demi-pointes, Monsieur, des demi-pointes ! — Bon ! Saluez. Souriez... On ne peut pas mieux.

2. *LE BOURGEOIS GENTILHOMME* ET *MONSIEUR DE POURCEAUGNAC*

{ On pourra rapprocher de la scène v de l'acte IV, la quatrième
{ scène de l'acte premier de *Monsieur de Pourceaugnac*.

Scène IV. — Eraste, Sbrigani, Monsieur de Pourceaugnac.

Éraste. — Ah ! qu'est-ce ci ? que vois-je ? Quelle heureuse rencontre ! Monsieur de Pourceaugnac ! Que je suis ravi de vous voir ! Comment ? il semble que vous ayez peine à me reconnaître !

Monsieur de Pourceaugnac. — Monsieur, je suis votre serviteur.

Éraste. — Est-il possible que cinq ou six années m'aient ôté de votre mémoire ? et que vous ne reconnaissiez pas le meilleur ami de toute la famille des Pourceaugnacs ?

Monsieur de Pourceaugnac. — Pardonnez-moi. (*A Sbrigani.*) Ma foi ! je ne sais qui il est.

Éraste. — Il n'y a pas un Pourceaugnac à Limoges que je ne connaisse depuis le plus grand jusques au plus petit ; je ne fréquentais qu'eux dans le temps que j'y étais, et j'avais l'honneur de vous voir presque tous les jours.

Monsieur de Pourceaugnac. — C'est moi qui l'ai reçu, Monsieur.

Éraste. — Vous ne vous remettez point mon visage ?

Monsieur de Pourceaugnac. — Si fait. (*A Sbrigani.*) Je ne le connais point.

Éraste. — Vous ne vous ressouvenez pas que j'ai eu le bonheur de boire avec vous je ne sais combien de fois ?

Monsieur de Pourceaugnac. — Excusez-moi. (*A Sbrigani.*) Je ne sais ce que c'est.

ÉRASTE. — Comment appelez-vous ce traiteur de Limoges qui fait si bonne chère ?

MONSIEUR DE POURCEAUGNAC. — Petit-Jean ?

ÉRASTE. — Le voilà. Nous allions le plus souvent ensemble chez lui nous réjouir. Comment est-ce que vous nommez à Limoges ce lieu où l'on se promène ?

MONSIEUR DE POURCEAUGNAC. — Le cimetière des Arènes ?

ÉRASTE. — Justement : c'est où je passais de si douces heures à jouir de votre agréable conversation. Vous ne vous remettez pas tout cela ?

MONSIEUR DE POURCEAUGNAC. — Excusez-moi, je me le remets. (*A Sbrigani.*) Diable emporte si je m'en souviens !

SBRIGANI, *bas à M. de Pourceaugnac.* — Il y a cent choses comme cela qui passent de la tête.

ÉRASTE. — Embrassez-moi donc, je vous prie, et resserrons les nœuds de notre ancienne amitié.

SBRIGANI, *à M. de Pourceaugnac.* — Voilà un homme qui vous aime fort.

ÉRASTE. — Dites-moi un peu des nouvelles de toute la parenté : comment se porte Monsieur votre... là... qui est si honnête homme ?

MONSIEUR DE POURCEAUGNAC. — Mon frère le consul[1] ?

ÉRASTE. — Oui.

MONSIEUR DE POURCEAUGNAC. — Il se porte le mieux du monde.

ÉRASTE. — Certes j'en suis ravi. Et celui qui est de si bonne humeur ? là... Monsieur votre... ?

MONSIEUR DE POURCEAUGNAC. — Mon cousin l'assesseur[2] ?

ÉRASTE. — Justement.

MONSIEUR DE POURCEAUGNAC. — Toujours gai et gaillard.

ÉRASTE. — Ma foi ! j'en ai beaucoup de joie. Et Monsieur votre oncle ? le... ?

MONSIEUR DE POURCEAUGNAC. — Je n'ai point d'oncle.

ÉRASTE. — Vous aviez pourtant en ce temps-là...

MONSIEUR DE POURCEAUGNAC. — Non, rien qu'une tante.

ÉRASTE. — C'est ce que je voulais dire ; Madame votre tante, comment se porte-t-elle ?

MONSIEUR DE POURCEAUGNAC. — Elle est morte depuis six mois.

ÉRASTE. — Hélas! la pauvre femme! elle était si bonne personne.

MONSIEUR DE POURCEAUGNAC. — Nous avons aussi mon neveu le chanoine qui a pensé mourir de la petite vérole.

ÉRASTE. — Quel dommage ç'aurait été!

MONSIEUR DE POURCEAUGNAC. — Le connaissiez-vous aussi?

ÉRASTE. — Vraiment si je le connais! Un grand garçon bien fait.

MONSIEUR DE POURCEAUGNAC. — Pas des plus grands.

ÉRASTE. — Non, mais de taille bien prise.

MONSIEUR DE POURCEAUGNAC. — Eh! oui.

ÉRASTE. — Qui est votre neveu...

MONSIEUR DE POURCEAUGNAC. — Oui.

ÉRASTE. — Fils de votre frère... ou de votre sœur...

MONSIEUR DE POURCEAUGNAC. — Justement.

ÉRASTE. — Chanoine de l'église de... Comment l'appelez-vous?

MONSIEUR DE POURCEAUGNAC. — De Saint-Etienne.

ÉRASTE. — Le voilà, je ne connais autre.

MONSIEUR DE POURCEAUGNAC, *à Sbrigani*. — Il dit toute la parenté.

SBRIGANI. — Il vous connaît plus que vous ne croyez.

MONSIEUR DE POURCEAUGNAC. — A ce que je vois, vous avez demeuré longtemps dans notre ville?

ÉRASTE. — Deux ans entiers.

MONSIEUR DE POURCEAUGNAC. — Vous étiez donc là quand mon cousin l'élu[3] fit tenir[4] son enfant à Monsieur notre gouverneur[5]?

ÉRASTE. — Vraiment oui, j'y fus convié des premiers.

MONSIEUR DE POURCEAUGNAC. — Cela fut galant[6].

ÉRASTE. — Très-galant.

MONSIEUR DE POURCEAUGNAC. — C'était un repas bien troussé.

ÉRASTE. — Sans doute.

MONSIEUR DE POURCEAUGNAC. — Vous vîtes donc aussi la querelle que j'eus avec ce gentilhomme périgordin[7]?

ÉRASTE. — Oui.

MONSIEUR DE POURCEAUGNAC. — Parbleu! il trouva à qui parler.

ÉRASTE. — Ah! ah!

MONSIEUR DE POURCEAUGNAC. — Il me donna un soufflet, mais je lui dis bien son fait.

ÉRASTE. — Assurément. Au reste, je ne prétends pas que vous preniez d'autre logis que le mien.

MONSIEUR DE POURCEAUGNAC. — Je n'ai garde de...

ÉRASTE. — Vous moquez-vous ? Je ne souffrirai point du tout que mon meilleur ami soit autre part que dans ma maison.

MONSIEUR DE POURCEAUGNAC. — Ce serait vous...

ÉRASTE. — Non, le diable m'emporte! vous logerez chez moi.

SBRIGANI, *à M. de Pourceaugnac.* — Puisqu'il le veut obstinément, je vous conseille d'accepter l'offre.

ÉRASTE. — Où sont vos hardes[8] ?

MONSIEUR DE POURCEAUGNAC. — Je les ai laissées, avec mon valet, où je suis descendu.

ÉRASTE. — Envoyons-les quérir par quelqu'un.

MONSIEUR DE POURCEAUGNAC. — Non, je lui ai défendu de bouger, à moins que j'y fusse moi-même, de peur de quelque fourberie.

SBRIGANI. — C'est prudemment avisé.

MONSIEUR DE POURCEAUGNAC. — Ce pays-ci est un peu sujet à caution.

ÉRASTE. — On voit les gens d'esprit en tout.

SBRIGANI. — Je vais accompagner Monsieur, et le ramènerai où vous voudrez.

ÉRASTE. — Oui, je serai bien aise de donner quelques ordres, et vous n'avez qu'à revenir à cette maison-là.

SBRIGANI. — Nous sommes à vous tout à l'heure.

ÉRASTE, *à M. de Pourceaugnac.* — Je vous attends avec impatience.

MONSIEUR DE POURCEAUGNAC, *à Sbrigani.* — Voilà une connaissance où je ne m'attendais point.

SBRIGANI. — Il a la mine d'être honnête homme.

ÉRASTE, *seul.* — Ma foi! Monsieur de Pourceaugnac, nous vous en donnerons de toutes les façons; les choses sont préparées, et je n'ai qu'à frapper.

3. LE RÔLE DE LA TURQUERIE

D'Arvieux, dans ses *Mémoires,* raconte comment l'idée en serait venue :

> Le Roi ayant voulu faire un voyage à Chambord pour y prendre le divertissement de la chasse, voulut donner à la Cour

celui d'un ballet et, comme l'idée des Turcs qu'on venait de voir à Paris était encore toute récente, il crut qu'il serait bon de les faire paraître sur la scène. Sa Majesté m'ordonna de me joindre à Messieurs Molière et de Lulli pour composer une pièce de théâtre où l'on pût faire entrer quelque chose des habillements et des manières des Turcs. Je me rendis pour cet effet au village d'Auteuil où M. de Molière avait une maison fort jolie. Ce fut là que nous travaillâmes à cette pièce de théâtre que l'on voit dans les œuvres de Molière sous le titre de *Bourgeois gentilhomme,* qui se fit Turc pour épouser la fille du Grand Seigneur. Je fus chargé de tout ce qui regardait les habillements et les manières des Turcs. La pièce achevée, on la présenta au Roi qui l'agréa, et je demeurai huit jours chez Baraillon, maître tailleur, pour faire faire les habits et turbans à la turque. Tout fut transporté à Chambord et sa pièce représentée dans le mois de septembre, avec un succès qui satisfit le Roi et toute la Cour. Sa Majesté eut la bonté de dire qu'Elle voyait bien que le chevalier d'Arvieux s'en était mêlé, à quoi M. le Duc d'Aumont et M. Daquin répondirent : Sire, nous pouvons assurer Votre Majesté qu'il y a pris un très grand soin et qu'il cherchera toutes les occasions de faire quelque chose qui lui puisse être agréable. Le Roi répliqua qu'il en était persuadé et qu'il ne m'avait jamais rien commandé que je n'eusse fait à sa satisfaction, qu'il aurait soin de moi et qu'il s'en souviendrait dans les occasions.

Ces paroles obligeantes sorties de la bouche d'un si grand Monarque m'attirèrent les compliments de toute la Cour. C'est une eau bénite dont les courtisans ne sont pas chiches. Le Ballet et la Comédie furent représentés avec un si grand succès que, quoiqu'on les répétât plusieurs fois de suite, tout le monde le redemandait encore ; aussi ne pouvait-on rien ajouter à l'habileté des acteurs. On voulut même faire entrer les scènes turques dans le ballet de *Psyché* qu'on préparait pour le carnaval suivant, mais, après y avoir bien pensé, on jugea que ces deux sujets ne pouvaient pas s'allier ensemble.

(D'Arvieux, Mémoires, 1735.)

Mais, dès 1645, faire parler le turc à des personnages de comédie était un élément comique. Le passage suivant (v. 1015-1023) de *la Sœur* de Rotrou en fait foi :

◆ Acte III, scène IV. — Lélie, Ergaste, Anselme, Horace.

ANSELME

1015 Il n'entend pas la langue, et ne peut te répondre.

ERGASTE

Eh bien, lui parlant turc, je sais bien le confondre.
Cabrisciam ogni boraf, embusaim Constantinopola[9] ?

LÉLIE, *à part.*

O rare, ô brave Ergaste !

HORACE

Ben belmen, ne sensulez.

ANSELME

Eh bien, que veut-il dire ?

ERGASTE

Qu'en vous en imposant son père a voulu rire,
Qu'il est d'humeur railleuse, et n'a jamais été
1020 En Turquie.

ANSELME

En quel lieu l'a-t-il donc racheté ?

ERGASTE, *à Horace*

Carigar camboco, ma io ossansando ?

HORACE

Bensem, belmen.

ERGASTE

A Lipse[10] en Nègrepont[11].

ANSELME

O tête vieille et folle !
Sachez par quel chemin ils sont venus à Nole.

ERGASTE

Ossasando, nequei, nequet, poter lever cosir Nola[12] ?

HORACE

Sachina, basumbasce, agrir se.

ERGASTE

Il dit qu'on vient par mer, sans passer par Venise.

◆ Acte III, scène v. — GÉRONTE, ANSELME, HORACE.

ANSELME

Le voilà.

GÉRONTE

Grâce au ciel, à mes souhaits prospère,
1060 Ayant passé chez moi j'ai rencontré mon frère,

Qui, me sollicitant d'accepter son logis,
M'oblige à revenir pour reprendre mon fils.
J'en usais librement ; excusez, je vous prie.

ANSELME

Géronte, un mot, de grâce : apprend-on en Turquie
1065 Ou dans le cabaret à jouer ses amis ?

GÉRONTE

En l'un ni l'autre lieu je ne l'ai point appris ;
Ce n'est point mon humeur.

ANSELME

                Non ! ma fille servante,
Un voyage en Turquie et ma femme vivante !
Tout ce conte à plaisir[13] est une vérité ?

GÉRONTE

1070 Je ne fais point de conte, et n'ai rien inventé.

ANSELME

Vous avez, dites-vous, vu Constance en Turquie ?
Vous osez soutenir qu'Aurélie est Sophie !
Vous parlez de Venise ! et vous avez le front,
N'ayant qu'été par mer de Nole en Nègrepont,
1075 De dire...

GÉRONTE

        En Nègrepont ! ô Dieu, la vaine fable !

ANSELME

Votre fils, qui l'a dit, n'est donc pas véritable[14] ?

GÉRONTE

Quoi ! sans savoir la langue, il peut vous l'avoir dit ?

ANSELME

Il nous a parlé turc, que mon valet apprit
Séjournant sur les lieux pour racheter ma femme.

GÉRONTE, *à Horace.*

1080 *Soler ?*

HORACE

    Man[15].

ANSELME

          Et bien plus [16], chose à votre âge infâme,
Que vous avez tantôt trouvé le vin si bon
Que vous n'en avez pas oublié la raison[17],

Mais, en la faisant trop, l'avez bien égarée[18];
Vos discours m'en étaient une marque assurée.

GÉRONTE

085 Dieu ! qu'entends-je ? (*A Horace.*)
Jerusalas, adhuc moluc acoceras maristo, viscelei, huvi havete carbulach.

HORACE

Eracercheter biradam suledi, ben belmen, ne sulodij.

GÉRONTE, *à Anselme.*

Croyez que votre serviteur
Doit être un maître[19] fourbe, un insigne affronteur[20].

ANSELME

Que vous dit-il encor ?

GÉRONTE

Qu'il n'a pu rien comprendre
A ce qu'un de vos gens lui voulait faire entendre.

ANSELME

M'aurait-il attrapé ? le trait serait subtil !
090 Mais, s'il ne l'entendait, que lui répondait-il ?

GÉRONTE, *à Horace.*

Acciam sembiliir bel mes, mic sulmes ?

HORACE

Acciam bien croch soler, sen belmen, sen croch soler.

GÉRONTE

Qu'il ne l'entendait point, et croit que son langage
N'était qu'un faux jargon qui n'est point en usage.
Croyez encore un coup qu'il est un faux vaurien,
Un fourbe, un archifourbe, et gardez-vous-en bien.
095 Je vous suis inutile et vais trouver mon frère.
Adieu.

ANSELME

Jusqu'au revoir ; le ciel vous soit prospère !

GÉRONTE, *à Horace, s'en allant.*

Ghidelum anglan cic !

HORACE, *le suivant.*
Ghidelum baba !

4. MOLIÈRE ET LES MŒURS DU TEMPS

Il ne s'agit pas de chercher des sources d'inspiration dans la vie courante du temps, mais de voir comment la comédie de Molière cadrait avec la société de son époque.

4.1. L'ACCUEIL FAIT AU *BOURGEOIS GENTILHOMME*

Voici la relation qu'en fait Grimarest dans sa *Vie de Molière :*

◆ Molière travaillait toujours d'après la nature pour travailler plus sûrement. M. Rohault, quoique son ami, fut son modèle pour le philosophe du *Bourgeois gentilhomme;* et, afin d'en rendre la représentation plus heureuse, Molière fit dessein d'emprunter un vieux chapeau à M. Rohault, pour le donner à du Croisy, qui devait représenter ce personnage dans la pièce. Il envoya Baron chez M. Rohault pour le prier de lui prêter ce chapeau, qui était d'une si singulière figure qu'il n'avait pas son pareil. Mais Molière fut refusé, parce que Baron n'eut pas la prudence de cacher au philosophe l'usage qu'on voulait faire de son chapeau.

... Le *Bourgeois gentilhomme* fut joué pour la première fois à Chambord au mois d'octobre 1670. Jamais pièce n'a été plus malheureusement reçue que celle-là; et aucune de celles de Molière ne lui a donné tant de déplaisir. Le Roi ne lui en dit pas un mot à son souper, et tous les courtisans la mettaient en morceaux. « Molière nous prend assurément pour des grues de croire nous divertir avec de telles pauvretés, disait M. le Duc de ... ». « Qu'est-ce qu'il veut dire avec son halaba, balachou ? » disait M. le Duc de ..., « le pauvre homme extravague; il est épuisé; si quelqu'autre auteur ne prend le théâtre, il va tomber : cet homme-là donne dans la farce italienne ». Il se passa cinq jours avant que l'on représentât cette pièce pour la seconde fois, et, pendant ces cinq jours, Molière, tout mortifié, se tint courbé dans sa chambre. Il appréhendait le mauvais compliment du courtisan prévenu. Il envoyait seulement Baron à la découverte, qui lui rapportait toujours de mauvaises nouvelles. Toute la Cour était révoltée.

Cependant on joua cette pièce pour la seconde fois. Après la représentation, le Roi, qui n'avait point encore porté son jugement, eut la bonté de dire à Molière : « Je ne vous ai point parlé de votre pièce à la première représentation, parce que j'ai appréhendé d'être séduit par la manière dont elle avait été représentée, mais, en vérité, Molière, vous n'avez encore rien fait qui m'ait tant diverti, et votre pièce est excellente. »

Molière reprit haleine au jugement de Sa Majesté, et aussitôt il fut accablé de louanges par les courtisans qui, tout d'une voix, répétaient tant bien que mal ce que le Roi venait de dire à l'avantage de cette pièce. « Cet homme-là est inimitable, disait le même Duc de ..., il y a un *vis comica* dans tout ce qu'il fait, que les anciens n'ont pas si heureusement rencontré que lui. » Quel malheur pour ces Messieurs que Sa Majesté n'eût point dit son sentiment la première fois !

(Grimarest, *Vie de Molière*, 1705.)

◆ Au mois de novembre de la même année 1670, que l'on représenta le *Bourgeois gentilhomme* à Paris, le nombre prit parti de cette pièce. Chaque bourgeois y croyait trouver son voisin peint au naturel, et il ne se lassait pas d'aller voir ce portrait. Le spectacle d'ailleurs, quoique outré et hors du vraisemblable, mais parfaitement bien exécuté, attirait les spectateurs ; et on laissait gronder les critiques, sans faire attention à ce qu'ils disaient contre cette pièce.

Il y a des gens de ce temps-ci qui prétendent que Molière ait pris l'idée du *Bourgeois gentilhomme* dans la personne de Gandouin, chapelier, qui avait consommé mille écus avec une femme que Molière connaissait et à qui ce Gandouin donna une belle maison qu'il avait à Meudon. Quand cet homme fut abîmé, il voulut plaider pour rentrer en possession de son bien. Son neveu, qui était procureur et de meilleur sens que lui, n'ayant pas voulu entrer dans son sentiment, cet oncle furieux lui donna un coup de couteau, dont pourtant il ne mourut pas. Mais on fit enfermer ce fou à Charenton d'où il se sauva par-dessus les murs. Bien loin que ce bourgeois ait servi d'original à Molière pour sa pièce, il ne l'a connu ni devant, ni après l'avoir faite ; et il est indifférent à mon sujet que l'aventure de ce chapelier soit arrivée ou non après la mort de Molière.

(Grimarest, *Vie de Molière*, 1705.)

Une *lettre sur Molière* montre, en accord avec le texte précédent, l'intérêt que les contemporains manifestent toujours pour les clefs :

Le portrait que fait Cléonte dans le troisième acte du *Bourgeois gentilhomme* est fait d'après elle [Armande Béjart]. Elle jouait tous les grands rôles dans les pièces de son mari, qu'il travaillait exprès pour ses talents. Elle avait de la voix et chantait ordinairement avec La Grange dans le second acte du *Malade imaginaire*.

4.2. STENDHAL

Stendhal, dans un écrit qui fait le lien entre le *Racine et Shakespeare* de 1823 et celui de 1825, fait une étude qui, centrée sur 1670, stimulera sans doute plus l'intérêt qu'un texte plus objectif ou plus spécialisé sur le même sujet : *De l'état de la société par rapport à la comédie, sous le règne de Louis XIV*. En voici le texte intégral :

Haïr n'est pas un plaisir ; je crois même que beaucoup de lecteurs penseront avec moi que c'est une peine, et une peine d'autant plus vive, qu'on a plus d'imagination ou de sensibilité.

La Bruyère a dit :

« Se dérober à la cour un seul moment, c'est y renoncer. Le courtisan qui l'a vue le matin la voit le soir, pour la reconnaître le lendemain, et afin que lui-même y soit connu. »

Même en 1670, dans les plus beaux temps de Louis XIV, la cour ne fut qu'un rassemblement d'ennemis et de rivaux. La haine, l'envie, y dominaient ; comment la vraie gaieté s'y serait-elle montrée ?

Ces gens qui se haïssent si cordialement entre eux, et qui mouraient après cinquante ans de haine, demandant encore sur le lit de mort : « Comment se porte monsieur un tel[21] ? », ces gens détestaient encore plus certains êtres qu'ils n'apercevaient jamais que pour les pressurer ou en avoir peur. Leur haine était d'autant plus forte, qu'elle était précédée par le mépris. Ce qui pouvait les choquer le plus au monde, c'était le soupçon d'avoir quelque chose de commun avec ces êtres-là. « *Ce que vous dites-là, mon fils, est bien peuple* », dit Louis XIV, un jour que ce grand roi jugea convenable de pousser la réprimande presque jusqu'à l'injure. Aux yeux de Louis XIV, d'Henri IV, de Louis XVIII, il n'y eut jamais en France que deux classes de personnes : les nobles, qu'il fallait gouverner par l'*honneur* et récompenser avec le cordon bleu ; la canaille, à laquelle on fait jeter force saucisses et jambons dans les grandes occasions, mais qu'il faut pendre et massacrer sans pitié dès qu'elle s'avise d'élever la voix[22]. Cet état de la civilisation présente deux sources de comique pour les courtisans : 1. se tromper dans l'imitation de ce qui est de bon goût à la cour ; 2. avoir dans ses manières ou dans sa conduite une ressemblance quelconque avec un bourgeois. Les lettres de madame de Sévigné prouvent toutes ces choses jusqu'à l'évidence. C'était une femme douce, aimable, légère, point méchante. Voyez sa correspondance pendant ses séjours à sa terre des *Rochers,* en Bretagne, et le ton dont elle parle des pendaisons et autres mesures acerbes employées par son bon ami M. le duc de Chaulnes.

Ces lettres charmantes montrent surtout qu'un courtisan était toujours pauvre. Il était pauvre, parce qu'il ne pouvait pas avoir le même luxe que son voisin ; et, ce qu'il y avait d'*affreux*, de poignant pour lui, c'étaient les grâces de la cour qui mettaient ce voisin à même d'étaler tout ce luxe.

Ainsi, outre les deux sources de haine indiquées ci-dessus, un courtisan avait encore pour contribuer à son bonheur, la pauvreté avec vanité, la plus cruelle de toutes, car elle est suivie par le mépris[23].

A la cour de Louis XIV, en 1670, au milieu de tant d'amers chagrins, d'espérances déçues, d'amitiés trahies, un seul ressort restait à ces âmes vaines et légères : l'anxiété du jeu, les transports du gain, l'horreur de la perte. Voir le profond ennui d'un Vardes ou d'un Bussy-Rabutin au fond de leur exil. N'être plus à la cour, c'était avoir tous les malheurs, tous les chagrins, sentir toutes les pointes de la civilisation d'alors, sans ce qui les faisait supporter. Il fallait, pour l'exilé, ou vivre avec des bourgeois, chose horrible, ou voir les courtisans du troisième ou quatrième ordre, qui venaient faire leur charge dans la province, et qui vous accordaient leur pitié. Le chef-d'œuvre de Louis XIV, le complément du système de Richelieu, fut de créer cet ennui de l'exil.

La cour de Louis XIV, pour qui sait la voir, ne fut jamais qu'une table de *pharaon*. Ce fut de telles gens que, dans l'intervalle de leurs parties, Molière se chargea d'amuser. Il y réussit comme un grand homme qu'il était, c'est-à-dire d'une manière à peu près parfaite. Les comédies qu'il présenta aux courtisans de l'*homme-roi* furent probablement les meilleures et les plus amusantes que l'on pût faire pour ces sortes de gens. Mais, en 1825, nous ne sommes plus ces sortes de gens. L'opinion est faite par des gens habitant Paris, et ayant plus de dix mille livres de rente et moins de cent. Quelquefois la *dignité*[24] des courtisans de Louis XIV se trouva choquée même de l'imitation gaie de ce qu'il y avait de plus ridiculement odieux à leurs yeux : un marchand de Paris. Le *Bourgeois gentilhomme* leur parut *affreux*, non pas à cause du rôle de Dorante, qui aujourd'hui ferait frémir MM. Auger, Lémontey et autres censeurs, mais tout simplement parce qu'il était dégradant et dégoûtant d'avoir les yeux fixés si longuement sur un être aussi abject que M. Jourdain, sur un marchand. Toutefois Louis XIV fut de meilleur goût ; ce grand roi voulut relever ses sujets industriels, et d'un mot il les rendit dignes qu'on se moquât d'eux. « Molière », dit-il à son valet de chambre-tapissier, tout triste des mépris de la cour, « Molière, vous n'avez encore rien fait qui m'ait tant diverti, et votre pièce est excellente. »

L'avouerai-je ? je suis peu sensible à ce bienfait du grand roi. Lorsque, vers 1720, les dissipations des grands seigneurs et le système de Law eurent enfin créé une bourgeoisie, il parut une troisième source de comique : l'imitation imparfaite et gauche des aimables courtisans. Le fils de M. Turcaret[25], déguisé sous un nom de terre, et devenu fermier général, dut avoir dans le monde une existence[26] dont le modèle n'avait pas paru sous Louis XIV, dans ce siècle où les ministres eux-mêmes avaient commencé à n'être que des bourgeois. Un homme de la cour ne pouvait voir M. Colbert que pour affaires. Paris se remplit de bourgeois fort riches, dont les mémoires de Collé vous donneront la nomenclature : MM. d'Angivilliers, Turgot, Trudaine, Monticourt, Helvétius, d'Epinay, etc. Peu à peu ces hommes opulents et bien élevés, fils des grossiers Turcarets, commencèrent cette fatale opinion publique, qui a fini par tout gâter en 1789. Ces fermiers généraux recevaient les gens de lettres à leurs soupers, et ceux-ci sortirent un peu du rôle de *bouffons* qu'ils avaient rempli à la table des véritables grands seigneurs.

Les *Considérations sur les mœurs,* de Duclos, sont le *Code civil* de ce nouvel ordre de choses, dont les *Mémoires de madame d'Epinay* et de Marmontel nous ont laissé une description assez amusante. On y voit un M. de Bellegarde, qui, malgré son grand nom, n'est qu'un fermier général ; mais il mange deux cent mille francs par an, et son fils, élevé dans le même luxe que M. le duc de Fronsac, se trouve son égal, pour les manières[27].

De ce moment, Turcaret fut sans modèles ; mais cette nouvelle société de 1720 à 1790, ce changement total si important pour l'histoire et la politique, l'est fort peu pour la comédie ; pendant tout ce temps, elle n'eut point d'homme de génie. Les esprits, étonnés de pouvoir raisonner, se jetaient avec fureur dans ce plaisir tout nouveau. Raisonner sur l'existence de Dieu parut charmant, même aux dames. Les parlements et les archevêques, par leurs condamnations, vinrent jeter quelque piquant sur cette manière aride d'employer son esprit ; tout le monde lut avec fureur *Emile,* l'*Encyclopédie,* le *Contrat social.*

Un homme de génie parut tout à fait à la fin de cette époque. L'Académie, par l'organe de M. Suard, maudit Beaumarchais. Mais déjà il ne s'agissait plus de s'amuser dans le salon ; on songeait à reconstruire la maison, et l'architecte Mirabeau l'emporta sur le décorateur Beaumarchais. Quand un peu de bonne foi dans le pouvoir aura terminé la Révolution, peu à peu tout se classera ; le raisonnement lourd, philosophique, inattaquable, sera laissé à la Chambre des députés. Alors la comédie renaîtra, car on aura un besoin effréné de rire. L'hypocrisie de la vieille madame de Maintenon et de la vieillesse de Louis XIV fut remplacée par les orgies du Régent ; de même, quand nous sortirons, enfin, de cette farce lugubre, et qu'il nous sera permis de déposer le passeport, le fusil, les épaulettes, la robe de jésuite et tout l'attirail (*contre*)-révolutionnaire, nous aurons une époque de gaieté charmante. Mais abandonnons les conjectures politiques, et revenons à la comédie. On fut ridicule dans les comédies telles quelles, de 1720 à 1790, quand on n'imita pas, comme il faut, la partie des mœurs de la cour que M. de Monticourt ou M. de Trudaine, gens riches de Paris, pouvaient permettre à leur vanité[28].

Que me fait à moi, Français de 1825, qui ai de la considération au prorata de mes écus, et des plaisirs en raison de mon esprit, que me fait l'imitation plus ou moins heureuse du bon ton de la cour ? Il faut bien toujours, pour être ridicule, que l'on se trompe sur le chemin du bonheur. Mais le bonheur ne consiste plus uniquement pour les Français, à imiter, chacun selon les convenances de son état, les manières de la cour.

Remarquez toutefois que l'habitude de conformer nos actions à un *patron convenu* nous reste. Aucun peuple ne tient plus à ses habitudes que le Français. L'excessive vanité donne le mot de cette énigme : nous abhorrons les périls obscurs.

Mais, enfin, aujourd'hui ce n'est plus Louis XIV et les impertinents de sa cour, si bien peints par le courtisan Dangeau, qui sont chargés de confectionner le *patron* auquel, chacun suivant les convenances de notre fortune, nous brûlons de nous conformer.

C'est l'*opinion de la majorité* qui élève sur la place publique le modèle auquel tous sont tenus de se conformer. Il ne suffit plus de se tromper sur le chemin qui mène à la cour. Le comte Alfieri raconte, dans sa *Vie,* que, le premier jour de l'an 1768, les échevins de Paris s'étant égarés, et n'étant pas arrivés dans la galerie de Versailles assez à temps pour recueillir un regard que Louis XIV daignait laisser tomber sur eux, ce premier jour de l'an, en allant à la messe, ce roi demanda ce qu'étaient devenus les échevins ; une voix répondit : « Ils sont restés embourbés », et le roi lui-même daigna sourire[29].

L'on raconte encore ces sortes d'anecdotes, on en rit comme d'un conte de fées au faubourg Saint-Germain. L'on regrette un peu le temps des fées ; mais il y a deux siècles entre ces pauvres échevins de Paris, se perdant dans la boue sur le chemin de Versailles, et de grands seigneurs venant briguer une bourgeoise réputation de bien dire à la Chambre des députés, pour de là passer au ministère.

Notes. — 1. *Consul :* membre du conseil municipal. Limoges était administrée par six consuls, dont la charge durait deux ans. 2. *Assesseur :* magistrat siégeant au présidial, tribunal de première instance sous l'Ancien Régime. 3. *Élu :* officier du gouvernement royal, chargé de répartir certains impôts (la taille et les aides) et de régler les contestations relatives à ces impôts dans une circonscription appelée *élection*. L'élection était une subdivision de la généralité. 4. *Tenir.* Sur les fonts baptismaux en qualité de parrain. 5. Il s'agit du *gouverneur* de la province, personnage fort important, représentant direct de l'autorité royale. Les gouverneurs étaient toujours de famille noble. 6. *Galant :* élégant, de bonne compagnie. 7. *Périgordin :* périgourdin. 8. *Hardes :* « Les habits et meubles portatifs qui servent à vêtir ou à parer une personne ou sa chambre » (*Dict. Furetière*). **9.** Il s'agit d'un turc de pure invention (voir IV, I, Ergaste : « Je ne sais quel génie, en ce besoin extrême, / Me dictait un jargon que j'ignore moi-même »). Molière s'est souvenu de ce passage, et c'est avec ce turc de fantaisie qu'il a commencé le discours latin de Sganarelle dans *le Médecin malgré lui*, II, IV : « Cabricias arci thuram... » — Rotrou, copiant ici textuellement le texte en prose de Della Porta, ne considère plus ce turc comme s'intégrant à la versification ; mais la finale en *-la* lui suffit pour interrompre quatre rimes féminines consécutives ; même chose après le vers 1022, où *Nola* semble rimer de loin avec *Constantinopola*. **10.** Ce nom n'est pas dans *La Sorella* et semble de l'invention de Rotrou, peut-être par une curieuse association d'idées avec Juste Lipse, le célèbre philologue de la fin du XVIᵉ siècle ; car il est peu probable que ce nom renvoie à Lipsi, la petite île du Dodécanèse. **11.** Ile d'Eubée, appelée Nègrepont par les navigateurs italiens du Moyen Age, au nord-est de l'Attique ; comme la Grèce, elle était sous la domination turque depuis 1470. **12.** Ce turc, à quelques différences près, a servi encore au latin de Sganarelle dans *le Médecin malgré lui*, II, IV : « Ossabandus, nequeys, nequer, potarinum... ». **13.** *A plaisir :* pour se divertir (voir Molière, *l'Etourdi*, III, II : tout ce beau mystère « N'est qu'un pur stratagème, un trait facétieux, / Une histoire à plaisir, un conte [...] »). **14.** *Véritable :* qui dit la vérité, sincère. **15.** Ici les mots en pseudo-turc entrent dans la mesure du vers, car ils sont courts ; les phrases qui suivent, en revanche, en sont exclues. **16.** Sous-entendre « il a dit ». **17.** La raison de ce que vous faisiez, de ce qui vous faisait boire : ils trinquaient *à l'honneur de leur chère patrie* retrouvée (vers 1044). **18.** Rotrou joue ici sur le mot *raison :* 1° *faire raison à quelqu'un* (d'une santé qu'il a portée) : boire à son tour avec lui à la santé de la personne (ou de la chose) désignée (voir La Fontaine, *Contes*, les Rémois : « Je bois, dit-il, à la santé des dames ! / Et de trinquer : passe encore pour cela. / On fit raison ; le vin ne dura guère ») ; 2° *égarer sa raison :* la perdre, devenir insensé ou fou. **19.** Titre donné dans les anciennes corporations à l'apprenti qui avait prouvé ses capacités professionnelles en exécutant ce qu'on appelait le *chef-d'œuvre* ; le mot s'appliqua par la suite à ceux qui se signalaient « par quelque mauvaise qualité » (Furetière, 1690 ; voir La Fontaine, IX, XVI : « nos deux maîtres fripons », et Molière, *l'Avare*, I, III : « maître juré filou »). **20.** *Affronteur :* celui qui trompe impudemment (voir la note du vers 498). **21.** Historique. Voir Saint-Simon. **22.** Mémoires de Bassompierre, de Gourville, etc. **23.** Lettres de Mᵐᵉ de Sévigné. — Détails sur la vie et les projets de M. le marquis de Sévigné, et de MM. de Grignan père et fils. **24.** Pour prendre une idée exacte de cette *dignité,* voir les mémoires de Mᵐᵉ la duchesse d'Orléans, mère du Régent. Cette sincère Allemande dérange un peu les mille mensonges de Mᵐᵉ de Genlis, de M. de Lacretelle et autres personnages du même poids. **25.** Ce soir, mon fiacre a été arrêté un quart d'heure sur le boulevard des Italiens par les descendants des croisés, qui faisaient queue pour tâcher d'être admis au bal d'un banquier juif (M. de Rothschild). La matinée des nobles dames du faubourg Saint-Germain avait été employée à faire toute sorte de bassesses pour s'y faire prier. **26.** Mémoires de Collé. **27.** Lever de Mᵐᵉ d'Epinay : « Les deux laquais ouvrent les deux battants pour me laisser sortir et crient dans l'antichambre : Voilà madame, messieurs, voilà madame. Tout le monde se range en haie. D'abord, c'est un polisson qui vient brailler un air, et à qui on accorde sa protection pour le faire entrer à l'Opéra, après lui avoir donné quelques leçons de bon goût, et lui avoir appris ce que c'est que la *propreté du chant français*. Puis, ce sont des marchands d'étoffes, des marchands d'instruments, des bijoutiers, des colporteurs, des laquais, des décrotteurs, des créanciers, etc. » (*Mémoires et correspondance* de Mᵐᵉ d'Epinay, t. I, p. 356-357.) **28.** Le rôle de *Récard,* dans une comédie en prose et en cinq actes de Collé, à la suite de ses *Mémoires* ; le *Mondor* des *Fausses Infidélités*, etc. **29.** *Vita di Alfieri*, tome Iᵉʳ, page 140.

JUGEMENTS
SUR « LE BOURGEOIS GENTILHOMME »

XVIIᵉ SIÈCLE

Le gazetier Robinet donne un compte rendu rapide qui laisse entendre que la pièce fut un succès, sans que, cependant, son éloge dépasse les termes d'une banalité convenue.

> Mardi, ballet et comédie,
> Avec très bonne mélodie
> Aux autres ébats succéda,
> Où tout, dit-on, des mieux alla,
> Par les soins des deux grands Baptistes,
> Originaux et non copistes,
> Comme on sait dans leur noble emploi,
> Pour divertir notre grand Roi,
> L'un par sa belle comédie,
> Et l'autre par son harmonie.

Robinet,
Lettre en vers à Monsieur
(18 octobre 1670).

Boileau, qui a défendu l'auteur du Misanthrope *sans jamais bien comprendre celui des* Fourberies de Scapin, *ne nous a rien laissé sur ce* Bourgeois gentilhomme *dont il ne devait guère goûter les mascarades.*

XVIIIᵉ SIÈCLE

Le XVIIIᵉ siècle nous apporte la comparaison de deux jugements opposés : ceux de Rousseau et de Voltaire. Pour le premier, le *Bourgeois gentilhomme* est une pièce immorale, comme toutes les comédies de Molière, puisqu'on rit aux dépens de Monsieur Jourdain et qu'on est ainsi complice de Dorante. Mais Voltaire n'a pas pitié de la vanité du Bourgeois.

J'entends dire qu'il [Molière] attaque les vices; mais je voudrais bien que l'on comparât ceux qu'il attaque avec ceux qu'il favorise. Quel est le plus blâmable, d'un bourgeois sans esprit et vain qui fait sottement le gentilhomme, ou du gentilhomme fripon qui le dupe ? Dans la pièce dont je parle, ce dernier n'est-il pas l'honnête homme, n'a-t-il pas pour lui l'intérêt et le public n'applaudit-il pas à tous les tours qu'il fait à l'autre ?

J.-J. Rousseau,
Lettre à M. d'Alembert sur les spectacles (1758).

Le Bourgeois gentilhomme est un des plus heureux sujets de comédie que le ridicule des hommes ait pu fournir. La vanité, attribut de l'espèce humaine, fait que les princes prennent le titre de rois, que les grands seigneurs veulent être des princes [...]. Cette faiblesse est précisément la même que celle d'un bourgeois qui veut être homme de qualité; mais la folie du bourgeois est la seule qui soit comique et qui puisse faire rire au théâtre : ce sont les extrêmes disproportions des manières et du langage d'un homme avec les airs et les discours qu'il veut affecter qui font un ridicule plaisant.

Voltaire,
Sommaires des pièces de Molière (1765).

XIXe SIÈCLE

Sainte-Beuve, qui revint souvent dans ses articles de critique sur Molière et son œuvre, a aussi défini les raisons profondes de son goût pour Molière.

Aimer Molière, c'est être assuré de ne pas aller donner dans l'admiration béate et sans limite pour une humanité qui s'idolâtre et qui oublie de quelle étoffe elle est faite, et qu'elle n'est toujours, quoi qu'elle fasse, que l'humaine et chétive nature. C'est ne pas la mépriser trop pourtant, cette commune humanité dont on rit, dont on est, et dans laquelle on se replonge chaque fois avec lui par une hilarité bienfaisante.

Sainte-Beuve,
Nouveaux Lundis (13 juillet 1863).

Plus tard, Gustave Lanson admire, entre autres, l'exactitude avec laquelle Molière a décrit les diverses classes sociales de son temps, et il explique pourquoi cette peinture garde encore sa vérité.

Les bourgeois sont nombreux et divers comme leur classe : M. Dimanche, le marchand, créancier né des gentilshommes, et né pour être payé en monnaie de singe; Mme Jourdain, toute proche du peuple par son bon sens, sa tête chaude, sa parole bruyante, et sa bonté foncière; Jourdain, Arnolphe, les bourgeois vaniteux qui jouent au gentilhomme, prennent des noms de terre ou frayent avec des nobles dont la compagnie leur coûte cher [...]. Voici enfin la noblesse de Paris et de la cour : le noble ruiné qui se fait escroc, Dorante [...]. Il est remarquable que Molière a si bien posé les traits caractéristiques des diverses classes de la société française, qu'à travers toutes les révolutions les grandes lignes de ses études restent vraies.

G. Lanson,
Histoire de la littérature française (1894).

XXᵉ SIÈCLE

La critique du XXᵉ siècle s'aperçoit qu'on a trop souvent négligé le divertissement qui accompagne et couronne la pièce et qu'on a jugé le Bourgeois gentilhomme en faisant abstraction d'un élément essentiel, le ballet, considéré jusqu'alors comme un ornement surajouté. Dans quelle mesure la composition de la pièce est-elle conditionnée par le divertissement ? Telle est à peu près la question autour de laquelle tournent les jugements portés au XXᵉ siècle, avec quelques nuances ou même quelques divergences dans les réponses.

Le roi avait dit : « Un ballet avec des Turcs ! » L'esprit de Molière part de là. Il se pose cette question naturelle : « Chez les Turcs, qu'est-ce qu'il y a de plus comique ? Le Grand Turc, parbleu ! Mais le Grand Turc fait bien vieux. Prenons le fils du Grand Turc. Et comme il s'agit d'une comédie, ce ne peut être qu'un simulacre de fils du Grand Turc ! Un jeune homme sous ce déguisement dupera le bourgeois qui lui aura refusé sa fille. » [...] Molière tient son sujet. Il lui a suffi de mener logiquement sa pensée. C'est toujours cette logique inattaquable qui donne à ses pièces leur premier ton d'éternelle vérité. [...]

Comédie-ballet, dit le sous-titre de la pièce, c'est-à-dire que la comédie s'envolera sur les ailes de la poésie, à la minute où elle entrera dans un ballet, ou que simplement le ballet sera la réalité haussée d'un ton, dans l'allégresse. Le comique des paroles illustrées par le geste ne suffit plus à Molière. Il veut une joie plus rayonnante. Il fait appel à la musique, et il invente cette apothéose qu'est la cérémonie. Le *Bourgeois gentilhomme* est ainsi le contraire d'une comédie mal équilibrée. C'est la fleur exquise d'une civilisation, qui a su quelque temps que l'art théâtral unit le plaisir des yeux et des oreilles à celui de l'esprit. [...] On peut l'étudier de toutes manières : on ne voit que bonheur dans la réussite.

René Benjamin,
Molière (1936).

Il [Molière] a devant les yeux un Monsieur Jourdain rubicond, chamarré, flamboyant, un magnifique Jourdain-citrouille, tout jubilant de l'habit qu'on lui présente comme une bannière de la Fête-Dieu, bourrant de pistoles les poches des compagnons tailleurs (ce qui ne l'empêche pas de voir qu'on le vole, car il a l'œil marchand), trop heureux d'ouvrir son coffre-fort à Dorante, dansant le menuet, faisant la révérence, appelant ses laquais, changeant vingt fois d'indienne, pestant contre Nicole, et s'étalant dans ses fauteuils de damas écarlate avec un bonheur qui, pour devenir complet, ne demanderait qu'à être partagé. [...] L'épaisseur de son ridicule est énorme, et jamais rien dans son attitude n'inspire le dégoût. On devine Molière content de le regarder, de le palper, de l'installer dans ses meubles, de planter un turban sur sa perruque, d'en faire un Mamamouchi, de le voir si prospère, si triomphant, si bien en scène. Au fond, ce gros bouffon à figure de pivoine lui est sympathique.

Pierre Brisson,
Molière (1944).

Le Bourgeois gentilhomme n'est ni une étude sociale, ni une étude de caractère. La pièce est bâtie à la diable. Les deux premiers actes ne sont rien qu'une série de *lazzi*. L'action ne commence qu'au IIIe acte. Elle reste extrêmement sommaire, d'une invraisemblance parfaite et sereine. La matière manque tellement que Molière recommence pour la troisième fois la scène du double dépit amoureux, qu'il avait déjà reprise en 1667 pour meubler le vide du IIe acte de *Tartuffe*. Les caractères ne sont même pas tous cohérents. Dorante commence par promettre beaucoup. Ce gentilhomme élégant est d'une indélicatesse froide. Il annonce le chevalier d'industrie. Il pouvait fournir la matière d'une étude très neuve. Mais Molière s'arrête en chemin et le Dorante du dernier acte est devenu un personnage sympathique.

Ces défauts seraient graves si *le Bourgeois gentilhomme* était une grande comédie. Ils n'ont aucune importance dans une comédie-ballet, et celle-ci, prise telle qu'elle est, avec les libertés du genre, dans son vrai ton et son exact éclairage, est une des œuvres les plus heureuses de Molière, par sa verve endiablée, la valeur amusante de Mme Jourdain et surtout la vie prodigieuse de M. Jourdain.

Antoine Adam,
*Histoire de la littérature française
au XVIIe siècle* (1952).

Monsieur Jourdain pousse à l'absurde l'ambition bourgeoise de tout acquérir à prix d'argent : la considération, les titres, les belles manières. Si son pouvoir défaut parce qu'il ne se voit pas comme les autres le voient, si son délire l'enferme dans une solitude totale, il se crée un univers à lui où tout devient déguisement : les beaux habits, le beau langage et les gestes élégants. Il est donc normal de finir en apothéose sur la cérémonie turque, jeu du travestissement avec ses oripeaux, son galimatias et ses salamalecs.

Alfred Simon,
Molière par lui-même (1957).

SUJETS DE DEVOIRS ET D'EXPOSÉS

NARRATIONS, LETTRES ET PORTRAITS

● Nicole raconte à Toinette (du *Malade imaginaire*) les événements qui viennent de se dérouler chez son maître, particulièrement la cérémonie à laquelle elle a assisté en cachette.

● Monsieur Jourdain et Chrysale (des *Femmes savantes*) se rencontrent, chacun d'eux se plaint des ennuis que sa femme ne cesse de lui susciter dans sa vie domestique. Mais ils s'aperçoivent bientôt qu'ils ne sont pas d'accord sur la façon de concevoir la vie familiale. Vous donnerez à leur discussion un dénouement de votre choix.

● Harpagon écrit à un de ses amis pour lui raconter les folies de Monsieur Jourdain, dont il a entendu parler.

● Ce qu'on dit de Monsieur Jourdain dans son quartier.

● Faites le portrait du Bourgeois gentilhomme à la manière de La Bruyère.

● Faites le portrait de l'un des maîtres à la manière de La Bruyère.

DISSERTATIONS ET EXPOSÉS

● Les jeux de scène dans *le Bourgeois gentilhomme*. En quoi contribuent-ils non seulement à rendre l'action plaisante, mais encore à préciser les caractères (en particulier celui de Monsieur Jourdain) ?

● Comparez la cérémonie du *Bourgeois gentilhomme* à celle du *Malade imaginaire*.

● Déterminez, dans *le Bourgeois gentilhomme*, la part de la fantaisie, de la farce, de la comédie profonde — et donnez votre impression sur l'art de Molière.

● Un critique de la fin du XIXᵉ siècle, Jacquinet, écrit dans la Notice du *Bourgeois gentilhomme* : « La dernière de nos révolutions (1870), sous le flot démocratique de laquelle tout s'est aplani, si elle n'a pas mis fin au sot besoin de se distinguer du commun par un nom de naissance ou par un titre, paraît bien en avoir effacé, sinon détruit, le relief comique sans retour. » Vous semble-t-il, au contraire, que le ridicule, si plaisamment raillé par Molière, garde, encore aujourd'hui, son relief comique ?

● Imaginez qu'un auteur comique d'aujourd'hui veuille reprendre le thème du *Bourgeois gentilhomme* et le moderniser. Résumez acte par acte l'action ainsi transposée.

● En quoi Monsieur Jourdain peut-il être considéré comme l'ancêtre des « nouveaux riches » ?

● A quoi servent les rôles de Covielle et de Nicole dans *le Bourgeois gentilhomme* ? Sont-ils aussi importants que les rôles des valets et des servantes dans les autres pièces de Molière ?

TABLE DES MATIÈRES

IMPRIMERIE HÉRISSEY. — 27000 - ÉVREUX.
Décembre 1970. — Dépôt légal 1970-4e. — No 22512. — No de série Éditeur 8958.
IMPRIMÉ EN FRANCE (Printed in France). — 34 657 X-11-78